The
Scarlet
Sentinels

A Novel

JOHN C. SMITH

Agio
PUBLISHING HOUSE

Agio Publishing House
151 Howe Street, Victoria BC Canada V8V 4K5

For rights information and bulk orders, please contact
info@agiopublishing.com
or go to www.agiopublishing.com

The Scarlet Sentinels
ISBN 978-1-897435-76-2 (hardcover book)
ISBN 978-1-897435-80-9 (paperback book)
ISBN 978-1-897435-77-9 (ebook)
Cataloguing information available from
Library and Archives Canada.

Printed on acid-free paper.
Agio Publishing House is a socially responsible company,
measuring success on a triple-bottom-line basis.

10   9   8   7   6   5   4   3   2   1

DEDICATION

This book is dedicated to the men and women who wore, and still wear, the uniform of the Royal Canadian Mounted Police. I tell this story like it is, through my eyes and experience as a detachment watch commander, to illustrate the complexities of police work – the tragic, sad, happy and sometimes satisfying events that are experienced by members of the Force, in their efforts to provide professional police service to Canadians. *Maintiens le Droit.*

ACKNOWLEDGEMENTS

I have the following to thank for their help and source material: B.C. Ministry of Attorney General, Prosecutors Office; retired Associate Chief Justice of B.C. Mr. Patrick Dohm; B.C. Conservation Officer Service; Paulina Sokoloski, RCMP Intellectual Services Unit; Mr. Reg Midgley (my grammar school teacher); Giovanna Greco, for translation; Bruce Batchelor, my publisher, for his invaluable help; my three sons – Greg, Jeff and Brad; my wife, Jean, for her knowledge of nursing and her enduring patience (*John, dinner's getting cold!*); my cat, Benny; and, not the least, to all the members of 'A' Watch, RCMP Kamloops, B.C., 1976–1979, for the fine memories.

NOTE TO READERS

Author John C. Smith, a member of the Royal Canadian Mounted Police for twenty-five years, served at six different police posts in British Columbia and was an instructor at the Canadian Police College, Ottawa. Much of his service was performed in what is called 'General Duty' policing, where most law enforcement is carried out.

The author, with his cat Benny who regularly insists on helping out on the keyboard.

The Scarlet Sentinels spans a period of one year at a large detachment in the Interior region of British Columbia. Although written as a novel, this story accurately reflects the kinds of events that typically occur in the police world, presented graphically and in the lingua franca that is particular to this work. Readers will enter the lives of members of this famous police force at the detachment level, learning how they operate in, and adapt to, continual challenge and change. Past and current members of the Force may well recognize a part of themselves and others, in this narrative, although it should be considered a work of fiction and all characters are composites of many individuals known to the author and his imagination.

PART ONE

1

It was early September, 1988. Sergeant Jack Sterling reported for work at 6:30 p.m., half an hour early as he wanted to do two things – check the 'still under investigation reports' (SUI) workload of his watch members, and to introduce them to the *Parkton News* reporter, Charlie Preston, as they reported for work and let them know what was happening. He'd have both corporals and twelve constables on duty tonight – three constables being away for a variety of reasons.

The reporter was being allowed, with the permission of Inspector Edwardson, the Officer in Charge of the detachment, to accompany members of the watch on patrol, over a four-week period, to learn how police work was carried out at the local level, with the idea of writing a series in the paper about his experiences.

The sergeant knew the idea would not be overly popular with his members. They were always guarded when the press was around. Most didn't like to feel inhibited in their speech and manner, out of the public eye. Sterling was going to explain to them the 'Rules of the Ride-Along' to try to ease their minds. He knew the reporter well enough, he thought, to know that the man would not betray a trust. He'd explain the situation to Preston, and felt he was mature enough to understand. If it didn't work out, Sterling would simply stop the ride-alongs.

He decided to take the reporter out initially himself – to assess how Preston acted and reacted during these outings – before turning him over to members of his watch.

Sterling would take it upon himself to debrief the reporter and the accompanying police officer at the end of each patrol, to assess the value of this exercise and whether to continue. Besides which, the inspector wanted frequent feedback too.

It was Monday night and statistically not terribly busy. After everyone had been introduced and dispatched to their patrol areas, he said to the reporter, "Okay, Charlie, ready to go out?"

"Sure, I'm ready. What kind of activity can we expect tonight?"

"It should be fairly quiet, but in police work, you just never know."

"I take it you'll fill me in on what to do during any emergency that you may get involved in – what I'm to do, Jack?"

"Absolutely. Let's get out on the road first," he replied as they walked to the parking lot. Sterling unlocked the doors to 10-Bravo-7, put the key in the ignition, started it up and checked all his lights, turn signals, emergency lights including the roof-mounted 'alley lights', siren and loud hailer. Opening the trunk, he checked off the equipment contained inside against a laminated list – a Remington .308 rifle with scope (in scabbard covering), tear gas gun and cartridges, first aid kit, a 24-feet-long retractable measuring tape, red reflectorized road safety triangles, road flares, rolls of yellow 'Police – Do Not Enter' tape, an axe and shovel, a yellow traffic vest in a plastic case and, last but not least, the spare tire (inflated).

"That's quite an arsenal of equipment in there," noted Preston as Sterling closed the lid. "Plus the shotgun."

"Yeah, you noticed it in the car."

"Why not have the rifle in the car too?"

"Well, a couple of things, I suppose. First, where to put it and, secondly, rifles seldom get used – they're for shooting longer distances, of course, whereas the 'scattergun' is more effective for close-range use. You ready to roll?"

They got in the patrol car and Sterling checked the gas gauge – almost full, he noted.

"Right, we're good to go. *Radio, 10-Bravo-7, 10-8 with Charlie Preston as ride-along,*" Sterling announced into the dashboard-mounted microphone. Turning to Preston, he added, "You'll get used to the call numbers we use pretty quickly. I don't stay on the road for more than an hour usually. I suppose I don't really need to since I have two senior corporals who remain out for most of the watch and keep an eye on things, but I like to keep a finger on the pulse of activity too. I also think it's good for the guys, and the one woman, to see me on the road. I can also assess how they are doing. I don't go about this surreptitiously, sneaking around, so to speak. I'd have no credibility if I did that. Every now and then I have to have a word or two with a member, usually something minor, and I never do that in front of other people."

"Sounds logical," Preston said.

"I have a lot of paperwork to do and keep an eye on a myriad of other things that go on during my watch. And, of course, I always keep an ear to the radio transmissions. I try to be available to help members when they bring in arrested people, and assist with locking them up if they get a bit boisterous. As well, I discuss issues with members of the other sections – General Investigation Section (GIS), Traffic, Identification people, and so on. On the night shift, all these people report to me when necessary. On some weekends, that number can amount to upwards of forty bodies, plus civilian staff."

Preston was making notes on a lined pad.

"You'll see as I drive that I also – if I'm near enough – cover a member attending a potentially dangerous call, and I usually stop and wait when I see someone doing a traffic stop. I position my car so that it is visible to the occupants of the vehicle and the member. That way, they both know another police car is close by – that will tend to brook any arguments or possible assault on the police person. You may see me do that tonight.

"Let's talk about emergency situations. One thing I need to remind you of is the insurance coverage. You've signed a waiver and are aware that you ride at your own risk?"

The reporter nodded.

"When I'm out of the car, I have my portable radio. If I get into a messy situation that in your view requires some assistance on your part, such as someone trying to kick the shit out of me, the first thing you need to do is report the incident to the dispatcher. When that happens, all the other cars on the road will hear. Someone, usually one of the zone corporals will direct help my way. That means, of course, that you have to say exactly where we are and ask for instructions. Again, a corporal will more than likely respond and you need to do as he asks, please, in spite of how you may feel about helping me. It all depends on circumstances and that mainly rests on how close, or not, police assistance is. That will be addressed by the NCO who may ask you to help until the police arrive. Okay with that?"

"Yes, I understand," replied Preston.

"Alright. You can see my radio microphone on the hook on the dash. The watch commander's car is always 10-Bravo-7. To radio the office say, 'Dispatch or Radio, 10-Bravo-7, emergency call.' When you get an acknowledgement, tell them as succinctly as possible about the situation. So, let's say I've made a stop at Columbia and 9th and two males bail out of their car and start pounding on me. What would you say and do?"

"Pick up the mic, call Dispatch and say, 'Sergeant Sterling being assaulted by two men at Columbia and 9th. I'm Charlie Preston, his ride-along.' I guess I'd listen to the next response or two to determine whether or not I should get out of the car and get into the fray."

"Good, and just to allay any worries you may have, it hasn't happened yet. Don't want you to think this is a regular occurrence. By the way, always wait for the dispatcher to acknowledge your call. Now, if I stop a car or a pedestrian, I'd like you to stay in the car and just keep an eye on things. Roll the window down if you want. I don't think I need to point out to you, but just to make it official, you have no police powers. What you *do have* is a citizen's power of arrest. That's defined in the *Criminal Code of Canada* under Section 494: 'Any one may arrest without warrant a person whom he finds committing an indictable offence.'

"Note the wording *any one* means just that. An indictable offence is a more serious criminal offence for which imprisonment is five years or more.

"I know what you're thinking – 'how the hell do I know which offences are indictable?' Don't worry about that. You have two things going for you in a situation like this. One is 'Common Sense' and the other more important one is called 'Reasonable and Probable Grounds.' So, if I'm in a fight, any right-thinking person could be led to believe that the fight or assault could lead to serious injury to me or my death, then that is certainly an 'indictable offence' and he or she would therefore be protected from later criminal and/or civil action, by taking appropriate steps in coming to my assistance. So, punching me is one thing, cutting me with a knife or using a weapon of some kind is serious. As you can see, there's no clear answer sometimes to these situations. Each incident has to be assessed and treated on its own merits. Sorry I can't be more explicit, Charlie. Now, if you want to call it a night now and leave, I'll understand."

"No no, I fully understand, Jack. You've explained it quite well. If a situation arises, I just hope I can do the right thing."

"Okay, to continue then. One of the most common things you'll hear on the radio is members checking vehicles and sometimes people on foot. It's a police responsibility to do that. For our info and the protection of the public, we need to know who's 'out and about', or to use the old British expression which I like, 'who's abroad in the land.'

"The overwhelming majority of those checks are benign and most people don't take exception to them and understand the need to do so. Most bad guys have wheels and it's good to keep tabs on them and to arrest when a warrant has been issued. I also firmly believe that these continual checks help prevent some percentage of crime – petty or serious stuff."

"Do your officers develop a sixth sense about vehicles and people they check? I mean, they do it so much it seems," said Preston.

"Good point. Yes, they do and acting upon it often pays off with an arrest. The civil liberties people call the checking we do 'harassment of the public' believing that we need reasonable and probable grounds or as you hear on TV shows, the American term 'probable cause.' I've had a Canadian kid say that to me, 'You don't got no probable cause.'"

"Bet that pumped up your heart rate a bit, eh?"

"Don't get me going on American TV cop shows. They're what I call the sanitized version of the gritty Canadian ones and don't get close to reality either."

By the time they reached Victoria Street, the main road through the downtown area, twilight had faded into darkness, but that did not affect this street. The City had recently installed bright new incandescent lights and those, together with bright store-front windows and illuminated multi-coloured business lights announcing the names of the stores, had turned the thoroughfare into a 'Vegas Effect.'

"The brighter the lights, the better we like 'em," said Sterling.

Just ahead was one of the better-known pubs − better-known to the police that is − the Stallion aka the 'Horseshit Saloon.' There were two pubs with similar labels on this street. The Stallion boasted a western motif, consisting of photos of rodeo events − bronc riding, barrel racing, taking down heifers with lassos, etc. − and items like western saddles, bridles and bits, horseshoes and old cowboy boots, hanging from the booze- and smoke-infused cedar walls. As Bravo-7 drove slowly past, the bat-wing doors were flung open to emit a couple of the 'inmates', the raucous blast of some twangy western music, and the stale smell of beer and burgers.

"Surprisingly busy for a Monday night. Wait 'til the weekend when it's packed," said Sterling. "We do good business there."

"Charlie-3, Radio," the Traffic patrol driver called in a clipped, urgent voice.

"Charlie-3, go."

"I'm west-bound passing the Thomson Valley Shopping Centre on the Trans-Canada following a car at over 160 K. He won't stop. Is there anyone ahead of me?" he said over the noise of his screaming siren.

His call was quickly answered by Corporal Bibermann who said, "Charlie-3, this is Bravo-8. I'm on Columbia Hill west-bound and can be on the TCH in about two minutes. Any other cars in the area?" he asked.

10-Bravo-12 responded that he was near the Sub Division building and would hold there. The dispatcher remained quiet knowing that the matter was being handled.

"Bravo-15, I'm in Riverside Park," called Marv Peterson. "I can get up to the highway in a few minutes, okay?" he said to Bibermann as he activated his emergency lights and siren.

"No, stay where you are," said the corporal.

Sterling said to Preston, "Charlie-3 is a city traffic car," he explained to his passenger. "He's got a 350 hp Interceptor motor and it'll go but it sounds like the pursued car is just as fast. I believe the traffic car has a set of roadblock spikes in his car but, of course, they're useless unless he can get ahead and roll them out onto the road. Let's see what happens," he said as he stopped talking to concentrate on his own high-speed driving.

On their way up to the highway, they listened to the radio chatter. Other patrols cars not involved stayed off the air. It was obvious the fleeing vehicle was trying to outrun the police and in terms of public safety, it was a question of whether to continue the pursuit or not – a call to be made in most cases by the constable chasing. In this case, it was on the four-lane main highway, in the middle of the evening with low vehicle density, dry weather, so the chase was being continued.

"The next detachment and available police car is at Ashville, about 35 miles west," explained Sterling. "They'd probably have one car out now. There is a Highway Patrol unit there too and he could use his spike block, unless the car turns south on Highway 8A, the winding country road to Highway 3, the southern, east–west trans-provincial route."

In thinking this through, Sterling called the city dispatcher and asked her to call the next detachment west, to put them on alert and to request the HP car assist if possible. He asked the driver of the chase car to try to keep the car in sight, and called off the two city cars that were following now. They'd soon be out of the detachment area and he didn't think that was necessary.

In a few minutes, Sterling pulled over onto the gravel shoulder and parked. He asked the dispatcher again to call Ashville and to ask how many cars they had to attempt a road block procedure and to confirm that they possessed a set of spikes blocks.

But Ashville's involvement did not become necessary. Charlie-3's driver came on the air and said that the pursued car had crashed. As it turned south on 8A without scarcely slowing down, the vehicle had rolled several times. Sliding to a screeching stop, the constable gave his 10-7 and asked for an ambulance and assistance from another police car.

A minute later, the city dispatcher received an update.

"Radio, Charlie-3."

"Charlie-3."

"No need for anyone to rush. The lone occupant appears to be deceased. Ask the Coroner and a Sub Division HP car to attend, please. This is way outside the city limit. I'll be out of the car."

"Well, that was short and sweet, and fatal," said Sterling to the reporter.

"I wonder why people try to outrun the police? He must know they set up roadblocks," observed Preston.

"There's lot of reasons," replied Sterling. "Maybe he's wanted, his DL is expired, not carrying insurance, HBD – that's short for 'had been drinking' – it may be a stolen auto, he may be carrying drugs, or simply the thrill of winning a race – take your pick. At least he won't be able to do that again."

"Isn't that a bit cynical? If you don't mind me saying."

"Yes, I suppose it is and police officers tend to develop a thick skin when it comes to fatals caused by stupidity, carelessness or outright criminal behaviour.

"We take the view that if the driver dies and doesn't take an innocent person with him, he won't get a second chance. Many men under thirty don't think about that concept. They *know* they are invincible. It's a shame, I suppose. Do you want to go to the scene?"

"No, thanks, I'll pass," Preston said.

Sterling turned the car around to head back to the 'barn' and drop off his passenger.

The reporter said his thanks for an interesting time on patrol and that he'd see Sterling next week, maybe a different night.

2

The evening was miserable, dark and cool with a steady drizzle. The scraping of the wipers across the windshield grated on Joe McKillen's mind and irritated him. He was feeling down anyway. His wife Jody and their two young children had been away from home for two weeks now, visiting her mother in Sydney, Nova Scotia, where he was from as well.

He was sick of his own cooking and lonely. He longed for the warmth and security of being in his wife's arms again, the good clean smell of her shiny hair – 'that was one of the things that attracted me to her,' he reflected – and of course, the touch of her warm responding body.

Scrape, scrape. Scrape, scrape.

"Scrape away, you bastards," he muttered at them. "In two weeks time you can drive somebody else nuts!"

That was when his car, a 1986 Ford Crown Vic, getting old by police standards, was due to be traded in. By now, with just over 160,000 kilometres on the clock, it was in the garage more often than not. The windshield wipers were doing nothing more than smudging the glass as they laboured their way back and forth. When McKillen had mentioned this to the Administration NCO, his reply was that he wasn't going to spend twenty-five dollars for a new set of blades when the car was to be traded so soon – "Live with it," he'd said.

The only thing that was good about the old Ford was the AM/FM radio. Joe McKillen tuned in to *Easy Listening* on CKPK, the local station, which had just finished a break with the 10 p.m. news and weather.

The background music penetrated his thoughts and he turned it up a bit. It was Barbra Streisand singing one of his favourite hit songs – *'People, people who need people….'*

Ordinarily, he didn't care that much for her singing. He thought her technique was too 'arty', too forceful and pretentious at times, but he had to concede that this was one song she could sing well and with feeling. He turned the volume up a bit higher and filled the car with beautiful sounds. In the privacy of his own little world, out on the rain-slicked streets, he raised his voice in harmony with hers and sang –

'Lovers, are very special people…'

The melody and lyrics resonated in his heart, but only served to make him feel even more depressed.

'A feeling deep in your soul—'

"All cars, North Zone! All cars!"

Judy Benson's voice cut through his self-pitying reverie halfway through the song. She had a different inflection in her voice and when she called 'All cars' twice he knew that she had something urgent to say. His was the second car to respond: "10-Bravo-3."

After the other general duty cars and one traffic unit had quickly responded, she came back on the air.

"All cars, report of a pedestrian hit-and-run, junction of Oak Crescent and Eighth Avenue. Vehicle described as older model, tan General Motors product, possibly Chevrolet, one head light and one tail light out, lone male occupant, heading north on Eighth at high speed. Ambulance dispatched. Member attending, please?"

"Radio, 10-Charlie-1, I'll take that," the traffic man replied.

It was 10:15 p.m. and McKillen had been on duty just over three hours.

'God, the drunks are out early tonight,' he thought as he pressed the mic button and said, "Radio, 10-Bravo-3, I'll take the suspect H and R car. I'm on Leigh at Eighth Avenue now, about ten blocks from the scene. Anybody cover me?"

Dick Ketchum, driving 10-Bravo-6, said that he'd back him up. No sooner had McKillen hung his mic back on the dashboard hook than he had to pick it up again as the offending vehicle, still on Eighth Avenue, came into view, on his left, travelling at speed. 'Boy, here we go again,' he said to himself. 'Wish I had a newer car.'

There weren't too many things that Constable McKillen did not like doing as a policeman, but high speed chases were not his 'bag'. He had been injured in one, a couple of years ago, and the experience had reduced his youthful zeal a bit. That was not to say, however, that he did not give the matter his best shot. It was just that his previous attitude of 'I'll get you, you son of a bitch, if it's the last thing I do' had almost become a tragic reality, and he was now somewhat more circumspect.

"Okay. I'm on his rear, Dick, still north-bound, speed one hundred plus. It's a gold Chev. Radio, I'll get you the plate number as soon as I can get close enough."

"Bravo-3, copy."

Dispatch said, "10-Charlie-1, ambulance should be there shortly. This is possibly a fatal. See the witness, Sheila Clark. Copy?"

Over the noise of the pulsating scream of his car's siren, the driver of 10-Charlie-1 answered, "Ten-four."

Ketchum said, "Joe, I'm on Railway Avenue North now, west of you near the City limit. Let me know which way he turns when he gets to the tracks."

"Okay. He's really moving. He'll have to slow down if he wants to make a turn," McKillen said as he got closer to the T-intersection.

A moment later – "Dick, the idiot didn't make a turn, he went up the bank at an angle onto the tracks!" McKillen shouted into his mic. "Christ, would you believe he's now driving along the bloody tracks!"

"Which way is he heading?"

"West."

"Are you following?"

"Yeah, I'm paralleling him along Leigh Avenue coming toward

you. Why don't you wait by the next crossing and I'll follow back here," replied McKillen.

"Okay, but—"

"Radio, 10-Bravo-3, Judy, call the railway dispatcher and ask him when the next train— never mind, there's one on the tracks now! Jesus Christ, they're going to hit!" he shouted.

The Chevrolet, bouncing and swaying along the ties, sparks spraying up from the undercarriage whenever metal scraped against the rails, was still moving at a fairly good clip. The car had entered a right-hand bend in the track just as the lead train engine was halfway through it. Driving a little bit back and to the left rear of the car, McKillen knew the car's driver had seen the huge single, oscillating headlight of the locomotive. The red light on the left rear of the car, the only one working, glowed a brighter red momentarily as the driver futilely applied his brakes.

The screech of the locked train wheels on the rails and the horrendous grinding crash of that head-on collision were clearly heard by those in the radio room and all cars on the air. In his disbelief at what was about to happen, Joe McKillen was still clutching the mic in his hand, in a death grip, button open, when the train struck the car.

◆   ◇   ◆

Later, just before dawn, when the mangled body of the driver, including a pair of separated feet, had been removed from the wreckage, came the post-mortem discussion of this event.

Half a dozen policemen, meeting in Mama Elsa's All-Night Deli, relived their respective parts in, and views of, one more momentous occasion.

Dick Ketchum said, "Jesus, Joe, I was gonna tell you the goddammed train was coming but you cut me off, not that it would've made much difference anyway."

"You got that right," replied McKillen. "That bastard was doomed as soon as he got on those tracks. Why the hell would he do that?"

"Good question," somebody said. "Wasn't he a bloody mess!"

"Just a mixture of hamburger and metal," replied Ketchum. "The only way I could tell it had been a human being was by the feet I picked under the mess after the CNR crane had pulled the wreckage off the tracks. I'm wondering why he went onto the tracks? Maybe it was a suicide attempt, it was such a crazy move, or maybe he was well over the alcohol legal limit. The autopsy blood test will reveal the latter, but not if he purposely meant to kill himself, unless he has a history of such crazy behaviour."

To the junior man on the watch, Constable Henry 'Hank' Deleeuw, those words represented the very essence of exciting police work. He took in every word with avid attention, and of course had to use his very limited opportunity to get his views in too, using the vernacular quite acceptable and expected among policemen.

"Yeah, shit, I had a look at the car just now. Man, the only way you could tell it was a Chevy was by the emblem still intact on what was left of the trunk lid."

"No kidding, Hank, that's very observant of you. You keep that up and you might make it onto the GIS squad." Those words, from Corporal Don Cliff, the Traffic Analyst Specialist, who had just finished his exhaustive examination of both the scene of the hit and run – luckily not a 'fatal' as it turned out – and the crash on the tracks, were not meant to be vindictive, and Deleeuw realized that.

"How bad was the pedestrian anyway, Corp?"

"She's still unconscious, serious back and head injuries but she'll live, I'm told. What gets me is she's only six years old, same age as Avery, my daughter, and that could've been her lying there," said Cliff.

Munching a bacon-on-a-bun and sipping an inevitable Coke, Joe McKillen had to agree. "You know, I can go to any fatal MVA and it doesn't faze me, so long as it isn't a kid. When that happens, my two little monsters get some extra lovin' from their dad when he gets home."

When they had wrung all they could out of the previous evening's events, the talk turned to other motor vehicle accidents, each, to an outsider listening in, seeming even more spectacular than the previous. Vivid adjectives to describe them and some degree of embellishment upon the actual facts were acceptable, but one had to be careful that none of the listeners had been at the same accident being described. After the last drop of beverage was finished, it was back to business.

♦ ◊ ♦

McKillen joined the Force at the age of twenty-four, having spent four years at Dalhousie University, getting his undergraduate degree. He really didn't know why he majored in history, except that he was good at the subject in school, and maintained his interest. In reviewing the usefulness of his degree as it applied to police work, he had to conclude that something like psychology, sociology, law or a sciences subject would have had better application. In any event, he was glad to get away from sixteen years of being a student and to get into some active, meaningful, paid work. He'd met his wife at the university. She graduated with a B.Ed. and wanted to teach. They were married right after both left university, and within six months, McKillen was in police training at Regina's Depot Division. He was the only man in his troop from Nova Scotia and was constantly reminded about his Cape Breton accent with laughable and sometimes irritating imitations.

After graduating from the Academy, McKillen was posted to the West Coast on General Duty policing and spent the next three years at a large municipal detachment, driving around in the rain.

Jody had found her teaching job at an elementary school, and by the time they arrived in Parkton a year ago, the family had increased to almost four. Jason was now two, and Mary-Ellen had just turned ten months.

McKillen came from a family of three brothers and two sisters and, as the eldest, had shouldered a lot of responsibility in his formative years, helping out his mother and crippled father, and extensively with his siblings. His mother spent five to six days a week away from the home, cleaning houses. He was bright enough to win entry to university on a scholarship. His parents could never have afforded the tuition. By the time he entered the Force he was a very mature and sensible person, well adjusted and most suitable in many ways for his new role.

Entering the Mounted Police, going through six months of very rigorous training and then on to active police work had been something of a culture shock, but after a few months of sober second reflection, he concluded that he had made the right decision. With no babies yet on the scene, both he and Jody had adjusted quite well to the different shifts and new lifestyle in a new province.

He had wanted to hold off for some time before having children. He told his wife he needed to 'dig the adult scene' for a while. A 'while' turned out to be two years before his first-born arrived, which under the circumstances, was just about right, he thought.

He was reasonably happy to be on the West Coast, much different than the Atlantic coast. The cost of living was expensive and it was a good thing his wife had a job. The incessant rain, forty-three days in a row one winter, and grey skies eventually got to him, to the point where getting a transfer to a sunny climate, even if it meant enduring sub-zero winter temperatures, was almost an obsession.

During his personnel interview two years ago, he told the Staffing Officer about his desire. Well, he had to stay three years he was told, so he persevered. Here in Parkton rainy days were few and far between, and the change in scene and climate was most welcome. Tonight was one of those exceptions, so that the inclement weather combined with his family's absence and some inner unease that McKillen couldn't quite put his finger on, made him somewhat morose and quiet. His mood was obviously reflected in his eyes, face and demeanour for, back at the office to fill in his notebook and write up a couple of complaints he had attended, the watch commander noted this and asked him if everything was okay.

"Yeah, sure, Sarge, I'm fine. Why?"

"Oh, I just noted you look a little down tonight. Did that train accident bother you?"

"No."

"Okay, if you say so. Just remember, uh, if I can help you any time, just ask, okay?"

"Okay, Sarge. Thanks."

His relationship with the other members of the watch and his sergeant was always positive. He was a likeable person, with an open, honest, forthright disposition, not given to speaking a great deal of bullshit and, in keeping with his Scottish ancestry, careful with his money. It just wasn't true, he told a few of the other members over coffee one night, that he squeaked while he walked and that he washed and dried his Kleenex. He just wasn't cheap like some other members he knew, looking meaningfully at the others around the table.

In a few months, McKillen would have to decide on whether or not to sign on again; 're-engage' as the official document called it. His original five-year contract was due then and in a way it was a turning point in his life. It was a time of taking serious stock, re-appraising one's service, experiences and so on, and deciding whether or not to break away and do something else, or go on. For most who made the choice of 'going on', it was almost in all respects a commitment to stay in the Force for a long time to come, at least until pensionable service at twenty years or beyond.

Even for many of those who did leave, life outside the Force, or 'civvy life' as it was referred to, was not at all what they thought it to be. In fact, it was often rather bleak, cold and unfriendly and some-times financially disastrous.

'Maybe that's what's nagging me tonight,' he pondered. 'Maybe I've got the 'five-year itch'. Okay, suppose I did get out. What would I do? Well, with a few more credits maybe I could teach, but that doesn't really grab me, and anyway, I have to eat. Sell insurance or real estate? No, I'm not the aggressive type. Somehow I need more, more than the daily grind of picking up drunks, breaking up fights, refer-eeing domestic disputes, investigating accidents and checking door knobs at night. I suppose what I'm saying to myself is that things aren't challenging enough....

'What's 'challenging'?' he asked himself. 'Maybe I should apply for a transfer to some other duty, say, General Investigation Section and do some detective work, or the Commercial Crime Branch and go after white collar criminals in the business world. Different kind of assholes to deal with but they'd probably be more polite.

'How about Security Service or the CPIC computer centre in Ottawa, or even Financial Services, where all the money is? I don't know. Maybe I should request to go back to university and get a de-gree in psychology or law; either of those would be more useful in the long term. Maybe I should shut up and be thankful for having a good, steady job, after all, there are lot of people out there who would pay to trade places with me. I wonder if everyone else, in any other work or business, goes through this kind of mental turmoil? What a dissatisfied bunch of bastards human beings are,' he concluded.

Joe McKillen went home to bed at 7:30 that morning feeling worn out, physically and emotionally – and lonely.

3

September 15. Tonight was to be his fourth Annual Watch Meeting, when most of his people were back on duty after the long summer holidays. Sgt. Jack Sterling felt it was important to review police matters with his people annually and to reiterate a few operational reminders. He smiled briefly when he remembered his first one, introducing himself as the new watch commander four years ago. Since then, half the people on his watch had changed including his two corporals. While his approach had also changed a bit, he still recalled it as being brief but effective, as his minutes reflected...

It was four o'clock in the morning in mid–September 1985 when that first meeting was called to order, if that was the right way to describe the motley gathering. Members of 'A' Watch were draped over chairs, filing cabinets and propped up against the one bare wall in the small office. The room had no drapes but did have one-way glass. No one could see in, even at night with the lights on.

The meeting was scheduled for now because Sunday night shifts were usually the quietest time in the week for criminal activity. Most of Parkton's citizens were in bed recovering from a multitude of weekend activities except for a half dozen inebriated ones in the detachment drunk tank, sobering up for an early Monday morning release. For a short period of time, all the patrol cars had been pulled off the road, after the sergeant was assured that thorough property checks had been conducted in the business areas at least once, earlier in the night.

Sergeant John Matthew (Jack) Sterling was born in the United

Kingdom in 1940. At 6-foot-one, 175 lbs, with light brown hair, blue eyes and according to the admittedly biased opinion of his wife, Jocelyn, 'good looking,' Sterling had taken over command of 'A' Watch one month earlier from E.R. 'Earl' Raymond, who'd been transferred. At the time of the change of command – mid-August – half the watch was not on duty. Several members were on annual leave, mostly those with school-aged children on summer break, one was on sick leave recovering from injuries received in a police car accident and one was on temporary assignment with 'E' Division Headquarters Joint Forces Operations Team in Vancouver.

This, then, was the first occasion where all but one of his team were working and, as the sergeant well knew, perhaps the last opportunity for some time to see most of his crew together. Shifts were chronically shorthanded for a variety of reasons. It wasn't uncommon to work a shift with half the authorized manpower; maintaining full strength was a constant battle. Anyway, he thought, it was an appropriate time for him to call his first meeting. Certain things needed to be said, so that all the members 'knew where he was coming from,' as the current expression put it.

"Okay, everybody, settle down, please," he said as he entered the noisy room and the chatting subsided to a murmur and then stopped. He went to the small desk in front of the window and stared at the occupied chair behind it. The occupant got the message and got up and moved. "Thank you."

Standing behind the desk, he looked around the room at all the faces and said, "Thanks for your attention, lady and gents," thereby including the one woman on his shift.

"This is quite an occasion, for me at least. It's the first time since I arrived that I've seen all but one of you under one roof at the same time. What I am about to do may seem a little bit unorthodox to you but I want to open this meeting with a brief prayer. Would you join me, please?"

Those who were sitting slowly stood and shuffled somewhat

awkwardly amid some looks that said, 'What the hell?' 'Do you believe this!?'

Someone at the back of the room whispered, "Shit, that's all we need, a goddamn evangelist watch commander. Gimme a break!"

The sergeant raised both his arms in the air, just like a TV preacher and said, "Dear Lord, I pray that all these people gathered before you tonight have the ability to use what little brains and talent they have been endowed with, to help me get through my term of office at Parkton without too many major screw-ups before I transfer out, or retire or get committed. In the name of Jesus Christ, Amen.

"I said it was going to be a short meeting," he continued as everyone sat down or leaned against a wall. "There are three items I want to discuss and for you to remember. First – diary dates. Some of you are in the bad habit of allowing them to lapse without updating your SUI files. Neither I nor the secretarial staff wish to go hunting for overdue files that are still under investigation. You *will* keep open files current. Failure to do so will mean a confessional period with me and, if that doesn't work, the matter will be reflected in your annual appraisal report, or a strong suggestion from me that you need to rethink and review your service in the world-famous Royal Canadian Mounted Police, and look for some other line of work."

The room had gone very quiet.

"Second – notebooks. I want you to ensure that you use them religiously and according to the Rules of Proper Use. You know damn well you may have to produce them in Court. Well kept and accurate notes reflect your police professionalism – or lack thereof if you don't maintain them properly. While I'm on the subject, make sure you have your caution cards in them, and, if you don't do it now, make a habit of reading the card to people under arrest; don't reel the caution off from memory. Why is that?" he asked, looking around the room.

"Well, so as to prevent making errors in giving verbal cautions and to avoid a hassle in Court with Defence Counsel," someone said in a voice that suggested the obvious.

"Yeah, you're right," the sergeant replied. "It could mean the difference in getting a conviction or not, and, it helps keep Judges happy too. As we all know, their happiness is paramount. And one last important thing; make a note in your book every time you caution someone. I go one step further. I tell the suspect that I've done that. If the matter goes to trial, a copy of your notes goes into the Prosecutor's file.

"Okay. Final point. Uniforms. I'm not expecting you to come to work dressed like graduation day in Regina. On the other hand, if you're going to have creases in your shirt, make sure they're straight ones and in the right places. I don't expect a spit shine on your shoes or boots, but I don't want to see blobs of muck on them either. Trousers are a free issue so trade them in before they get to the point they're so shiny that light reflects off them. Once in a while an application of polish to your leatherwear would make it feel good."

Looking around the room, he asked, "Any questions? No? One more thing; you know that I've just arrived from the Canadian Police College as an instructor on the Senior Police Administration Course. I'm a bit rusty on my General Duty responsibilities after four years in Ottawa and I'm counting on *all* of you for your help. I'm not new to this line of work, having spent most of my service at the detachment level and ran my own shop in the Okanagan. So you could say I've 'been there, done that.' Alright. Thanks for your attention. Don't forget my catchy little saying – 'the watch that prays together stays together.' Now go out and do good things in the world. Would the two zone commanders stay, please."

On their way out to the police parking lot to resume patrols, one of the members said to his companion, "Well, what do you think of the new sergeant? Is he weird or isn't he?"

"I think he'll be okay. He's got a different sense of humour. He may have just arrived from police academia but he's got lots of general duty experience in a variety of detachments including being in charge of his own for four years. He'll eventually come around to our way of thinking just like we trained Earl."

"I don't know about that. I think he's very much his own man and won't put up with any sloppy shit from us. I wouldn't want to press him on the issue. I think we've entered a new era. Time will tell, I guess."

♦ ◇ ♦

By 1988, Parkton City Detachment had a complement of 110 sworn (regular) members, of whom 72 were attached to four watches – A, B, C and D. The remaining were engaged in a variety of work in eight sections – Traffic, General Investigation (GIS), Drugs, Identification and Forensics, Community Relations, Court Liaison, a Police Service Dog Unit and a few responsible for Administrative duties.

Currently, on 'A' Watch, Corporal Al Hawkes was in charge of North Zone and Corporal Walter 'Walt' Bibermann in charge of Centre and South zones. Both had arrived in the past two years.

North area included most of the City north and west of the Thompson River and was a mix of light industrial, residential and the International Airport complex. Hawkes also had the main Canadian National Railway station, plus the CNR track ran through his territory for several miles.

Centre included the very busy city business centre, the Canadian Pacific Railway station, most of the major hotels, and older residential homes, while South area, much more spread out, was a combination of light industry, newer and new houses, in large subdivisions.

Further out were hay fields, smallish horse and cattle ranches, orchards and, more recently, fields of a new crop, called ginseng. This land was bisected east-west by the Trans-Canada Highway and included a small First Nations Reserve on the north side. The two corporals' population numbers and work loads were about even.

In spite of their distinct personality differences – Hawkes was a 'hail-fellow, well-met' kind of guy with a loud laugh while his peer was reserved, religious (he never swore but tolerated it with his men) and soft spoken – they got along quite well. They didn't socialize off duty except when some special occasion called for having a beer or two, generally with other members of the watch. Bibermann was a non-drinker and would have soft drinks.

As he normally did after each meeting, Sterling asked his corporals to stay for a quick discussion and any recommendations they may have. This year, he needed their views about the 12-hour watch system.

"Sure, I like it, how about you, Al?" asked Bibermann looking at Hawkes, who nodded his assent. "Why do you ask, Jack?"

"Well, the inspector has been quietly reviewing the issue. He's a bit of a traditionalist and had a hard time changing from the 8-hour ones a year ago. I think he still thinks that the members getting three full days off after each four 12-hour shifts, and then five days off after they've finished, is too much. He also believes they are too tiring.

"I think he's going to call a meeting of unit heads soon about the matter and I'd like to go prepared with my arguments to continue this system. He's partly right about them possibly being a bit tiring. I see a few of our guys looking a bit bleary-eyed around four a.m. but the graveyard shift is only for two nights. I can recall, as I'm sure you can, feeling quite tired after working five night shifts in a row on the old 8-hour shifts, from twelve midnight to eight a.m. Am I right?" he asked rhetorically.

The corporals nodded their heads in agreement.

"Listen, I'd appreciate a short note from each of you listing the positive aspects of this system. It would be good to go to the meeting, when and if one is called, with your support and reasons. I do value your help and advice. Thanks."

4   Jack Sterling was home alone; Jocelyn was with their three sons downtown at the Y pool taking swimming and lifeguard courses. It was three o'clock and he was watching the end of the B.C. Lions vs. Calgary Stampeders football game coming from Calgary. With 20 seconds to go in the last quarter, the Stamps were ahead 21–15 and the Lions had just gained possession of the ball at the Calgary 47-yard line. It was now or nothing, thought Sterling, eyes glued to the screen. Quarterback Matt Dunigan took the snap, ran back five paces, when Sterling's phone rang.

'Damn!' he thought. 'Helluva time to call. Pick up or let it ring until the play is finished?'

Dunigan let go with a 'Hail Mary' pass, sending the ball in a high arc toward the Calgary end zone. The ringing continued insistently. A bit exasperated, he grabbed the receiver and quickly blurted, "Yes?!" – not his usual response in taking a call – as the ball was dropping rapidly into a crowd of players behind the goal line.

"Jack, that you?" Staff Sergeant Hall asked.

Sterling replied quickly, "Yeah, gimme a minute," as he saw one pair of hands reach higher than the rest and snatch the ball. *Who caught it!?* Watching the referee eventually throw both arms straight up indicating a touchdown for the Lions, Sterling yelled, "Yes, yes!" A tied game!

Turning his head to speak into the phone, he said, "Excuse me, who's this?"

"Jack, it's Jim Hall. Sounds like you're watching the game."

"Oh, hi, Jim, sorry. This is a nail biter. Only a few seconds on the clock for the final play, a convert attempt coming up. If Passaglia makes the kick, the Lions win 21–20."

"Okay, I'll stand by. Let me know what happens, then we can talk," said Hall.

The kicker took a few paces back, the ball was snapped and placed, a boot made contact and the ball sailed through the goal posts for the single point. Game over.

"Yes!" shouted Sterling, punching his fist in the air and picking up the phone. "Go ahead, Staff. I guess you heard me, eh?"

"I suppose you could consider my call pretty good timing, eh? Right at the end of the game. Anyway, you and your crew are going to have to go to work early today. There's been a prison break from the Regional Correctional Centre and three bad people have escaped. They knocked a guard out on the way. They may have been met by someone outside the main gate – that's unconfirmed.

"We need extra manpower out now to help 'D' Watch members set up roadblocks and help handle normal calls. Get your zone supervisors to call their people and get them to the office ASAP for a briefing before being dispersed. Tell them to hurry the calls. I'd like you to come in right away. Can you do that?"

"Sure, Jim. Let me leave a note for my wife and get into uniform. See you there," he finished. He called Hawkes and Bibermann and set the wheels in motion.

♦ ◊ ♦

Al Hawkes was at home. It was just after three o'clock on Saturday, a nice fall day in October, with the afternoon temperature at a warm 21 degrees centigrade. On his transfer to Parkton two years previously from a small detachment in the North, he'd been promoted to corporal.

He and his wife purchased an older home, almost a 'fixer-upper' in a modest area on the North Shore, 'modest' in this case meaning cheap. It was their first house and all they could afford. He'd been making improvements to the property ever since. These 12-hour work shifts allowed him to have several days off consecutively and really get things done.

For the past two days he'd been putting up a four-feet-high cedar fence, a kind of lattice style that Shirley, his wife, had seen in a gardening magazine. It was a bit 'picky' to work on, but he liked 'messing around with wood' as he put it and was satisfied with the look of what he'd achieved so far. He was about half finished. Today, he was putting in concrete footings for the four-by-four posts for the remainder of the fence. He was particular with measurements. He followed the rule his carpentry instructor in high school told them – 'measure it twice, to make it nice.'

Shirley was at work as a pharmacist assistant in a small shopping centre located close by on Adanac Avenue, just off the Airport Road. She walked to work and their two children, Sandra, 8, and Shaun, 6, walked to their school only two blocks from the house, with either Mom or Dad – all very convenient for everyone. Today they were off and visiting friends down the block. So, for Hawkes, it was a quiet time which he appreciated. He was a contented individual, reasonably happy with his job and his private life.

The house phone rang. Dropping his shovel, he ran up the back steps into the kitchen, grabbing the phone off its wall cradle on the third ring. It was Sergeant Sterling.

"Al, it's Jack calling. Sorry to bother you at home but we have an emergency situation going on. There's been a break-out at the provincial jail and three nasty fellows are on the loose. Inspector Edwardson wants our watch in pronto to augment 'D' Watch members. You'll get the details when you arrive. Now, I've called Walt Bibermann and he is calling his people in and I'd like you to do the same. Emphasize promptness. Round up as many as you can. Don't waste time explaining. What this means, of course, is that we'll start our shift early and go on through to 7 a.m. tomorrow. You okay with this?"

"Yeah, Jack, will do," he replied. "I'm going to call Shirley and put her on notice so that she can pick up the kids from their friend's house when she gets off. I'll be as quick as I can."

He was lucky to contact six out of his seven people. Constable Kart didn't pick up, so he left a message. In twenty-five minutes he reported to the office and eventually all but two members of 'A' Watch arrived and immediately went into a briefing given by Staff Sergeant Jim Hall, the Operations NCO. Inspector Edwardson was not present as he was at the TV station talking to the news media.

Hall began by introducing the *Parkton News* reporter, and saying thanks to 'A' Watch members for coming in, then handed out photocopies of the mug shots and descriptions of three escapees.

"These three," he said, "are from Montreal and members of the gang underworld in that city. As you may know, they were being held without bail at the RCC, awaiting a preliminary hearing on charges of Possession for the Purpose of Distribution – methamphetamine, coke and heroin. They were picked up by Salmon River Detachment two weeks ago at a road check and transported here pending the preliminary hearing.

"These bastards are as bad as they come. All have records for armed robbery and serious assaults and one got off on an attempt murder charge. They all travel armed and while it is believed they were not so when they broke out, there's no doubt they soon will be, or are already. The utmost caution then must be exercised, particularly around our citizens. I won't go into the escape details except to say they injured a guard at the main gate. Because of this, no one saw how they got away – on foot or by vehicle. At the moment, we don't know if this was an inside job or whether anyone picked them up. GIS are investigating at the jail. If I had to guess, I'd say they'll try to make it to Vancouver where they were headed with their load of drugs when stopped. Of course, knowing we know that, they could be trying to head back to Quebec.

"Okay, concerning operations. Because we have a finite number of vehicles, I'm sending you out in pairs, and of course, for safety reasons. For this operation, I'll be in overall charge, while 'D' Watch commander will be responsible for the North Zone and 'A' Watch commander for the Centre and South areas. There will necessarily be a mix of members from both watches in all areas of the City and you'll be assigned a car shortly." Looking at them meaningfully, he added, "There will be no 'watch rivalries' on this mission, ladies and gentlemen.

"In case you don't know, this escape is being carried on local TV and radio stations, together with the pictures and full descriptions of the escapees. We are already receiving a fair number of tips.

"Two cars with four members are stationed east and west on the TCH for roadblock duty, and you will relieve them in due course. As well, we have members at the downtown bus station, both railway stations and one at the airport although it's unlikely they will fly out of Parkton. Roving patrols in designated areas will be made. Obviously, we have to continue responding to regular calls and complaints, MVAs, etcetera – the routine stuff.

"We have extra complaint and dispatch staff on duty. I'll be here as long as it takes to coordinate matters and get this thing over with. Naturally, I'd like to see us get lucky and the sooner the better. I don't like having people like these roaming around our community. Members of 'D' Watch will stay on duty at least until midnight if required. Before you get your assignments, any questions, observations?"

Sergeant Sterling stood up and asked, "Staff, I'm wondering if it might be timely to review the Force's shooting policy, given the background of these individuals?"

"Okay, Jack, wouldn't do any harm. Just so I get it right, would someone bring me a copy of RR&O's and the *Criminal Code*."

Both were produced. Hall quickly began by reading Section 25, sub-section 1, sub-para (1)(b) of the *Code* which said, "*Everyone who is required by law to do anything in the administration or enforcement of the law... as a peace officer is, if he acts on reasonable grounds, justified in doing what he is required or authorized to do and in using AS MUCH FORCE AS IS NECESSARY FOR THAT PURPOSE,"* said Hall, emphasizing the last nine words. "I'll read sub-section 3. In essence, it says that *you cannot use excessive force* – and I'm going to again emphasize these words – *UNLESS HE (the police officer) BELIEVES ON REASONABLE AND PROBABLE GROUNDS THAT IT IS NECESSARY FOR THE PURPOSE OF PRESERVING HIMSELF OR ANYONE UNDER HIS PROTECTION FROM DEATH OR GRIEVOUS BODILY HARM.* Rules and Regs more or less reiterate the same thing, including the term 'good judgement.'"

He paused a moment to let that sink in and continued, "This is NOT an easy position for you to be in because of what does, or does not, constitute 'reasonable and probable grounds.'

"I note that Section 25 does not use the word 'imminent' and to me, that is the key. Of course, even that word is subjective. What the hell does 'imminent' mean? In other words, the onus is on you to determine 'imminent threat of death or bodily harm' as quickly and accurately as you can. The answer to your decision is settled by the Courts later on. The Force's policy on this issue is predicated on Section 25. So, if you do have to use your weapon, remember your firearms training – aim for centre mass.

"Alright, if there's nothing else, hit the road and let's see if we can pick these bastards up. Oh, and remember Sergeant Jablonski's parting words to his people on *Hill Street Blues* before they hit the streets," Hall said, raising his right hand and right index finger, "Be careful out there!"

♦   ◊   ♦

"Bravo-9, your Twenty?"

"Bravo-9, TCH and Carson Drive," Al Hawkes replied to the dispatcher's call.

"House B&E in progress, 1176 Greenwood Drive. Possible escapee suspects involved. Time 23:29. Your ETA?"

"Radio, we're about three minutes away."

"Ten-four. Closest other members, please."

"Bravo-13, we're about four minutes. Will cover."

"Roger. Coordinate with Corporal Hawkes."

"Bravo-9 and -13, go to Tac-three, cars and portables," instructed Sergeant Sterling, monitoring the conversations. "No sirens or lights. Stop short of the house. Advise when arrived. Bravo-7, Delta-1, what's your twenty, Dale?"

The Dog Master replied that he was on the Trans-Canada Highway, in mid-city, and that his ETA would be seven minutes or so. "I heard the previous transmissions," he added.

Racing along the highway, Hawkes instructed Constable Oliver to meet him on Greenwood – lights out. And to the Dog Master he asked if he could meet them, same place. "Walk Shadow towards us."

"Delta-1, ten four."

"Bravo-9, Bravo-7, I'll be there in less than ten minutes. Keep me apprised, please," said the Sergeant. The air waves went silent for sixty seconds, enough time for each officer en route to the scene to ponder what was ahead for them. They didn't get many calls like this.

♦ ◇ ♦

At 1176 Greenwood Drive, a man, dressed in a pair of tartan boxer shorts and an old work shirt, was standing in his garage, breathing heavily, with a gun in his hand pointing it at a male lying prone on the concrete floor. "You move, you son of a bitch and I'll shoot! You hear me!" he exclaimed. "The cops are on their way. You and your buddies – are you the three who escaped from jail?" No response.

To emphasize his position of authority in this case, he added, "You might wanna know I'm a retired infantry sergeant and I've killed people in my service. It won't take much for me to blow you away.

You got that?" he yelled again, which elicited a feeble nod of the head from the man.

Marty Williams and his wife June had retired for the night to their bedroom at eleven p.m. after watching the ten o'clock *News*, as was their custom. The TV station had carried a clip about the escape.

They lived in a split-level house with three upstairs bedrooms. The two other rooms were occupied by their seventeen- and fifteen-year-old daughters. Both parents usually read in bed, as they had tonight. Williams had served twenty years as a soldier in a Canadian Light Infantry Regiment and had seen active service in Cyprus and Bosnia.

He'd retired and was now a transit driver in the city. He was also a member of the Parkton Rod and Gun Club and owned a Remington 12-gauge shotgun and a Glock 17L, a 9mm, competition 'longslide' handgun. Both were locked in a gun cabinet in the master bedroom. At 11:25 p.m., they turned off their matching set of bed lamps and settled down.

Not yet asleep, Williams heard the muffled noise of a door closing somewhere downstairs. In quickly getting out of bed, he glanced at the large red, luminous numbers on the bedside clock – 11:27. Flicking on his light, he nudged June, who was almost asleep and whispered loudly, "Honey, there's someone in the house, downstairs. I'm going down. Go get the girls and bring them into this room and lock the door. Be very quiet, okay?"

Coming alert very quickly, she started putting on her dressing gown while Williams unlocked his cabinet, took out his Glock, rammed in a magazine of pre-loaded 9mm ammunition and set the gun. "You ready?"

She nodded and he could see she was shaking a bit. Putting both hands on her shoulders, he said, "Don't worry, it'll be okay, Sweetheart. Put the light out before we leave the room."

With his gun in his right hand and a small penlight flashlight in his left, Williams slipped out as June opened the door for him. She went left along the landing while he crept slowly down the short first flight of stairs into the main floor hallway and turned left down the next set of steps that led to the door into the garage. At this point, he heard a 'Shh!' from upstairs and a *click* as a door closed. Putting his left ear close to the thin wooden garage door, he heard something drop and another 'Shh!' from the other side, followed by a couple of low voices. 'So,' he thought, 'at least two people in there. Be careful,' he told himself.

◆ ◇ ◆

The three men had entered the garage by jimmying the side door by means of a small garden shovel they found stuck in the earth near the door. Having no flashlight, they had to resort to turning on the garage light momentarily to get the layout and to find the door into the house. The place was big enough for two cars but occupied by just one as the other was in the driveway. Spotting a wall-mounted tool rack over the work bench, one of them took down the largest, long-shafted screwdriver to open the inside door into the house. Switching off the light, and leaving the side door open for some limited light and a quick escape, they made their way around the car. With the three of them in close proximity to each other, it was inevitable that they would collide, resulting in the screwdriver being dropped on the concrete floor, the sound amplifying in the half-empty space.

"Ssh. Prenez garde!" said the lead man, in a loud whisper.

On the other side of the door, Marty Williams, gun ready in his hand, took a deep breath. Steeling himself, he gripped the door handle and slowly turned it.

'Here goes nothing,' he thought as he violently shoved it open.

The door swung outwards, hitting the first man in the chest and sending him crashing into his two companions behind him, knocking both to the floor as well.

Williams's flashlight picked out surprised looks on three faces as he yelled, "Hold it right there or I'll shoot!"

The two who were behind the leader quickly scrambled on all fours around the front of the car toward the door they had entered by. The man in front had been struck by the door and lay winded on the floor.

"You move, you son of a bitch, and I'll shoot, you hear me!?" pointing his gun at the man's chest from three feet away. Turning his head slightly, he shouted through the doorway, "June, call the cops – 911!"

The auxiliary wall phone by the work bench had a red light to indicate when the house phone was in use. It came on, indicating to him that his wife had heard and was making the call. He needed to secure the guy for the police. Keeping his flashlight directed at the prone man, he stepped over him, placing his gun on the roof of his car. He reached up to the wall on his immediate left, and felt for some electrical cords that hung there. His fingers curled around one length and he pulled it quickly off the nail.

He thought about turning on the garage light, reconsidered momentarily and decided against it. Make him too easy a target if the other two returned. He placed his flashlight in his mouth and knelt down beside the man, putting his right leg across the man's thighs. "Put your hands behind your back," he said.

"Quoi?"

Williams realized then that he was a French Canadian with little English and took both arms, crossing them behind his back, tying them with the cord. He stood up and took another cord from the wall and tied the man at his ankles. During the two minutes it took to do this, he had been listening for the sound of approaching police sirens and for any movement behind him in case the other two men had returned for their buddy – but it was eerily silent.

Picking up his gun, he tried to remember the French for 'stay here' and it came to him – "Restez ici!" he said forcefully. Satisfied that the individual was not going to move very soon, Williams slowly walked to the open side door and peeked out.

There was some ambient light from the nearby street lamp but he could see or hear nothing.

'Damn,' he thought. 'What's keeping the police – I need them here *now*.'

Just as he was about to go back to check on his prisoner and to shout to his wife to call the police again, he caught a glimpse of the silhouettes of two men at the end of his driveway. Thinking they were the two men who had run away, he raised his gun at them and was about to yell, 'Hold it!' when he was bathed in bright light, momentarily blinding him.

A voice, in North American English, loudly commanded him to, "Drop your weapon – do it now!"

Williams immediately did as he was told by placing his gun on the pathway, stood up and raised his hands. "Are you the police?"

"We are," a voice replied.

"We're the people who called in," said Williams, hands still in the air. "I've captured one of them and he's in my garage."

"Okay," said one of the officers, "we're going to walk toward you. Step back from your weapon and stay as you are, please."

When the two officers got to him, Williams said, "Jesus, it's good to see you guys. I didn't hear any sirens and I was going to get my wife to call you again."

One of the constables picked up his gun while the second gave him a quick pat down and let him lower his hands. Seemingly satisfied he was who he claimed to be, the constable said, "It's standard police practice for us to approach situations like this as silently as we can, so we don't spook the burglars. Sorry about the pat down but you understand? Let's see who you've got here," he added, returning the gun.

Before leaving Williams, with the prisoner in tow, Corporal Hawkes, who had covered the rear of the house, shook his hand and thanked him for his citizen's services, telling him he would be asking the Officer in Charge of the detachment to consider sending him a letter of commendation.

By one o'clock it was all over. The other two escapees were found by the police dog hiding under an old tractor in a lean-to shelter in an apple orchard at the end of Greenwood Drive. Like most people, these two had a healthy respect for German Shepherds and gave up quietly.

◆ ◇ ◆

Al Hawkes called his wife at daybreak, apologizing for waking her up, to let her know he was okay, would be home at the usual time and reminded her about his favourite breakfast. He was home, tired, at 7:30 Monday morning. Walking into his house, he immediately smelled pork sausages frying, and the aroma of fresh-brewed coffee.

"Ahh, smells good!" he said, hugging his wife closely and then his two kids. They examined him with looks that seemed to be checking to see if he still had two arms and two legs – a whole human being. All three went to work and school respectively, feeling good about the day and proud of husband and father.

As Hawkes went to bed after his great breakfast, he reflected on the night's activities and was very thankful that no police officer had had to rely on Section 25 of the *Criminal Code* last night to 'do his duty.'

'I just hope I never have to,' he thought. He slept well.

5

She drifted across the wooden floor in full battle dress – a 'Ferrari red' silk one. The manufacturer had obviously run out of material. The top started just one inch above her areola and the hemline one inch below her – you know. She was literally just two inches from legal arrest for a violation of the indecency section of the *Criminal Code*. No foundation garments either – nil, zip, nada. A man can tell. The only other apparel was a pair of matching red high heels. Out of those shoes stretched a pair of identically shaped legs that looked as though they had been turned on the same lathe. Her upper right arm boasted a tattoo of a heart with 'Love Mom' inside. Hair: bottled blond and spiked. Face: smothered in 'Tammy Faye' powder and eye lashes with similar amounts of mascara, complete with lip-glossed, dress-matching lipstick and large, matching red-plastic hoops on her ears. Age: rough guess, twenty-eight.

All conversation in the pub quickly ceased. Not to carry a meta-phor too far, the silence was pregnant. It was six o'clock Friday eve-ning and most of the tables were full.

She selected one of the remaining stools at the bar and sat. As she did so, the red dress rose even higher and legs and thighs became unbearably prominent.

The bartender was the first to recover. Summoning all his will-power, he looked her in the eyes and asked for her order. Tapping her long red stick-on fingernails on the bar, she ordered a Coke and paid for it from a red clutch purse.

The buzz of conversation slowly resumed.

"What the hell were we talking about?" Ray said to his three friends, sitting at a small round copper-covered beer table no more than six feet from *her*.

"Goddamned if I know. Who can think rationally sitting this close to heaven?" one said.

♦ ◇ ♦

This was the first day on her temporary assignment that Constable Alice Conway had gone 'fishing,' as Corporal Kenneth Brandt, in charge of the Detachment Drug Section put it, earlier that evening. "By the time we dress you up—"

"—More like down," she interrupted.

"—You can get information about drugs from anyone. Men will bare their hearts and souls to you," he finished.

"It's not their hearts and souls I'm concerned about them baring. Looking like this, I'll have to fight them off," she replied.

"Alice, we've schooled you in drug dialogue and dealing activities. You've already shown you can be cool under pressure when you were in uniform. Look at this exercise as just another bunch of ignorant, low-life assholes you have to deal with. You'll be amazed at what they tell you. Just keep the entrapment rules in mind and the gist of your conversations for your notes later. You'll be fine and although you have no wire, for obvious reasons, we're close by. Again, you know the 'assistance needed' signal?" he asked.

"Yeah, scratch my right ass," she said.

"Well, close enough. Your right ear would be more ladylike," he laughed.

"Listen," Brandt continued, "don't worry if you don't score this evening. As much as anything, this is a trial run for you. We need to find out if our info about an increase in illegal drug activity at this pub is true or just fiction, okay?"

Turning to her two back-up people, he asked them if they had anything to add before they left on this assignment.

They said no, they'd already gone over the plan and were ready.

♦ ◇ ♦

It took a minute or two for his eyes to adjust to the dark interior, even though two TV sets were showing an NHL pre-season game. It was the Vancouver Canucks versus the L.A. Kings, and Wayne Gretzky, recently traded to the Kings in August, had just scored his first goal. The pub crowd roared in approval, still uncertain though whether to cheer for the 'Great One' or their own team.

As bars go, the Pioneer Pub, decorated in a western theme, wasn't too shabby, and mostly inhabited by clientele from working-class backgrounds and close to where the policeman lived. As he went forward toward the bar looking for his buddy, Wally Rheingold, he spotted a female sitting on a bar stool, wearing a bright red dress. There were two vacant seats to her right so he slid onto the one next to her with the words, "This taken?"

She gave him a cursory glance, shook her head 'No' and went back to her drink, a Coke, he thought.

Constable Alan Burns was 28 years old, occupied a six-foot frame, weighing a proportionate 190 pounds, with his head covered in a short brush cut of black hair. He was relatively good looking, grey eyes, his nose a bit on the large size, the result of minor league hockey games action. He was also unmarried and very heterosexual.

After ordering dark ale, he leaned forward over his folded arms on the bar to get a better look at the woman's face and said, "Busy tonight, eh?"

No response.

He tried again. "Hi, my name's Al. Yours?"

At first glance, he took her to be about his age and she certainly had a beautiful profile, at least in the dim light. He detected a slight but very agreeable perfume coming from her body, and the dress she was wearing, showing a lot of cleavage, especially in her position slightly bent over the bar rail, left absolutely nothing to the imagination, top and bottom. Sitting up straight, she turned her head slightly to the right and eyeballed him for a second or two and said, "I don't think you need to know that."

"Oh, sorry," he said, a bit nonplussed by her reply. Not one to give up easily and like many men, he was convinced that he had a 'way' of chatting to women. This was reinforced in his mind by the fact that he'd managed a few 'affairs of the heart' as he liked to put it, meaning mostly one-night stands.

Not willing to give up – the next stool was for his friend and there were no others available, nor tables either – Burns just couldn't sit there in silence. With five years of service, he'd learned quite well, through osmosis as much as with training and experience, about human psychology and how to 'read' people. In two or three seconds, he diagnosed, by judging her body language, attitude, limited use of words and by the important fact that she was alone and apparently not expecting anyone – she could have lied about that – that further effort was worthwhile. He noticed her scanning the room and he thought that she may be looking for another seat away from him – time to strike again.

"Look, once again I'm sorry. Let me buy you a drink, on one condition."

Looking at him straight on, she asked, "And what's that?"

"That you don't have to talk to me."

A slight smile crossed her face momentarily and she replied, "In that case, it's a deal: a glass of Chardonnay."

Keeping his silence, Burns dutifully waited for the drink to be delivered and watched her take a sip.

"Hmm, that's quite good. Thanks," she said.

"Permission to speak?" he asked with a straight face.

She nodded.

"Glad you like it. I don't always drink beer."

"Come here often?"

"Not really," he replied, limiting his language. He'd learned, through interviewing hundreds of witnesses and suspects, that silence, on his part, often induced people to fill the void with talk, and it worked once again.

"So, I take it the friend you are waiting for is a male, or you wouldn't be trying to pick me up – or would you?" she asked.

He laughed and said, "No. Surely I don't look that needy?"

"How needy are you?"

Al Burns was not sure where this was going, and he was a bit surprised at the tenor of the question. Was this just verbal sparring or more than that?

Deciding to escalate the conversation more into the realm of physical needs, he said, "Well, on a scale of one to ten, I guess I'd be approaching ten, truth be told."

She had a beautiful laugh and he was about to continue when he felt a hand on his right shoulder. "Hi, Al, how's it goin'?" Wally asked. "This seat for me?"

"Hi, Wally. Yeah. Go ahead," he responded and at the same time thought, 'Goddamn, Wally, poor timing.'

Rheingold, having seen his friend talking to the lady in red, sat and reached across in front of him and extended his hand to the woman saying, "Hello, my name's Wally," and then, a bit lamely, continued, "Of course, you already heard that," as she peremptorily took his hand and said, "I'm Alice."

Rheingold picked up on the awareness of the situation for his friend and said, "Look, excuse me for a few minutes. I have to make a call and I'll do it on the exterior phone; it's too noisy in here." With that, he left.

Turning to face the lady in red, he said, "So, it's Alice, is it. Nice name."

"Thanks. What's Al short for – Alan, Alexander, Aloysius?"

"It's Alan with one L – similar to Alice with one L."

"What do you do, Alan-with-one-L?"

When asked that question by a stranger, he preferred not to say what he did for a living because by doing so, it put a different dimension on any subsequent conversation with someone he did not know and who was not a member of the Force. He generally said he worked for the 'Government' and when pressed for further information would say something like, 'Oh, it's mostly clerical work, not very interesting,' which was only a tiny part true. He was responsible for preparing the monthly statistical Crime Report for his watch, a job which took an hour at most.

Alice Conway knew he was hedging and merely said. "Oh, sounds exciting," in a slightly sarcastic way.

Before he could ask the same question, Conway asked him if he was from Parkton. She's 'fishing,' he knew and his verbal guard increased. He needed to be truthful but careful as well. It was just too early to divulge much information should this 'association' progress further.

"I'm from Trona," he said.

"Trona?" she said quizzically, screwing up her face. "Oh, you mean *To-ron-to.*"

"That's what I said – Trona."

She laughed. "Reminds me of a famous line from an old George and Ira Gershwin song, *'Let's call the whole thing off.'* You know the line? 'I say to-mah-to and you say to-may-to.'"

"Oh, yeah," he replied, vaguely wondering what she was talking about. Before she could probe further, he asked her what she did for a living.

"Oh, just taking some time off between jobs."

"I take it you live here then?"

"No, I'm from the Vancouver area but I have a cousin who lives here."

Burns was about to press for more information when the room erupted into cheering and whistling as his team, the Canucks, scored an early goal in the first period, evening-up the score.

When the noise settled down, he felt he had lost the momentum on the personal stuff that she, like him, didn't want to discuss further.

Looking into the mirror on the wall behind the bar, he noted two men looking at his reflection and when he made eye contact, they both quickly averted theirs. A 'caution' flag appeared in his brain as he studied them a few moments longer.

Both were maybe slightly older, stocky builds, one with black long hair, the other with shorter dirty blond (at least in the pub light) and both verging on 'scruffy'.

One was wearing a referee's vertical black-and-white striped shirt and the second, a nondescript high-necked grey sweater, all this information gleaned from a two-second scan. He diverted his eyes, but his suspicions had been aroused and he stole another quick sideways glance at them.

'Alice' was saying something to him and he said, "Sorry, Alice, what did you say?' as he looked at her, face-on. He liked what he saw.

"I said you look a bit distracted."

"Oh, I don't mean to be, certainly not with you. If anything, I'd like to be a bit more preoccupied."

Just as Burns was about to get that way with her, Rheingold sat down next to him again.

"Can I get you guys another drink?" he asked before ordering one for himself.

She said, "Look, I have to go – sorry. Nice meeting you, Al. Maybe we'll run into each other again. See you, guys."

With that, red purse in hand, she slid off the stool and walked toward the exit.

Burns watched her as she did so, noticing her shape from the rear and saying to his partner, "There goes a classy-looking lady. You really have lousy timing, Wally Rheingold."

As she swung open the big, wide front door, letting bright sunlight stream in, he also saw the two guys seated close to the door get up and leave, one throwing a brief glance in his direction.

"Come with me, Wally," Burns said, throwing some cash on the bar and getting off his stool.

"But what about our drinks?" he protested.

"The hell with the drinks. I think something may be going down outside, maybe with Alice," as he walked quickly to the exit, Rheingold tagging along.

As they reached the exit, two people entered the pub and the two policemen both stood aside to let them pass, and at the same time, took a quick glance outside. 'Alice' was near the far end of the parking lot while the two men were continuing in that direction.

Not wanting to reveal himself yet, Burns pushed the door open slightly for another look and now saw the woman and the two men talking beside a nondescript grey sedan.

Rheingold took a peek over his shoulder and asked, "Whad'ya think?"

"Don't quite know. Two or three things, I suppose. She could be a hooker and these guys want a threesome or she's an addict and/or a pusher and she could be making a sale to them or a buy from them. Somehow though, I don't feel those possibilities fit her character."

"Well, you know the old saying, Al," Rheingold said as they continued their surveillance, "Love is blind and I think you're a bit mesmerized still by the sight of her ass, old buddy."

"That's true, but I don't think it's clouded my instincts about her that much."

"Okay. What now?"

"Let's see what they do."

What the three did was confer for a few minutes. The two Drug Squad members, sent up from Vancouver to help the small local Drug section with assistance from GIS, decided that the time and effort spent at this pub would produce no tangible results and that they had other targets to check out.

'Alice' returned to her car, a new black Mustang and Burns watched her get in. As she sat down, he caught a glimpse of the long, luscious, naked left leg before she closed the door and drove away. In spite of this, he remembered to note the plate number.

He and Rheingold made their way across the parking lot, trying to stay low profile by walking between parked cars until they got closer to the two men and their car, an '89 Plymouth Gran Fury, dark blue. Burns wanted to get a look at the license plate number and 'run' it through the detachment dispatcher to get the RO – registered owner's name and address. Although neither of them were on duty, he felt it might be prudent to get this information quickly and then check with Corporal Ken Brandt or the NCO in charge of the GI Section.

He asked Rheingold to stay and watch the men and walked quickly back to the pub to make his call, from the small, less-noisy foyer area. Reaching the dispatcher, he identified himself – she knew who he was – and requested the information. A minute later, he had his answer, or rather, the lack of one. Sheila Mason told him the Motor Vehicles Office had placed a 'block' on this information from being released. It was enough, however, to tell him that the Plymouth had been rented by the RCMP for use in undercover operations and that the two men and 'Alice' were more than likely from the Greater Vancouver area. They were back in the car now.

He walked back to Rheingold with the information.

"So," Wally said, "they're running an operation here."

"Yeah – you know, until I saw the car, I thought they were just some dick-heads. They certainly looked the part. I'm also sure that Alice, if that's her real name, is undercover as well. In any event, we don't get involved, but I'd still like to confirm this somehow and I'd sure like to meet her again."

6   The buzz of conversation quickly died down as Sergeant Sterling entered the room. He stood, in uniform, at the front of the class and said, "Good evening, gentlemen," – there were no women present – "good to see you all here. The gentleman standing with me is Charlie Preston, a reporter for the *Parkton News*. He is doing a series of articles called *People in the Public Service* and will talk about that when I've finished my introduction. Some of you may know him and he will be attending a few of these sessions" – as he indicated with his hand for Preston to take a seat.

"You've all met me, of course, as I've taken your applications and interviewed you for the RCMP Auxiliary Police Program. This class of fifteen is a fairly big one and when you've all passed," he emphasized, "you will complete our full complement of forty auxiliary positions. I don't believe you've all met each other and I'd like you to stand and state your name and, if you wish, what you do for a living. You will certainly get to know each other over the next ten weekly sessions."

After they were finished the introductions, Sterling continued.

"This is the first session and will only last for an hour and a half while I cover the curriculum in a bit of detail and any questions you may have. I reiterate the need for you to attend all sessions. Each of them is equally important and will go some way toward making you knowledgeable and somewhat competent in police matters before we cut you loose on the unsuspecting public."

A small chuckle from the group.

"You will find, however, that much of the time you are in the public eye in uniform, they do not see your auxiliary shoulder patch and may mistake you for a regular member. Most of the time, it will be to your advantage. I have a question: Why?"

One person raised his hand and got the nod to reply. "Well, I suppose it gets around the problem of being identified as a 'rent-a-cop', a somewhat derogatory label, but more importantly, gives us an air of having full police authority. Public perception is important, I think."

"Good point. Hank Williams, isn't it?" said the sergeant.

"Yes," replied Williams, whose day job was that of a grade school teacher.

Sterling continued, "Having noted that of course means that you have to 'assume the role' but let me also point out that if asked, you must not hold yourself out to be a regular member.

"It's important your curriculum then is similar to that used in recruit training in Regina, but obviously not as long and intense. You aren't being paid to do police work, per se, but to assist when necessary. The training you receive, the information you learn, will certainly enable you to perform your work in a competent manner. Of course, the more time you put in, the more self-confident and self-sufficient you will become, to the Force and to the citizens who live here. It's an honourable job you are about to undertake and, while you're all here together tonight, let me thank you for volunteering in a worthwhile cause.

"This isn't everybody's 'cup of tea' and some of you may see it that way. It's certainly okay if you do and no shame is attached if you want to discontinue.

"I do ask you to focus fully on the training program. As well as being necessary, the information you learn will be enlightening and interesting. Your duties for assisting regular members will be covered in detail on your last session. These are important to know. At the conclusion, you will be paraded in uniform before either the Officer in Charge of this detachment or the Officer Commanding the Sub Division. This is a very special occasion where you are sworn in and receive your badge and police ID card and can then begin patrol work and other duties. Family members are, of course, invited."

At 9:10 p.m. he dismissed the group, after his guest had said a few supporting words about citizenship and the importance of volunteerism. When the last man had left the room, Sterling said to the reporter, "Well, what do you think?"

"Do you mean about the individuals or the curriculum?" asked Preston.

"Well, both, I guess," replied Sterling.

"I'd rather not pass judgment on the men except to say they all appear keen about the prospect of becoming a 'quasi-police' officer if I can use that expression, but your training program looks fairly comprehensive and interesting as you pointed out. What's the drop-out rate, Jack?"

"It goes in two stages. The attrition rate in the training period is about twenty percent and climbs to about thirty-five after a few weeks of doing patrol work."

"So," continued Charlie, "that's an average loss of three people initially, out of this class of fifteen, rising to about five after being on the road for a while. Why is that?"

"A variety of reasons," the sergeant replied. "In this initial training phase, a few decide they may have been a bit ambitious, or conversely, that they wanted more authority – be more like a real cop, so to speak. Where most of them do their introspection about being an auxiliary is after they've done a few uniformed patrols and some assistance work. They begin to get the idea that this kind of activity, this kind of contact with the public, especially the negative stuff – being sworn at, spat on, shoved and occasionally assaulted – is definitely not for them.

"As well, other things impinge upon whether they stay or not; like family support, especially if they are married and more so if they have kids. Some wives tend to increasingly worry about their husband's safety – all wives do, for that matter – *but if you're not earning your living at it, why do it?* is their rhetorical question.

"For a few auxiliaries, their work interferes with attendance and they have no choice but to quit – just to cite a few reasons. Over time, these losses add up and we have to recruit to fill vacancies."

"So tell me," the reporter asked, "in the grand scheme of things, are they really worth all the effort and expense in terms of being a real, tangible value to the detachment, and, of course, by extension, the general public?"

"My answer," replied Sterling, "is an unqualified 'Yes'. I can say that, after two or three years of field experience, most of these guys are as good as regular members. We simply can't do without them."

"Well, that's a ringing endorsement. Listen. Remember that project we talked about three or four weeks ago, about me writing a book about my experiences with 'A' watch? I've done some serious thinking about it and I'd like to discuss it further with you. Now that I've finished my newspaper articles on the four ride-alongs that I did recently, I'd like to continue with them. When would be a good time, Jack?"

"Anytime, I guess. How long will you need?"

"About an hour I should think – how about over lunch somewhere?"

"Okay. It'll have to be on a day off. There're too many interruptions at work."

"How about if I call you, say, for next week?"

"Sounds good. Perhaps we can get together with Inspector Edwardson for a review?"

"Good. Look in the paper tomorrow. Good night, Jack."

7

Jim Portal got home early for a change – fifteen minutes past seven, having worked a 12-hour day shift. After gassing up, he'd returned to the office when the late afternoon rush-hour traffic had subsided and finished writing up his various complaints and other paperwork by seven. He lived fifteen minutes from the office. Married to Lillian for four years, they had no children although they both wanted one, or possibly two, they had decided recently. She was a registered nurse and worked in a local medical clinic on the South Shore.

Prior to being transferred to Parkton two years ago, he had been stationed at a Lower Mainland municipal detachment for three years, right after he left Regina in 1983. Not long after he left the training establishment, he and a buddy went to a house warming party where he met Miss Walsley. At the time, Portal was twenty-two and had had a few 'steady dates' as he called them. They did not lead to anything and he was not anxious to get 'tied up' at that time on a permanent basis, besides, as he said to his friend, "None of my women appealed to me to that extent."

But this one was different – completely. To Constable Portal, she was gorgeous, shapely, personable and 'seemed to like me – a lot,' he confided in his friend. "What did you think of her?" he asked, looking for approval.

"She's not bad. Wouldn't kick her out of bed," he replied, a bit facetiously.

"Whaddya mean 'not bad'? She could qualify as Miss Canada any day. Besides, you won't have the opportunity to do that."

"Okay, okay, settle down, friend. She's all yours."

"Well, let's hope so," replied Portal, sounding a bit placated. A year later, Portal and Lillian Walsley were married and two years after, transferred to Parkton.

♦   ◇   ♦

Entering his house, he said, "Hi, Lil," and got a 'Hi, Sweetheart,' in return as he removed his shoes just inside the back door and took off his Sam Brown belt and revolver, which he removed from the holster and placed in a bolted-down lock-box in the hall closet. He washed his hands in the bathroom and went into the kitchen, hugged his wife, gave her a light kiss on the lips, turned her around and, cupping his hands, pulled her back against him and gave her another hug. She turned her head and, looking up over her shoulder at him, said, "Do you love me or these?"

"All three," he replied diplomatically.

"Good answer," she said, disengaging and entering the kitchen. "Like a Molson's?" she asked. "Dinner'll be ready in ten minutes."

"Be great, thanks," as his wife removed the can from the fridge, cracked it open and handed it to him.

"How was your day?" she said.

Taking a long sip from the can and wiping the foam off his lips with the back of his hand, he said. "Unremarkable."

Lillian gave a little chuckle and said, "So, you've adopted some of the language I have to use," she noted. Doctors often used that word to describe someone's medical condition and it came out in her conversation occasionally. Naturally enough, she too discussed her work with her husband and, like him, only in a general sense. Both avoided 'naming names' as that was deemed unprofessional.

"So," she said, "a slow day, was it?" as she opened the oven and checked on his baked chicken supper.

"No, no, not at all. Fairly busy but mostly 'chicken-shit stuff' – no pun intended," he said, nodding at the chicken, "just the 'same old, same old'. That smells delicious, Lil," noting the large Idaho potato that he liked to slather lots of sour cream on.

"You seem a bit reticent with your language this evening," she noted. "Holding something back, Jim?"

"No, I'm just trying to enjoy my beer. My day definitely got off to a different start though."

"Tell me about it."

"Around 7:30 a.m. I was patrolling the back road, you know, the one that runs west along the north shore of Parkton Lake, before I had to go and do school patrols around eight. Over the past couple of years I've found the odd stolen vehicle abandoned along there and sometimes piles of trash, old fridges, broken furniture, mattresses. I don't know if I've told you before but I actually search trash to try to find a name and address and when I do, I invite those people to come out and clean up their mess under the threat of prosecution. I tell them I've taken a photo of it and their address and it seems to work. Anyway, I digress.

"So, I'm driving along, admiring the view of the lake and the hills, turn a corner and spot a fairly new car parked on the side of the road. It was a cool morning today and the windows were fogged up, so someone was inside.

"Silently drifting to a stop thirty yards or so behind it, I walked quietly on the grass verge, stopped at a rear door, bent over and tried to peek in. In spite of the steamy window I could see inside. And what did I spy, with my little eye?" he asked Lil.

"A couple going at it?" she quickly responded.

"Yep. 'Au naturel' they were too. So, I said to myself, 'What should I do?'"

"Let me guess," said his wife. "Being the voyeur that I know you to be, you also elected to get enough 'evidence' by watching the action?"

He laughed. "Well, what could I do when it was presented so

graphically? I weighed my options. Disturb them and cause 'coitus interruptus' or walk away?

"I decided to leave them – there was no traffic on the road at that time of day – and I was about to do that when the woman, about 25, I'd guess, who was in the submissive position, opened her eyes and saw me, or at least my face and head. She screamed. I stood up revealing my uniform and tapped on the window. After some quick re-arranging of body positions, she covered herself with her slip, while he fished in his trousers, which were draped over the back of the driver's seat, for his ID."

"How embarrassing for them," she said.

"Well, as the old saying goes, 'you pays your money, and you takes your chances.' Anyway, I told them they needed to be a little more circumspect in where they chose to have 'relations' and left."

"Good choice, sweetheart. Come on, supper's ready. Let's eat."

Between mouthfuls of delicious food and sips of beer, he completed his list of activities for the day – the usual school patrols until nine a.m., picked up a stolen bike – Lil interjected with, "Wow! How did you manage that one?" – arrested two drunks, attended a shoplifting complaint at the liquor store (committed by a known 'wino'), attended two minor fender-benders (no traffic cars on today), theft of a front step flower box, probably late at night or early in the morning, and issued two traffic tickets. "That was the sum and substance of my day's efforts, for which, at my current pay grade, amounted to two hundred dollars, minus income tax, pension and U.I. premiums," he concluded.

"Want an early night?" she asked with a smile.

"Letmethinkaboutit. I'vethoughtaboutit – Yes!" he quickly replied. Life was good.

8

Shelley Prentice was fifteen minutes late arriving for the start of the seven a.m. watch. The rest of the members had left for early morning school patrols. It was Friday.

She apologized to the watch commander and told him, truthfully, that she had closed her eyes for a few minutes after her alarm went off. Bent over his desk in the sergeant's office, he grunted something like, "Okay, but don't make a habit of it," while she grabbed the keys for her assigned patrol car, 10-Bravo-10, from the peg board and headed into the parking lot.

She felt 'pissy' today and a little worried. Starting her 'beast' as she called her car, she headed into the steady stream of in-bound city traffic to her area of patrol, the North Shore. Her period was late. Three days she figured and that, for her, was getting to be a significant amount of time to be overdue.

Someone behind her honked his horn and she realized with a start that she was still stopped at light that had turned green with no one in front of her. She waived her hand 'sorry' to the guy and quickly got her car up to speed.

Turning onto the bridge over the Thompson River, the two west out-bound lanes were relatively clear and she had some time to further ruminate about her 'condition' before she arrived at her school patrol zone.

She and her boyfriend, Rob, an instructor in electrical mechanics at the local community college, had taken pains to be careful with their intercourse. They lived separately and 'dated' only once or twice a week and these meetings didn't always involve sex. She was old enough to clearly know that 'shit happens' to put it crudely and mistakes occur.

'God, if I'm pregnant,' she thought, 'it'll drastically change my life! Will I have the baby or not? What will Rob think about this?' For that matter too, what will the male members of her watch think and say, knowing that she was not married or even living with a man? She could imagine the small talk – *'Have you heard? Shelley's 'up the stump'* or similar stupid chauvinist expressions. As well, how would Mom and Dad react?

Arriving at her assigned school, she told herself to try to put the situation out of her mind, at least until the end of the day, and concentrate on her job. Easy to say, sometimes hard to do. Constable Shelley Prentice was normally emotionally stable and fair-minded in her work. With four years of service, she'd learned that tolerance with people was a useful strategy to adopt, at least most of the time, and tried to remain equanimous in her interaction with them.

Not today. At least, not first-off. She'd followed a woman driver through the thirty-kilometre school zone at almost forty, pulled her over and wrote a ticket, a fifty-dollar voluntary penalty and two points against her license. In these circumstances, she would normally give a verbal warning, unless of course the driver was being an asshole with her, in which case she would start writing. It was nice to have that kind of authority and choice, but she realized too that she had to treat people as equally as she could.

As soon as she got back into her police car, she knew she had failed in this case. She'd let her emotions and disposition get the better of her and regretted her actions. This was clearly, in her view – the guys on highway patrol work might think differently – a case for leniency and the friendly 'please be careful driving through school zones' talk that she frequently used.

Today she did not attend the usual 9:45 a.m. coffee break with the guys – there were no other women on her watch – at a shopping mall McDonald's. She couldn't face up to them and put up with the

BS that usually flowed, and really wanted, needed, her time to herself. She chose instead a small, comfortable non-chain coffee shop on the Airport Road. It was quiet.

Prentice used to smoke and this was certainly one of those days she could have used a cigarette. She picked a corner of the café that had four empty tables and placed her portable radio on one of them together with her black, sugar-only coffee. She took a sip and then turned down the volume so that only she could hear the radio chatter and, of course, in case her car received a call. On urgent matters, she'd have to abandon her coffee and hit the road.

'How long can I wait?' she pondered, 'before I have to drag myself in for a test?'

Tomorrow, Saturday, was the last day of this day-shift watch, and she was off for four days. This created a bit of a dilemma for her. It was the weekend and she could not get to see her physician until Monday, if she could get in then. That meant she'd be at least five days overdue, six days on Monday if she had calculated the time correctly and knowing her rhythms, she was fairly certain she had. 'Christ, what am I going to do?' she agonized.

She had no time to answer that rhetorical question as the radio dispatcher interrupted her thoughts by saying, "All cars, all cars. North Shore, possible bank hold-up in motion, National Bank, 4000 block Airport Road. 10-Bravo-10, I believe you are the closest unit. What would be your ETA?"

"City Bravo-10, I'm about two minutes away," she said into her radio as she quickly exited the café, leaving her coffee cup half full. She noted the time – 10:05.

"Ten-four," the dispatcher replied. "Advise when you arrive and wait for backup. Use extreme caution. We are trying to confirm this call."

Shelley Prentice had rolled on a half dozen bank hold-up calls, but they'd been false alarms, usually caused by a careless teller setting off the system.

"All cars, this is a confirmed armed robbery, possibly two suspects. Descriptions follow. North Shore cars, copy?" she asked.

Five patrol cars replied and the watch commander who was downtown. He said he would be on site as soon as possible and requested Constable Prentice to give him a situation report as soon as she could. He also instructed a city-centre car to take up a position at the east end of the bridge. He called Corporal Hawkes, the area zone commander, to confirm his location relative to the scene and then instructed the dispatcher to go ahead with the further information.

"All cars. Further info. Two suspects armed with handguns. One shot fired. Unknown if any person shot. Suspects described as one short, one taller, both wearing masks, dark clothing and quite agitated. Copy?"

All replied, "10-4."

Upon hearing this information, Sergeant Sterling cut in and said, "Prentice, what's your location now?"

"I'm about one hundred yards from the parking lot. Not using siren," she replied.

"Good. Wait at the edge of the lot if possible until the first back-up arrives, but preferably for me to get there if possible. Copy?"

"Ten-four, Sarge."

"Corporal Hawkes, your twenty?"

"I'll be with Prentice less than two minutes."

The Tac-Team, always on call, usually arrived on these occasions after the action was over. They were called to attend as a matter of routine.

For a few seconds, the air waves were silent. On some calls, for some unknown reason, it could be an ominous silence. It was in this case.

Prentice saw the other units arrive and place themselves strategically around the lot, one going down the lane at the rear of the bank. Corporal Hawkes pulled in behind her and got out, crouching as he ran to the right front fender of her car.

"See anything?" he asked across the hood.

"No, nothing, Corp," she replied.

She was about forty yards from the bank's glass double doors, just back out of sight. The other two PC's that had just arrived were stopped on the road-side of the parking lot facing the bank, with customer cars blocking their presence to some extent, from the bank. No police cars then were in sight from the bank premises, or so they thought.

Hold-up situations always had the real potential for violence. Most 'hold-up artists' were not known for their careful planning and calmness, unlike the cool, calm and calculating ones portrayed in the movies. Many of them were 'junkies' on a 'high' and therefore, most unpredictable – as was the case now.

Two muffled shots were heard and no more than three seconds passed before both front doors burst open and the bandits emerged, guns in hand. One was indeed short, the other tall and they were dressed as described. Prentice and the corporal had the best view. He said into his portable radio, rather obviously for the two members out front and more pertinently for the one at the rear, that the two men were leaving the bank with their guns out. Hold your fire.

As near as Prentice could recall later, in writing up her notes, the following was the sequence of events as they unfolded:

'The two police officers in front of the bank, on the road side, exited their cars and drew their weapons.

'One of the robbers, the taller one, spotted them and pointed his weapon forward as he started to run across the lot and fired, at the same time yelling to his partner, "It's the fuckin' cops!"

'Someone yelled, "Drop your weapons! – It's the police!"

'The number two man did just that, like it was a hot potato, raised his hands and stopped.

'The first guy shouted, "Fuck you!" and fired a volley of rounds toward the same officer, who by now had taken shelter behind his car, leaving the door open.

'*The member who had been in the alley now peeked out from around the corner of the bank building.*'

Corporal Hawkes yelled into his radio, "You guys surrounding the parking lot, DON'T SHOOT! You don't have a clear background."

He said to Prentice across the hood of the car, "He's got a semi-automatic of some kind and he's empty."

Just as he said this, the shooter stopped a few yards from his companion, went down on one knee, and ejected the empty clip. His partner hit the ground too.

Corporal Hawkes, squatting beside the fender, had an unobstructed side-shot across the lot. He shouted, "Police! Drop your weapon or I'll fire!" and aimed his gun at the suspect, who stood up, banged his full clip of ammo into the butt, primed the gun, raised it and pointed at the hidden officer.

As the first round left the barrel of the shooter's gun, in the same instant, a 9mm bullet left the muzzle of Hawkes's Smith and Wesson in a pall of smoke. The gunman dropped to the ground and lay still.

Sergeant Sterling pulled up behind Hawkes's and Prentice's police cars in a cloud of roiling dust and squealing brakes. All of this was followed by several seconds of silence as the dust cleared.

It was the strong, acrid smell of the blue cloud of gun smoke from Hawkes's weapon and the explosive noise as the bullet exited the barrel that Shelley Prentice would remember most later on. He must have been a helluva shooter, she thought, to hit the man standing sideways-on, to kill him at a distance of about forty yards, or very lucky, if that was the right adjective to use in a case like this.

As well, all of this activity took place within the space of twelve seconds, she estimated.

Later, when she had calmed down and had time to reflect on matters, she couldn't help but feel grateful to the corporal in taking responsibility for ending it quickly and preventing more bloodshed. Had he not been there, the outcome might have been different – even more tragic. She'd never know. And all this drama for the lousy sum of $850 dollars that they left the bank with.

The Tactical Team arrived ten minutes later but there was really nothing for them to do and they were dismissed by the sergeant. Shelly Prentice spent the remainder of the morning and lunch hour helping safeguard the scene. The whole parking lot was sealed off with 'POLICE LINE – DO NOT CROSS' tape, and the bank and one small grocery store ware asked to close their doors for the day.

Apparently the shots fired in the bank were aimed into the ceiling as warning shots.

The second suspect was taken into custody, handcuffed, read the 'Police Caution' card and taken to the detachment office. The coroner attended at the site, pronounced death and authorized the removal of the body to the hospital morgue when the investigation was complete.

General Investigation detectives arrived shortly to determine what happened, as did Staff Sergeant Jim Hall, the Operations NCO, in part to find out how the members were bearing up, especially Corporal Hawkes, who now, tragically, had been forced to rely on Secion 25 of the *Code* to 'do his duty'.

The Identification Section had two members on site, taking photographs, dusting inside the premises for fingerprints, bagging the two guns, picking up the empty shell casings, after photographing them in place, putting the 'loot' in a small canvas bag, measuring the scene and creating a diagram.

GIS conducted preliminary debriefing interviews of the members at the scene, separately and talked to the witnesses. The veracity of what members had to say had to be checked against what physically occurred, with that of the evidence at the site and the civilian witnesses' accounts.

This was routine, in order to determine whether or not the shooting had been 'righteous' in police parlance – was it justified? Their statements would be recorded later at the detachment, on tape.

When the GIS and Ident people had finished, out of sensitivity to the general public, one of the 'A' Watch members was delegated to clean up the pool of blood, which by now had coagulated in the late fall sunshine.

At the end of the day, when she finally got home to her apartment, Constable Prentice experienced an overwhelming sense of relief – for two reasons. First, that she would be forever thankful that it wasn't she who had had to make the decision to shoot and kill someone. 'I wonder what I would have done if Corporal Hawkes had not been present?' It bothered her immensely that she had seen a human being killed in front of her and she resolved that she should take advantage of the assistance available through a local psychologist on retainer by the Force. Second, her ovulation had started. She wondered if it had been induced by the dramatic events of the day.

Grabbing her open bottle of Crown Royal, she poured a half inch into a glass, muttered to herself once again 'helluva day!' and swallowed it all, coughing as the golden liquid burned her throat on the way down.

Her phone rang. It was Rob.

9

Constable Hank Deleeuw arrived at 06:45 for the start of his first day back after four days off between night shift and day shift. Members were required to report in a bit early on these occasions to have their respective zone commanders bring them up to speed on the more serious criminal activity – rashes of break-ins, stolen autos, robberies etcetera – that had taken place on their days off, and some BOLFs – be on the lookout for – people and vehicles.

After the short review, Corporal Hawkes called Deleeuw over. "Hank, your trainer won't be with you today and possibly tomorrow. Dick is home with a bout of the 'flu so I'm going to cut you adrift and set you loose on the public solo, God help them. You ready for this?"

'Shit, am I ready!' Hank thought, 'been ready for months now' but simply answered, "Sure, Corp, I'm ready."

"Good. I have three words of advice for you. Guess what they are?"

"Um – don't mess up?" he replied with a smile.

"Well, that's a less succinct way of putting it but you get my drift. Don't forget your pre-check of the patrol car. See you later."

Deleeuw went to the patrol cars key board and unhooked the keys to 10-B-6. He was feeling good. Great in fact. 'On my own, at last.' He was only two months away from the completion of his one-year training period and he had been separated from Constable Ketchum, his designated trainer, on only two previous occasions, but then another trainer had accompanied him on patrols.

He'd heard another new recruit would be arriving soon from Depot Division to join 'A' Watch and he was glad about that. He'd had enough of the 'shit' jobs for the junior member and those included having to attend autopsies, which he was definitely not fond of.

In the parking lot he checked his patrol car for any defects, that it had been gassed up and the emergency equipment worked. Everything was good and he was ready to roll. Ketchum had only allowed him to operate the car on a few occasions, not because he was scared of Deleeuw's driving – he wasn't – but simply because he liked to drive.

He sat still for a few seconds gathering his thoughts and reflected on how much power and authority he had as a federal law enforcement officer – the only Force in Canada that granted its members the power to arrest anyone, anywhere, for any arrestable offence under God knows how many *Acts* the RCMP could enforce. Like all his predecessors who'd gone on their first lone patrol – as he was about to experience – he had to wonder if he was really up to it. At this very moment, if at no other time in his service, he realized the weight of authority that he carried and the responsibility to do his job *'Without Fear, Favour or Affection'* and he was a little bit scared.

Taking his mic off the dashboard hook, he said "Radio, Bravo-6, 10-8, Deleeuw, North Zone," thereby letting his watch mates and anyone else who might be listening in, know there was a 'new sheriff in town.'

♦ ◊ ♦

Hank Deleeuw, second generation Canadian, of Dutch descent, had recently turned 21, the youngest member of 'A' Watch. He was big – 6-foot-two, 200 pounds, blond short hair, blue eyes, pale skin, strong, well muscled – and hailed from Douglas, Manitoba, Dutch farm country since the late 1800s. Growing up on his parents' dairy farm (Holstein cows – 'you know, the black and white ones,' he liked to tell city folk who were deplorably ignorant about dairy cattle), he was allowed to 'sleep in' one day a week – Sundays, until seven.

During his police training in Regina, reveille – wake up call – was 6 o'clock during the week. He was invariably up before then, as much as anything to be first in the shower room and so that he could spend time making sure his bed was correctly made and kit laid out exactly in the approved manner. It was always the city boys who bitched and complained about the early wake-up call and who had the hardest time during their first two months in training, especially the Phys Ed stuff.

On Sundays at the farm, after his milking and cleaning chores were done, and breakfast over with, it was into the bath tub, then into his Sunday church clothes and the thirty-one kilometres drive into Brandon with his parents, brother and sister for services at the Christian Reform Church downtown.

When Deleeuw left high school at age 18, he continued to help out on the farm, his father paying him a stipend for his work, but he knew it wasn't to be his life's vocation. He needed something a tad more challenging, interesting, but what?

His epiphany came in very common circumstances, a wedding. His mom and dad had been invited by long-time friends and fellow church members, to their daughter's wedding, to a member of the RCMP stationed at Brandon. Deleeuw knew the young bride-to-be as she had attended the same school and had invited him to come along with his parents. The groom, dressed in his bright red 'Walking Out Order' uniform, struck an immediate chord with young Deleeuw, who, after a brief discussion with the constable, knew exactly what he wanted to do with the rest of his life.

He discussed the matter with his parents who gave him their blessing. They'd be proud to have a son as a Mountie. Hank needed to be sure his dad would manage without him and he was reassured that his older brother, Ralph, was quite content to remain on the farm.

Now, although he had less than a year's service in the Force, he was sure it had been the right decision.

Waiting at the police parking lot exit for traffic to clear, a motorist stopped to let him into his lane. He waived his 'thanks' at the man as he pulled out. 'There's some nice people out there,' he thought. 'Maybe this is going to be a good day.' He was soon to find out.

After school patrols were completed, he spent an hour working on two of his files, one a grocery store B&E a week ago and the second regarding an injury hit-and-run accident.

A member of 'B' Watch had found the offending vehicle and had it impounded at a North Shore towing company lot. He needed to examine it and take photos.

At 9:45, he called Shelley Prentice, also working in his area, but there was no response and he had not heard her give her 10-7. Not wanting to drive all the way back to the eastern end of the zone to meet Al Kart and Joe McKillen for coffee, as that would put him a bit too far from his patrol area, he stopped at the A&W in a small shopping centre adjacent to the main road, giving his 10-7 to the dispatcher.

He ordered a bacon and egg sandwich, potato patty, orange juice and a coffee, black, no sugar. Grabbing a copy of the *Parkton News*, he settled in a booth to eat and read, his portable in front of him. Finishing the last bite of his delicious bun, followed by the last swallow of his coffee, he was wiping his fingers with a napkin when the portable radio came to life announcing a bank robbery – in his area! Looking at his watch he saw that it was 10:05, just after bank opening time. As he took his radio and stood up to leave the restaurant, he heard Prentice acknowledge the call and say that she was responding as she was fairly close.

Deleeuw figured he was about a mile away. Back in 10-Bravo-6, he told Dispatch that he'd be there shortly, as he tore out of the parking lot, his red and blues on and siren screaming. He heard Corporal Hawkes in Bravo-9 and McKillen in Bravo-3 responding to the call and a reminder from the corporal to use caution. As he approached the shopping centre, he turned off his siren.

About 200 yards away, he heard Dispatch say shots had been fired inside the bank. 'Holy shit!' Hank thought. As he arrived at the parking lot he got a glimpse of Prentice's and Hawkes's patrol cars parked on one corner close to a building. He pulled in with a squeal of tires and stopped about forty yards away, facing the doors to the bank across the lot. As he did so, he saw McKillen pull in several yards away on his right. Both got out of their cars at the same time and knelt behind their respective car doors, revolvers drawn and pointed at the bank.

At that moment, the glass doors of the bank burst open and two masked men, both with weapons, began to run across the near empty parking lot – toward them! One of them shouted, "It's the fuckin' cops!" and began firing – at them! – one round zinging past his right ear.

Deleeuw heard a male voice over to his left shout, "Drop your weapons or I'll shoot!" followed a few seconds later by one shot. Peeking over his car window sill, he saw one man kneeling down and the other falling.

"Holy shit!" he exclaimed out loud this time. Neither of the bandits moved and once again there was no sound in the air, and just the slightest whiff of gun smoke.

It was like the tableau of a theatre play before him, where the movement of the actors was frozen in time as the play ended and the curtains closed. It was a scene he would always remember.

10

Al Burns had seven years service in the Force. He had dual citizenship – Canadian and American. His Canadian father was currently a colonel in the Air Force, stationed at National Defence Headquarters, Ottawa. He was an electronics warfare expert and twenty-eight years ago had been posted as Liaison Officer at North American Aerospace Defence Command (NORAD) in Boulder, Colorado, at that time specializing in radar telemetry.

There he had met his wife, Susan, who was a young second lieutenant in the USAF, also stationed at NORAD, as a registered nurse. Al was born a year later, in 1961 and spent his first four years in Colorado before moving to Canadian Forces Base Comox, in British Columbia, with his transferred father. His mother elected to leave the U.S. Air Force and continued her nursing career at the Comox General Hospital. Al Burns often referred to himself as an 'air force brat' but he was proud of his dad.

The family was later transferred to the largest Canadian Air Base at Trenton, Ontario, where Al Burns finished high school and, a year and a half later, joined the RCMP.

With a firm grounding in the mid-west American dialect and with his mother's ever-present Colorado accent, he was often mistaken for an American but he was used to it and okay with it too. He was an easy-going, likeable individual, and fitted in well with his watch mates at Parkton. At twenty-seven, he was feeling the early need to settle down and he definitely wanted children.

Trouble was, he hadn't found a woman yet with whom to share that kind of responsibility. He knew it was important to find a 'soul mate'. Confiding in his partner, Wally Rheingold, he was told, "Shit, you're too young, Al. Good lookin' guy like you needs to play the field a bit longer. Wait 'til you're in your thirties before you start getting serious, man."

Burns said something non-committal like, "Yeah, maybe you're right," but he could not shake the image and presence of the woman in red he'd run into at the Pioneer Pub a couple of days ago. To him, she was the perfect '10', certainly physically and, he suspected, in her character as well, from the way she presented herself. She seemed too well bred to be a hooker or someone pushing drugs – maybe an undercover operator? Before she drove out of the pub parking lot, he took down her license number and ran the plate. It was registered to Alice Conway, residing in Richmond. No criminal record. On the off-chance, he'd called that detachment and asked for Constable Conway, and was told no one of that name was stationed there. She wasn't listed in the Vancouver area telephone directory. He thought about calling the 'E' Division Drug Section people but decided against that. He did phone the local hotels and motels in the Parkton area to maybe pickup on where she was staying but struck out again. Okay then, she must be staying with her cousin whoever that was. After this conversation with his partner, she'd come back into focus again. His interest was definitely piqued.

They were on the Trans-Canada West on general patrols. South area was short two men – Portal and Oliver – and they'd been assigned to cover it today.

Rheingold was driving and Burns had made much of the fact that he was 'senior man' of the duo – by six months – in a joking kind of way. Rheingold played along, occasionally called him 'Boss'. They'd been paired up for just over a year and could read each other's minds and anticipate their actions, a good combination at times, very useful in tense situations.

Suddenly Burns said, "Turn around, Wally!" as he activated the emergency roof lights.

"What the hell, Al, what did you see?" Rheingold turned the wheels hard left and made a one-eighty. Luckily there was a gap in the traffic as he accelerated back toward the City.

"Okay, slow down," directed Burns, turning off the roof lights and, in reply to Rheingold's question, said, "I think that was Alice who passed us. I didn't get much of a glimpse of her but I'm sure that's her in that car, that black Mustang three cars ahead. Hang back and let's see where she goes."

"Jesus, we shouldn't be doing this on company time, you know."

"Yeah, I know. I'll put some extra time in if it'll make you feel better."

They were heading downhill now on Columbia Street and the Ford sportscar turned left onto Second Avenue – First Avenue being a one-way uphill – going into the downtown area. At Seymour, the car made a left turn. From his position two cars back, he was able to catch a read of the license plate and knew then it was Alice's car. His heart rate rose even more. "Not too close, Wally. Don't want to spook her."

"Okay, already. Man, you got it bad!"

The Mustang stopped again at a red light. On the green, it went straight ahead and made a right-hand turn into the police/public parking lot in front of the detachment. As the police car passed, Burns was able to see the woman get out of her car.

"Go into the back of our lot, Wally."

He did as he was told and Burns said, "I'm going in for a minute or two, okay?" as he quickly got out of the patrol car and entered the detachment via the rear garage door.

Rheingold switched off the motor, turned the key to the accessory position, and listened to some light rock on Radio CKPK. He had noticed 10-Bravo-7 on the lot and knew that the watch NCO was in the building. 'Hope you've got your excuse ready, Al, if you run into the sergeant,' he muttered to himself.

Opening the back door allowed Burns a clear view through the ground floor office area to the front counter. 'Alice' was on the public side of it talking to a male, who, from the back, looked like one of the Drug Squad members. He went to the side door and let her in. Burns stood where he was, not sure what to do. As she got closer she saw him, and stared, with some hint of recognition. The Drug member walked into their section's office.

'Say something,' Burns said to himself and he did. He said, "Hello, Alice."

She replied, "Hello, you're um…."

"Al. Al Burns, 'A' Watch. Nice to see you again. What're you doing here?" He held out his hand and she shook it lightly with a cool hand.

"Sorry," she said, "don't have time to stop right now. I'll – I'll give you a call," she hesitatingly replied, and entered the same office, closing the door.

She looked altogether different today. Dressed in a mid-grey no-lapels suit jacket and matching knee-length skirt, worn over a pale blue, white-buttoned silk blouse, and standing in a pair of black patent leather four-inch heels pumps, she was as tall as him. Even in this much toned-down suit, she still looked as gorgeous as in her 'Ferrari dress' as he called it when trying his best to describe it to his mates.

Seeing Sergeant Sterling leave his office with a civilian, Burns quickly turned around and walked out. He knew he was walking on air.

Back in the car he sat still and looked straight ahead, mesmerized. Rheingold started the car, turned down the AM radio and stated, "Well, it *was her*, wasn't it?"

Two or three seconds of silence.

"Wal, I think, I *know*, I'm in love. This is the one," he replied, looking his partner in the eye.

At the driveway exit, Rheingold looked left and right and did a left turn back onto Seymour to continue their patrol. Once over in the right lane, he spoke. "I don't know what to say, mi compadre. Felicitaciones? Good luck? Be careful? Is she married? This is such a sudden declaration on your part. There's a little bit of a problem though—."

Before he could go on, Burns interrupted by saying, "What do you mean – a problem?"

"Well, no big deal, I suppose, but this is only the second time you've met. How the hell can you be so sure?"

"I don't know. I can't put how I feel into words, but she *did* say she would call me. Would she say that if I didn't appeal to her, at least a bit?"

"Yeah, you may have a point. Anyway, I'll shut up and let you dream. Talk to me when you're ready, eh?" he said as they drove up First Avenue to get back to the TCH. Sneaking a quick glance at his partner, he definitely noticed a glow on the man's face.

♦ ◊ ♦

She'd called and said, "Hi, it's Alice Conway – the woman in red. Remember me?"

Burns said, "How could I forget?"

They met at a new Tim Hortons. The coffee and doughnuts were excellent and the chain was becoming a Canadian coffee icon, with rapid expansion. It was Conway's idea and she made a standard joke about cops and doughnuts. He loved her laugh.

They started the conversation together with both of them saying 'So?' at the same time.

"No, you go first," he insisted. He wanted to hear her speak.

"A bit of a coincidence us both being members of the Force, isn't it?" she began rhetorically. "I've just transferred here from Division DS to Parkton DS as an additional member. Corporal Brandt made a case for an increase in the Drug Squad here with his stats."

"You know, I wasn't sure when I saw you at the Pioneer the other night. I had a feeling you might be doing undercover work. Did you decide to wear that dress?"

"No," she chuckled, "it was the corporal who prevailed on me to wear it. What did you think?"

"I think I'd better be careful about what I say," Burns replied, smiling. "You were just barely legal, you know."

"Yeah, it was a bit over the top," she replied, and then realizing what she had said, she blushed and said, "Nearly *out* of the top!"

"I almost didn't sit next to you, you know. Those two bar stools were the only seats left, but as I walked across the floor, I reconsidered my feelings and said, 'To hell with it, let's see what's up.' Very glad I did. You looked so different yesterday when I met you at the office, and today."

She wore slim blue jeans with a high collar, open neck, cream-coloured blouse under a shortie, flared black leather jacket.

"Before I continue, I have a confession to make," Burns continued. "When you left the pub, you were followed by two scruffy individuals who, at first glance, made Wally and I think they were your pimps or drug contacts. I took note of your car plate and ran it. Of course, the information was blocked. If that offends you, please excuse me," he said with an inquisitive glance at her.

She considered his remarks for a few seconds and replied, "Being a policeman here, you have a right to find out what's going on in the community, off duty or not, so no, I don't mind. If I had been what I purported to be, I would imagine you would have reported the incident to the Drug or GIS section?" she said rhetorically.

"Thanks, but I'm not finished my confession. It was no accident when you saw me at the office on Thursday morning. I was on patrol with Rheingold and spotted you in a Mustang heading into town and followed you. Is that your car? You surprised me a bit when you pulled into our parking lot, so we also drove in and I walked in the back door. Once again, hope you don't mind."

"No," she said, "it shows you have initiative and perseverance. So, Alan Burns, who are you?"

◆ ◇ ◆

That evening, when Shelley Prentice returned to her apartment, she found her new roommate, Alice Conway, preparing some supper.

"What's for dinner, Alice? Smells good."

"I thought we'd have steamed salmon, Basmati rice, fresh peas and a mixed green salad. Alright with you?"

"Sure is. Alright, so tell me, I'm dying to know, how did your meeting with Al Burns go?"

"Went well. Let's open some Chardonnay," said Conway.

"Oh boy, is this a celebration? Are you going to marry him?"

"Don't push me, Shell. You were right, he's a nice guy. Let nature take its course." Then, realizing what she had said and implied, she blushed and quickly said, "You know what I mean."

"Yeah, sure I do," replied her friend with a slight smile on her face, putting a music disc in the CD player.

◆ ◇ ◆

A week later, Al Burns knocked on the door of apartment 301, an end-of-the-hall, two-bedroom suite, at exactly 6:45. The door was opened almost immediately and Alice Conway said, "Hello, Alan."

"Hello, Alice."

For a few seconds, neither of them said anything further. He stood outside the door and she just inside. She spoke first. "Oh my God, I'm sorry, please come in," as she stood aside.

"Sorry," he said. "It's not like me to say nothing. It's just that I can't get over how gorgeous you look this evening."

"Why, thank you, Sir. You look pretty good yourself. Jeez, we're sounding like a mutual admiration society. Would you like a drink?"

"Sure, rye and seven if you have it, please. Is Shelley not home?"

"Oh, she's out for the night with a friend. What are we going to see tonight?"

"There's three new releases at the Capitol Six Theatre and I made a note. *Fatal Attraction* with Michael Douglas and Glenn Close; *Good Morning, Vietnam* with Robin Williams and Forest Whitaker and *The Witches of Eastwick* with Jack Nicholson and Cher. Any preference?"

"*Fatal Attraction* sounds good. Hopefully it won't apply in our case," she jested.

"Should be interesting. Show time is 7:30."

After the movie they walked to Rosie's Restaurant nearby and over hot chocolate and pastries, discussed the merits and otherwise of the film, and whether or not it and or the actors would be nominated for an Academy Award. Certainly worthy of it, they agreed.

Nervousness pervaded the air around them. Both were attuned to the nearness of each other and wondered if it would be the beginning of a lovely relationship.

And indeed it was, for later, back at her place, after a half bottle of Zinfandel each, their inhibitions rapidly declining, Conway whispered to Burns from very close up, if he 'wanted any brains left?'

At first he said, "No," but followed quickly with a slight change of mind – "Well, maybe a couple so they can regenerate. I do have to go to work in the morning."

The Lady in Red dutifully complied.

11

The Harding family could be described as middle class. They lived about twelve blocks from the downtown area in a wood frame, white stucco, three-bedroom, 1960s house on one floor with a sub-basement. The only addition they'd added was a flat-roofed garage for their two vehicles. One was a 1986 Ford Taurus and the second, a 1980 Toyota pickup.

At age forty-four, Gerald (Gerry) Harding was employed as a supervisor at the sorting station in the main Post Office and had twelve years service. His ambition was to become the Postmaster. He drove the Toyota.

Geraldine, his wife – they were kidded about their matching first names when they were first going out often being called the 'Gerry twins' – had just turned forty-three. Like many people reaching this age, she suddenly felt depressed – life was passing her by, so to speak, and what did she have to show for it, she would ask herself. She wasn't discontented nor was she contented, rather she seemed to live in some dull middle ground in between. She hoped she would soon get over this 'mental' condition, as she thought of it, as it was affecting her family, she felt sure. She didn't think it was the onset of menopause. Her job as a Safeway cashier paid quite well and her co-workers and surroundings were pleasant enough, but after three years of ringing up groceries, it had become mundane.

They had one child, a daughter – Mary Elizabeth, named after her two grandmothers – just turned sixteen. Geraldine and Harding had wanted another child – he hoping for a son, her not caring one way or the other. They tried for five years and after a visit to an obstetrician and some tests, learned that her endometrium was no longer able to accommodate a fertilized ovum and they were terribly disappointed. This condition did not help her mindset either.

Mary was in grade ten, an average student. She was nice enough looking, a little on the plump side like her mother which caused Mary some concern.

One thing that disturbed her parents a bit was her mood swings, more down than up lately. She'd had a propensity toward this kind of behaviour most of her life but lately, her dark moments had become more pronounced and often lasted several days. The Hardings discussed the matter recently, thought about taking her to the school counsellor, but put it off, attributing her moods to her age more than anything. Harding remarked to his wife about the increasing number of 'spats' that she and their daughter were having – shouting matches at times, and the use of foul language by Mary.

"I'll give her a few more months," he said, "and if she doesn't smarten up, we'll have to take her in for professional counselling," to which his wife nodded her agreement.

"Is she out with Ralph again this evening?" he asked.

"Yes, I told her to be home no later than midnight. It's Friday evening so I thought that would be okay?" Geraldine replied.

"I guess. What do you think of him?"

"He's alright. Not the brightest star and I'm not sure I'd want him for a son-in-law, but he's nice enough to Mary and she tells me she 'loves him.'"

"Hmm, I wonder what that means?" said Harding. "Do you think they're having sex?"

"Oh my God! I hope not. I think we need to talk to her, don't you?"

"Jeez, I hate to do that but I suppose we'll reach the day when it becomes inevitable – soon now. We'll have to think about our approach and what to say."

"I'm taking her shopping tomorrow to look for a new dress for the school dance next weekend. We've already had a row about that. She wants something 'off the shoulder and low-cut' but I said, 'No, not at your age.' Hope she's not late home tonight."

Later, in bed, Mrs. Harding was awakened from a light sleep by the closing of the front door. Looking at the bedside LED clock, the large red numbers glowed 02:00.

'Damn!' she thought. 'Another argument at breakfast.'

♦ ◊ ♦

Constable Andrew Oliver was born in 1966 at the Regina General Hospital.

Due to complications, his mother's physician advised her to go there for the birth, as it had the best obstetrics unit. The event went well and in two days, Mrs. Oliver took her baby home to Pilot Butte, Saskatchewan.

In those days, policing was carried out by the rural detachment based out of Regina, and it was his contact with one of the members who coached his local Pee Wee hockey team – the Pilots, their hockey shirts displaying a skate with a wing attached, for speed – that eventually led him to join the Force.

On leaving high school, he went to a nearby community college to take a few courses that might prepare him for a university program. One of them was simply called Statistics 101 and was a generic overview of the subject. It was interesting for him because, early on in his life in Pilot Butte, he had often been driven or walked by the population sign underneath the name of the community, on the highway at the edge of town, which never changed from its painted-on number of 1,800. He might have been ten years of age when the next door neighbour, old Mister Ladouceur, died. He noticed that the sign did not change then to 1,799, nor when his mother's friend, Sarah Watkins, had her twins did the number increase to 1,802. He understood that statistics could be skewed, even by simple neglect.

On graduation from police training, his first posting was Parkton Detachment. He currently had two years service, which included the six months spent in training at 'Depot' Division.

As yet, he had never seen a real dead person, only one on a video in recruit training because, as their instructor made it quite clear, members often have to attend autopsies 'so you need to know, and see, what is involved.' It was gross to watch and three of his classmates had to quickly leave the classroom. So far, he had avoided that onerous duty but things were about to change for him in a most dramatic way.

It was Saturday morning and he was on day shift, in Centre Zone for a change, when the dispatcher said, "Closest car to twelve hundred block Hemlock, respond, please."

Oliver picked up his mic and said, "10-Bravo-13, Eighth and Centre."

"Report of possible gunshot at 1260. Called in by neighbour at 1264."

"I'm four blocks away," he replied. "Anyone close to cover me?"

"Bravo-8, I'll be there in couple of minutes," said Corporal Bibermann. "Just take a quick look but don't approach until I get there."

Pulling up to the white stucco house in the middle of the block, Oliver eye-balled the place, noting the absence of a vehicle on the street in front or in the driveway and no apparent activity within. 'Maybe a car backfiring,' was his initial thought. He noted the time: 11:45. He gave his ten-seven to Dispatch but kept the motor running and his radio on.

Bibermann pulled up behind him and both got out of their cars.

"Anything?" asked the corporal.

"No," replied Oliver. "No sign of activity and no vehicles around."

"Stay here while I make a quick check with the neighbour."

On his return in two minutes, he told Oliver that the complainant next door had heard a muffled shot – not sure what kind of weapon.

"Apparently the house is owned by a Mr. and Mrs. Harding and they have a teenage daughter. Both their cars are away and he thinks no one is home."

The living room drapes were closed. Bibermann banged on the door and called out loudly, "Police, open the door, please."

No answer and he repeated the command. The door was locked.

"Okay, let's look around the side and back for another entry."

They found a side door, with a small curtain covering the one window pane and repeated the same routine. No response. Turning the door handle with his left hand and with his right hand on his uncovered revolver butt, Bibermann slowly pushed the door inward. It took a second or two for him to exclaim, "Oh my God!"

Looking over the corporal's shoulder, young Andy Oliver saw his first dead person and started to gag, his stomach violently clenching in and out.

It was the kitchen they were entering and sitting in a wooden chair next to the table and facing the door was what remained of a human being, a young female judging by her clothing. Almost the whole of her head was missing, most of it splattered over a nearby wall and on the ceiling. Thick, dark red venous blood had flowed down from the gaping wound and had formed a pool around the chair legs. It was still dripping from her clothing. A single barrel, twelve-gauge shotgun was between her legs with the muzzle resting on her chest.

Bibermann called out, "Hello, anyone at home?" – a useless thing to do he thought upon reflection, but, you never know. "Are you okay, Andy?" he added.

Oliver could only nod 'Yes' as he tried to regain his composure.

"Stay here a minute while I check the house," the corporal said, stepping around the blood to the dry flooring to avoid the obvious. Returning in less that a minute he found the pale-looking constable staring at the corpse.

"Alright, Andy, make a call to Dispatch. Use the wall phone here. We need to do five things right away. Get Ident Section, GIS, Forensic,

the doctor on call at the hospital – he has to 'pronounce' death regardless of the obviousness of it – and notify the coroner. Got that?
While you make the calls, I'm running next door to have a word with
the neighbour. After the calls, make some notes. Back in a jiff."

Oliver recovered a bit from the shock, and called Dispatch. 'I
wonder where the parents are?' he thought as he hung up the phone
and prepared to make the other calls. 'We need to find out ASAP.'

As if in answer to his question, he heard a couple of footsteps
sounding like they were running down the cement walkway at the
side of the house. As he was about to go to the door, it suddenly
opened and there stood Mr. and Mrs. Harding. A moment of complete silence ensued as they took in the scene and then Geraldine
Harding let out an ear-piercing scream and collapsed on the floor.

Gerald Harding didn't do anything for what seemed like long
moments, continuing to stare at the remains of his only child, his
mouth working but no words coming out. Ignoring his wife sob-
bing on the floor, he noticed the constable and uselessly asked, "What
happened?"

Constable Andy Oliver's emotions were in a turmoil. This was a
lot of dramatic activity to absorb in such a short period of time and
he didn't know how to respond. Luckily his corporal arrived and
took over the situation.

After all the different people had come and done their required
thing, the body was finally removed and the local press given their
'pound of flesh.'

Bibermann said to Oliver, "Come on, Andy, let's find a quiet place
to have a coffee and go over our notes. You feel a bit better now?"

Oliver nodded.

"Nasty business is police work sometimes," said his colleague.

♦   ◊   ♦

Two weeks later, 'A' Watch was back on day shift. Other than the death of Mary Harding, it had been a relatively uneventful time for Oliver except for attending her autopsy – his first 'live' one, so to speak, as he put it to his good friend and confidant, Rick Taylor, a few days later. He also patrolled Centre Zone, which included all the downtown area. They both liked doing duty here. There was lots of activity and the work was quite varied. They sometimes rode together, but not today. The watch was a bit shorthanded and the watch commander wanted as many cars on the road as he could manage. It was almost lunch time and Oliver was getting hungry. He was about to call Taylor to pick a spot for lunch when Dispatch called, "Centre car."

Oliver answered quickly before anyone else. With only three of his files in the Still Under Investigation stage, his work load was light and he was on the prowl for more work. He got it.

"Need you to attend at Golden Heights Rest Home on Columbia. Report of a sudden death. ETA?"

"Er, 10-4. Be there in two, three minutes," he replied, with an obvious degree of reluctance in his voice. 'Shit, I would open my mouth!' he thought.

On arrival, he gave his ten-seven, grabbed his clipboard and note pad, got out of his car, locked it and climbed a flight of stairs going up to the main entrance of the home. Again, he noted the time: 11:55.

Entering the wide front doors, he encountered a middle-aged woman in some kind of uniform who introduced herself as the manager of the facility. He noted a bit of a skeptical look on her face. Removing his cap and tucking it under an arm, he followed her into the building.

"I'm afraid one of our residents has ended his life. Would you come with me, please?"

'Good God, not another suicide!' he thought. 'I shouldn't be so quick in answering dispatch calls,' as he followed the woman up two flights of stairs.

"His name is – was – Matthew Alexander Fraser, born in Dundee,

Scotland in 1898, making him ninety now," she said, doing the math for the young constable. As they rounded the stairs to the second floor, he could see a pair of slippered feet sticking out from under a bed-sheet, the body lying across four steps at an angle.

"Alright, let me explain what happened. Matthew has – had – been quite depressed lately and about thirty minutes or so ago, hung himself. He did that by placing a length of yellow nylon rope around his neck, which he cut from one of our aluminum extension ladders in the storage room, which is open during the day, and tied the other end around the rail as you can see and climbed over it, letting himself fall a few feet. The reason for him being on the stairs now is that two of my staff pulled him back up and tried to revive him but he was quite obviously deceased. The men could not untie the knot and had no knife to cut the cord, although I doubt they would have tried. I instructed them to leave the noose on him and not to take the rope off the rail knowing that you would require photographs. As well, I found this note, in his writing, on his bedside table," she said, handing the small piece of white notepad to Oliver.

On it, Mr. Fraser had scribbled the last eight words of his life:

I cant take it no more

Goodbye Alex

After reading it, a feeling of pity momentarily overcame Oliver and he thought, 'Two suicides in two weeks – at the opposite ends of the age spectrum. I don't understand it.'

He excused himself and moved several steps down to have a bit of privacy while he called for a doctor, notified the coroner's office and asked Dispatch for a member of the Ident section for photos.

Sergeant Sterling called to ask if he needed assistance.

"No, thanks, Sarge, I'm okay for this one. Drop by if you have to though."

Oliver did a brief sketch on his clipboard paper showing the relative position of the body and its location. Going back up the few steps, he raised the sheet to confirm death, noted the cord around the man's neck and the dark blue death mask of his face.

It was general police policy to initially regard all reported suicides as potential homicides. Someone may be 'rigging' the death to make it look that way. It very rarely happened but had to be investigated, initially.

He took verbal statements from the staff while waiting for the doctor and police photographer, telling the civilians that he would return later for written statements. He also decided to ask the doctor to cut the cord which was deeply embedded in the flesh.

Later, in the afternoon he met his buddy at the downtown McDonald's. He was ravenous and got an order of the three major food groups that sometimes sustain police officers – Big Mac, fries and a Coke – and commiserated with Rick Taylor about the morning's event.

"Poor old guy. I wonder what kind of life he lived? This one makes two suicides for me in less than two weeks, one young and one old."

"Yeah, well like I often say, 'Shit happens' and 'Things always seem to come in threes,' so beware, my friend."

Sure enough, three days later, on night shift, Andy Oliver attended another death, a fatal motor vehicle accident. Afterwards, he thought, 'Well, I've had my third one, and three autopsies, so maybe I've got them out of my system for a while. Hope so. I don't want to become an expert on these things and get them assigned to me because of 'increasing expertise'. No, thanks!'

12

It was 7:30 on a Friday evening in mid-October when Jack Sterling and reporter Charlie Preston left the detachment office and went 10-8 in the watch commander's patrol car. Fall in south-central British Columbia could be quite warm with afternoon temperatures sometimes in the high 20s Celsius. By this time of the day, it was down only a few degrees. With the air on at full blast and all the windows closed, the temperature was just bearable in the patrol car.

Fridays were late shopping evenings, stores closing at nine. It was also payday and the downtown area was full of traffic and pedestrians which predicted a busy police night. Sterling was short three constables, two on leave and one ODS – off duty sick. It meant he had to do more patrol work than usual and take a few calls. That was generally okay with him and, after all, he did still enjoy doing a bit of general police work.

"Guess we could be in for a busy night from the looks and sounds of things," said Preston.

In the space of the first hour, 'A' Watch, with a complement of fifteen regular members, had been called to three MVAs (one with an injury), two shoplifters, two domestic disputes ('God, the family fights are starting early tonight,' remarked the sergeant), a 'gas and dash' at a service station on the highway and the first impaired driver of the evening.

"I think I'm going to stay in the downtown area for now. It's still teeming with people and traffic. I'm going to have to handle a call or two, so be prepared. You can accompany me outside the car but hang back a bit as if I'm alone. Call for assistance if I get into trouble," he reminded Preston. "Okay with you?"

Preston nodded and settled back in anticipation.

The dispatcher called, "Centre car," and Sterling answered, "Bravo-7."

"Report of a fight at the Grand pub in the alley."

"Bravo-7, 10-4."

They were three blocks away.

"We don't usually hurry to these things. By the time we arrive, they're generally over and dispersed and no harm done. If the combatants are drunk, we call for the Bun Wagon and take them to the Tank to cool off. 10-Alpha-1 usually attends."

What they found was a bit more serious. One person, a young male, was lying still in the back lane surrounded by a group of people. As Sterling got close, he saw one of them kick the inert individual in the ribs. He said to Preston, "Stand by near the car," and jumped out, using his portable radio to call, "Bravo-7, need assistance. Assault in progress." He didn't hear Ketchum, driving 10-Bravo-6, give his 10-7 about ten seconds later.

The guy doing the kicking was about to use his boot again when Sterling grabbed him from behind, putting him in a headlock, bent him backwards and started to drag him toward the police car. Out of the corner of his eye, he saw a fist just before it hit him in the face, almost knocking him off balance as he continued to pull his prisoner along.

Just at that moment, Ketchum grabbed hold of the guy who'd punched the sergeant, dragged him to the back of the prison van, making what could only be described as a 'forcible entry' of the individual into the back and slamming the door, just in time to help Sterling, who'd become aware of his presence, do the same thing with his man.

A little winded, Sterling told Ketchum to wait by the van and call an ambulance while he checked on the unconscious guy. "When you get back to the office, put the one who did the kicking in the holding cell by himself. Don't want him getting marked up. Wait until I check the guy on the ground before you go."

Seeing two police officers and two police vehicles, the remainder of the group of people prudently started to leave while Sterling knelt down to check the man. His left cheek was gaping open, revealing the sides of his teeth and he was bleeding profusely. Without undressing him, Sterling couldn't tell what other injuries he suffered. With the small crowd departing, the sergeant signalled to the constable to leave and called his ride-along to come over.

"This guy's unconscious, Charlie. I hear sirens so the ambulance should be here shortly. I'm going to have to go to the ER for a preliminary check on his condition and get some indication from the attending doctor when I might be able to talk to him. I'll come back later and check in the pub as to what may have caused this. Be nice to have a witness but most of these assholes 'didn't see nothin' when you ask – bartenders too."

"How's your face, Jack?" said the reporter, examining it from close up.

Sterling touched his right cheek tenderly and said, "After I get some ice on it at the hospital, it'll be fine. Let's go."

With the individual on a gurney and into the ambulance, they returned to Sterling's car. They'd had left the car running and it was welcomely cool inside.

Sterling was sweaty and apologized to the reporter. It didn't help to have to wear the recently-issued body armour.

"No problem," Preston replied. "As you so eloquently put it, 'shit happens'."

Five minutes later, Sterling went 10-7 at PGH. "Bravo-7 at hospital."

"10-4," Dispatch confirmed.

Much later, when the stupidity and complaints had subsided, the two men were able to talk a bit over Cokes and a couple of apple pies at the Golden Arches on the TCH east.

"So, whaddya think?" asked Sterling. "Want to be a cop?"

"Thanks, no, but I have to say it's an interesting, fascinating job. Is it always like this on weekends?"

"Not generally, except for payday weekends, and the season or time of year. Hot weather obviously makes people drink a lot more liquids, especially beer and all of this very much impacts on human behaviour. Our stats increase enormously in the summer and fall months and correspondingly decrease in the winter. Long weekends in the summer, from Victoria Day in May to Labour Day in September, produce the largest number of complaints."

"You mentioned a lack of manpower sometimes. It's my observation that you cope with that to some extent with the assistance of your auxiliaries?"

"Yeah. Thank God for them. One of the best things 'E' Division did was to implement that kind of program. Helps us out enormously. Take tonight, for example. I've allotted one auxiliary to a regular member per car. That way, I can have more of a police presence on the road and be able to answer complaints more quickly. Works quite well. Whenever I have the luxury of a full complement of members on duty, eighteen of us, plus say eighteen auxiliaries, that puts thirty-six warm bodies and pairs of eyes on the road in eighteen cars in addition to, say, three Traffic Section cars, two GIS people and one Dog Master, we can respond to anything quickly. That's what I call good, effective policing. It's happened to me all of four times this year.

"By the way, while I think of it, how did you make out interviewing Constable McKillen last weekend? Sorry I didn't get to check with you before you left."

"Good. He's a bright, interesting individual with a good thinking head on his shoulders. He has what I call a 'command presence' when dealing with people. He gives off vibes to assholes that say, 'Don't mess with me,' and he's big enough too. We had to stop by his house for something and I met his wife and their two little kids. Delightful people."

"Good. When do you want to go out again, Charlie?"

"In a couple of weeks. I'll call you."

"Alright. I'll put you with someone on the North Shore for a change. You may notice a different class of police clientele there."

Preston chuckled and said, "I can imagine. Can't wait!"

13

At the start of the watch early Friday evening it looked to become a busy night. Three cars were patrolling the Centre Zone and all were occupied with complaints when the call came from Dispatch asking a car to attend a report of a sudden death at 1022, 8th Avenue. No details available. Sergeant Sterling, accompanied by Charlie Preston, took the call, as they were in the downtown area, showing the flag on the main street, to let the citizens know – law abiding and otherwise – that there was a police presence. Time of call: 10:10 p.m.

They arrived at the address two minutes later, met at a broken down wooden gate by a woman of about 50 years. Preston stayed in the car while Sterling spoke to her. She identified herself as Monica Fairhurst, who lived across the street.

"Thank you for getting here so promptly. There's a deceased person, a man in the house and he may have been dead for some time. His wife is there too. I'm their neighbour and I've been checking on them for the past year and have just returned from Puerto Vallarta. Mrs. Brownlee – that's her name – assured me that she and her husband, Arthur, would be okay for the two weeks that we were away. Anyway, when we got home this evening I walked over to tell them we were back and found Arthur dead on the couch. I'm an RN and work at the hospital so I know the procedures and quickly called your office. I know what you are going to ask, so let me continue with what I know?"

"Please, go ahead, Mrs. Fairhurst."

"Both the Brownlee's are in their nineties with no relatives in

Parkton, only a daughter in Toronto. I have her address and telephone number. They are both in failing health but managed okay. When I knocked on their door about six or seven minutes ago, she opened it and I was immediately hit by the overpowering smell of death. I had to hold my nose when I walked in and noted Arthur on the living-room couch. The only light on came from the kitchen but enough for me to see that his skin was black and a cursory glance indicated to me he had been dead for some time. Edna asked me if Arthur was okay. I asked her to come to the front door so that I could breathe fresher air and she told me that her husband hadn't risen from the couch for over a week. In her confused state, she thought he was napping and didn't want to disturb him. So that's the situation. If you don't need me now, I'd like to go home and shower and change if that's alright?"

While she had been describing the scene, Sterling could smell the very pungent odour from his position at the gate and dreaded the thought of having to go in. He went back to the car to tell the reporter what the problem was, noting he'd be here for some time, unless he could get one of his watch members freed up to come and take over.

"I can't afford to spend much time here. I'd suggest you stay at the car or I'll get you another ride. The smell in the house is awful."

He called the Identification man on his portable radio and asked Dispatch for someone from the coroner's office to attend. Taking a big breath, he entered the house.

◆ ◇ ◆

Constable Deleeuw was about to see his first, really dead whole person, not the pieces of one he'd seen at the train-car wreck of some weeks ago. He and his partner/trainer Dick Ketchum, had just gone 10-8 on his radio from a suspected house break-in, unfounded as it turned out, and had been asked to take over the sudden death file in Centre Zone.

"Why didn't the sergeant stay on this case?" he asked.

"Well, rank has its privileges and besides, he's got the *News* reporter with him tonight. Had to go home, shower and change, as I imagine we have to do too. Christ! I hope I never go out this way," said Ketchum, after learning more of the circumstances en route.

Arthur Brownlee's decomposing body, zippered up tightly in a rubberized bag, was removed by the coroner's representative to the morgue. Edna Brownlee was taken in care by the Eldercare Society, her daughter in Toronto was notified, and the house secured.

An unpleasant task for all concerned and cause for some introspection. What investigators had learned confirmed the neighbouring nurse's story: that his wife, in an obvious state of mental disability, had thought Brownlee had simply laid down on the couch to have a nap and she, being a very kind and considerate person, did not want to disturb him. As the autopsy later showed, he'd been lying dead all this time, undisturbed.

♦ ◇ ♦

"Geez, you stink, Jack!" remarked Preston as Sterling got into the patrol car.

"Not for long, I hope. Come home with me while I shower and change?"

"Sure, sounds good. I have a question. How do the police go about trying to determine how a person died?"

"Hmm. Let me answer as I would in a training setting...."

"The death of a human being occurs by one of four means – natural causes, accident, suicide, or homicide. Determining which of these causes was responsible can be problematic. An 'accidental' death can appear natural, suicidal or, rarely, homicidal. A desperate individual can mask his or her suicide by making the death appear to be natural – for some important reasons – ill health, or say financial worries, with the idea that the life insurance company will pay out the benefit to the next of kin.

"Murder, of course, can be made to look natural, accidental or suicidal. So, anticipating your next question, how do we find out the truth about how an individual died?

"Very briefly, it takes a combination of a medical examination by a pathologist through an autopsy, a toxicologist for the presence of toxic, lethal substances, and forensic specialists for other different causes. All of this is overlaid by a thorough police investigation. So, the police generally start out by asking the question 'was this death a homicide?' and, if not, move on down the list. Occasionally however, a coroner will rule a death as 'undetermined', leaving the cause open to speculation. That cover it okay?"

Preston nodded his head and said, "Thanks."

"You know, you seem to be getting a bit sanguine about police work now, Charlie. Rubbing off on you, is it?"

"Yeah, maybe. Kind of creeps up on you, doesn't it?"

Sterling said, "Radio, Bravo-7, 10-7 residence, thirty minutes."

◆   ◇   ◆

On the road again, fortified with hot apple pie covered in melted cheddar cheese and washed down with fresh coffee, both men felt better.

"Thanks, Jack, that was good. Where to now?"

"I have to nip back down to the office to take a reading on things and then we'll go over to the North Shore for a while. I need to be on the road a bit tonight, being short of people."

At the office, the reporter asked and was given permission to sit in the dispatch centre for thirty minutes or so, on the understanding that none of what he saw and heard was reported – he could only write in the abstract – no names or locations, until Sterling was ready to go out again. He was impressed with the manner and speed with which the two female operators carried out their tasks. Men, Preston was sure, could not do this job with the same dexterity.

It was after midnight and they were out near the airport. "What time do you want to quit, Charlie?" asked Sterling.

"Oh, I can go for another couple of hours. Jean's visiting her mom on the Coast so my time's my own," he said.

They had, in the past hour or so, responded to minor complaints – a noisy party, squealing tires and a possible prowler and Preston hadn't been able to ask about Sterling's time in the Force. Things had quietened down a bit now.

"What do your notes say about our last discussion?" asked Sterling.

"Let me check," Preston replied, pulling out a three-by-six-inches, coiled-spine notebook from his jacket pocket. After glancing at it, he said, "We finished up at the point where you were in training in Regina."

"Okay, I don't know if I can put my experiences and observation in chronological order, but not to worry. We can review that later. One thing I have to mention about our training was the fact that we rode horses – equitation training. Because of that, training time generally ran to nine months."

"Did you like riding?"

"Not at first. It was physical torture for the first couple of months, trying to get our legs and feet in the right position, trying not to bounce up and down, especially at the trot – very hard on the arse – trying to get the bastards to go where we wanted them to go, but most of all, not falling off. If you did that, you'd have to run around the riding school behind your horse. On top of that we had stable duties. Monday to Saturday, we were up at 6 a.m. and ran over to the stables building, cleaned out the tons of horse shit accumulated from about 48 animals overnight, then groomed and fed them. Grooming included scraping the horse shit out of their horseshoes with a pick, and cleaning their docks. By the way, do you know what a 'dock' is in relation to horse anatomy?"

"I can guess – its ass?"

"Close enough. Then we'd run back to barracks and from there go to breakfast, still wearing our 'fatigue' uniforms. At that first meal of the day, the Mess Hall was a strange admixture of the smells of bacon and eggs and horse manure. Didn't matter. We were so hungry, we'd have eaten the latter if it had been put on our plates. With respect to riding, I have to say that as we learned to ride we felt much more competent, much less tired and most of us enjoyed eventually making our animals walk, trot, canter and gallop at our command, not that of the riding instructor. It was a proud day for me when he called out, 'Sterling, you can put your spurs on.' I was a real Mountie, or so I liked to think."

"There's no more equitation training now, is there?"

"No, I think that ceased in 1966. I can anticipate your next question. There's three or four reasons: it added three months on training time and therefore cost money, our economy was floundering at that time and budgets were cut, but I believe more than anything, it was a change in training philosophy. There must have been some anguish over that decision in Ottawa though, to cut riding; after all, horses defined who we were as an organization, from the beginning, on the Long March West in 1874."

"Yes, an epic journey as I've read. How was training changed then?"

"Much more emphasis was placed on imparting police-related knowledge and skills, more academics, more time on investigative skills, public relations and, of course, a quicker turnaround time for producing recruits for the field by reducing the training time to six months.

"I may have mentioned this to you before, Charlie, that 'Depot' Division later created a small mock village and trainees spend time manning the 'detachment office' investigating complaints. As well, when they graduate now, unlike me in my day, they're placed with a trainer on a Recruit Field Training Program for a year.

"Graduation Day, also known as 'Pass Out,' was a milestone for all those who survived. It was held in the gym and consisted of a physical training display and fifteen minutes of silent foot drill performed, of course, in our Red Serge Review Order of Dress, without a single word of command.

"We had to practice these movements for better than two months by means of using a 'count' system in our heads and remembering the movements we practiced. After all, it was being performed in front of a crowd of parents, brothers, sisters, friends and girlfriends – none of us was married then – and we did not want to screw this up."

"How did the drill system work?"

"Well, take for instance when we were marching and had to halt – stop. After we halted, there was no sound. We'd count in our heads to four then do an 'eyes right' by moving our heads to the right, shuffle ourselves until we were lined up straight, all eyes on our Right Marker – who was at the right end of the front rank – to ever-so slightly nod his Stetson and we'd snap our heads to the front in unison. We even did a bit of revolver drill, all again by silent numbers. These kinds of movements, done properly, blows the minds away of the spectators. There were some pretty expanded chests that day, I can tell you. To a man – it was another eight years before women were allowed to join the Force – we felt invincible and ready to take on the world of crime. We were trained, we told ourselves. In hindsight, what we knew was pitifully little, as we soon discovered.

"I can remember well how much I felt let down when I stood at attention in front of the sergeant at my first detachment and have him tell me that, quote, 'Sterling, you're no goddamn use to me 'til you've got your first five years in,' as he gave me a set of car keys and told me not to screw up.

"I felt offended by that remark but, of course, remained silent. After all, I was a brand new product of RCMP training, where discipline was everything. In hindsight—."

"Bravo-7, Bravo-4," crackled from the radio.

"— the sergeant was right," continued Sterling, ignoring the call from Constable Smith. "It takes a long time to build up that very necessary ingredient of police work – a 'sixth sense.'"

Sterling removed his mic from the hook on the dash and said, "Bravo-4, go ahead."

Frank Smith said, "If you're not 10-6 and 10-12 (busy and someone in the car), can we make a meet?"

"I am 10-12 but I can meet you, if you like." He did not ask why, knowing that the reason for the request was probably no one else's business.

The two patrol cars met at a Safeway parking lot near the bridge into downtown.

As his car pulled up alongside Bravo-7, Smith could see the newspaper reporter still present. "Hi, Sarge, sorry to bother you. Can you spare a couple of minutes?"

"Sure. Let me join you," Sterling said and excused himself from the reporter.

"What's up, Frank?" he asked as soon as he'd sat down in Smith's cruiser.

"I don't know if you heard that last call for me to land-line the office."

Sterling nodded.

"It was my sister in Surrey. My mother just suffered a major heart attack and is on life-support in Memorial Hospital. The prognosis is not good, I'm told. I need to get down there ASAP. Do you mind if I leave?"

"I'm very sorry to hear that, Frank. Of course. Go. Do the paperwork when you get back and keep in touch with me. I'll give you my home phone number," he said, scribbling it down on his clipboard pad, tearing the paper off and handing it to Smith. "And I'll let the OIC know. Hope everything turns out okay. Take care on the way down to the Coast."

'Shit!' Sterling said to himself as Smith pulled away in a hurry, 'that's all I need, another absent member. Gotta let him go though.'

"Everything okay?" asked Preston as Sterling returned.

"No," he replied, telling him the reason for the meet. "I had to cut him loose and send him on his way tonight."

"That's too bad. Let's hope she pulls through. Can you go on? I believe it was on the Island where you met your wife, Jocelyn?"

"Yes, at a Legion dance. The community was too small to have anything like a night club or a private dance hall. It was okay though with a bit of interior decoration. We got married after three years and a year later, Greg was born, just before I was transferred to S&I – Security and Intelligence Section – in Vancouver. I really didn't want to go. I was happy enough doing general duty work, but in those days, one did not have a choice. Well, I guess you did: take the transfer or leave the Force.

"We lived in Richmond, just south of Vancouver and I had to commute into the city, a chore I disliked. Commuting may save money by ride-sharing, but it becomes a pain when the driver of the week is late arriving, or a person we stop to pick up is late. I have a thing about being late anywhere. I finally quit the car pool."

"I take it you weren't too keen on the work, whatever that was, Jack?"

"No, it certainly wasn't my cup of tea. I had to spend the first six months as a 'Reader' sitting across the desk from my boss, a corporal, reviewing very mundane files, mostly about applicants for federal government positions, and for those in government service being promoted to higher positions, especially in the military. My work improved a bit when I was transferred to a multi-ethnic section, with responsibilities for checking on members of the CPC – the Communist Party of Canada – and the Fascist and Nazi parties. Some active surveillance was required and that was a bit more like regular police work but it did mean sitting and watching people or a place, day or night, with binoculars, for hours and for tracking visiting delegations from communist bloc countries, including Cuba, and of all things, groups like the Moscow Ballet. That was fun actually. Some of the females would walk around in their hotel rooms topless, drapes open and we became what I called 'legal voyeurs' – after all, we *were* performing our duty.

"During this time, I had a great deal of reading to do. About the rise of the Communist Party, first in the Soviet Union – you know, Lenin 'et al' – then in Canada, and the creation and growth of the Fascist and Nazi parties. Dry stuff.

"Anyway, I lasted in the job just under two years and asked for a transfer back to general duty. By the way, being in the reporting business, you probably recall the creation of the Canadian Security Intelligence Service – CSIS – which took over these kinds of responsibilities from the RCMP in 1984. My view of that move is that the new agency hasn't done so well in the past four years. Time will tell."

"So where'd you go?"

"Well, I think because I was living in Richmond, I got a 'paper' transfer there. The detachment was, for all intense and purposes, just another municipal police operation, surrounded on three sides by Vancouver, Delta and New Westminster police forces, the fourth side being of course, part of the coastline of the Straight of Georgia. It was largely a bedroom community, with little industrial business.

"Police work was pretty routine stuff. Traffic patrols – Highway 99 ran through on its way to the U.S. border where it became I-5 – with lots of MVAs and fatals, juvenile crime – now called 'Young Offenders' probably so as not to offend their sensitivities – and stuff like shoplifting, serving summonses and warrants for other detachments and lots of family fights.

"At one time, we could reckon on attending one of these every time we went on shift. That was where I had a rifle pointed at me from close up. The end of the barrel appeared huge in my vision and I thought I was a goner. Hated those god-damn calls.

"Oh, yes, and we worked six shifts a week. Overtime did not exist. But you know, in spite of all that, I considered myself lucky to be in the Force and would never have moved to a city police force, although clearly, it would have been economically better."

"Municipal salaries were higher, I suppose?"

"Yes. They were all unionized and worked a forty-hour week, with paid overtime. Importantly though was the fact that you remained in one geographic location – in the Lower Mainland – for all your service, whereas we were subject to long distance transfers and in those days, generally suffered a loss on the sale of your house. I could not afford a house until 1979. Most members, however, did not mind the transfers and enjoyed being at a new detachment periodically. Also it was a chance for promotion and with approximately 4,000 or so members stationed in British Columbia around that time – 1970 – a larger 'gene pool' to pick from, so to speak."

"When were you first promoted, Jack?"

"In 1975, but you're getting ahead of me. I have another detachment to get to yet. Look, it's 1 a.m. and quietened down now. I think I'll return to the office. Let's continue next week if we can, okay?"

PART TWO

14

It was a cold, moonlit Monday evening in late fall with, unusually, three inches of new snow on the ground. At the Sterling residence, the sergeant's three sons – Greg, 17, Jeff, 13 and Brad, almost 12 – homework finished, were hunkered down in the TV room watching one of their favourite shows – *Columbo*. Their dad was fond of the show, especially Peter Falk as Detective Columbo, in his dirty old creased raincoat and the 'shuffling' but effective way he did police work. It was 8:15.

Sterling was in Vancouver for the week, instructing at a supervisor's course for senior police NCOs. Mother was up at the community college taking a night school course in Accounting. She was employed by the local school board.

The faint sound of breaking glass broke through the sound from the TV set. Greg quickly got off the couch and said, "Quiet! I think someone's trying to get into the house downstairs. Follow me."

The three of them entered the kitchen where a door led to the basement stairs. Without turning on the light, and opening the door slowly, Greg peered into the stairwell and heard movement.

"Jeff," he whispered, "call the police and tell them what's happening. Brad, you come with me," and grabbed his baseball bat standing in the corner of the small landing. The two of them, Greg leading, started to slowly make their way down, the steps creaking as they went. The intruder, hearing this, scrambled back over the window sill, cutting the palm of his hand on a small broken piece of glass remaining in the frame and started running downhill.

Greg, a few seconds behind, ran out the basement door, yelling to

Brad to 'stay there.' Still carrying the bat, he started chasing the individual, who by now had a head start. In the bright moonlight, Greg
saw the person disappear into the apartment complex at the bottom
of the hill. Sensing that it might be hopeless to try to find him, and a
bit worried about his younger brothers, he returned to the house. As
soon as he saw Jeff, he asked him if he had contacted the police.

"Yes, they said they'd send a car up ASAP – I think that means as
soon as possible."

"Did you tell them it was Dad's house?"

"No, sorry, I forgot," replied Jeff.

"That's okay, they should be here soon," and just as he said that,
he heard a car door slam in the driveway, followed in a few seconds
by the doorbell ringing.

Jim Portal worked the South Zone, largely on the west side and
uphill of the downtown area. The City stretched a mile or so into the
high hills to the south and about six miles on a high plateau to the
west. The busy Trans-Canada Highway cut through here and he had a
fairly large area to cover, especially if his was the only patrol car working, as it was tonight. Fortunately, when the call came in, he was less
than a mile away from the address given – 246 Beston Drive, not far
from the Hudson's Bay shopping mall.

"Hmm," he'd said to the *Parkton News* reporter, who was accompanying him tonight, "that's Sergeant Sterling's street," as he raced
along, emergency lights on but no siren. He asked if anyone was near
to cover him. One of the City Centre cars responded and said he
would be there shortly – "That's 246, right?" he asked.

Dispatch came on the air immediately, confirmed the number
and said she believed it was Sergeant Sterling's residence and one of
his boys had called in. 'I believe he's in Vancouver."

"Ten-four. Would you call back and confirm that all is okay at the
house. Mrs. Sterling must be out," he said, pushing the accelerator to
the floor and saying on his radio, "Be there in thirty seconds."

Pulling into the driveway, he quickly told Dispatch he had arrived.

Yes, it was Sterling's house. He asked Charlie Preston to stay in the car. Jumping out, he shone his flashlight down the side of the premises and around the empty carport. Going to the front door, he opened the bug screen and knocked hard. It was opened immediately by a kid about sixteen or so and at least as tall as Jim.

"Hi, I'm Constable Portal. I work for your dad. You are?"

"Greg. My brother Jeff called the police station. Come in, please."

Shaking his hand, Portal entered the house, and asked if Mrs. Smith was at home.

"No," replied Greg, "she's at night school."

"Okay, I have two quick questions for you. Are you okay, and where was the break-in?"

Greg said they were all okay and explained what happened, telling the policeman that that he had two brothers and introduced Jeffrey and Bradley. He then led the constable down to the basement, show-ing him his room and the smashed-out window. Portal noted the blood and asked Greg if he had cut himself, and Greg said that he had noted the blood and assumed the culprit had cut his hand.

"Don't touch anything, Greg. The Ident Section guy is on his way. You scared the guy off, did you?" noticing the baseball bat on the bed.

"Yeah. He ran down the hill toward those apartments near the highway. He had a bit of a start on me so I didn't follow him far and came back to the house."

"Can you describe him for me?"

"He was a little shorter than me, medium build and was wearing a black toque, dark jacket and pants. He looked young from the way he ran."

"May I use your phone?" Portal asked.

"Sure," said Greg.

While calling the office, he heard another car enter the driveway. It was Constable Wardlow who had driven over from the east side of the zone to assist.

On the phone, he said to Shirley, the operator, "All's okay here and Bernie is with me. Can you confirm the dog man is on his way? We have a good set of footprints in the snow and a bit of blood to follow. The boys scared the intruder off. No, Mrs. Smith is at the college," he replied to the question. "No need to call her. I'll talk to her later. Thanks for your help."

"Okay, Greg, Constable Wardlow will stay with you and get a statement if you don't mind. I've sent for the Dog Master who should be here shortly and he and I will look for the culprit. See you later," he said, going outside to his car to make a few notes. He told the news reporter what had happened, while he awaited the arrival of the dog.

Constable Sheldon Barker – a fitting name for a Dog Master, thought everyone who met him – and 'Bruno' arrived at the house shortly. Barker and Portal took the dog to the back of the house for a smell of the broken window and blood – there was no glass outside as the window had been broken inward – and set off down the grass and snow covered hill. The footprints and blood trail led to a townhouse and when the door was opened, a young lad – aged 18 as it turned out and therefore an adult in criminal law – stood before them with a bloody bandage around his right hand. As soon as he saw Bruno, he admitted the offence. His parents were not home and as the wound looked like it needed suturing, the Dog Master arrested him and took him to the General Hospital for treatment and then to the detachment for a mug shot, fingerprints, statement and subsequent release to his parents.

Later, at the office near the end of their shift, Portal and Wardlow discussed the incident, Jim making the observation, "Jesus, talk about picking the wrong place to B&E."

"It's a good thing young Greg didn't bean him with that bat," replied his partner. "Lad probably doesn't know his own strength and could have done serious damage. Anyway, the sergeant will be interested in what happened and the outcome. For their ages, his sons are big buggers, eh? Good thing Greg didn't catch that guy."

15

Sergeant Sterling had placed the reporter with Constable Frank Smith in North Zone. It was a Saturday evening and so far, at 9 o'clock, it had been relatively quiet. Two of the reasons for that may have been due to the fact that it was *Hockey Night in Canada* and the Vancouver Canucks were at home to the Calgary Flames, game beginning at 7 p.m. MST, and it was a non-payday weekend.

In the two hours they had been on patrol, Smith had responded to two minor complaints, one of excessive noise from a BBQ party and the second, of a suspicious person in a backyard at about 8:30. He'd called the dog man in to have a look around but they found nothing and the complainant was satisfied with the action taken.

The reporter, of course, wanted to know about the man or woman he was patrolling with and always asked the question, "Do you mind giving me a little bit of your background?"

"No. What would you like to know?" replied Smith.

"Well, the usual stuff. Where were you born, your ethnic background, where you worked before you joined the Force, when did you sign on and why, single, married, kids and anything else you think is relative. I assure you that the information will go no further than me and will be treated with respect. You okay with that?"

"Sure," responded Smith, as he slowly drove south along the road from West Side and was returning to the more populated area in the North Shore. "Well, I'm 27 with seven years of service, married, no kids — yet. Born in Vancouver of English heritage and have one younger sister. My father arrived from Plymouth with his parents in

1955 and married my mother whose family, coincidentally, also emigrated from the U.K. Mum and Dad took me for a visit there when I was eleven, so that would have been 1972. You could still see the scars on the landscape from the Second World War. When I got home, I felt good and lucky, about being a Canadian. Um, what other things did you ask?"

"Well, did you work before you joined the Force and I'm always interested in what motivates people to do the work they do. I hope you don't think I'm being nosy?"

"No, no, not at all. I understand. When I graduated high school at 18, like most kids, I didn't know what I'd like to do, so I did a couple of mundane jobs while I tried to sort out my working life. One was as a construction worker and when I got laid off in the fall, got a job at a grocery store chain – Safeway – stocking shelves. One day I saw an ad in the *Vancouver Sun* newspaper about considering a career in the RCMP – 'Apply at the recruiting office in downtown,' it said, giving the address.

"So I went, not with the intention of applying so much, as to find out more about the job. I had never seen a live member of the Force, only on TV news. The constable doing the recruiting was really persuasive and after a good hour of discussion, I thought, 'What the hell, I think that might suit me. Give it a go.' So I completed an application form. I was a bit surprised when I got a call in three months to go for an initial interview.

"By then, I'd read all I could about the Force and its interesting history and realized that it was a career kind of job that required a commitment from me. I was impressed with their training program, which looked a bit difficult, the uniform – I have to admit I wondered how good I'd look in red serge – and the big variety of jobs available, so I decided to go for it. As for motivation, I needed work!"

"Interesting," replied Preston. "So, with seven years of service, I guess it's a career for you now."

Before Smith could reply, Dispatch called, "North Shore car closest to Tranquility and Greenfield Avenue."

Smith replied that he was on Tranquility Road, close by.

"Okay, Bravo-4, report of a loud disturbance, possibly domestic at
126. ETA?"

"Bravo-4, less than two minutes."

Shelley Prentice in Bravo-10 said she would cover, "be there in
three."

The reporter observed that the street name was a bit of a misnomer for a call like this.

The short road had no lighting and it was pitch black out. Frank
Smith used his roof top side-lights as he drove down the street. At 122
he slowed down further to look for number 126 and found that he
didn't need to – he heard the screaming and yelling through his open
car window, stopped in front and gave his 10-7. To his companion he
said, "Charlie, you can come up to the front door with me but don't
enter, okay? If the occupants see two of us, there's less chance of any
rough stuff."

The small stucco house was on two floors, with an in-ground
basement and front steps that led up to the second floor. The livingroom window was too high off the ground to get a look inside, so
Constable Smith was a bit disadvantaged by not being able to do that.
He rapped on the door and said loudly, "Police – open up!"

A woman screamed as he said that, drowning out his voice.

Trying the door, he found it locked. He banged much louder
again and shouted the same command, waited a few seconds, during
which there was more shouting by a male and female and another
scream. Not wanting to break the door down, he said to Preston, "I'm
going round the back to see if there's another entrance."

The reporter followed him around, where they found another
set of steps up to a back door. The policeman pounded on this door
and repeated his demand. No response and the house had gone quiet.
Smith tried the door and found it unlocked.

Turning the handle slowly, he pushed the door open and once again said, "Police. I'm coming in," motioning to Preston to hold back as he stepped into a hallway, walking slowly forward, still no sound. He felt uneasy. At the end of the hall, the light went out and before he could react, he received a blow to the head that knocked him out and he fell heavily to the floor.

The reporter, still standing at the open door, witnessed the assault. Unsure of what to do and apprehensive about entering, he ran down the steps and around to the front of the house, intending to call it in to the dispatcher. With great relief he saw another patrol car pull up behind Smith's.

Running to the driver's side he said, "Quick, Constable Smith's in trouble. He's been knocked down!"

The policewoman inside picked up her radio and said, "Radio, Bravo-10, officer down at 126 at that last domestic call. Need ambulance ASAP and cover, please. 10-7 out of car and on portable."

To the reporter she said, "Which way into the home? Show me!"

He led her round the back and up the stairs, Shelley Prentice drawing her revolver after replacing her portable radio on her belt.

"Stay outside," she said over her shoulder.

In the dim light she could see Smith lying at the end of the hallway. She advanced cautiously, in a semi-crouch position, gun held in a two-hand grip pointing directly ahead.

"Police. Show yourself!" she yelled and at that moment, a very large man appeared, holding something in his raised arms.

Prentice immediately knelt on the floor and aimed her weapon at the centre mass of the figure and at the same time, on her portable radio heard Joe McKillen give his 10-7 outside.

"This is the police. Drop your weapon or I'll shoot!" she said.

When she reflected on her actions later, she was surprised at how acutely sensitive the human ear becomes in tense situations. She distinctly remembered two things – hearing a car door slam and the heavy breathing of the man in front of her, followed by a moment or two of utter silence. 'I was in the eye of a potential deadly storm,' she thought later. 'Christ, this was the second time I've ever drawn my gun, right after the bank robbery episode a few months ago.'

The man stood motionless, with the piece of wood she'd discerned in the dim backlight still raised.

In a hard voice, Prentice said, "Don't be an idiot, man. Drop it or I'll shoot." Then, for effect, she added, "I'm a female cop and you know how trigger-happy we can be. I don't take any shit!"

Her words must have sunk in for the man slowly lowered the length of two-by-four lumber and put it on the floor.

By the time she stood up she heard McKillen rush up the back steps and enter the hallway behind her. While her partner handcuffed the man, Prentice bent over Smith and quickly checked his vitals. His heartbeat, while elevated, was strong. She entered the livingroom and found a woman collapsed on the rug with blood running out of her head and beginning to pool around it.

After briefly checking the woman for a pulse, she asked Dispatch on her portable to call a second ambulance ASAP and PGH to advise them of two incoming people with head injuries, one in serious condition. Corporal Hawkes then came on the air and said he would be there in two or three minutes.

With the suspect cautioned and in custody, Constable Prentice led him out to her car, put him in the back and then released the spring-loaded plastic shield that sprung up just behind the front seat, separating her from the prisoner while she drove.

In her account of the incident to boyfriend Rob later the next day, in response to his question, 'How did you feel?' she thought for a minute and said, "You know, I was angry and scared and so pumped up in those few seconds, it felt like my veins were full of adrenalin instead of blood. Took me a while to recover."

"You'll be okay, sweetheart. You're a good cop," and gave her a hug.

◆ ◇ ◆

Smith's injury was not serious and he recovered consciousness as he was loaded onto the stretcher at the house. However, the woman, the suspect's common-law wife, was in bad shape and had to be fed oxygen on her way to Emergency.

Later, at the office, Charlie Preston recounted the incident to Sergeant Sterling and said that he admired the actions taken by the two responding officers and that he now fully understood the potential for violence.

People's emotions are raw at a time like this and therefore their actions are most unpredictable, he noted. He didn't mention Shelley Prentice's threat to the suspect. As funny as he found it, he didn't think he needed to share it with anyone else.

"That's why we try to have not less than two members attend at the same time if possible. If there's an indication that someone is about to suffer grievous bodily harm or that death may be imminent, then the lone police officer must go in and take the risk. You can see why this kind of call is not one of our most favourite," Sterling said.

"I hope Frank will be alright."

"Yeah, he'll be fine. I reminded him he's lucky to have such a thick skull. He'll be released tomorrow."

"How's the woman?"

"She's critical. Frank was lucky in that he was struck by the flat side of the two-by-four whereas it appears she was hit by a corner. We checked on the husband and he was convicted four months ago of assaulting her, put on probation and had to sign a Restraining Order which prohibited him from making contact with his wife without another neutral adult present. Most of these assholes violate the Order anyway and often they're not worth the paper they're written on. Damned shame. Many women have died over the years."

16

McIntosh Brothers had been in the construction business in Parkton for the past twenty years, largely building residences and some commercial structures. They had slowly gained a good reputation for the architectural finesse in their designs and quality building. Their latest residential project was called Thistle Heights and was located in the hills to the south, just inside the City limit and was to consist of a group of townhouses and single dwellings, set on a small plateau. It was called 'Thistle' because the two brothers who owned the company, while Canadian born, were the children of Scottish immigrants. To give the dwellings a bit of a Scottish flavour, they had planned to put three things in place in each unit – one wall in each kitchen done in a mild plaid design, the kitchen countertops would be advertised as 'Scottish curling rock granite' and, when completed, every residence would have a few plants of thistle growing near each entrance, a touch that one of the wives of the brothers came up with. The project was about half finished with most of the townhouses completed.

The company, having previously experienced thefts of materials from their sites, employed the services of a security company which placed night watchmen at the premises in the non-construction hours. It had paid off as there had been no thefts over the past several months. Tonight, however, there was no guard on duty.

◆ ◇ ◆

In the Greater Parkton area, fully one quarter of all motor vehicle registrations were for pickup trucks. Outside the City limits, where the main source of income was derived from farming and ranching, the utility pickup was ubiquitous. As was the case in point.

The rusted sections on the body of the black 1975 Ford F150 looked like an old man's age patches. And it creaked and rattled as it slowly crept up the newly-paved, sidewalk-less road, lights out, stopping about one hundred yards short of the new subdivision. The road surface was covered with hard-packed snow pounded during the day by large construction vehicles.

Turning off the motor, the driver, dressed in a black toque, jacket and pants, sat still for several minutes, observing the area with a pair of Zeiss Icon binoculars, 7 x 35 wide angle, night vision lenses, valued at $250.00 and stolen a week ago from the camera shop in town. They were excellent for night viewing, he found. When he was driving, the strap was around his neck and the glasses tucked down inside his zippered-up coat. It was just after one a.m. A bright, almost full moonlit, cold, early Monday morning. He could see no activity through the glasses and noted the absence of any vehicles. It was his first visit to this site and he was expecting to see a watchman's transport of some kind, as he had at the two other places he had canvassed over the weekend.

'Hmm, that looks good. Maybe I'll do it tonight. I'll walk up and have a closer look to check for sure as the guy could have driven it around the back. If there's no one around, I'll bring my truck up closer. That way, I can get away faster if I have to,' he said to himself.

Bending forward, he pulled on a pair of low-cut rubber overshoes over his ankle boots. He would discard them when finished with his night's work. He did not want to be found in possession of any incriminating evidence, including the 'tools of his trade,' as he liked to think of them.

A few weeks ago, he had been browsing in a second-hand book store that also sold used videos. He was looking for material that essentially was about vampires and ghouls – he especially liked watching video scenes of fire and destruction – when he found a college textbook, five years old, entitled *Criminal Investigation*. Looking at the contents page, he noted a chapter dealing with arson that got his attention. He bought the book for three dollars and took it home and read the chapter several times, including how police investigations are conducted. 'Very revealing,' he thought. 'Good to know.' He realized how sloppy he had been on his previous 'adventures' as he liked to call them and vowed to be so careful as to avoid being caught.

Taking his two-cell flashlight from the glove box, one where the beam could be changed from a wide arc to a pin-point light, he put it in his coat pocket. 'Probably don't need it tonight,' he thought. 'It's so bright out. I guess that's both good and bad. Oh well.'

The urge drove him on. Getting out of the truck, he closed the door quietly. Sound carried farther at night he knew. Walking quickly to the unfenced site, his eyes and ears were sensitive to visual and atmospheric changes. He stood very still for fully two minutes assessing the situation and then walked around the back for a quick check.

No sound – no activity – no vehicle. He looked at his watch again – 1:15. Satisfied, it was time to go to work.

Returning to his vehicle, he drove it to the edge of the construction area, stopping on the pavement on the packed snow, rather than enter the property and leave a set of tire tracks in the new snow – however worn the treads were, that could be traced to him. Leaving the motor running, he asked himself, 'Okay, you up for this?' and answered, 'Yep, let's do it.'

Pulling on a pair of rubber gloves, he got out of his truck, went to the back, opened the canopy, reached in and pulled the tailgate down. His means of accelerant was a 4.5-gallon jerry can of gasoline, sitting in the bed of the truck, lashed to the side with two rubber tie-downs. He had carefully considered this important aspect of his work. If stopped by the police and his vehicle searched, his very reasonable explanation for its presence was that the gas was for his vehicle and he wasn't hiding it. After all, most people carried a spare can in this country.

Reaching in, he unstrapped the full can of gas and the long screw-on nozzle and lifted it out. It was really heavy. Taking one more quick look back down the road and one more check for sound, he carried the big can, walking one-sidedly to the end of the row of units. Uncapping the can, he took the nozzle, screwed it on tightly and put the cap into a long plastic bag, wrapping the end around his right index finger. Picking up the can of gas he started carefully pouring the liquid against the lower part of the wooden wall so as to prevent splash-back on his shoes and bottom of his pants. Continuing to pour, he slowly walked along the front of each connected residence. Reaching the end of the row, he put down the can out of the way, removed the nozzle, laid it on the deck, took the cap out of the bag and screwed it tightly back on the can, throwing the bag against the wall. He next took two loose long wood matches from his jacket pocket, scratched the end of one on the rough-timbered deck floor, waited for the flare to die down, bent over and ignited the gasoline, throwing the second match into the flames. No means of ignition on his person.

The effect was immediate. Instant fire, rapidly spreading along and up the walls. Not waiting to see the results, he picked up the nearly-empty jerry can and nozzle, walked quickly back to the Ford, replacing and securing them in the bed of the truck, closing the canopy. Then, taking off his gloves he balled them up and flung them as hard as he could into the nearby trees, followed by each overshoe.

He didn't think they'd be found and wouldn't yield any useful evidence even if they were. Getting into the cab, he took a quick look at the quickly rising flames, a smile of complete satisfaction on his face and drove the battered old pickup back down the hill toward Rose Hill Estates, lights out.

When he turned right to go back toward the City, he put his lights on. He hadn't driven far when he saw, around a gradual bend in the road a mile or so away, through some thinly spaced trees, the flashing red and blue lights of an approaching emergency vehicle, most probably a police car, he thought.

'Christ, that was a fast response! I wonder if someone seen me?' he thought. Realizing he was the only vehicle on the road and absolutely not wishing to be stopped, he doused his headlights again and made a sharp left turn at the last street back into Rose Hill, went down a block, made another left, parked, turned his motor off and sat, his heart beating fast and, in spite of the cold, his hands feeling sweaty on the steering wheel. He'd wait here, he told himself, until the fire trucks got to the scene, before heading out onto the main road again.

◆ ◇ ◆

Constable Portal took the fire call as he was the closest patrol car. The City's fire department was on the way from their sub-station on the west Trans-Canada Highway, but it was an uphill drive and they'd be almost ten minutes before they arrived. The address given was Thistle Drive, a new road to a sub-division under construction, the dispatcher advised.

"Okay, I think I know where that is," replied Portal. "It's uphill from the Rose Hill Estates. I'll be there in five or less."

He'd been up there before on a break-in complaint. There was no traffic about so he didn't think it was appropriate to wake up people unnecessarily with his siren. 'Sounds like a pretty big one,' he thought, given the details he had received. Reaching Dogwood Street, the top road in Rose Hill, he made a hard left turn onto Thistle, the rear end of his car sliding around in a 180-degree arc on the hard-packed snow. He corrected by yanking the wheel, steering into the skid.

The sight that greeted him was startling. A row of townhouses fully engulfed in flames. He knew right away there was no saving them. As he quickly approached the scene, he noted four or five people standing nearby, staring at the huge fire. They did not hear him arrive, with the roaring of the flames.

Before giving his 10-7, he thought about asking Dispatch to get the Ident and GIS people up to the site, but remembered, looking at his watch, that they had both gone home. 'I'll take a few pictures and they can do more in the morning.'

The onlookers heard his car door slam and turned around.

"Any of you folks see what happened?" he asked loudly.

One man said, "No. I reported the fire and gave your office the name of the builder. I was awakened by the bright, flickering light from the flames. My bedroom window faces up this way."

"See anyone?" asked Portal.

"No, I didn't see anyone or any vehicle."

"Yeah, same with me," said a woman. "These places are brand new and as far as we know, no one lives in them yet."

He asked if they knew whether or not there was a night watchman on duty and no one knew. He was thinking of the obvious. He observed the building site sign giving the name of the builder and a couple of telephone numbers. He used his portable to ask Dispatch if they had been able to contact them.

"No, we're still checking. There's no reply to the one we called – 479-2703," she replied.

"Okay, try this one. If you get someone, ask them if they have a night guard up here. There's no car around and I'm assuming there isn't one, but I don't know that for sure. He or she may have been dropped off. This place is a write-off by the way. Suggest you don't tell the person that. Ask if they can let me know about the guard, and if they can get here right away."

He took the names and addresses of the witnesses as a matter of routine and would turn them over to the Investigation Section at the end of the watch in the morning. He was a bit concerned that the heat from the end townhouse unit next to the first house might cause it to catch fire and spread to the others. 'C'mon, fire department, get your asses here!' he thought and then caught the faint sound of approaching sirens.

He heard his call sign on his radio and responded, "Bravo-12, go ahead."

"Jim, we got the building owner on the line. He advises there is supposed to be a night watchman on duty and that he does have a vehicle as far as he knows. He's going to call the guy's home to check and will be on his way then. By the way, do you want me to call GIS?"

"No, it's okay. It can wait until morning, thanks."

As the first fire truck rounded the corner onto Thistle, Dispatch called him again to advise there was no guard there tonight. He was home sick and did not call his boss. "Copy?"

"Got it. Thanks again."

"Jim, just to let you know I'll be at your location in three, four minutes." It was the watch commander.

Just as Portal got off his radio, a member of the local print media – a reporter from the *Parkton News* – rolled up to the site, followed several minutes later by the TV people.

'Christ,' thought Portal, 'just what the arsonist wants and needs!'

And he did.

17

Ernest Emile Austmann, born in 1960, was from Kitchener, Ontario. His father, Reverend Bernhardt Kurt Austmann, had been born in the same city, to which his father, Emile, had immigrated in 1920 as a former German soldier in Kaiser Wilhelm's army of World War I. The city had been originally called Berlin by earlier German immigrants, but because of the unfortunate linkage to its namesake city during the hostilities, the place was re-named Kitchener in 1916.

Bernhardt Austmann was the minister of the Lutheran Church in the city centre and had four children. Ernie was the youngest. Growing up in a religious atmosphere, he had to, when old enough, attend his father's church three times on Sundays – Bible class, then morning and evening services. His was a straightforward upbringing with emphasis on obedience and knowledge of church doctrine and education, his father owning a master's degree in Divinity. Humour was not valued a great deal. His oldest brother had entered church service, but young Ernie had no such inclination, rather, he thought about a career in the military or perhaps with a police force. He really didn't think he could emulate his father's lifestyle. He needed something a bit more exciting, challenging.

Upon graduating high school, he entered Eastwood Collegiate Institute to take some general course work leading to an undergrad degree in 'something,' he told his dad. 'At least he's continuing his education,' thought the father.

Near the end of his first year, the college held a Student Career Day and it was here that he picked up two pamphlets – one from the

Royal Military College in Kingston and the second, a generic one published by the RCMP.

Looking them over, he was surprised to find that RMC offered a four-year degree program and a commission in the Canadian Armed Forces – his choice of Army, Navy or Air Force, on graduation. 'Good deal,' he thought.

The police pamphlet, while not offering free schooling, did seem promising and the money was quite good. Like the Armed Forces, service was open to men and women. The man on the cover certainly did look imposing, dressed in his red serge Review Order uniform complete with silver spurs on the back of high, very shiny brown riding boots. He was surprised too at the multitude of jobs in the Force, as they called themselves. They even had their own 'Navy' and 'Air Force' – many different kinds of coastal and inland patrol boats and several kinds of airplanes, including small passenger jets and helicopters. 'Not too shabby,' he thought. 'What to do? I'll apply to both.'

The Force was the first to respond to his application. At the time, they were short of personnel and were on a bit of a recruiting drive.

He told his father of his decision. Dad agreed that while both jobs served the public and were therefore laudable, he was disappointed that his son did not consider the ministry as a career. Within six months, having passed his written test, two physical examinations, a dental check, an intensive psychological test and a one-hour interview, Ernie Austmann was sworn in and reported to 'Depot' Division, Regina for six months of rigorous training.

A visiting major from the U.S. Marine Corps training base at Camp Pendleton, California, present to assess the Force's training program, allowed that the physical training – martial arts, cross-country running, physical education, swimming and water rescue, foot drill and firearms training – were at least as tough as that given to Marine Corps recruits.

A very proud Austmann family attended the colourful and exacting graduation ceremony. They had never seen a 'real live Mountie' before, as his father said, and in spite of his reservations about his son becoming a member of the RCMP, he was even prouder when he heard the drill instructor say when the 32-person troop marched off the parade square in front of all the visitors, "There they go, ladies and gentlemen – *Canada's Finest!*"

This was followed by loud, prolonged clapping. A day to remember.

◆ ◇ ◆

Even with eight years service, Austmann's general demeanour was still a bit reserved. When he joined in 1980, he did not swear and was a bit taken aback about what he heard, even from women, who, in some cases, swore more fluently than the 'gentlemen' of the troop. As time went by and given the nature of police work, he did allow the odd swear words to creep into his language repertoire, especially when he lost a particularly egregious Court case that he knew he should have won and the bastard walked out of Court all cocky and with a smile on his face. He'd put the dismissal down to the incompetence of the Prosecutor – usually through lack of preparation and review – or to the Judge, for a variety of reasons including the fear by some, of convicting a person of a serious offence and then having the conviction overturned by an Appeals Court, with perhaps some blameworthy remarks included in the 'Reasons for Judgment.'

As one of his buddies said, "Hey, win some, lose some. Makes you more careful in your investigation and case preparation. Instead of asking 'How can I win this case?' it may be well to ask 'How can I lose it? I always look for the loopholes and try to cover those bases, together with a heart-to-heart with the Crown lawyer before trial. Usually works for me."

Since graduating, he found General Duties police work satisfactory. He'd looked at specialty sections and while plainclothes investigations seemed promising, in the end he'd stayed in uniform. He was ambitious and wanted to rise in the ranks as high as he could go and to that end, acquitted himself in a professional manner without revealing his desire to his workmates. They were decidedly different individuals and he got on well with them in spite of what he thought were weird idiosyncrasies that some of them had.

He excused these thoughts by rationalizing, 'We're all human, I suppose. I guess I have my foibles too.' He'd received good annual appraisal reports and he felt that his zone NCO and watch commander could rely on him to get a job done. In his eight years, he'd been stationed at a large Lower Mainland municipal detachment and a small, four-person one on Vancouver Island before arriving at Parkton two years ago.

He felt that he had two more years or thereabouts to serve here before his next transfer when he'd have two, five-year Service Stars on the upper left arm of his jacket. 'By then,' he'd told himself, 'I'd like to be in line for my corporal's hooks.'

He had seriously considered applying for the Force's A250 University Program that sent selected members to school for an undergraduate degree. It meant three to four years away from police work except for the summer months when students were temporarily assigned to a variety of duties, some of them quite mundane. However, 'events' got in his way. The event in this case came in the form of a female, and at the age of 26, he knew that his time as a 'free man' was nearly up. He was deeply in love.

As coincidence would have it, Julia Rheinhartt was also of German origin, four generations removed. She and Ernie Austmann were a match, intellectually and in their perspectives on life. When he discussed the police university program with her, she was enthused about the idea, especially since she held a B.Comm. degree. Going that route would mean that he would have to leave Parkton and go to Vancouver to one of the two major universities there, for a period of three to four years. He didn't know if he could do that alone and leave her in Parkton to which she replied, "Not a problem, Sweetheart, I can go with you and find a job down there somewhere."

He considered the ramifications of what she said and replied, "That's nice of you but we could not afford to live apart. It may sound a bit old fashioned but my conscience won't allow me to live together, to say nothing about how my parents would feel. We'd have to get married and we've only known each other a few months – a bit too soon for such a major step in our lives, don't you think? But there is another possibility and that's doing my degree by something called correspondence programs. A few schools now offer this method of study and the obvious choice for me would be that offered by University of Waterloo in Kitchener/Waterloo, Ontario, which, as you know, is my home town. The courses are home study but there are three things to the down-side of doing it this way."

"What are they?" she asked.

"Well, it would take almost twice as long to earn the degree. While working full-time, I could only accommodate two courses per semester – and that would include a lot of study time and writing assignments and papers – for a max of six courses per year. It takes 32 courses to complete, so do the math. Secondly, as you don't attend classes, you study alone and there's no class interaction – no classmates to bounce your ideas back and forth and take a measure as to whether your understanding of the course material is right or not. You're on your own. Thirdly, I'd have to pay my tuition and buy books, although that's not a big consideration."

"No, it may not be easy, darling, but if you want to advance your education," said Julia, "why don't you go for it? You'll only be thirty-four or thirty-five when you finish and the piece of parchment will be nice to have and may help your career."

That had been several months ago when he'd had this discussion. Since then, he had applied to, been accepted and had finished his first two courses – Psychology and Sociology 101. He found the material easy to comprehend and received good marks.

♦ ◊ ♦

Back on night watch. Unlike a few of the other members of his shift who complained about the long, twelve-hour shifts and who often took 'forty winks' in some out of the way spot, their radios turned down to half volume in the event they were called, Austmann did not. He was always 'on the prowl.' After he did his property checks in the business and industrial parts of his zone, he'd show the flag – to very few people at night he realized – by patrolling the residential streets, looking for anything out of place or house parties that may be a little noisy, when he'd make his presence known to the occupants and ask them to 'tone the noise down a bit in consideration of your neighbours' and checking the names and addresses of people seen on foot.

He'd had some feedback from a few residents who appreciated police presence in their neighbourhoods at night. "Part of our responsibilities," he told them, pleased that they had noticed.

North Zone was different in make-up, topographically and size compared to Centre and South zones. Consisting mostly of blue collar workers employed at the pulp mill, a nearby ore mining operation and in the forest industry, it, unfortunately, had a higher criminal activity rate, particularly among the juvenile (under 18) population. As well, family problems were more common, with alcohol and drug use often at the centre of them.

Austmann knew his area intimately and had had contact with a number of its residents. He had patrolled every street, back lane, dead-end and sundry pieces of wasteland; he knew where the trouble spots were and all the shortcuts to get to them.

The main thoroughfare running through, to end at the Airport, was originally named Brock Street, after an English immigrant of that name who settled in the area in the late 1800s, but everyone called it the Airport Road.

The further out one went, the sparser the homes became. Most of the early settlers were of British stock and, coming from Kent and Surrey counties where apple, pear, cherry and plum orchards were a source of livelihood, brought that knowledge and seeds with them, creating hundreds of acres of fruit trees in the fertile, flat-bottomed valley, where an ample water supply was nearby in Lake Parkton. While suburbia had encroached over the past hundred years or so, there were still small holdings of orchard land remaining.

Driving Bravo-16, he checked his watch – 2:05 a.m. His partner, Frank Smith, was riding shotgun tonight, while Constable Prentice was covering the east part of the zone, closer to the downtown area. Except for the odd vehicle, there was no traffic activity, and of course, the Airport was closed at this hour. One patrol along this part of the road was usually enough – there were few calls out here.

They had to drive into the Airport property for a quick look as part of the new security measures. There was a commissionaire on duty and he waved 'hello' to them on their way around the terminal. They knew that he made a note of their presence.

"Okay, Frank, what say we meet up with Shelley at the Golden Arches?" Austmann asked.

"Sure! Sounds good. Nothing going on here," Smith replied, so they headed back the way they had come.

It was a cold, clear night with a bit of black ice shining on the road surface, so they drove under the fifty km speed limit. They were still in the small orchards area when Austmann slowed down, stopped the car and reversed.

"Whaddya see?" asked Smith.

"See that black pickup truck on the right?" he said. "I'm pretty sure that wasn't there half an hour ago when we came by and note the way it's parked – not quite in the driveway. Also, no frost on the windows. Worth a check?" he asked rhetorically.

Pulling off the gravelled portion, they both got out, and with flashlights, approached the truck, an older model Ford F150, with a dark coloured canopy.

It was parked at an odd angle at the entrance to a dirt driveway which led to an old, run-down, two-storey house, probably eighty to one hundred years old, no lights on, situated amid a group of about three dozen fruit trees arranged in rows down the sides and rear. They walked down both sides of the pickup, which was rusting out, and looked in the cab. Empty. Smith went around to the front and taking his brown leather glove off, put his bare hand through the grill to feel the radiator – still quite warm. He looked down and noted the license plate number and then moved around to the driver's side where Austmann was still shining his light inside.

"Doors locked, no key in ignition, looks clean and window is down a couple of inches. No smell of booze or anything. Maybe the guy works late," he said. Going to the rear, he asked Smith if the rear plate number matched the front.

"Yeah, it does." Smith then shone his light through the smoky brown rear window of the canopy and spotted a 4.5 gallon U.S. Army style gas can with a pouring spout strapped to the side with a short bungee cord. Trying the canopy handle, it would not turn. Locked. "Let's run the plates."

"I wonder if there's gas in the can?" said Austmann. "Let me shake the truck a bit and listen for the slosh." He did and they could hear liquid splashing.

"Okay, no big deal here," he said, writing the details on the foolscap paper on his clipboard. The time was 3:10.

"Radio, Bravo-16, RO check, please," called Smith.

"Bravo-16, go ahead."

"B.C. plate, L-Lima 27902."

"Lima 27902. Standby," said the dispatcher.

In fifteen seconds, she replied, "Bravo 16, ready to copy?"

"Go ahead."

"Registered Owner is Mark A. Rifell – R I F E L L – 4815 Airport Road. Do you want an Indices check?" she asked.

"Er, yes, thanks," said Smith, noting the same house number on the roadside mail box.

"Bravo-16, DOB is 28-10-64, same address. Record. Minor in

possession of liquor, *G.L. Act*, Parkton, 11–07–82. CC in your drawer. Copy?"

Just a government liquor act offence, noted Austmann, as they made their way to rendezvous with Prentice.

At the end of the watch, Austmann entered the details of the check, along with six others, on the DPR report and threw it in the GIS basket, along with the paperwork from the rest of his team.

18

The members of the four watches at Parkton City Detachment each had a drawer, built into a long counter against one of the interior office walls, for their files, messages, etcetera. Files in this case consisted of blue covers for 'Concluded' investigations and pink covers for files 'Still Under Investigation'.

When 'A' Watch members returned to duty on day shift three days after the latest arson at the Thistle Estates, they found the following three-page information sheet from Sergeant Jones, GIS. It had, of course, been distributed to the whole detachment. Sergeant Sterling took his copy out and read the following:

TO ALL DETACHMENT MEMBERS –
CONFIDENTIAL
RE: ARSON, THISTLE ESTATES 4/5-12-88

This fire, set at approx. 2:15 a.m. Monday night last, caused about $1.2 million in damages. 8 townhouses were demolished.

Evidence found at the scene by the Captain in charge of the fire crew indicates it was set with an accelerant, most likely gasoline, which appears to have been ignited by at least one long wooden match. A charred one was found on the deck of the end unit, suggesting that was the originating point of ignition and that the suspect walked along each adjoining deck, from his right to his left, pouring the accelerant as he went. Luckily, the front wall of this end unit collapsed inward, rather than onto the deck.

Chemical analysis of the fire starter is being conducted. No suspect vehicles were seen at or near, or leaving the scene. The five on-lookers have been ruled out as suspects, each providing a reliable alibi. While there was a couple of inches of snow on the ground, it had been compacted on the road surface. Several decent tire impressions were left on the construction site, measured and photographed in case the suspect's vehicle did enter the site. We believe the individual drove to the site — it would be too far to walk and carry the accelerant — unless of course he lives just below in the Rose Hill Estates, but it seems unlikely at this time.

We believe we are dealing with someone who is very careful about his activities and thinks things through. Because of the slim evidence to date, we have not been able to develop a profile of the individual.

The Provincial Fire Marshall's investigator, Malcolm Wood, is responsible for further investigation of this fire, in conjunction with my Section and that of our Identification people. He has more or less ruled out profit and insurance fraud by the Company, who are currently in good financial standing. They have experienced thefts of materials from the sites in the past and generally, unless much material is stolen, don't file an insurance claim.

That is why they have gone to the expense of hiring security people, although in this instance, unfortunately, it didn't work as the night guard failed to show up. He is being investigated re: possible collusion on his part with a suspect but the possibility of some kind of gain is remote.

With the little evidence we have, we cannot make a connection to other past fires. The only two similarities that remain the same are the facts that a vehicle was believed used and the approximate time frame of the fires — 2 a.m. *IF* this is the same person setting these fires, in the latest one, he's upped the ante, going for dwellings, even if they were apparently empty. He may have thought about this and reasoned that, with the absence of vehicles and no lights on in the building, none of the units were occupied, a reasonable assumption to make given the circumstances but unless he checked the doors and entered to confirm – the builder claims they are locked each evening – he could not be certain of this. His actions therefore are highly irresponsible with potentially deadly consequences. People have died, inadvertently, because of such carelessness, which makes it imperative that we stop this individual. To that end, I'd like every member who is engaged in night patrol work – Watch people and other Units – to become much more vigilant and inquisitive. By that I mean more checking of moving and stationary vehicles and people on foot.

We now have the Daily Patrol Reporting – DPR – system in place and I'm asking you to be diligent in its use. When times are quiet, particularly in the early morning hours, to use the STOP, OBSERVE & LISTEN tactic, as been suggested after you have completed your property checks. By doing this, you may well pick up on other criminal activity. My Section does not mind how much paper work you generate. It's been a bit sparse recently.

I will keep you posted with the results of the fire investigation findings and any correlation that might arise between this and the other fires.

Thanks for your attention and efforts. Unit Heads, please ensure a c.c. of this Memo is read by every member.

Thanks – Trevor Jones i/c GIS

Sterling checked each drawer to see that his members had a copy. Based on what Jones had said, he felt that he had covered very adequately what needed to be known, and felt that there was really nothing to add. It all came down to diligence and maybe a little bit of luck which occasionally, but not often enough, happened in police work.

Mostly, it was a case of plodding along (from which derived the name 'Mr. Plod', the name given to the British police counterpart – a derisive one for a slow, somewhat dim-witted constable on patrol) but this was in reality how many cases were solved – unlike the TV cop shows which seemed to be solved in one hour, including time for commercials.

Sterling believed that the 'beat cop' was the heart and soul of a police organization and that everything should revolve around that individual. 'I'll talk to each one of my people about this arson case,' he thought. 'It's a challenging one that I know they'd like to crack. Wouldn't do 'A' Watch's reputation any harm, and for that matter, mine neither.'

19

"It's for you, Sarge," the dispatcher said on the office intercom.

"Thanks, Shirley." Pressing the button down, he said, "Sterling here."

"Hi, Jack, it's Charlie Preston. Got a minute?"

"Sure, go ahead."

"Just wondering when we can get together. What shift are you on this weekend?"

"I'm on days until Monday," replied Sterling. "Any time would be alright with me."

"Okay, good. How about Sunday, say, after lunch sometime?"

♦   ◇   ♦

Parking his car in the police staff parking lot – with permission – Preston arrived at the appointed time for his sixth ride-along with Sterling.

Sterling had spent the morning on administrative matters – reading criminal reports, reviewing and signing off finished complaints, checking members' files that were still under investigation and reading two PERS forms, just completed. These were annual reports required of all members of the Force. In part, they formed the basis for future promotions and were taken seriously. They were completed by corporals for constables, sergeants for corporals and so on, in the same unit of operation.

When the reporter arrived, he was directed to the detachment coffee room at the rear of the building. Sterling was just finishing his canned salmon with lettuce and tomato sandwich and was about to eat some dessert when the reporter walked in.

"Hello, Charlie, care for a piece of fresh-baked cherry pie?" asked Sterling.

"Thanks, but no. Just finished lunch at home. Take your time. How've you been? Haven't seen you for almost a month, I believe."

Outside in the police car parking lot, they both settled into Bravo-7 with Sterling giving his 10-8. "I don't have to remind you of procedures, do I?" he asked his passenger with a slight grin.

"No, I think I've got them down by now. Basically, if you get into shit, I bail and run," he said with a smile and Sterling said that that was probably the most prudent thing to do.

"Where will the wind carry us today?"

"Well, I thought I'd give the South Zone a look. While it's Sunday, it can be busy, especially for traffic if it's a nice day, as it is. There's a lot of traffic on the Trans-Canada Highway, people out for a drive, shopping, golf and so on, so I'll ride herd on them for a bit and give a hand to the three units out here, a General Duty car, a City Traffic car and Highway Patrol unit. That might sound like enough but they do cover an eighteen-mile stretch. Because of the 110-km speed limit in parts, it can lead to some horrendous crashes and often fatals. It's good to have Traffic and HP units around when that happens as these people have specialized training in accident investigation, called 'traffic analyses' and take a more forensic approach to their work. If we have a fatal MVA in the City, they take over the investigation." Changing the subject, Sterling said, "So, what's new on the news front?"

"Oh, you know, same old, same old. One thing I am interested in is the Thistle Estates fire. Any leads? Suspects?"

"Yes, we have one but not much in the way of evidence, more a feeling really. Part of the problem as you're probably aware is that fires usually obliterate physical evidence, and secondly, it is difficult to develop a time pattern for the perpetrator. Our consensus at the moment is that without more to go on, it probably wouldn't help to bring him in without something substantive to confront him with. I can say that we're trying to do a surveillance of sorts, but that's difficult too and manpower- and time-consuming, and it becomes inconsistent over time."

Just after entering the highway, Sterling saw a police car ahead stopped on the side of the road, with its emergency lights on, checking a vehicle. As was the custom with most police officers in other patrol cars, they would stop and observe, ready to offer assistance, their time and circumstances permitting. Preston knew this from previous outings with Sterling and did not engage him in conversation, thereby distracting his attention.

When the stopped vehicle left, the constable got out of his vehicle and walked back.

"Hi, Sarge, thanks for checking," said the driver of 10-Charlie-3, nodding his head at Sterling's passenger.

"No problem," replied Sterling. "Speeder?"

"Yeah. Actually it's a two-for-one day. Two cars were having a bit of a race east-bound, doing over 130 kph. My guy stopped but the other kept going, not knowing that a Highway car was ahead of me, and he got him. That'll cost them both three hundred dollars and three points. If traffic was any heavier they'd both be facing possible 'dangerous' charges and arrest, as was pointed out."

"Good stuff. See you later," said the sergeant.

Resuming the patrol, Preston said, "As you know, Jack, I've talked to some of your crew by now and got some of their work-life history. It's a pretty eclectic group of souls you have with you, most interesting from a human relations point of view. So, how about you? As a maestro says to his musicians, 'from the beginning.' Okay if I record the personal stuff?"

Sterling chuckled and said, "Well, since you put it that way, what choice do I have? Yeah, go ahead." He didn't particularly liked talking about himself and somewhat reluctantly began by quoting the first three words in the Holy Bible: "In the beginning... I was born in the United Kingdom in Surrey County, in an old town called Leatherhead, 40 miles south of London."

"Yes, I notice the slight trace of an English accent. Go on, please."

"My mother was a nurse's aide and father, an accountant. We lived in a semi-detached – called a duplex here – on the outer edges next to farmland. As I got a little older, I did a lot of pathway walking – trails if you like – and at around 8 or so, got my first bike and that considerably enlarged my area of travel, to the point later, on weekend days, I would take a lunch and ride for several hours, mostly on my own, exploring the countryside. For me it was a new sense of freedom. Got knocked down twice and quickly learned how to deal with traffic.

"My father was transferred to a seaside city in Essex County and I was good enough to be admitted into a Grammar school at age eleven, a pre-requisite in England to enter university. One thing stood in the way of that next step – National Service – mandatory two years in the military beginning at age 18, in the Army, Navy or Air Force, no choice as to which.

"I was conscripted into the Army, the Royal Artillery, and went off to gunnery school near Wales. Five months later I found myself attached to the 26th Field Regiment in Egypt for the next one and a half years, close to the Suez Canal Zone. It was a time of great upheaval in that country and at times our regiment was used in an infantry capacity to guard vital military establishments – ammunition depots, water reservoirs, transportation compounds and so on. We actually got into combat situations – more like skirmishes really – with the Egyptian military. Several Army personnel were killed in my time there. Okay, I think we've gone far enough east, Charlie, let's turn around and head back," Sterling said, as he made a wide U-turn with Bravo-7.

While they had been driving Preston noticed the sergeant's eyes, as he had with other members of 'A' Watch, constantly moving, left, right and checking the rear view mirror, always watching. A necessary trait, he mused.

"That's interesting. What did you think of the ancient civilization?"

"What I saw wasn't much," he replied, "except for the relatively new Suez Canal, a marvel of British and French engineering, and I did wonder otherwise, what those people in the time of the Pharaohs would have thought of the canal. It was pretty much a scrub desert area we were in, sprinkled with a few small villages and towns except, of course, for Port Said at the north end of the canal and the Port of Suez at the south end. No military people were allowed within fifty miles of Cairo. In spite of that, I did get a sense of the country, its ancientness, its biblical connections and vowed to return someday to see Egypt's antiquities.

"At one point, our whole Army Division went on a week-long military exercise, called manoeuvres, across the Sinai Desert almost to the border with Israel. We were also only about 75 miles from Saint Catherine's Monastery in the mountains to the south – a Greek Orthodox Church dating back to about the year AD 384.

"I remember reading about the place in religious studies at high school. It intrigued me and I wanted to see it. Someday I will. Anyway, what got me interested in Canada was that we had a Canadian sergeant major, named Bill Hogan, from Vancouver. I got talking to him – loved his accent – and quickly became fascinated with the country, to the point where I felt the urge to emigrate when I returned home and see it for myself.

"Back in the U.K. after my service, I worked for four years piddling around in a variety of jobs and decided to emigrate. I saved every penny I could for my fare, by sea, and some money to tide me over until I found work there."

Sterling's reminiscences were interrupted by a radio transmission.

"Bravo-13, report of a disturbance at 200 Bestwick Drive; possible family fight. ETA, please?" asked the dispatcher.

"Bravo-13, about 5 minutes or so."

"B–13, Bravo-7. I'll cover you, Andrew," said Sterling, and said to his passenger, "It's our policy to do this on family matters."

"Yes, I know, I've had the pleasure before, remember?"

On his arrival, they saw Constable Andy Oliver's car parked in the driveway. The entrance to the house was around the side and as Sterling rounded the corner on foot, he heard a male voice yell, "Shut up, you fuckin' bitch! Why'd you call the cops anyway!"

Oliver was standing on the top step, his arms outstretched and the palms of his hands facing outward in a placating gesture trying to get a word in with the man facing him in the doorway.

"Okay, okay," said Sterling in a loud voice. "Calm down, please, you're disturbing the neighbours."

On seeing and hearing him, the man slammed the door shut. Both police officers stood for a few moments on the step on either side, listening, but it was quiet inside.

Then suddenly, a loud scream followed by two words, "No, no!" in a panicked female voice.

Sterling banged loudly on the door and shouted, "Open up now!"

With his ear to the door, he could hear loud moaning and said to Oliver, "We've got to go in. No time to be nice or legal. Let's shoulder the door open," and they did, with one double shove, splintering the frame as the door swung violently inward.

They found the woman, about forty years of age, lying on the living room floor in a fetal position, her face bloodied. Sterling immediately knelt down beside her to check her vital signs. Meanwhile Oliver started searching for the male, and soon determined he had fled through the back door, now open.

Fifteen minutes later, Sterling was back at Bravo-7, having left Oliver to see the woman off to the hospital in the ambulance, and secure the house as best he could.

"What's up, Doc?" Preston asked in his best Bug Bunny accent as Sterling stepped back into the patrol car. Before filling him in with the details, the sergeant put out an APB for the male.

"We'll probably pick him up soon," he said and filled the reporter in on the details. He took a drive around the immediate area looking for the culprit, but no luck. After fifteen minutes or so Sterling said, "I need a coffee and to de-stress. Want one?"

On the way, he said, "You know, occasionally, only too rarely, I'm afraid, family disputes can turn out to be humorous and it reinforces my view that if the police can inject a bit of levity into a situation, the end result can be positive.

"I'm reminded of one such case. It happened here in Parkton on my first tour of duty. I was directed to a family disturbance up in the Aberdeen Hills estate, a new neighbourhood of expensive homes set in immaculate surroundings. The home I was called to was large, with big, solid, polished, double oak doors.

"As I walked up the fancy rock-walled steps I could just hear shouting inside. I knocked on the door but got no response as the shouting continued. This time I pounded on the door with my fist and yelled, 'Police – open up!' The door was not opened and I tried the door knob, turned it and opened the door. Just inside, under a set of chandelier lights stood a man and a woman, in their forties, standing very still after seeing me enter, holding a Chippendale-style dining-room chair by its legs, between them at arm's length, an obvious disagreement over furniture ownership.

"Looking briefly from one to the other, I said, 'Looks like I arrived just in time to referee the dispute.' With a smile on my face – it did look stupid and funny – I stepped forward and took the chair from their hands.

"'Who shall I award this to?' I said.

"Both burst out laughing, to their credit, seeing the humour and the silliness of it.

"I went back to check up on them a couple of weeks later, using an unmarked car to drop by. They were gracious, laughed with me about their actions and said they had made up, come to terms with their differences and thanked me for the way I handled the situation. Made me feel good."

"You know, Jack, it seems to me that marriages can be a bit like living in an arena – not unlike the Roman ones, where happy summer fêtes are held or the more usual grim fights to the death – husbands and wives being the gladiators."

"Never thought of it what way, Charlie – good analogy."

The new Tim Hortons chain of coffee shops turned out to be busy and noisy so he told his companion that he'd continue with his 'life's saga,' as he put it, when they hit the road again.

◆ ◇ ◆

"Let's see, where was I?"

Traffic was light on Highway 5 north and the radio had gone quiet.

"I think you were on the point of leaving the U.K.," Charlie Preston reminded him.

"Right. Well, with my parent's sad blessings, I took a train to Liverpool and stepped aboard one of the Cunard Lines Steamships, the *RMS Franconia*, built and outfitted similarly to the cruise ships of today – luxurious travel. Next stop – Quebec City, Canada.

"As we got close to the Canadian coast we found ourselves in 'Iceberg City' – huge chunks of the stuff everywhere. It was 'slow speed ahead' for two days until we entered the mouth of the St. Lawrence River, only to run into pea-soup fog for another two days.

"There were a lot of young men and women on that ship, all presumably going to look for a new life in the Colonies, an exciting and apprehensive time for all I would imagine. A two-day train ride took me to Winnipeg where I was met by friends of the family who took me under their wing. I was 25 and it was May and the countryside was just getting out of the icy grip of winter. Spring was imminent and people were cheerful and friendly. I was to discover later that many people suffer from 'cabin fever' over the long, cold winters. I take it you know what that means?"

"Sure do. I lived in Toronto for fifteen years. Nice city, horrible weather."

"It was in Winnipeg that I saw my first real-live Mountie, driving a black and white Highway Patrol car, and that piqued my interest. I went to 'D' Division HQ and picked up a couple of brochures, talked to a constable at the front desk about a career in the Force and that did it for me.

"I didn't know the selection process would take so long – nine months to a year then – or how selective it was. Someone told me only five out of one hundred applicants were admitted and made the analogy that it was a bit like getting into the priesthood. 'Fat chance I stand,' I thought to myself, but, 'nothing ventured – nothing gained' and filled in the application forms in the hope of becoming one of 'Canada's Finest'.

"I had a preliminary medical and dental exam, went for my initial interview, wrote an exam – questions about the Canadian parliamentary system, Canadian history, geography, wrote an essay of my choice of topics – this I realized later was a method for them to see if I could string a few words together to see if I made sense and that my grammar was passable – and completed the test with questions on math, algebra and geometry. Did well on the written stuff but failed the math. Luckily I was allowed to re-write that in three months and passed handily. All this was followed by a series of short psychological tests and a final one-and-a-half hour penetrating interview with an inspector. He gave me some hope by saying that I had done well, but that the decision to admit me into the Force was not his alone, but by committee although I was told later that his recommendation carried a lot of weight. By now I was in Alberta working for the Bank of Commerce as it was then known.

"I was at my tellers cage in the main branch of the bank in downtown Edmonton on March 18th, 1964 and was called away to the phone. It was the recruiting corporal from 'K' Division HQ who said, 'Jack, can you come to our office tomorrow?'

"Nervously I said, 'Yes' and he said, 'Good, wear a suit and tie. You're to be sworn in at ten. Okay with you?'

"What a question. I was speechless and he said, 'Jack, you there?' and I muttered that I'd be there. The 19th of March turned out to be the most significant day of my young life."

"What an exciting time for you," said his passenger. "Did you celebrate?"

"Yeah. A half dozen of the bank staff took me to a local watering hole. I got shit-faced and had to be driven home. Anyway, I think I've said enough for now. Let's head back to the Barn. I've got paperwork to finish. Hope you don't mind?"

20

Gerhardt Adolph Bibermann was born in Salzburg, Austria in 1916. With the City's Mozart legacy and its history of music accomplishments, it followed that every school was imbued with the spirit of teaching classical music – instrument, voice, composing and conducting. Bibermann took up the violin in school and eventually became good enough to join the renowned Vienna Symphony Orchestra in 1937, the year before the annexation of his country by the Germans. During World War Two, he was exempted from military service in the German armed forces because of his position with the orchestra. In 1944 the V.S.O. was shut down and the musicians sent to work in munitions factories in a last-gasp effort by the Nazis to avoid defeat. He returned to the orchestra after the war in 1945, but the atmosphere had changed. The quality of music was not the same. He and his new wife decided to immigrate to Canada and joined the wave of post-war European people in 1946, settling in Coburg, Ontario. He was lucky in obtaining work with the Toronto Symphony Orchestra, but the work was sporadic and could not support him very well and eventually he found a job with the Department of External Affairs as a translator in Ottawa, moving there in 1948. Their son, Walter, was born in 1949.

In school, the lad did not excel in things musical, to his father's deep disappointment, who had realized that Canada was a different society, where the European tradition of son following in his father's footsteps was not followed.

It was much freer and egalitarian, far less hide-bound than Austria, but Mr. Bibermann senior was slowly acclimatizing to his new culture.

In his twelfth year at school, Walter – Walt to his friends, a name his father could not call his son – went on a field trip to 'N' Division RCMP at the north end of St. Laurent Boulevard adjacent to the Ottawa River. It was home to four completely different police operations – the Crime Detection Laboratory, the Equitation Branch (where the world famous Musical Ride trained), the Canadian Police College and an Air Detachment. Young Bibermann was able to visit the stables and see the men undergoing their 'Ride' training and was even allowed to sit on a horse – the RCMP, if nothing else, were ever with an eye to recruiting and what better way to lure young people. Suitably impressed, his wish to become a 'Redcoat' came true on his twenty-second birthday when he was sworn in at 'A' Division headquarters in downtown Ottawa.

To date, his seventeen years of service had seen him transferred to four different police posts. From training he was sent to a Traffic Section in the Fraser Valley east of Vancouver where he rode 'herd' on miles of motor vehicles commuting back and forth to Vancouver, issuing traffic tickets, conducting roadblocks and attending approximately four hundred accidents, including many fatal ones in his three years of this kind of police work. It made him wonder if his decision to join the Force had been a wise one.

His luck, as he saw it, changed when he was sent to a four-member rural detachment in central British Columbia – a world of difference he found to his liking. It was a relief to get away from the crowds and incessant traffic. He often had to patrol alone and was forced to consider his decisions and actions much more carefully, not only for his safety – there was seldom any backup assistance – but especially for his place in the small community, where, for the most part, he was respected and by only a few, feared or reviled. He commiserated about this one day with his corporal after three 'difficult' encounters he had experienced in one day, with local people.

"In this business, Walt," he was told, "you sometimes have to take people's money away from them in fines, or their freedom. Not a popular thing to do but you have a duty to uphold the law 'without fear, favour or affection' as our unofficial motto goes and if people 'shit on your parade' as my saying goes, then so be it. We're not married to the Force and can leave it if we wish. I don't read you as a 'quitter' though. You're just having a 'bad hair day' as my wife puts it. Feel better now?" the corporal added with a slight smile.

Before his transfer to Parkton, Bibermann found himself in Williams Lake in B.C.'s Cariboo Region, the land of 'cowboys and Indians' in the literal sense.

Vast tracks of the area consisted of rangeland where tens of thousands of beef cattle were raised on huge ranches. Interspersed in this country were a number of sizeable Indian Reserves, mostly home to the Northern Shuswap tribe. Forestry occupations were another source of income. It was a busy office and his first prolonged interaction with native people. He found that generally, he got along with them quite well and learned to accommodate to their particular lifestyles, although he found it a bit disturbing to discover a disproportionate percentage of them involved in petty and serious crime. Assaults and the odd murder were mostly intra-band in nature and by doing a bit of study about their culture, he began to understand why and sympathized with their problems.

On his arrival at Parkton he was promoted to corporal and became a zone supervisor, the junior of two, on 'A' Watch, with responsibility for eight constables patrolling the South area and the City Centre. Corporal Bibermann was a bit of a taciturn individual, not given to frivolity but he still could enjoy a good joke, at least a 'clean' one. He attended the Lutheran Church, rarely swore and his subordinates respected him for that and tried to keep their language in check in his presence. They'd let the word 'fuck' slip out on occasion and then say, 'Oops, sorry, Corp!' And he would reply, 'That's okay, don't worry about it.' He was not a prude.

Until recently, things had been going relatively well in his life. He and his wife had two children, Robert and Tracey, both healthy and doing quite well in school. Then, about three months ago, things began to come apart, privately and at work to the point where he felt 'down' and was often frustrated.

The thing that hit him hardest was his mother's phone call from Ottawa three months ago, that his father, now aged 72, had developed prostate cancer and that it was in an advanced state.

The other aspect of his life that was concerning were problems with his work responsibilities. He was short of people for a variety of reasons – two people off sick (both injured – one on the job, the other from playing hockey), one member quit, and his new constable, Andrew Oliver, was glued to his trainer for another couple of months before he could be cut loose and begin patrols alone. All this reduced his strength by fifty percent in his zones. Centre Zone required more people because of the volume of work involved, while South Zone, less so. At times, however, he had no one patrolling the south area for periods of time and he would try to cover that off by attending calls himself. He didn't mind that too much but he felt he was not supervising his guys adequately and checking the quality of their work. He also often worked an hour or more after his watch ended, just catching up on paperwork. He did his best to keep his nose 'above water' but lately 'A' Watch had received more than its usual share of complaints, as police calls were labelled and the pressure was mounting.

Al Hawkes, the NCO in charge of North Zone, had two people away but his patrol area was considerably smaller, had less of a population and he was able to handle the load. As well, over the past two weeks, the watch commander had been away teaching a supervisor's course on the Coast.

Bibermann was not a complainer, and felt that he could manage his section okay. He'd talked to Al one day recently, over coffee, and was offered one of his members to assist with the work, but he said, "Let's wait until Jack returns and get his okay, if I still need someone."

He did and the sergeant approved moving Constable Ketchum to work the City Centre area until Bibermann's section had recovered its manpower. Ketchum had started his policing in Parkton working the downtown area and knew its little idiosyncrasies. He'd fit right in and he had a fairly new recruit with him.

Two weeks later, Corporal Bibermann had to take a bereavement leave of absence of two weeks when his father died. It was a heavy psychological blow for him and his mother, who would have to live alone. There were no siblings. When he returned, he discussed with his wife, Paula, the possibility of transferring to a position in Ottawa to be near her. She asked him to think about it carefully – she knew he liked the Parkton area and the work he did – before making a decision. She would support him fully, regardless, she said. That night, in his daily prayer, he asked God for His guidance. A couple of days later, his decision, to stay, was predicated on that.

21

Another set of headlights slid around the corner a half kilometre away and stabbed his side mirror with bright halogen light. Constable Ken Jackson in 10-Alpha-1 knew the vehicle was really moving.

"You can tell," he said, "by the vehicle's motion and at night, the headlights bounce less at high speed."

As they rapidly approached his patrol car, he glanced at the radar clock mounted on the dash. The digital readout glowed red at 162 unequivocal kilometres per hour. He was right. In the ten seconds it took to grab the mic and alert the pickup man ahead, the vehicle rocketed by him, shaking his car in its turbulence.

It was a bright red Porsche Carrera 911. 'Another goddamn wannabee Grand Prix driver,' he thought as he relayed the description ahead.

The radar unit, operated by the Sub Division Highway Patrol, was set up about 5 km east of the City limits on the Trans-Canada Highway east-bound, in a 100 km speed zone. It was 7:30 p.m. in early January. Traffic had been light.

Constable Jim Portal, General Duty, 'A' Watch', the pickup man and ticket writer, was parked on a bend half a kilometre further east in 10-Bravo-12. He had just enough time to bail out of his car and wave his red-wanded flashlight at the glaring pool of light almost upon him. He had to step back smartly however, as the German import didn't even slow down, much less stop.

Wrenching open his car door, Portal did several things almost at once: flipping on the emergency roof lights and wailer, reaching for the mic, and throwing the engine in gear. The police car – parked on the shoulder – sprayed gravel in a double rooster tail as he punched the pedal to the mat and yelled, "10-Alpha-1, he's running on us – call ahead!"

In a follow-up call, he added, "If radio traffic gets busy, we'll go to Tac-3, okay?"

Constable Jackson, having abandoned his position and driving east-bound, did the necessary radio work for Portal, calling the detachment dispatcher with the information. She was alert though, having overheard the transmission and was about to call the police at Salmon River, sixty kilometres east, for back-up. A patrol car from that area responded, gave his 10-20, which was about fifty km away and said he would head west.

Portal had his police car quickly at maximum speed, but knew of course that he could not match that of the Porsche. He'd have to rely on the help of his unknown partner ahead to try to get it stopped.

In spite of what the general public think about the seeming thrill of high speed chases, most police officers don't like to engage in them. Instead of one vehicle hurtling down the road, there are two or more and the potential for disaster is very real, particularly at night.

Several things can happen to put the driving public and the officer in real danger: tires can blow, wildlife cross highways, the presence of other, slower moving vehicles, intersection traffic, and the agitated state of the driver being pursued. Weather can obviously play another deadly role in this mélange of highway conditions.

Portal knew the landscape ahead. Rolling hills and flat ranchland made up the bulk of it going east with a number of scattered ranch houses. There were a few side roads, some paved, some gravel. Highway 5, south-bound, exited the TCH about twenty km east. He was doing some quick, strategic thinking. He called Ken Jackson behind him and told him to slow down to normal speed or less and use his side-mounted dual spotlights to take a quick look down any turn-offs or cross roads in case the Porsche had 'deeked off' onto one of them to wait for the police cars to continue east-bound. The driver's objective, of course, would be to pull out, head back to the City and hang around out of sight for a couple of hours before continuing his journey, sure that the police cars had abandoned the chase and returned.

Portal also asked Dispatch to call the small Pine Creek Detachment on 5 South to see if they could spare a patrol car to start north toward the main highway.

With this car going north, another one coming west and Portal's car going east, he hoped that between them they would get lucky and stop the son-of-a-bitch. It would take some luck and manoeuvring to do that though. He knew that the *Motor Vehicle Act* provided for the arrest of a driver if circumstances permitted. Really excessive speed, as in this case, could, but not necessarily, constitute such grounds. Much depended on those circumstances – for example, the type of terrain a highway passed through, city or rural, the posted speed limit, the presence of school and playground zones, density of traffic, time of day – night-time more than day because of limited visibility – intersecting roads and weather conditions all had to be taken into consideration before a decision was made to arrest or not to arrest. More egregious circumstances than these could slide over into the offence of dangerous driving under the *Criminal Code of Canada*. Arrest actions always had to be justified. Sometimes, though, it was the toss of a dice, so to speak, that made the decision. Portal had arrested a few drivers under both pieces of legislation, provincial and federal, and had obtained convictions. He did tend to err on the side of caution however.

Jackson switched on his white side-lights. As he was driving, he glanced fleetingly to his right and left whenever there was a turn-off road or lane, in hopes of catching a glint of reflection off the chrome, glass or paint of their adversary. Sure enough, he eventually did!

All four tires on the patrol vehicle suffered identical flat spots as they stopped in a cloud of burning rubber. He called Portal to advise him and rammed the car into reverse, leaving another low blue, acrid cloud of smoke as he backed up down the road to the spot where he had noticed the flash of reflected light and saw evidence of tire tracks turning off the highway onto a gravel road. The gravel had been cleaned off by spinning tires leaving exposed dirt as the Porsche had churned up the loose stones. As he turned onto the road, Jackson's headlights picked up the not-quite-settled dust as he slowly drove along. In a few seconds, he spotted his quarry in the cow pasture about fifty feet to his right, sunk right up to his little 'red-ass' axle, wheels spinning and filling up his wheel wells with thick, gooey muck. Jackson started to enjoy doing traffic work again!

He called Bravo-12 who responded immediately.

"Call off your hounds and turn around. You'll see my lights. I have something good to show you. Also, please call our Dispatch and ask them to cancel the other two cars, with our thanks."

Later, when he and Portal discussed the incident at the office, naturally with other members present, they couldn't help but almost feel sorry for the guy. He didn't know it, but he could have had a free tow out of his predicament, as both police cars carried short tow chains and could have easily pulled the small car out of the mud.

The tow-truck operator charged the would-be Formula One speedster a one hundred dollar bill, took an hour and a half of his time, and the driver got a Court appearance ticket – no voluntary penalty for this lad! They also informed him that had the circumstances on the highway been different, he might have had a free ride back to the city, in handcuffs, in the back of the police car.

Portal told Jackson that by the time he got up to maximum speed, the Porsche was long gone, figuring the driver had floor-boarded it to well over 200 km, probably in order to get sufficiently far enough ahead to pull off and hide, knowing that a roadblock was likely being set up for him. As it turned out, a good guess.

"He made our day," the members agreed.

22

Mrs. Erickson said, "Alright, children, settle down, please," as Constable Rick Taylor, a member of 'A' Watch, entered the classroom. It took a minute to go from screechy noise to a murmur, then quiet. The grade one kids of Parsons Elementary School in the downtown area, watched as Taylor shook hands with their teacher and put his material on her desk. He was dressed in his patrol uniform, blue bomber-style jacket, tan shirt, blue tie with a bar holding it to his shirt, blue pants with a one-inch yellow stripe down the sides, and black shiny shoes. He was also wearing a Sam Browne complete with holstered gun and handcuff case.

Mrs. Erickson introduced him, asked the children to pay special attention to what he had to say and to ask questions. As Taylor removed his jacket she took it from him and placed it over the back of her seat. He put his overheads next to the projector already set up and placed the first one on the glass plate.

Turning to face the class he said, "Good morning, boys and girls. Thank you for inviting me into your class."

A ragged chorus of 'good mornings' was returned as he looked at thirty-six expectant faces.

Taylor had given a dozen such talks in his four years of service and didn't mind, as some members did. He felt it was better to do this than not, as much as anything to try to dispel the 'cop image' so aggressively and inaccurately portrayed on the TV screen, and the 'attitude' factor often depicted against the police, especially by young people. The RCMP had a policy of promoting these sessions with children and youth, concluding with a Career Days booth for the grade elevens, and the *Safe Driving* program a month or so before graduation.

There were no statistics to say whether this approach to understanding the police function in society was beneficial. How do you measure this and how do you track over a period of twelve years? It could be done perhaps, but what an enormous task, he thought. He comforted himself by 'doing the job' and hoping for the best. He also made an effort to use simple language with six-year-old kids to try to retain their interest in his twenty-minute talk. He was a believer in the KISS principle, 'Keep It Simple, Stupid.'

"I know you want to ask questions and I am going to ask you one now. First, what is the name of the police force I belong to?'

"The Mounties," one boy quickly responded.

"That's right. We are also known by a much longer name," and turning on the projector, he showed the first of fourteen pictures on the wall screen – the words ROYAL CANADIAN MOUNTED POLICE in bold red letters and underneath, in brackets, (RCMP), which he read to them. Below that appeared the badge of the force in full colour.

"Okay. Where do you suppose the word 'Mounties' came from?"
No response.

"You see the word 'Mounted' here?" Taylor asked rhetorically, touching the screen with his retractable pointer. "This meant that policemen used to ride horses on their patrols. 'Mounted' means to sit on a horse.

"The reason for this is simple – cars, automobiles did not exist because the 'Force' as the Mounties were also known, was formed, or created way back in 1873, over one hundred years ago. Horses were the only means of transportation – getting around – in those days."

Taylor continued by showing his overhead pictures to illustrate, in simple terms, the evolution of the RCMP from a cavalry unit into a modern police force of 25,000 men and women, with a fleet of patrol cars, airplanes, helicopters, and boats of all shapes and sizes to patrol rivers, lakes and the ocean. He also mentioned an extensive computer system, and the use of dogs for police work.

In mentioning this, he said that Corporal Dale Marinaro, the Dog Master and his dog, Shadow, were outside exercising and would be in the classroom soon.

One boy asked if he could see his gun. Anticipating this, Taylor had unloaded it prior to entering the classroom. He said that he would hold the gun and walk around the room and show them. While he did this, he continued his presentation with Mrs. Erickson turning the overheads at his nod.

"Alright, boys and girls, now that I've finished my talk, do you have any questions?"

Several hands shot up.

The first selected kid said, "How many people have you shot?"

The room went silent quickly, all ears and brains waiting for his reply.

"That's a reasonable question, I suppose, since I am a policeman but I may disappoint you by saying, 'No one,' and I hope I never have to. It's a terrible thing to have to kill another human being. It would be something that would bother me for the rest of my life. This is a good time to talk to you about police shows you watch on TV. I would hope that you boys and girls understand that most of what you watch is called 'play acting' and not real. They make them seem real so that the shows are exciting and that you will continue to watch them. Please try to remember that when you watch police stories like, say, *Miami Vice* and *Hill Street Blues*, for example."

A few minutes later, Taylor ended by saying, "If there are no other questions, let me say thank you for paying attention. I hope you found what I had to say interesting about the most famous police force in the world, the Royal Canadian Mounted Police, and that someday, some of you will think about becoming a Mountie, too."

♦   ◊   ♦

Taylor met Marinaro in the hallway who asked how it went.

"Oh, the usual. Pretty good, attentive bunch of kids with the same questions including, 'How many people have you shot?' I felt like saying for once, 'hundreds, I've lost count' – just to see their reaction.

"I suspect they'd probably take that answer in their stride today with what they're watching on the idiot box and some of the games they play. I wonder just how inured they are to violence? I do speak briefly about TV and film violence. It makes me wonder how someone like me doing this talk in ten to fifteen years from now would answer that same question," said Taylor.

"I hear you," said Marinaro. "I'll go let Shadow drool all over them now. I'm always asked how many bad guys has he chewed up. See ya, Rick."

23

At 27, Janice Smith (née Samuels) was a beautiful woman. Average height, slim but not skinny, full breasted, with big brown eyes and long black shiny hair, she had been first runner-up in the Miss Canada contest seven years ago in Toronto. Her life for a while was filled with exciting things, people and places.

It was shortly after this event that she met her future husband, Frank, who was standing guard in his red serge uniform, outside the front doors of the Governor General's residence at Rideau Hall, in Ottawa one warm and humid summer evening. It was a formal gathering and Miss Canada and Janice Samuels had been invited. Finding the atmosphere inside very stifling, she shook her chaperone and slipped outside for a walk around the grey limestone mansion and grounds, in the cool of the early evening.

The sun was on the horizon, a huge red ball of fire which cast, through the city haze, an amber glow on the building, making it look like a picture postcard of one of those stately old baronial English estate houses seen in travel brochures.

Constable Franklin James Smith, age 21, four weeks out of recruit training, looked impressive standing there – 'pretty', as she was to tell him later – an adjective that only a female would apply, he thought. The glow of the sunset certainly enhanced his appearance and attracted Samuels to him.

She purposely walked slowly and as she approached she looked at him and said, "Hi, beautiful evening, isn't it?"

Smith had been instructed that he was not to fraternize with tourists and guests, and to limit his conversation to being polite but restrained. 'Don't say anything your mother wouldn't be proud of,' the staff sergeant in charge of the Governor General's Security Detail had said. Smith's primary duty was one of watchfulness, not chatting.

Looking at the vision of beauty in front of him now, dressed in her pale blue, formal gown, he was literally lost for words and couldn't say a thing. Samuels, sensing perhaps that she had embarrassed the man, was about to move on when Smith finally came alive and blurted out, "Er, yes, great evening, Miss."

Holding her right hand out toward him, she said, "I'm Janice Samuels."

Smith, knowing that the staff sergeant was not on duty, nevertheless flicked his eyes quickly off to his right where the guard house was located, to ensure that no one was about to see him shake hands with Miss Canada. 'Wait 'til I tell the guys about this! They won't believe me. I'm not sure I believe it myself.' All that thinking and motion took the space of only a second or two before he held his brown leather glove-covered right hand out to take hers and say, "I'm Constable Smith; pleased to meet you."

There was another moment of awkward silence until Smith asked Samuels if she was really Miss Canada. He knew that Canada's number one beauty queen was part of delegation visiting this evening, and assumed that she was the woman as she was wearing a white silk sash under her powder-blue evening jacket, covering up the words 'Miss Canada' as he thought.

Janice Samuels gave a sophisticated kind of laugh and said, "No, unfortunately I came in second but you know what they say about number twos," as she uncovered the sash to show him the words 'First Runner Up.'

Warming up to her quickly, Smith said, "Well, that's too bad. I think they made a terrible mistake; must have been a bunch of blind people on the judges panel."

Samuels, although she couldn't consciously know it at that moment, was being struck down with 'scarlet fever,' a saying in the Force as old as the Mounted Police. "Why, thank you, Sir," she replied demurely in an imitation southern accent, "the next time I run for the title I'll ask for you on the panel."

Smith was about to say something else when he heard the noise of an approaching vehicle down the driveway and noticed it was a 'black and white.'

'Oh, Christ, what lousy timing,' he said to himself, knowing it was the shift corporal returning from a patrol of the grounds. Seeing him look over her shoulder and catching the slight narrowing of his eyes, Samuels turned to look and realized that it might not be healthy for the Mountie if she hung around any longer. Turning casually to stroll away, she called back to Constable Smith it was nice talking to him, and walked back toward the Hall.

A few seconds later, the police car stopped beside him. The corporal, leaning his head out of the window, looked at Smith and then the woman now disappearing through the large oak doors and said, "Jesus, Smith, I leave you for fifteen minutes and already you're making time with the girls. Who was that chick anyway?"

"Miss Canada," he lied.

"Wow. You don't fool around do you? Wanna trade places?"

Smith was just about to be flippant and say something like, 'Yeah, I'll take your job any day,' but thought better of it. Being just out of training, he thought it prudent to still be polite to corporals.

For the remainder of the evening, his mind just wasn't on the job. When the visitors left, he was back in the guard house on a break and couldn't watch them leave. He told the other members of the guard unit about his encounter with 'Miss Canada,' embellishing the story a bit, even going so far as to say that he had made a date with her, tomorrow, his day off, figuring he'd be safe enough to say that.

Needless to say, he was found out and it happened in a somewhat ironic way, for, the next evening, Janice Samuels called the guard house, on the pretext of being Frank Smith's sister from 'back home'.

The member answering the phone had been on duty the previous evening and knew Smith did not have a sister, or a girl friend.

Sensing something, he spoke with her for a minute or two and then asked, "Are you really his sister or by any chance are you the Miss Canada he met last evening and claimed he had a date with today?"

Samuels, caught by surprise, had to pause for a moment and do some fast thinking. Honesty is the best policy, I suppose, she thought, and said, "I'm sorry, you're right. I'm not his sister, neither am I Miss Canada. I'm the runner-up, Janice Samuels. I feel so silly for saying what I said."

"That's quite okay. I understand perfectly, Miss," the constable diplomatically replied.

"Look," she asked, "would you mind giving me Constable Smith's phone number?"

That night, Franklin Smith was the happiest man in Ottawa. Now he really did have a date. Of course, he had a little bit of explaining to do, but then, so did Janice Samuels.

Now, seven years later, six of them married to Frank, she stood in her kitchen, alone, in her new house high on a hill overlooking the river and the City of Parkton. It was 5:30 and she had just returned from work where she was the senior secretary in a large law firm downtown. She didn't know why, but she felt down and had been so for a number of days in succession and she could tell it was affecting her relationship with her husband.

Mixing a gin and tonic, she sat down in the livingroom and her eye caught the coloured wedding photo of her and Smith, on the mahogany lamp table. 'We looked so young and handsome and innocent,' she thought. She reflected on the past six years of their lives in part to try to pinpoint the reason for her uneasy and negative feelings.

After marrying, they had been transferred within a couple of months to British Columbia and for four years, Frank had been posted to a large municipal detachment adjacent to the City of Vancouver, working general duty shifts.

The first couple of years had been great. Both worked and they had a good income. Much of it was spent on clothes – mostly for her – eating out, discos, and trips to Seattle, Portland and San Francisco. She really enjoyed the big city life and loved visiting boutiques and fashion houses. She was always dressed in the latest style. In fact, she read the national fashion magazines to keep abreast of what the new clothing trends would be, and then diligently searched for them in stores. Dressing in the 'latest' became a compulsion. Of course, she had to dress 'decently' as she put it to Smith, because of her job.

Frank Smith, in turn, was beginning to tire of the 'same old BS' as he put it, both at work and at home. A steady diet of attending motor vehicle accidents and family fights was not his idea of what police work should be. In these two examples, he'd 'been there, done that' many times over. As well, steak and lobster had begun to pall on his palate. Home cooking and more time at home was what he wanted. Besides, he was now 27 and had a strong desire to become a father. That desire however, was not shared by his wife and sex had become somewhat of a psychological battleground between them. It was just at this time that he was transferred again.

Janice Smith knew that the move to this large Interior detachment had pleased Frank considerably. The work was far more diversified and for a while he seemed reasonably contented. On the other hand, life for her in the smaller city was beginning to seem vapid and wearisome. Fashions were a year behind; people seemed less sophisticated and 'hip' to her way of thinking, and she missed the excitement of the bright lights. As well, her current job, while well paid and interesting at times, had become only a 'means to an end' – to save enough money for occasional trips, often alone, to the Coast. Lost in her thoughts, she did not hear Frank Smith's car enter the driveway and was startled when she heard the side door open.

"Hi, Hon!" Constable Smith said as he entered the livingroom. "How's everything?"

"Great, Hon. Just great," she replied mechanically.

"Good. What's for dinner?" he asked, giving her a peck on the cheek that was turned for that purpose.

"Well, I've got nothing ready yet. Let's order a pizza."

24

Surplus Harry's was exactly the kind of store that the name implied. It sold almost any commodity or item that the general public might find useful. Its range of goods extended from rubber dinghies, fishing equipment, rifles and shotguns, tools of every kind, surplus paints, underwear, cans of outdated sardines and boxes of cereal, to cowboy boots and Stetsons, auto parts, nails, pots and pans, candy, and so on. All this stuff was purchased at low cost and sold at low cost – 'NO REFUNDS' noted the sign at the till. It was a popular and busy establishment, open six days a week (not Monday) from 10 a.m. to 7 p.m. – 6 p.m. on Sundays. The place smelled old because it was old, but was nevertheless a fascinating place to browse.

Mark Rifell was a browser tonight.

The building was an old Canadian Pacific Railway (CPR) freight shed, built barn-like at the turn of the twentieth century alongside the tracks, with a long freight platform at the rear adjacent to the tracks, about half a mile east of the City Centre and the main CPR station. The smell of creosote, emanating from the wooden floor, pervaded the inside, adding to the musty but not altogether unpleasant smell. It had the look and feel of an old wild west general store.

Aficionados who visited the establishment included much of Parkton's society. One need not feel ashamed to be seen there. Rifell was not.

He had shopped here on occasion – indeed purchased his cheap red plastic gasoline can here – but this was his first visit as a non-shopper. He was an assessor today.

As he entered the building on Sunday, January 8th, he noted the store hours again. Good.

The pick-up dock was down at the east end of the building. He walked through the store to that end and made note of the two bay doors and an exit side door for customers. No interior bars on this door, just an ordinary lock. No sign of an electronic alarm device. In one corner he noted a pile of cardboard boxes, wrapping paper and a few wooden pallets. 'I wonder when they get rid of this stuff?' Thinking for a minute, he realized that, with Sunday being an unlikely day for trash pickup, there should be a lot of this stuff left over from Saturday's business. Also good to note. Saturday then, was going to be his night.

He needed to check out the back of the store and the platform area next to the tracks. Finding a closed door which said 'No Exit' on the inside, he quickly looked back and, seeing no one, opened it wide. Stepping forward a pace onto the platform, he looked quickly each way and, again seeing no one, closed the door and decided to walk to his left along the building.

If he was stopped and checked, he'd use the excuse he was looking for a washroom, but no one challenged him. On the way along, he checked for exits and found two doors.

Satisfied, he re-entered the building through the same door and went for another walk around the vast interior, getting some ideas about where to light up. The place was busy and he was inconspicuous among the shoppers. 'Just a couple of other things for me to check,' he said to himself as he walked out. It was 5:30. As he continued to his pickup, parked on Railway Street a block away from the store, he noted the parking signs – '2 hours parking 8 a.m. – 6 p.m. Mon-Sat' That resolved one issue – where and how close to park to the target. The second was lighting – no street light in the immediate area and no lights on at the front of Surplus Harry's, at least not yet. It wasn't quite dark enough. Across the street from him was a row of old, run-down houses, which had been part of the early Italian community going back 80 years or more. It was said they were slated for demolition. He felt safe to park here.

Getting into his vehicle, he decided to wait until it got dark, which should be around six. Sure enough, four lights came on along the front of the store but they were quite dim. It didn't matter though, because the end of the building, where the bay doors were, was in darkness. Feeling satisfied, he drove away.

25

The previous Saturday evening, Mark Rifell left home at 2100 hours. He was going to refer to time now as the military do, because he viewed his 'operation' in this light – carefully planned and executed. He had taken his check list and ticked off each item as he prepared.

Before leaving, he put the overshoes on over his boots, and tucked the two matches inside. The candles and rubber gloves went in his shirt pocket, string and flashlight in the glove box, and the small cardboard lighting box inside the newspapers which he left on the front seat. He read the paper daily, he'd explain if stopped. The tire iron was where it normally would be – on the floor behind his seat. The gas can, filled, was lashed to the inside of the truck bed. Nothing incriminating. He was ready to roll.

Driving past the CP Rail station in the downtown area, he decided to enter the parking lot on the west side. He noted eight to ten vehicles parked, a mixture of SUVs, passenger cars and pickups at the far end of the lot. Must be railway employees, he thought. 'Good, I can park here for a while and watch my work when I'm done.' A great view down the curving tracks to the surplus store. Leaving, he then canvassed the area around his target, the parking lot at the end, and along Railway Street. Apart from the odd vehicle passing through, there was no other activity, no one on foot. The dim outside lights were on and still no light at the loading dock end. A few cars were parked on the street where he had parked previously, during his look around the store last weekend. By the time he had parallel parked on

Railway Street behind a brown van, it was 2140 hrs – twenty minutes to ten – almost Zero Hour for him.

He decided to stick with his plan and stay there until 2200 hrs.

The temperature had moderated over the past two days and he reckoned it was about ten Celsius under a cloudy sky, with a slight easterly breeze. Each time a vehicle drove by, he ducked down out of sight. As it got closer to ten, he could feel his pulse picking up. At exactly that time, he got out of his truck and quickly went to the back and retrieved his gas can and spout, closing the canopy but not locking it.

Returning to the cab, he gathered his paraphernalia including his tire iron, locked the door and put on his rubber gloves. Standing still for a minute, he looked all around him – no vehicles, no pedestrians – quiet.

Carrying the newer, small jerry can tucked in behind him, he walked the half block to the loading dock and climbed the five wooden steps to the platform and the customer service door. It was very dark here.

Just on the off-chance the door may have been left unlocked, he tried the door knob. Locked. Putting the gas can down, he took the straight V-shaped edge of the tire iron and wedged it between the door and the frame, just below the handle, banged hard on the top curved end of the iron with the palm of his hand a couple of times, forcing the end in further and levered the iron bar back toward him.

In two tries, he heard the lock snap open and ten seconds later, he stood inside the pitch black interior, closing the door. He placed the iron bar on the floor to the right of the door and the gas can beside it. No loud alarm device went off and he had no idea as to whether or not the building had a silent alarm. He suspected it didn't but to be sure, he waited a full five minutes outside the door in case security or the police showed up.

Back inside, and taking his penlight out of his jacket pocket, he turned it on, keeping the wide-angle beam pointed at the floor.

Moving over to the right-hand corner, he took a large, folded card-board box, re-shaped it into a box again and stuffed it full with loose brown wrapping paper. He carried the box and as many flattened boxes as he could carry into the centre of the store, using the flash-light still in his mouth to guide the way. He placed the paper and boxes under a set of wooden stairs that led up to a small suspended office. Returning to the dock area, he gathered more folded boxes, one wooden pallet and returned to the steps, piling them on top of the paper-filled box. Nearby were several racks of men's and women's outer clothing, on small wheels. He pushed them around the staircase. Going back to the dock again, he picked up the gas can and returned.

He prepared his fuse system. Tying one end of his string around the bottom of the candle, a quarter of an inch from the end, he dipped the yard of string into the gas can and laid it in a straight line on the floor with two feet of it under the loosely piled paper and boxes.

He took the second candle and, with one of his two matches, heated the bottom of it to form a small puddle of wax on the floor and stuck the end of the first candle into the prepared wax, placed the small cardboard box over it, making sure the string passed under the V-exit. Satisfied it was laid out as he had planned, and taking one last look around, he lit the candle with his second match, and put the charred remains of both matches and the other candle on top of the newspaper. He had three minutes to get away.

On the way back to his truck, he removed his gloves and over-shoes and threw them over an embankment into tall grass, fifty yards or so from the building. He put the gas can in the back, locked the canopy door, and placed the tire iron behind his seat. Driving back along Railway Street, he glanced at Surplus Harry's as he passed. No sign of fire – yet. That made him wonder if his attempt had failed, but he said to himself, 'Patience.'

At the railway station, he again pulled into the parking lot, facing east down the track, turned off his motor and sat, watching. He did not have to wait long.

◆ ◇ ◆

When Rifell got up at 10 o'clock on Sunday, January 15th, he turned on his TV and watched the account of the store fire. It showed the huge fire burning during the night, gradually engulfing the whole of the store, the smouldering ruin giving off tons of smoke still at news time. Later on, he went out and bought the Parkton newspaper which showed the high, vivid flames across the whole of the front page. Cutting it out, he taped it on his bedroom closet wall, along with other pictures of his work. In a way, he felt a little bit sad. He liked browsing the old Surplus Harry's store.

'Oh well,' he thought, 'they can always rebuild with the insurance money.'

PARKTON NEWS
JANUARY 15, 1989
By Charles Preston

One of the biggest fires in the city occurred last night when Surplus Harry's store on Railway Street was demolished, a smouldering ruin as we go to press. Asst. Fire Chief Will Caglioni said at a press conference this morning that it appears to be a case of arson. "More will be known when we are able to do a closer examination of the scene. The Provincial Fire Marshall's office has been advised." Caglioni said that as the fire progressed he had to call in for more assistance from the two Fire Sub-Stations but they were not able to contain it."

The fire is believed to have started at about 10 p.m. but was not spotted until 10:30 when interior flames blew out several windows, allowing smoke to billow out. Eventually thick black smoke covered much of the downtown area, the source of which is believed to have come from the creosote-soaked timbers which made up much of the old building.

I interviewed RCMP Sgt. Jack Sterling, watch commander of the police unit on duty. He said that one of the by-products of this fire was the massive disruption of rail traffic on the CPR Line. As the store was next to their main line tracks, trains could not proceed, east or west. It was not until 4:30 a.m. that they began to move. By then, the line stretched about six kilometres in each direction and included the transcontinental passenger train, *The Canadian*, en route to Vancouver. It was not possible to shunt these west-bound units onto the CNR tracks as the railway bridge over the river to the CN Junction was just beyond the fire, he said. I asked the sergeant about ammunition explosions and he confirmed that several boxes of shotgun and rifle shells were stored which 'cooked-off' – exploded. The fire fighters had to stand down while the ammo was expended, again a dangerous situation. Railway and Park streets at Sixth Ave are still closed to traffic at press time.

The photo above, taken from an 8th floor window in the News building, shows the fire at its peak, with flames reaching as high as thirty-five metres.

♦ ◇ ♦

Ray Davis was the junior man on the General Investigation Section. Although he had six years of service, he was fairly new to the unit, having been transferred from General Duty, Burnaby Detachment, on the Coast. He didn't mind. He always wanted to be in plain clothes and dutifully served his requisite five years in uniform as was the general policy of the Force. GD was considered an excellent training ground for almost any specialist job.

When he came to work Monday on day watch, his first duty was to review the DPRs – the Daily Patrol Reports – for any useful information. 'Intelligence' was the new buzz word. He found that about

ninety-five percent of the information submitted contained just routine stuff – mostly automobile and pedestrian checks. Occasionally
someone was arrested for an outstanding Warrant, mostly local area
people. All of this information was recorded by one of the secretaries
on the new computer system which had the ability to cross-check
the information entered. To save on computer storage space, most of
it was purged from the system two months later. The entries that remained were a mix of 'known criminals', their known associates and
vehicles, persons arrested for more serious crime and something labelled 'persons/vehicles of interest.' It was also Davis's job to review
the monthly computer printouts for mainly two reasons – any trends
that may seem to be developing, for example, a person or vehicle
checked repeatedly in the same general area, time of day and any associates – possibly connected to reported break-ins, armed robberies,
assaults, etc. – demanding follow-up investigation and/or surveillance,
which occasionally led to a successful conclusion. The second reason
was to dump the rest to try to keep the system clean.

He was the right person for the job. He had an excellent memory
and a keen eye for detail. He worked in a small milieu of people whose
specific work was to investigate all serious crime in the detachment
area – mostly the more serious so-called 'Indictable Offences' which
carried a minimum five years in jail. GIS people were like city police
detectives, although unlike them, the work was diversified, making
them generalists, investigating anything that came across their desks.
That's what Davis found interesting and challenging.

With the latest arson case at Surplus Harry's over the weekend, he
began paying more attention to vehicles and people checked during
the hours of darkness. Few fires were lit, it seemed, during daylight.
His investigator's course at the Canadian Police College had spent
one morning looking at arson – often difficult to prove categorically, he'd learned. 'Serial' arsonists, as this person had been tentatively
labelled, tended to do their work by fits and starts. For most, there
was no financial gain and he'd learned the most inconsistent of them

would light two or three fires in a short period of time then nothing for a long period. The latest two fires were large and separated by only six weeks.

Mounting surveillance on this kind of activity was difficult, mainly due to manpower requirements – a 24-hour watch would require upwards of six members, something that even larger detachments could ill-afford for more than a day or two. Sure, they could use the services of uniformed members (in plain clothes) to help out but that meant removing them from patrol duties.

This kind of investigation required some fair degree of luck – catching the perpetrator in the act (a rare event), good witnesses, good patrol work and the checking they did, and, above all, good evidence. Putting fires out tended to destroy much of the physical evidence. It was a painstaking job to pick around in the debris of fires and one that required specialized training. 'Thank God for fire department and the fire marshall's investigators,' thought Davis. Police were not trained in the forensics involved; they were more limited to follow-up stuff involving vehicle checks, individuals' movements, searches and taking statements, all very much a co-operative effort.

'Okay, what've we got in Saturday and Sunday nights offerings?' he asked himself as he scanned the first sheet. 'A' Watch had been on duty. Twenty-four sheets had been left in the tray. After perusing them, nothing except maybe one short entry seemed really worth a follow up. A pickup truck had been checked out by a constable near the Airport at 12:10 a.m. Sunday. The driver said he was returning from a friend's house downtown. HNBD (had not been drinking), the officer noted, and was polite but nervous. Gave license number as L-27902 attached to a 1975 black Ford F150 in the name of Mark Rifell.

This was the first 'repeat' item he had noticed for a while. 'Okay, let's check the first report of this vehicle,' he decided. Taking the sheet of paper over to Shirley, the data entry clerk, he asked her to look for the previous license plate matching entry. She found it fairly quickly

– it was about to be deleted, she said. License plates stayed listed for only two months. It was a benign check and Davis studied the brief notes. *Where did the driver come from at that hour on a Monday morning?* 'A friend's,' Rifell had said, but there were no other details on the sheet.

"Shirley, what date was the last arson fire, you know, the Thistle Estate?"

"Just a sec," she replied, and then said, "December 4th and 5th."

'Well,' Davis wondered, 'is this a coincidence? Same vehicle and checked on the same days as the last two fires. Other than that, there's nothing suspicious whatsoever. Should be followed up though.'

"Run off a couple of copies of that entry, please, Shirley, and thanks."

He kept one on the DPR file and sent one to Sergeant Jones with a brief note and finished it with a request to be able to work on this file.

Permission was duly received.

26

This was their eighth patrol ride-along and, for a change, was on day shift, a Saturday near the end of January. Sterling was cruising the North Shore area. A question that the reporter asked was, "Why do you need to do patrols, Jack? Don't your two corporals take care of things and keep you in the loop?"

"Yes, they do and, no, I suppose I don't really need to go out, except for a major crime incident and even then, probably not. I guess I'm a General Duty guy at heart and still like to be 'out and about' and get out of the office for an hour or two but it's more than that I think. For me, it's 'showing the flag,' in my case the watch commander's flag – an imaginary one – to my people, let them know I'm around, to help if necessary, to show my concern and, occasionally, ride with them. Of course, my intent is not always that sublime. What I'm also doing is looking at my watch members' capabilities and performance. It's part of my responsibilities to do that in order to assure myself, and my superiors, that I have a capable group of people who do the job they're paid to do. I don't 'spy' on them – they know I'm around. I know that sounds a bit self-serving, but that's how I feel and what I do."

They were stopped at an intersection one car back at a red light. As their light turned green, Jack noticed a car on his right drive quickly through the just-turned red light and make a quick right.

"Did you see that? Trying to beat our line of traffic. Worth a stop," he said as he turned on his red lights and the car pulled over. After giving his 10-19 car check call to Dispatch, he said to his passenger, "Back in a few minutes."

Preston heard the sergeant ask for a license, registration and driv-er's record check on his portable radio. The information was returned quickly – negative on previous traffic violations.

When Jack Sterling returned to Bravo-7 he explained what hap-pened. "The young woman was very nervous, her first stop, she said. She knew what she had done and apologized. I hate it when people apologize to me. It's as though the offence was personal, committed against me. Anyway, I wrote her a warning ticket, actually a check-up slip that we issue for vehicle defects and wrote WARNING across the page and told her that if she transgressed again in the near future, she'd likely get a real ticket next time."

"I guess she appreciated the break?"

"Oh yeah. I tend to issue more warnings than tickets. I think often it does the trick in making people more careful and consider-ate in their driving habits than arbitrarily laying a violation ticket on everyone. People appreciate a break and it's good for PR. Ready to roll again?"

"You bet."

"Alright, I'm going to continue along Airport Road as I want to look at a certain house and vehicle, if the vehicle is there. You re-member the two recent arsons – the Thistle townhouses and the more recent Surplus Harry's?"

Charlie Preston nodded.

"Well, our G.I. Section recently came up with a new patrol check-sheet. It requires documenting all vehicles and pedestrian checks made, mostly during the hours of darkness, not ruling out daytime checks, of course. These sheets of paper are checked daily and the information is fed into our computer system.

"You understand, Charlie, that this info is strictly confidential?"

"Yes, I know about that. I saw the system used a couple of week-ends ago when I was out with Constable Rick Taylor. Good idea," said the reporter.

"As you may be aware," Sterling continued, "arson is difficult to investigate and prove, and often, unfortunately, never gets solved so we tend to take any lead, however slim that may be, and work it dry. That means careful examination of that information is made to try to determine its veracity – is there anything to it or not?

"A couple of days ago, GIS came up with an anomaly that they thought worth a follow-up. This was a vehicle checked on the nights of both fires, but not *at* the fires. Not much, I know. The vehicle resides at a house out near the Airport and I just want to drive by for a look, then we'll stop for a coffee at the Terminal Café."

After a few minutes, Sterling asked his companion to start looking for and calling out house numbers. They were in the four thousand block going west.

"I'm looking for 4815. It will be on the left."

After a minute, Preston said, "Next one coming up, Jack."

Sterling drove past at normal speed and glanced to his left, noting the small house set well back on the two-acre, apple-treed lot. No vehicle in driveway. 'Okay,' he thought, 'I'll have another look on the way back. How can we do surveillance if necessary?'

On the way back from the Airport, the truck was still not there. Preston was going to ask Sterling more questions about his past but there was a lot of radio chatter that he knew the sergeant was listening to and felt it was an inappropriate time to do this. Sterling dropped him off at the detachment parking lot having made arrangements to go out again soon.

♦ ◊ ♦

At 5 p.m. Corporal Al Hawkes entered the office to do some paperwork from the day's activities. Jack Sterling saw him and asked if he had time to talk for a minute. Sitting down in front of Sterling's desk, Hawkes asked, "What's up, Jack?"

"It's about the two big arsons we've had recently. GIS is working on them but with so little information to work on, there's not been much feedback. Our one and only suspect, if you can really call him that, lives out on Airport Road. I drove by his place this afternoon to have a look and to see what the surveillance possibilities were like. Not good. There's no place where we can hide a police car. We'd have to use an unmarked one and sit down the road a bit and use glasses.

"I'm going to see Jones on Monday to see what's happened, if anything, and talk about maintaining a watch on the house or at least keep a log of his comings and goings – establish a pattern. Whichever of your people patrols that area at night, have them make a note on the DPR sheet. Agreed?"

"Sure, Jack, we can do that. I take it you don't want to spook him, if possible?"

"No, not until I discuss surveillance strategy with Jones and get his okay, so hold on to the thought for now."

27

The telephone was answered on the second ring: "Parkton City Detachment, Constable Austmann speaking."

"Hello, Constable, my name is Arthur Wardlow, in Toronto. I wonder if I might speak with my son, Bernard, please. Is he there?"

"Yes, Sir, he's just coming on shift. Just a moment, please."

Placing the speaking end of the receiver in the palm of his right hand and squeezing it, he yelled into the office intercom, "Hey, Bernie, it's long distance. It's your old man on the line. Wanna take it in the sergeant's office? He's not in yet."

Wardlow pressed the intercom button in the main office and said he would, then walked into the sergeant's office in time to pick up the transferred call.

"Dad, is that you?"

"Hi, Son, yes, it's your 'old man' calling."

They both laughed about the slightly indelicate use of the title by Austmann, and Wardlow apologized to his father. The attempted muting with his hand hadn't worked, and Wardlow Senior had heard the conversation just the same.

"It's quite alright, Bernie. I've used the same expression before. Don't give him shit for it okay?"

"Okay, Dad. How are you?"

"Fine, thanks. I won't keep you. I tried calling you at your apartment and with no answer, I thought you might be at work. I wanted to kill two birds with one stone on this call. First and foremost, happy twenty-third for tomorrow. Wish the hell I could be there.

There's something on the way for you. Secondly, I got the inspector's position!"

◆ ◇ ◆

Wardlow's father had joined the Metro Toronto PD as a twenty four old, twenty-five years ago. As a result, his son had spent all his life in the big city, living in suburban Richmond Hill. Raised in a policeman's home, it was not at all surprising that his desired vocation in life would be the same as his father's. Like most police fathers, however, Inspector Wardlow did not push his son in that direction, having a number of very real misgivings about the job, not the least of which was the constant threat of serious injury or death, and the 'BB' or bureaucratic bullshit as Wardlow Senior put it, together with the long term stress that seemed to be part of the baggage of the job. If anything, he'd have preferred his son to go into something much more safe and potentially rewarding, such as accounting, surveying, architecture or something like that. Because of his experiences and these feelings, he was both proud and apprehensive when his son was sworn into the federal police force, at the tender age of twenty.

That was the trouble with Bernard Oscar Wardlow. Although six feet one inch in height and a slim 175 pounds – or as the new application forms would have it, 185.5 centimetres and 79.37 kilograms – and with thick black wavy hair, large brown eyes and a boyish face, he didn't look twenty; he looked sixteen. Even now, at twenty-three, after three years of service of hard livin' and drinkin' as he put it – which really wasn't the case, he had to put it that way – he still looked like a teenager. A moustache didn't do anything for him either. Older members on the detachment would call him 'son' or 'boy' and he was constantly asked to produce his ID in drinking establishment or restaurants serving liquor. He'd really get upset when he stopped someone to write up a ticket, give a warning or make an arrest after getting smart-assed remarks like, 'Jesus, when did they start hiring kiddie-cops?' or from thirty-year-olds, 'I'm old enough to be your old man!'

It wasn't until only fairly recently that he had learned to come to terms with his youthful appearance. He'd had another exasperating, 'You're too young to be a real cop,' diatribe from some loud-mouthed forty-year-old, difficult-to-arrest logger he had taken in for impaired driving earlier in the evening. Marvin Peterson, his partner, had long been aware of Wardlow's anguish over the issue but hadn't said anything, believing the experience and the aging process would take care of it, but it hadn't. Wardlow's body refused to look older!

On this night, Peterson knew that Wardlow had come very close to losing his cool and lashing out at his prisoner. He had to step in and ease Wardlow out of the breathalyzer room before things got out of hand. Later, when they had resumed their patrol and Wardlow had calmed down, Peterson thought it an appropriate time to bring the matter up. In spite of his farm boy background, Peterson could be remarkably diplomatic if he had to be.

"Feelin' alright now, Bernie?' he asked. He never used 'Bow Wow', the name bestowed upon his partner by other members because of his full initials – Bernard Oscar Wardlow.

"Yeah, I'm okay, thanks."

"You know, no matter how much you try to control yourself, there's always some asshole out there who can get under your skin, quite often on purpose to see how far he can push you," said Peterson sympathetically. "Used to happen to me a lot you know."

"Oh, how come?"

"Well, I had a different set of problems when I joined the Force. Where do you think I got my nickname 'Starvin' Marvin' from? I'm as tall as you but weighed only 151 pounds. Skinny. I almost didn't make it in, as weight had to be proportional to height. In other words, your body had to have some beef on it which is a good thing if you're going to be manhandling difficult people and I've had a bit of trouble doing just that. I've got a few scars and stitch marks to show for it. I have fifteen years service now and only just recently I started to put on weight.

"That was my curse. One day, Sergeant Bill Shaw, my detachment commander at the time said, "Marv, ever heard of that old English saying, 'sticks and stones may break my bones, but words will never hurt me?' I recall my dad saying that a long time ago to one of my kid brothers who was being picked on at school because he wore glasses with coke bottle lenses. I'd forgotten until Shaw reminded me. You ever heard it?"

"No, can't say I have, Marv, but I sure get the meaning. I guess I got a little bent out of shape tonight, eh?" he replied.

"Well, you were getting a little bit agitated, but it happens to the best of us. You know, if you want to stay and survive in this business, you've got to 'roll with the words.' Know what I mean?"

Wardlow did. After that, he developed an increasing equanimity toward taunts, of all kinds including those made against his mother and his own legitimacy. Hard to do but had to be done.

Since arriving in Parkton from Regina, Wardlow had been partnered with Constable Peterson, with whom he had completed his field training program. They were soon tagged the 'Odd Couple' by other members. In spite of their obvious differences in age, appearance, deportment, dress and upbringing – in or out of uniform Wardlow's shoes were always shiny, while Peterson was often accused of having horse shit stuck to his – there was an indefinable chemistry between them that allowed them to operate as an effective patrol team.

One seemed to feed off the other for support, mentally and physically. They had been together, for the most part, for over two years, during which time they had quickly learned to read each other's minds to an uncanny extent and to correctly and quickly size up an enforcement situation and the appropriate action to take, or not take, as the case may be.

The beginning of their partnership, however, did not portend well. What happened, of course, was in a sense classical, because it was both hilarious and potentially deadly serious at the same time, as is often the case in police work.

The incident served to quickly crystallize the pair into their eventual efficient, amiable working relationship.

Wardlow had been paired with Peterson frequently for the last few months but on this night, had been delegated to take out car 10-Bravo-10 alone, as the watch was 'thin on the ground,' the sergeant had said. He wanted more coverage with the extra car in this area.

The young constable was the first to respond on his radio to a domestic complaint at eleven-thirty on a cold, snowy Friday night in January, near the City Centre Zone area. Peterson, in Bravo-14, told the dispatcher he would cover Wardlow. Unknown to each other, both arrived at the house, on an unlit street, at almost the same time, Wardlow at the rear and Peterson at the front.

The dispatcher advised that the man was believed armed and according to the female complainant, in a frenzied condition in their bedroom. Wardlow elected to drive to the rear, figuring that's where the bedroom would be, and if he could, to take a peek before taking any action.

Because of other radio transmissions, Wardlow had not heard his partner say he was covering him. He'd given his 10-7 – out of service – first, and because of that had failed to hear Peterson give his. Peterson, of course, could not ask Wardlow where he was and presumed him to be around the back of the house in the lane.

Wardlow got out of his car. He had just over three years service and had gone to only a few of these 'family bitches' as domestic complaints were called. He didn't respond on his portable radio to Peterson's whispered calls, as the senior policeman approached the front of the house, gun drawn. As Wardlow said after, he had the damn radio in his winter parka pocket.

Also with gun drawn, he groped his way in the dark along the bush-lined path from the lane toward the rear of the house in a heavy snow fall, heart pumping like mad. Reaching a lighted window and crouching down, he slowly rose and peeked over the sill into the room, a bedroom containing a dishevelled bed and a mahogany dresser with a smashed mirror.

No one was there but a great deal of shouting and screaming was coming from somewhere in the house, probably in one of the rooms at the front, he judged. He decided to make his way around to the front just as Peterson, who could not see in the front window as the blinds were drawn, decided on the same tactic, but in the opposite direction.

They met – literally head-on. Although the blow was certainly not hard (they were both wearing fur caps), their foreheads met, causing both of them to crash to the ground on top of six inches of heavy, wet snow. In the pitch black at the side of the house, they hadn't seen or heard each other approaching, the snow masking their footsteps.

Both policemen for a split second thought it may have been the man with the gun from the house and the automatic response, the 'fight or flight' syndrome was, in this case, to be prepared to shoot if necessary. Only they couldn't.

Both had dropped their weapons after the impact. It doesn't require much imagination to picture the absolute frantic groping around with bare hands for a couple of wet, snow-clogged, Model 10 Smith and Wesson service revolvers by a couple of cops on their knees, still with the belief that the other person was the gunman! There was so much adrenalin being pumped, it was running out of every pore!

When they finally stopped for an instant, eyes adjusting to the dark, and recognized each other's blue winter parkas, they both shouted simultaneously "Jesus Christ, Bernie!" – "Jesus Christ, Marv!" and a second or two later, realizing the humour of the situation, broke into convulsive fits of laughter.

Later, after they'd managed to get the lunatic out of the house and to the cells, without the loss of anyone's blood, they reviewed what had happened and knew that in this case, they had been lucky. There were so many things that could have gone wrong leading perhaps to someone being injured or even shot to death. Wardlow admitted he hadn't done things right, particularly in not waiting to ensure back-up had arrived and not checking his portable radio.

Peterson allowed that perhaps they were a bit hasty in drawing their weapons in this case. The guy did have a rifle because he was a hunter, but it was still in the rack in the basement when they got into the house.

The woman complainant, asked by the radio dispatcher if her husband, boy friend or whatever, was armed, took it to mean did he have access to a weapon and not, as the intent of the question was, did he have a gun in his hand or at least within easy reach.

"I hate these goddamn domestic calls, Marv; they're a pain in the ass!"

"Yeah, you're right, and in our case, in the head too," replied Peterson, as he felt the slight bump on his forehead, "but it's all part of the job. You'll attend a lot more yet if you stay on general duty, but you know, you never get used to them and you can never be careful enough. People are so bloody unpredictable and so supremely agitated in these situations that their reasoning powers seem to completely shut down, leaving them almost at the animal stage at times. You wouldn't believe some of the totally hilarious and devastating domestic complaints I've attended. Sometimes I'm ashamed of being part of the human race. Anyway, let's talk about our future approaches to these kinds of call, eh?"

The result was that they became much more circumspect in their approaches to not only domestic calls but to other potentially hazard-ous ones as well.

That one incident, more than anything, had forged their relation-ship into a solid, trustworthy, respectful, productive liaison.

28 Paulo Marco Rifelli was born in Palermo, Sicily in 1943 in the middle of World War Two. His father, Antonio Rifelli, was conscripted into the Italian Army in 1942 to help the German occupiers defend the island from the soon-to-invade Allied Armies from North Africa. He took the prudent step of sending his wife Viola, daughter and new young son Paulo, to a cousin in Sorrento on the Italian mainland, where he thought they would be safe.

"Addio, mio amore. Che Dio vada con voi," he said to her as they stood on the dock and kissed goodbye. "Vi vedro di nuovo." *May God go with you. I will see you again.*

He never did, as he was killed in action in 1944, in that invasion.

Subsequently, Viola emigrated with her two children to Canada in 1946 and settled in Toronto's 'Little Italy' district. She found work as a presser in a laundry and barely made ends meet. There was no government 'safety net' then. In 1951, she moved once again at the invitation of her first cousin from Amalfi, just around the coast from Sorrento. Like her, the cousin had taken refuge in Canada, in this case, in Parkton, B.C., which also had a small Italian community.

In 1964, Viola's son married a second cousin, Teresa Gandolfi, born in 1941 in Positano, and Paulo became a father a year later, naming his son Marco Antonio after the kid's father and grandfather. The marriage was one of economic convenience as much as love and respect, as was still the case in much of the Italian community in those times.

The union disintegrated when Paulo moved away to a mining

job at the smelter in Trail when Marco was five. The child grew up bouncing around among different relatives while his mother went from job to job and bottle to bottle.

He eventually went to live with his grandmother, Viola, leaving at 16 when he quit school.

When he was growing up, his mother had a wood stove to heat the house. She'd light the paper under the wood with long wooden 'Eddie' matches. Marco loved to watch, fascinated by the sudden flare of the match head when she scratched it on the side of the box or the metal stove, and by the smell of the phosphorous and the clear flame when the match started to burn. His mother allowed him to light the fire one day, cautioning him about the use of 'raw matchees' as she called them. She left the matches on top of the woodpile next to the stove. Not able to resist, he took them and started lighting them, one by one. Realizing his mother might notice some were missing, he stole a box from the local hardware store and kept it in his room.

One day, he decided to light several at once to see the effect. He put about ten in his hand and closed it, with the tops sticking out between his right thumb and forefinger. He ignited a separate match and touched the edge of the bundle. The effect was an instantaneous flare-up and the concomitant flash-back effect slightly scorched his hand, making him drop all the matches on the floor. He quickly stamped them out and little damage was done. What he didn't think about was the strong cloud of phosphorus smoke that permeated the room. His mother discovered the smell a little while later and scolded him.

"No lighta da matchees inna da house!" she yelled. "Iss a danger," slapping him alongside his head and removing the box from the woodpile and hiding them.

But he knew where there was a limitless supply.

As a youngster, Marco experienced his first Hallowe'en at a local community event, complete with a large bonfire. He was fascinated and mesmerized by this and the sight and sound of exploding fireworks and rockets. Later, as a teenager, he joined a like-minded group of youths who used the celebration as an excuse to commit random acts of vandalism and setting small fires.

Marco didn't do well in high school partly because his grandmother didn't place a high value on education and was too busy in her daily life trying to make ends meet.

At school, he was called 'Marco the Eye-tye' by his classmates, because of his Italian heritage. Later, after leaving school, he took to calling himself Mark Rifell, dropping the 'c', and 'o', substituting a 'k' in Mark and taking the 'i' off his surname, anglicizing it to avoid embarrassment. Now twenty-three, Mark lived alone in a small bed-sitting room out on the Airport Road.

He was watching an evening news report on TV of a huge out-of-control fire, taking up much of a block of homes in Vancouver. Initial reports indicated arson as the cause and he watched avidly as the firemen battled the blaze, and reflected on the fires he had set, which, until the last one – the townhouses – had been quite small. He could feel the urge coming on again; knew the signs – agitation, compulsion, restlessness, an URGE TO BURN! Since reading the investigator's textbook and especially the long, interesting chapter on arson, he'd also thought about his methods of operation – modus operandi – as the book referred to them. 'I've been sloppy,' he thought.

He'd come to realize that if he didn't want to get caught – the punishment for arson was 14 years and if a person died as a result, the *Criminal Code* provided a penalty of life in prison – he had to be extremely careful. He'd need to rethink his – what word did the book use? – oh yes, 'strategy'. He'd checked that word in a dictionary and found that it meant, among other things, 'a plan or a design for achieving one's aims.'

'What are my aims? Simple. To light big fires, watch them burn and not get caught – but are they simple?' he asked himself.

His need for care became ever more important two nights ago. Around two in the morning, at home in his basement accommodation, he had heard a car door slam. Something prompted him to get out of bed and take a look through the high window in his room. What he saw scared the shit out of him!

Two police officers were checking his truck, parked at the end of the driveway, next to the road. His first thought was, 'How the hell did they find me so quickly!? I was real careful.'

They spent three or four minutes looking in the cab and the back, trying the doors and the canopy window, all of which were locked. He saw them shine a flashlight in and they must have seen the gas can. They did a check on their radio and shone a light on the front of the house, almost catching him looking out. In another minute, they left. When they drove away, he noted the sweat on his brow, how clammy his hands were, his shallow breathing and fast-beating heart. The police hadn't returned and his nerves calmed down but there'd be no more sleep that night. He couldn't understand why they had checked his vehicle.

It wasn't until two nights later that he figured it out. Returning from his shift at the mill at 1 a.m. he parked in his usual spot and locked up. Three other vehicles were parked nearby and he could see they were covered in heavy frost but because he'd been driving, his wasn't. Bingo! The cops were just doing routine checks – he hoped – and felt somewhat relieved.

Mark spent some time thinking about how he operated. He knew he was being careful, but careful enough? He didn't think so. After the townhouse fire, he'd been lucky in seeing the approaching police car and had time to get out of the way. He wasn't sure how he'd handle himself if he had been stopped.

'I need to think about that and have a story to cover my presence in any given area. Maybe I'm too far away from home.' When he started 'lighting up' as he called his activity, he thought it would be safer to go out in the early morning hours, as there'd be little traffic about – less people to see him. Most everyone would be in bed.

Now he was thinking that maybe that wasn't such a good idea: made his vehicle more obvious at that hour and more of a likelihood of being checked by the police. They did some late-night drunk driving checks he knew – usually around 11 p.m. to 1 a.m. but most of the checks were near the pubs. 'Maybe I should do my stuff around, say, ten when there is still a lot of motor vehicle activity on the streets?' He'd just be another pickup truck on the road. Safety in numbers? With regard to his shift work, though, he'd be legit, he told himself.

'Drink no booze, have my license and registration ready, be polite to the officer etcetera – a model citizen. Don't want to lose my license.' He smiled to himself. 'Okay, four things to re-consider – where, what, when and how do I light up?'

'I need to reduce my area of operation. No more long drives. Leave the binoculars at home – don't want to get caught with those on the road at night.' Getting his map of Greater Parkton from his truck, he spread it on the kitchen table. He had a choice of basically five kinds of buildings – 'structures' the fire department called them – to choose from and he wrote them on a telephone pad:

Private houses (dwelings) including apartments
Busineses – almost any kind
Public buildings – city or provincial
Wearhouses – almost any kind
Schools
Satisfied with his all-inclusive list, he reviewed and modified it a bit.
Dwelings – NO. Don't want to kill no one.
Busineses – must be unoccupied. Check for alarms. Look for back entrances. Note: TRY one by breaking in – sit in the weeds and wait to see if and when police or security people show up.
Public buildings – leave (sure to be alarmed)
Wearhouses – must be unoccupied – how do I check? Have to enter somehow. Lots of possibilities in several wearhouse areas – spread out all over.
Schools – tempting; because of alarms would have to light outside the building. Choose carefully – not near houses.
Next thing is: WHERE? Check a MAP.

He spent the next hour scouring the map which covered over 1600 square miles of the metropolitan area including some of the countryside. The reverse side showed the street map of the City.

There were seven warehouse areas, he noted as he circled them; two on this side (north) of the river, a large one on the Indian Reserve on the east side, one adjacent to the CPR track near downtown, two out in the east valley and one uphill to the west, next to the TCH. The last two he ruled out on account of distances to drive. In his mind, he made a note to start driving around the first three areas to get the 'lay of the land' and began to make plans for his next 'expedition'.

The next and equally important consideration, were the methods to be used. He'd already decided that the best time to start would be in the late evening time frame, on weekends when he was not working and there was much more traffic around at that hour. He'd try that anyway. He had reviewed several ways of starting a fire and decided that the one that fit his needs best was the 'time-delay' fuse. Just pouring the gas out and lighting it may not give him enough time to get away cleanly. He was lucky on the Thistle fire.

There were basically three fuses that he read about, and thought that the simplest and most effective was using a candle and a gas-soaked piece of string which would give him maybe five minutes to leave the area safely after lighting up and before the flames took hold. He thought it would be good to experiment. He bought two kinds of small candles – one that was four inches high and a quarter-inch thick and the smallest kind, slim and two inches tall, used for birthday cakes. He had to buy them in boxes of twelve each, but that was okay. He could use them.

At home in the basement, he lit both and timed them to flame-out. It was immediately obvious that the four-inch one took too long – twelve minutes – while the two-inch candle took three – just right, he thought. The next step was to tie a three feet long piece of gasoline-soaked string to the bottom of the candle. To do this, of course, meant going outside. At the rear of the house was an upper floor outside deck with a large space below at ground level for the lawn mower, hoses and garden tools, ideal for his experiment. The upper part of the house was rented to a retired elderly gentleman and Mark rarely saw him.

Under the deck, he cleared a space on the dirt floor, and tied one end of the gasoline-soaked three feet of string to the base of the candle and stuck the candle in the hard-packed soil, enough for it to stand upright. He lit the candle and stood back but after a few seconds, a small breeze blew the flame out. 'Damn!' Lighting it again, the flame flickered sideways a few times but eventually reached ground level, where it immediately ignited the string which flared up quickly along its whole length, the flames rising to a height of about eight inches. 'Okay, it works,' he thought. 'And no evidence left.'

There were two minor problems. He'd have to protect the candle flame from the wind and he'd have to wear rubber gloves when he soaked the string and tied it to the candle. No problem with the second; he'd have to think about the first.

When he thought about it, the solution was simple. He took a cardboard box and cut a piece out, forming it into a six-inch square with the sides about four inches high, no top or bottom, enough to hide the candle and flame from the wind and anyone who happened by while it was burning. Windy weather would be good anyway; help fan the flames once they got started.

The next evening, under the deck, he tried it again, placing the small box over the candle and lit it. The flame was nice and steady, but when it reached the candle bottom and the string caught alight, the bottom of the box resting on the ground and on the string, delayed the advance of the flame along the rest of the string. Okay. He took the box and cut out an inverted V at the bottom of one side so that the string could pass through. He replaced the candle and string and lit up. Worked perfectly this time. Only one minor thing to think about. Again, he had stuck the candle into the ground but realized that in most cases, if not all, he would be placing the candle on a hard surface, which would require hot-waxing the bottom to make it stand up. He felt very satisfied with his work.

The next thing to consider was the equipment to carry in his pickup when he went 'operational', another word he'd picked up from the textbook.

'Everything I carry I should be able to explain if stopped,' he thought, 'with the exception of the latex gloves and candles. I can put those in my shirt pocket. They take up no room.'

He made a note in point form of what he needed:

2 candles, 2"
2 wooden matches
Small cardboard box - top and bottom removed
1 piece string - about 3' long
A newspaper
Pair rubber or plastic gloves
Rubber low cut overshoes
Pencil flashlight
Tire iron – in truck
Gas can and nozzle stay strapped in the box in plain view.
No maps.
Places to be surveyed before.

And finally, what to wear. 'Easy. Dark jacket and pants, shoes with no-pattern soles and heels, and a plain, no-name, no-crest ball cap.'

'Don't forget – put the gloves on BEFORE you enter the building!' he reminded himself. 'Oh yeah. One other thing. Before you go out at night, check all the lights on the truck. Don't want to get stopped for a chicken-shit ticket.

'So, now I can go hunting again!'

PART THREE

29

The meeting consisted of six GIS members, Sergeant Miller of 'B' Watch (currently working day shift), two Identification Section members, the Parkton Assistant Deputy Fire Chief and the investigator from the Provincial Fire Marshall's office, Vancouver.

Sergeant Jones had asked these people to attend to discuss the current situation about the last two major arson events, and to develop some strategy to try to determine responsibility and prevent further fires.

"That's the essence of this meeting," he said. "By reviewing what we know, we can perhaps make some assumptions about our possible suspect and his M.O. As you know, we have little physical evidence to go on and even less about the perpetrator. Nevertheless, we're bound to make some kind of assessment of what we have and what we think. In cases like these, we very much have to rely on the eyes and ears of field personnel, mainly General Duty and Traffic members. We'll examine some recommendations a bit later.

"As you can see, I've invited Deputy Fire Chief Vince Carruthers and Inspector Pete Howard of the PFM's office to review their actions and findings, followed by discussion and a possible Plan of Action." Looking at the fire officer, he said, "Would you like to go first, Vince?"

"Thanks, Trevor. To refresh your memories, I'll do a brief recap of the Thistle and Surplus fires and my impressions. Both fires caused complete destruction of the premises and seemed to have been planned, rather than a random effort. In other words, the suspect 'cased' the locations, probably for size of structures, access and egress of the property, means of escape, but above all, for effect – how big a blaze could he cause? Both fires were well underway and the buildings irretrievably lost by the time our equipment arrived. That may or may not have been intentional on his part.

"The reasons for us to assume these fires were intentionally set are two-fold. First, these housing units at the Thistle were to be heated electrically but the power to them had NOT been connected. Second, the fast and uniform spread of flames strongly suggests as accelerant had been used. This assumption was reinforced when we found the remains of a burned wooden match on what remained of the front deck at the end of the row. 'Accidental' combustion was absolutely impossible.

"The Harry's Surplus fire was unequivocally set. The door at the loading dock had been forced and the fire started in the centre of the store, again by an accelerant. Trace elements of gasoline were found on a not-quite-burned piece of fabric. What slowed our response to the fire was because of the nature of the building – 90 years old, built like a large, long barn with few, and rather small, windows. The centre of the store was surrounded by all kinds of partitions, cabinets and display cases effectively hiding where the fire was set. Its late reporting was for good reason. Added to that is that Railway Street is not much used in the evening or night and few people live nearby. As a result, the flames had a good hold by the time we arrived. Of course, when the ammunition started to explode, we had to vacate in haste until it fully cooked off. That took almost a half hour.

"The reason the building was gutted, beside the unavoidable delay in responding, was, as I mentioned, its age and the fact that the timbers and wood-slat-sided interior walls had long ago dried out and therefore burned readily. The perpetrator had obviously examined his target beforehand. From his perspective, it was quite well done and he must have achieved a great deal of satisfaction – both at his perceived cleverness and the end result. It's a good thing there were no other buildings nearby. It leads me to conclude that he's not going to stop

THE SCARLET SENTINELS ♦ 199

and may be looking for bigger targets. The larger the fire the prettier it is to them. Any questions? No? Okay," he said, turning to Pete Howard, "I'm done for now."

"Alright folks, I haven't much to add. I've examined both scenes and come up with very little evidence. The single match found only tends to indicate arson and is virtually useless for comparison purposes. Even if the suspect was arrested at the scene carrying wood matches, they would only be an indicator at trial. It would carry little weight, I believe, in the preponderance of evidence.

"Just for the hell of it, though, I did speak to the six company construction employees who work there and the night watchman – who as you know, was absent that night – regarding their smoking habits, and of the three who smoked, all said they use, and produced, lighters. Having been 'bitten' by Defence Counsel once before on this point, during cross-exam, I do try to cover all my bases. At the Surplus fire, I examined the remains of the door frame beside the loading dock for tool marks, but they were quite indistinct – certainly not useful for comparison.

"To prove where the fire started, I had two of the store staff look at the area and they pointed out the melted remains of metal racks and clothes hangers, which categorically proves their movement to the stairway below the office where the fire was set. The suspect did use, I think, paper and cardboard from inside the loading dock area as there was very little ash evidence in that corner where this stuff was stored pending pickup by waste management people. I also believe he used a delaying fuse or device in order to give him time to leave the store. No evidence of the fuse was found.

"I've turned over my findings to Sergeant Jones, along with photos and lab results, as further investigation now rests largely on your shoulders. If, in reviewing the file, you have any questions, please give me a call.

"While this is only two fires, large as they were, they haven't yielded much evidence or point to a particular person with any degree of certainty. I think we can rule out arson for gain – usually insurance. Both the builder at Thistle and owner of Harry's are financially sound.

"There's been a space of six weeks between these events, which suggests our arsonist fits in the 'serial' category. We find these individuals tend to be sporadic in their need to set fires and, generally, are quite good at planning and executing them and take great care to avoid blame.

"Now, regarding the one individual on your radar screen, a guy named," he paused a moment to read it – "Mark Rifell, there's really nothing I can say. The indicators are very slim and I'm going to leave whatever approach you think may be necessary to confirm his involvement or eliminate him; up to Sergeant Jones and you. You definitely need to evolve a strategy and perhaps I could ask if you would share that with me. I've been in this business for five years after serving 25 years with the Burnaby Fire Department.

"How many of you have attended the Advanced Investigators Course at the CPC in Ottawa?" Several hands went up. "Good. You may recall the half-day session on arson. Your textbook identified the so-called 'four degrees of arson' as identified by the American agency, the National Center for the Analysis of Violent Crime – NCAVC. The first two – burning of a dwelling or a building – are what we're concerned with here. Our *Criminal Code of Canada* does not make these distinctions but lumps arson and arson causing death together into one offence, Section 433, punishable by life in prison. Serious stuff.

"Three things are usually the outcome with serial arsonists – the individual ceases his activities suddenly or does so slowly, over a period of time, or until some event in his life stops him or he is caught. We have found that they tend to give up after a person is killed as a result of their 'work'. Most do not intend that kind of outcome and try to take steps to avoid loss of life. So, you need to think about this. It takes a combined and sustained effort to catch a fire bug – it ain't easy. This kind of investigation can often be frustrating to deal with,

where patience, perseverance and persuasiveness need to be practiced
– the epitome of 'Mr. Plod, the policeman' if you don't mind me saying so – but that's the approach that wins the battle at the end of the
day. Naturally I offer the services of my office. Questions?"

With none being asked, Jones thanked the speaker and said,
"Please feel free to stay if you wish. Take a 5-minute break, everyone."

◆   ◇   ◆

"First," said Jones, after the group reassembled with coffee cups in
hand, "let's talk about Mr. Rifell briefly. Constable Ray Davis has
made enquiries and confirms his address at 4815 Airport Road and
that he works shift work at Techmark as a cleaner. He does two weeks
of days and two weeks evenings, Monday to Friday. The shifts are 8
hours and start at 0800 and 1600. Stating the obvious means that he
gets off work at 1600 or midnight, and he has weekends off. Note that
both fires were started on weekends. The Thistle fire was lit around
two o'clock early Monday and Harry's Surplus at ten on a Saturday
evening.

"Rifell is 24 years old, of Italian extraction and born Marco
Antonio Rifelli.

"He anglicized his name to Mark RIFELL, no 'i'. By the way, if
you re-arrange the first four letters of his surname – you get the word
'FIRE, something that an enterprising member of 'A' Watch discovered – surely just a coincidence for us?

"His mother lives in Vancouver – the father has left home. No
problems at work apart from being late a few times and he stays pretty
much to himself which can be a trait with arsonists. The two occasions he came to our attention – first with a check of his pickup
outside his residence and the second time during a stop-check – there
was *nothing* to arouse suspicion. The second check found all in order; no smell of alcohol or marijuana on him – he claims he doesn't

smoke and there was nothing in his truck save for a gallon can of gas strapped in the box.

"Most pickups carry extra gas around here. We may well be way off base with this guy, reading too much into the little we have. Constable Davis and I have discussed the value of doing an interview with him.

"We'd like to take a look at where he lives, but we have *no* evidence on which to base an application for a Search Warrant and, in arson cases, it's better to go in with a Warrant, even if the person gives permission to do so without. Talking to the man creates two possibilities. One, we interview him and we get lucky and he admits the offences – unlikely we think. By attempting to talk to him he may well deny his involvement, which would tend to make him even more cautious, or to cease his activity. That aspect may be good – no more fires at least by him but we'd never know and of course, it would not solve the two major fires we've had. This puts us in a difficult position.

"It's a perfect example of where the police are damned if they do and damned if they don't. So we have to figure out a Plan 'B' using the Mr. Plod approach mentioned by Inspector Howard.

"In my view, I think that essentially means maintaining a discreet watch on his movements. I don't want him stopped without reason – i.e., traffic offences – but more to do with a check of his pickup and his physical condition than with, say, a ticket. If and when anyone does make a stop, please ensure the details are recorded on the DPR sheet. Providing he's not on his way home, it may be possible to tail him with a GIS unmarked car. What I am suggesting now will be distributed to all watches and the Traffic section and I want this matter to be treated with the utmost confidentiality, switching radios from Channel 5 to 3 if necessary. Do NOT use his name. Suggest using 'Subject 1'. My guys will attempt to get a car in place as soon as possible.

"As well, let's try to maintain a discreet log on his residence. Just drive by and note the time and whether his vehicle is parked there.

We've got his shift schedule, a simple one, which means we can eliminate his presence on the road during those hours. Watch commanders need to keep this in mind and remind their members when on duty. Whoever is doing this seems to plan his fires and that includes, I would think, scouting out his locations.

"The last two fires can be compared in these three aspects: the structures were large and empty of people and on the second, a fuse type of device was employed. Using fuses, of course, gives the culprit time to arrange his fire for maximum effect and, importantly, time for escape. He can afford the time to wait until the flames are well under way, as evidenced with the second fire.

"Thirdly, his presence was not noted upon review of the video tapes of the people at the fires. That does not mean he wasn't there. He may have been parked down the road a bit, watching his results. Pretty thin evidence to say the least of it.

"With the Thistle fire, he must have assumed that the units were unoccupied judging from the absence of vehicles at the site, but he could have been wrong. What if, for example, the night watchman – although absent on this one night – had been dropped off and was staying inside and asleep after his periodic checks. The suspect's vehicle was exposed to view on the street at this location and he would not take the time to walk around to make a check. Make sense?" he asked the group. A few nods were given. "Both fires as we know were done over the weekends.

"The one major difference between them was the time – one at 2 a.m. and the other at 10 p.m. Why the difference? Can we read anything into that?"

"Possibly two different people?" suggested someone . "Or a change of tactic. Maybe he felt more vulnerable during that early time in the morning with less traffic about and more prone to a police check. There's usually much more traffic before midnight, certainly on weekends."

"Yeah, good points," continued Jones. "Inspector Howard

mentioned that serial arsonists usually do three or more fires, consecutively, with time off in between. Looking at the two fires recently set,
it seems to fit this kind of profile, which means we can expect more?"

"Yes, you could very well be right," said Howard.

"That's why we've got to be vigilant," continued Jones. "Fires are
routinely videotaped and reviewed to see if the same person appears
in them on more than one occasion. That in itself is not great evidence but it can go toward the 'weight' of other evidence that Crown
Prosecutors like to refer to in trying to secure a conviction.

"Someone asked me about static surveillance. Love to be able to
do that but it's a non-starter. First, there's no place to 'hide' out of
sight along that road. Open fields come right up to the pavement, but
more importantly, we just don't have the manpower and how long do
we keep it up? No one knows if or when this guy will strike again –
even if he is the arsonist.

"As I said, our best option for now is to keep up a loose surveillance and try to establish a pattern of movement of some kind. As
well, with any fires reported from this point on, we must know Rifell's
whereabouts immediately – that is to say at his home or parked near
the scene. Watch commanders must keep this in mind and I'll send a
copy of our discussions to them. One final reminder. Keep an open
mind; this may just not be our man.

"Thanks for your attendance here, Vince and Pete. Good input
and let's stay in touch. If there's nothing else, gents, I'll let you go."

30

Ray Davis pulled both the arson files from the system and put them on his desk. They were gaining some volume now with the inclusion of reports from the Parkton Fire Department, the Fire Investigator's office, photos, and witness statements but nothing that amounted to anything. He also had photocopies of the two DPR log sheets showing the checks on the Rifell vehicle. 'I need to know about this individual, but I don't want to talk to him yet,' he mused. 'Guess I should try the owner of the house first – hopefully not related.'

He checked the City Tax Assessment Rolls to get the owner's name – Mikhail (Mike) Dubcyk. 'A Slavic name of some kind?' he wondered.

Davis called Mr. Dubcyk and the phone was answered by an older man, he judged, with a heavily-accented East European voice. With a great deal of difficulty, he got the message through to the man that he was the police and wanted to see him, assuring him repeatedly that 'nothing was wrong.'

The outcome of the conversation at the house with the man confirmed that he rented the basement of the house to Mark Rifell but did not see much of him and indeed, didn't appear to be interested. He said the tenant worked at the mill, worked in shifts and kept pretty much to himself – "Don't cause me no trouble."

Davis had a difficult time in asking the man not to let the renter know the police were asking about him and that, "No, he wasn't in trouble. He may be a witness to *something*," which seemed to mollify the man's suspicions somewhat.

Outside the house, he made a call to the mill on his new, hand-held Motorola mobile phone for an appointment to see the Human Resources people there.

'Okay, next stop the mill,' Davis said to himself.

The Techmark Pulp Mill was a huge conglomeration of buildings, built on a hillside overlooking the city, one of the largest mills in the province and a major employer in the community, over 700 people. On certain days, when there was a temperature inversion sitting over the city, like a blanket, the smoke emissions, smelling strongly of sulphur, could not escape the valley and the smell permeated everything. Those who didn't mind – mainly employees probably, thought Davis – called it the 'smell of money.'

Parking his unmarked car in the visitor's parking lot outside the administration building, he walked in and asked the clerk where he could find the Director of Human Resources, Miss Hannah Priestly.

"Next floor up, end of hallway," he was told.

Finding the office, he knocked and was invited in. Miss Priestly came forward to meet him and shook his hand. "Constable Davis, I presume?" she said.

Ray Davis had a hard time letting go of it. 'Wow!' was the only word he could immediately summon up to describe her. "Yes – Miss Priestly?"

"Call me Hannah, please. Have a seat and may I offer you a coffee?"

After ordering the beverage from her secretary she sat down at a low, round coffee table and crossed her shapely legs. No rings, Davis also noted; she was 'neither promised nor owned.'

"What can I help you with? You mentioned an employee but didn't give me a name."

"That's routine police practice, I'm afraid. Not meant to be disrespectful," he replied, his face turning a bit red.

"No disrespect taken."

He was about to continue when the door opened and the

secretary appeared with a tray containing a carafe of coffee and saying, "Excuse me, please," she placed it on the table and left.

Pouring a coffee for him, Priestly asked, "Cream, sugar?" and he shook his head with a "No, thanks."

"The employee I'm enquiring about is named Mark Rifell – R I F E L L," he spelled out. "We're just making routine enquiries about this individual with the view to confirming his employment with the company and the nature of his job. I'm sorry I can't be more explicit than that but I would appreciate you keeping this matter confidential until I advise you otherwise. Is that okay?"

"Well, I suppose so. Will this matter you are investigating affect his employment with us?"

"No, I believe it won't but I'm not sure at the moment. Can you tell me what he does and what hours he works? Oh, and by the way, can you give me his date of birth please?"

"Let me check. Mark Rifell, you say," as she moved to her desk and tapped in the name. "Here he is. He's what is called a 'Dust Control Engineer' – DCE – and works both shifts – day and evening. He's been with us close to a year. His birthdate is October 28, 1965."

"Hmm, I'm not at all sure what the title means," said Davis. "Does that require an engineering degree or diploma?"

Priestly burst out laughing. "Oh my God, no. He's a cleaner – of machinery. He uses a vacuum to keep the various pulp and paper making machinery clean."

"Then why the word 'engineer' in his title?" Davis naturally asked.

"A simple answer. The union prevailed upon the company to change a few job description titles, believing the old ones to be a bit demeaning, like a 'cleaner'. The company acquiesced as no wage increases were involved. The only *engineering*," she said, putting up her fingers in quotes, "is to know how to turn off a piece of machinery before vacuuming it and how to turn it on again."

"How's his work? Any problems?"

"No, I've just skimmed through his employment record sheet and apart from being late a few times, there's nothing."

"Okay, one last thing. How long does he work day shift and night shift?"

"Two weeks on days and two on nights respectively. Let me check my computer again. Yes, he started the PM shift yesterday. Anything else I can help you with, Constable?"

"Please call me, Ray. I don't think so at the moment. If there is, may I call you again?" thinking that he'd have to find another reason to pay her another visit.

"By all means," she said, "I'd like that" – with what the police officer thought was a most lovely smile. *Promising….*

"Thanks, Hannah. If you'd remember the confidentiality bit," holding out his hand to once again to shake that most graceful extension of her right arm, holding it a second or so longer than needed.

He knew, absolutely knew, that he was being mentally seduced and loved every second of it. As he was turning to leave, he remembered his business card, slipped his hand in his jacket pocket and gave her one.

Driving the unmarked car back to the office was a bit like riding the Pegasus horse – it felt like the car had wings.

31

"Goddamnit!" shouted Mark Rifell as he pounded his steering wheel on his way home through the back streets of the North Shore on Saturday evening. "What a fuck-up!"

After lighting his fuse at the store, he'd gone to the back door to wait and ensure the flames took hold. They did, in that the clothing racks that he'd pushed together quickly flamed and reached the ceiling in about a minute, but then the stupid sprinklers came on and started spraying water all over everything, quickly dousing the fire. Reluctantly, he was forced to leave.

Calming himself down a bit, he reflected on his night's activities. 'Did I leave any traceable evidence?' Pondering his question, he was sure he hadn't. No fingerprints and no footprints.

He'd thrown the gloves and overshoes into a bin two or three blocks from the scene. The only slight possibility was that the marks left on the door frame could be traced to his tire iron. He'd get rid of that tomorrow.

Coming up to the stop sign at Crest Street and Airport Road, he looked left and right. Seeing no traffic in either direction, he turned right and drove the one block to his house, turning left and parking in the driveway. Locking the truck, he walked down the three steps and entered his basement suite. Looking at his wall clock, he noted the time: 2250 hours.

'Helluva night,' he thought.

♦ ◊ ♦

The call came in to the police office at 7:55 a.m. Monday, February 27, from the Miss Congeniality store, close to the downtown area, saying that the place had been broken into and a fire lit, which had been put out by the store sprinkler system, sometime over the week-end. The business, a woman's store catering to young women, had been closed on Saturday evening at six.

The store manager said, "We didn't know who to call first, you or the Fire Department. There's no fire damage to the building itself – but several racks of clothes have been burned and everything else inside is still soaking wet and unsellable."

She was asked to wait for the police to arrive and not to touch or move anything. The building, called the Commercial Block, was a brick and wood, 3-storey structure, circa 1930, situated at 8th and Pine streets, a block off the main street. It contained two businesses on the ground floor and both upper floors were offices.

A GIS member was dispatched who was joined a few minutes lat-er by a senior member of the Parkton Fire Department, and Sergeant Sterling, whose watch was now on duty. The three of them entered the front door and were met by Monica White, the owner. Not want-ing to crowd the area or contaminate it with more footprints, Sterling decided to wait by the door for a while and observe. Monica took the other policeman and the fireman to the centre of the shop where she showed them eight display racks, crowded together with burned and soggy dresses on metal clothes hangers.

She pointed out a three-sided dressing screen used as an extra change area, that she said had been rolled away from a corner to the middle of the floor in front of the display racks which hid them, and the start of the fire, from any passers-by on the street.

The police officer made a mental note to ask the Ident man when he arrived, to take several photos of it including from outside the store, looking through the front window.

Constable Ralph Todd began asking a few questions of Mrs. White, while the fireman further examined the centre of the store.

"How did you enter this morning?"

"As I usually do, through the front door."

"Was it locked?"

"Yes. I believe the person entered via the back door. I'll show you," she said, walking toward the rear.

"Were you open yesterday, Sunday?"

"No, we're closed. I locked up at 6 p.m. on Saturday."

As they reached the back door, Todd asked her if the store had an alarm system.

"No, unfortunately we don't."

"Do you routinely leave a light on in the store before you close up?"

"Yes, the two in the centre of the ceiling – oh, they were both off today when I came in."

"Did you check the wall switch?"

"No, I was so upset with what I saw, I forgot to do that. Let me check now," she said looking at the panel. "Well, two of them have been turned off," she noted, putting her hand up.

"No, don't touch that, please," Todd said quickly, "we need to check for fingerprints. You're sure you turned these lights on?"

"Yes, absolutely."

"Okay, let me look at the door," said Todd, sitting down on his haunches at eye level to the door knob. No damage inside the door. Culprit must have left the same way. He also noted the absence of lock bolts and suggested to Mrs. White that it would be a good idea to have them installed. He was about to open the door to look outside when the fire investigator, who was kneeling on the floor in the centre of the shop, called him.

"Look at this," he said, pointing to the burned down remains of a thin candle, and the remains of a soggy piece of cardboard lying next to it. "It's a fuse," and explained how it worked. "Simple but effective except in this case it seems. The stupid bugger didn't look up when he came in."

"Well," replied Todd, "he may not have noticed anyway because he turned off the only lights – there were two right above – in order to work in the dark."

He called Sergeant Sterling, who was talking to the owner by now. "Excuse me, you need to see this, Sarge" he said, pointing to the floor.

Sterling said, "Yeah, there's a possibility this kind of fuse was used in the previous fire," after examining the residue of evidence. Certainly could be the same person. I'm going to leave you guys to it and return to the office. I'll let Trevor Jones know what we've found."

As the sergeant was leaving, Constable Brownley, one of the Identification Branch members, arrived carrying his kit in an aluminum box. "What's up? Where would you like me to start?" he asked, removing his camera and stand.

Todd asked him to take a few snaps of the scene, both inside and outside the store – looking in – and close-ups of the apparent 'fuse' and asked him to join him at the back door when he was finished.

At the door, he knelt down on the floor and placed the fingertips of both hands at the bottom, where there was a slight gap between the door and the sill, and managed to pull the door open inwards. The door frame revealed a half-inch pry mark in the wood just above the lock. He also noticed a smattering of thin pieces of glass on the back step. Looking up, he saw the overhanging light bulb had been smashed, the screw threads still in place, small jagged pieces of glass hanging from them. Walking out, he noted the back door was in an alcove several feet off the alley – well hidden. He wondered briefly who did the property checks in this zone over the weekend. He told the Ident man about his findings.

A brief examination of the sprinkler system revealed it to be a common make, called a wet pipe sprinkler system with a suppression control mode where a few, or all, of the sprinkler heads could be activated over small or large areas of rising heat and flames. In this case, only three of the sprinkler heads were activated, but they produced enough water to cover the whole floor, no doubt running down the floor heater vents into the basement. In any event, they did the job. Without it, the building may well have burned down.

Before Constable Todd left, he spoke to the owner again, asking if she carried insurance. She said that she had to as required by her rental contract.

He also said that because this was an arson offence, the police were obliged to look into her business accounts to examine the company's financial standing – to eliminate the possibility of 'arson for gain.' Did she understand that necessity?

She did.

♦ ◇ ♦

Sergeant Jones sat in his office with Constable Todd and discussed the Commercial Block fire as the latest arson was now called. As a result of Todd's findings they both believed it was the same individual who lit the two previous ones, only this time he was unlucky and the building was still standing.

Todd said, "I think he slipped up with this one. He apparently may not have done a pre-check of the inside of the ladies store. He also put the store lights off with the back door switch. No prints. Must have worn gloves. I'm surprised – he should have noticed the sprinkler system, don't you think, Sarge?"

"Well, he didn't and that may have been because the sprinkler heads were recessed into the ceiling, but we do have a complete understanding of his fuse method. Quite good. The little V-cut into the bottom of what was left of the box, to allow the string to pass through, is a good example of how well thought out his activities are. I notice that this building is only three blocks away from the Surplus fire, although that may not mean anything – just a coincidence. I take it that the tool mark left in the wood door frame was too indistinct for comparison?"

"Yes, the wood is old and soft from weathering and doesn't allow for nice sharp edges to be left."

"I suppose that area is fairly pedestrian-free at night?"

"Uh huh. The building is on the edge of the commercial area and there is a small playground between it and the residential area."

"Don't forget too that it was Saturday night – hockey night," said Jones.

"I wonder if this son-of-a-bitch actually thinks of things like that. Anyway, not much evidence to go on," Todd replied.

"Did you check the weekend DPR sheets, Ralph?"

"Yes. Rifell's truck was seen in his driveway on Saturday evening at 2000 hours and on Sunday morning at 0200. No note of a physical check. Also, of course, no checks were made between those times so that gives him six hours to have moved around. I've checked the incoming complaints for the evening and 'D' Watch was quite busy, so they probably didn't have time and it's probably not a real priority for them."

"Okay," Jones said, "but for two nights, no one checked the back door of the shop or noticed the broken light bulb, which suggests to me that whoever covers this area for premises checks did not do them – maybe just drove by. It's always better for the police to find a place broken into than the owner."

"I'll speak to Sergeant Dunn about this. Seems to me it should have been found. I don't suppose the fire investigator has any thing to add?"

"No."

"Alright, before you go, Ralph, remind me of the time space between these three fires."

"There's been one every six weeks. Too early to tell, but maybe a time pattern developing?"

"Check the dates again. Let's be exact. Can you do that now?"

"Sure. I know the dates. Thistle fire started on Sunday night December 5. Surplus was set on January 14, and of course this latest on February 25 or 26. Let's see – to repeat, that's exactly six weeks separation."

"Again," asked the sergeant, "is this what I call 'coincidental randomness' or do the times correlate with something taking place in his life or did any of the stars line up that we don't know about? I think this situation is now going to need some surveillance planning. I'll talk to the Ops NCO about it and see what we can do."

32

"Horse shit!"

That exclamation came from the mouth of Marvin Peterson.

He was in conversation with his partner for the evening, Constable Bernie Wardlow, while patrolling Centre Zone in 10-Bravo-14. The brief statement was certainly a debatable one, for the topic under discussion was one dear to the hearts of both: money. Bernie, some twelve years younger than his companion, had led the topic off in a very forthright manner, when they decided it was time for a 10-61 break.

"Jeez, Marv, I'm tapped out tonight. Can you lend me a twenty until the eagle shits?"

"Uh, yeah, I guess so. I might point out that you only got paid seven days ago. Christ, Wardlow, what do you do with your money? Guy like you ought to be rolling in hay."

It was fairly obvious early on in a conversation with Constable Peterson that not only was he a 'queen's cowboy', but that at heart at least, a real one too. His speech was littered with phrases, nouns and adjectives coming from that special milieu.

"Well, I'm the one who's usually lending stuff out," said Wardlow, "but I just bought myself a set of wheels today and that kind of set me back to square one financially."

"Yeah, I guess it would," said his friend. "Whaddya get?"

"Brand new Bronco."

Peterson's eyes lit up. That was exactly what he wanted, complete with a bright, shiny hood ornament of a galloping horse. He owned a pickup truck but it looked like, in his words, a Hereford cow, it had been patched up so many times in shades of brown. The Bronco represented for him the very epitome of a motor vehicle, and he was slightly resentful that a young punk like Wardlow was able to afford such luxury, even if he only owned one wheel and the bank owned the rest.

"God, I wish I had one of those," he said.

"Well, it's relatively easy to get and painless, too," said Wardlow. And that led to the expletive that was a favourite of Peterson's.

"No, I mean it. Alls you do is simply apply for funds at your local bank and they'll be happy to oblige. They're shovelling the money out the door these days to anyone, even to those who are half a risk." Realizing the implication of his last remark, Wardlow hastily added, "Of course, Marv, I didn't mean to imply you are."

"Well, in a way, you know, you're right. I'd have trouble paying them back. My mortgage payments take damn near a third of my net income, and having two young kids at home, the old lady can't work, so we have to live pretty close to the bone at times."

Wardlow gave a chuckle and said, "Yeah, I wondered why you always carry a tin cup around, Marv!"

"And you're asking me for money?" he replied, as they swung into the McDonald's parking lot and gave their 10-7. "You better let me have a drive of the new beast you bought, for the interest you owe me!"

Marvin Andrew Peterson, at age forty (39, he liked to say), was an eighteen-year veteran of the Force. When he joined, he was thin, as he had said to Bernie. The NCO in charge of the small detachment in his hometown in Alberta had suggested when Marv applied to join, that he put on a bit of weight.

"The only good thing about you right now," he said, "is that if you stand sideways, a criminal would have nothing to shoot at. On the other hand, you're gonna have trouble bringing someone in who doesn't want to come along."

This was a bit disconcerting to Peterson, who said to his best friend after the interview that 'A – he didn't want to get shot at whether he was thin or fat, and B – he didn't want to get his lights punched out because he was too skinny.'

While he was in fact a bit of a beanpole still, he did have a great deal of sinewy strength and in his time in police service, no one had yet bested him in a fight, although he'd come close on occasion. That was largely due to his growing up on a combination farm and ranch and having to become, at a fairly early age, self-sufficient.

He was the eldest of six children and at the age of twelve was driving a tractor, helping his father at round-up time, catching cows and branding them, riding the horses bareback, loading hay bales, and feeding hogs and chickens. His dad tried raising turkeys one year but the constant gobbling sound drove them all crazy, and, as Marv was fond of repeating, 'There's nothing like the smell of turkey shit to clear the sinuses in the early morning,' and that was it for that enterprise. All of this made him tough.

He saw his first Mountie close up at that age when policemen used to give talks at schools on bicycle safety. Notwithstanding the fact that he and many other kids had no bikes to ride (they rode horses instead), he found the talk fascinating and the Mountie even more so. He resolved then, that would be his career when he graduated high school.

As it turned out, he had to wait for a while. His father had done rather well with his cattle and especially grain sales. China was becoming a major importer of Canadian grain and farmers couldn't grow enough. As a result, Peterson senior had expanded his acreage from a half section of land to a full section by the time Marvin was ready to leave school. As he was the oldest son, the next being three years younger, the father had prevailed on Marvin to 'stay on the farm for a year or two, until I can afford a reliable hired hand.' When young Peterson re-applied again, at age twenty-two, he hadn't gained an ounce of weight.

Near the end of his twenty-third year, he was sworn in at the Calgary Sub Division offices, taking the Oath of Allegiance to Her Majesty, swearing the *Official Secrets Act* and his consent to serve in the Force for the next five years, signing his enlistment papers in front of Inspector Garth Simpson. He was *in*!

One week later he found himself a member of Troop 16, Depot Division, Regina, Saskatchewan – 'the most eclectic bunch of misfits to ever walk through the gates,' their Troop Leader told them on their first ragged parade. None of them knew what 'eclectic' meant, but from the tone of the voice and their leader's body language, they knew it wasn't meant to be complimentary. Life was about to change drastically.

Only one thing upset Peterson initially, and that was the fact that he had missed out on equitation training. Riding horses as part of recruit training had been a tradition for over ninety years but was discontinued in 1966. It was considered somewhat of a redundant activity in view of the rapidly changing times, and besides, it reduced training time by three months, and time was money.

Another factor was an emerging change in training philosophy, which recognized the need to emphasize the academic side of police work, and downplay the physical. If he had joined at age eighteen, which was more the rule than the exception in those days, he would have been in time to take equitation training.

Upon leaving Regina, he was posted to a large municipal detachment in British Columbia, which he didn't like, for a couple of years. He couldn't stand the crowds, heavy traffic and the kind of police work, which included many family fights. His luck changed when he managed to get a place on the Musical Ride.

It meant three months of sweating it out at the riding school located at the 'N' Division grounds in Ottawa, learning to ride all over again, the way the Force wanted him to and practicing constantly the intricate manoeuvres of the various riding formations. He had to learn to use a double bridle called a 'Weymouth' and English-style saddle introduced in 1971, called the 'Stubben', made in Germany. He found riding with this equipment gave more control over his animal than with the western style single bridle and found it easy to learn the right touch he needed to direct and control the animal. It was 'a piece of cake' for Marv and he was the first in his class to 'earn' his spurs.

His time on the Ride included the year 1973, the one hundredth anniversary of the Force, and saw the Ride travel Canada from coast to coast doing almost eight months of back-to-back shows, including a performance for Her Majesty, The Queen and Prince Phillip at Regina. In a Calgary performance, his mother, father and siblings had the immense pride of seeing him ride.

Next year, the Ride toured parts of the eastern United States, including New York City, Washington, D.C. and Churchill Downs, home of the famous Kentucky Derby, where members were treated like royalty.

Peterson liked to talk about those experiences and would tell how people vied with each other, sometimes to the point of almost coming to blows, about who was going to have the honour of entertaining a Mountie for an evening.

The glamour of these occasions, and the near adulation in which they were received in American communities was worth all the hard work and sweat that went into the daily exercise rides, and cleaning stables, horses, riding tack and uniforms. It was indeed the life for a single man. In all that time, he never fell off his horse, Cindy, and only once lost his Stetson, when some jerk in the final charge down the field, bumped into his horse. It cost Peterson a dollar for that, a voluntary penalty members of the Ride paid if they lost a hat or worse yet, fell off their horse. The money went into a slush fund for a huge final party at the end of the season, when half the Ride would returned to the various detachments and units, their three years of duty completed and another sixteen new faces would begin training.

He was transferred back to British Columbia and served at two small Interior detachments, before being sent to Parkton, four years ago.

His years of association with horses had made him a knowledgeable and expert horseman. Although he wouldn't admit it, the two years he spent on the Ride, had only served to enhance those skills. To see him ride was poetry in motion. Now that he was stationed in Parkton, in the heart of interior British Columbia's cattle country, he could once again indulge in his first love.

He did that by purchasing a two-year-old mare Quarter Horse. It wasn't exactly a very prepossessing looking animal – an odd colour with an odd gait – but it could sure move. Living as he did not far from the racetrack and knowing the manager on a first name basis, Marv was able to exercise the horse regularly and put it through its paces to see what it could do. He re-named her Cindy. His original intention in buying the animal was strictly for recreational purposes. He wanted his two sons, Billy and Blake, to learn to ride and enjoy the outdoors and to acquire that certain sense of pride in owning, grooming and riding a horse. He quickly found out that Cindy could keep up with the best of the other race horses on the practice circuits and asked one of the regular jockeys to take her around the track for a timed run. She came within five seconds of the track record.

Thereafter, Peterson was persuaded to have the animal trained for the track and to enter the race circuit. To do so meant changing the registered ownership to his wife's name so that she could legitimately race the horse and keep any money it made. This kind of activity represented a bit of a grey area, but he complied anyway. Members of the Force were not allowed to own a business or be in the employ of someone else, due to conflict of interest possibilities, the unseemly nature of being so involved and, of course, the need to assure that their minds were focused on the job.

The twelve-hour shift system was very helpful in allowing Peterson to follow some of the racing circuit around the province. With four days on shift and four days off and after every fourth shift, an extra day off to make up for the extra hours worked in this kind of watch system, he was able to visit many racing points. Using a few days as well from his annual leave tacked on to his days off time meant he could run Cindy in most events during the racing season. He enjoyed his life. He liked police work, loved the track and got paid for doing it all, especially when his horse won, which as it turned out, was better than fifty percent of the time. He did comply with the 'rules' and handed the money over to Susan who promptly put it in their joint account.

So, upon reflection, the fact that he didn't own a new Bronco with a shiny silver horse emblem on the hood, didn't cause him much envy. He was happy for Wardlow, and his partner would undoubtedly let him drive it a bit, but, someday, his own Bronco would come in.

33

Constable Allen Kart lived in what he considered 'nice digs,' a top floor corner apartment of recent construction on the east side of North Parkton. It was situated at an angle and had corner windows that allowed two views – one looking northeast toward the Cariboo Mountains in the distance and the other looking southeast overlooking the confluence of the two Thompson rivers. The southeast direction also afforded a view of the downtown area with its bright night lights. He was a city boy at heart – from Winnipeg – where, coincidentally, his parents owned a house near the confluence of the Red and Assiniboine rivers. It was almost déjà vu.

His girlfriend, Pamela Harris, who often shared the space with him, agreed. It even had two bedrooms and his parents stayed with him on their first visit. Pamela didn't share space with him then, but she did last night. He was in a magnanimous mood this morning, almost 'chipper' to use one of his father's adjectives.

On school patrols today, he'd issued two 'verbals' as they were called, in lieu of tickets. There was no 'written rule' about speeding – when to issue a citation and when not to.

Canada had adopted the Metric system for measuring distance and speed, in September 1977. Prior to that, most police officers would issue a speeding ticket at 10 miles per hour over the posted limit. With the change to kilometres, many started issuing them at 10 kilometres per hour– approximately six miles per hour – over the limit.

While technically and legally it's still speeding, many officers thought it was 'too close to the bone' to prove categorically in Court and did not take any enforcement action for 10 kph only, perhaps issuing a verbal only in school zones.

Kart belonged to this second school of thought on this matter and often would not stop a vehicle unless it was going 16 kilometres over the limit – with exceptions. He was about to make one of these.

After coffee with his mates, he decided to take a spin northwards on West Side Road and show the flag in the community of the same name, five miles north and just within the city limit. The two-lane road hugged the bottom of the grassy hills on the left with the river on the right. Posted speed limit was 60 kph and this time of day there was little traffic.

He saw one car ahead which seemed to be gaining. Checking his speedometer, he saw he was doing 65. Pushing his speed to 70 he still wasn't catching up so he sped up to eighty, then ninety, coming to within a half kilometre of the car. At that point, he hung back in order to 'pace' the car and to check his speed. With a few bends in the road, he momentarily lost sight of it several times. In order to 'prove' the speed in Court, he had to keep the vehicle in sight for at least a half kilometre at a steady pace. A straight two kilometre stretch came up and he was able to accomplish this, with a steady clocked speed of 75 kph. That was enough for a stop and check.

Turning on his emergency lights, he pulled up closer. There were two occupants, both possibly males. Rather than use his siren, he liked to first honk his horn to attract the attention of the driver.

"Radio, Bravo-14," he called.

"Bravo-14, go ahead."

"Checking BCL 763-Bravo-Yankee-Delta, West Side Road, about mile three. Two male occupants."

"763-Bravo-Yankee-Delta, 10-4. Will call with RO," replied the female operator.

Overhearing this, the driver of Traffic car 10-Charlie-3 started along the same road. Whenever and wherever he could, he backed up General Duty drivers doing vehicle stops. Along with bar fights and spousal assaults, checking motor vehicles was a potentially hazardous occupation.

Kart parked his patrol car at an angle behind the stopped car, leaving his emergency roof lights on, grabbed his ticket book and clipboard and got out of the car. His intention was to issue a verbal warning. There had been little traffic on the road and he felt this action was appropriate.

As he approached the driver's side and was about to stop just short of the driver's door (a usual precaution), the window was lowered and a hand and arm came out and flicked away a cigarette butt across the road. The young driver looked up and over his shoulder at Kart and uttered the often-heard question presented to police officers: "What the fuck do you want?" The driver was a greasy-looking, pock-marked, unkempt, long-haired individual, whose comment induced a giggle from the second occupant.

By now, Kart had his face close to the open window, the more ready to smell the distinct aroma of marijuana or alcohol. There wasn't any. What he did notice was the distinct smell of foul body odours.

"Good morning, Sir, thank you for stopping," he said, trying to keep the sarcasm out of his voice. "I'm glad you asked that question. There's a number of reasons. First, throwing a lighted cigarette onto the highway is an offence under the *Motor Vehicle Act,* as is of course, speeding. You were clocked at 75 kilometres per hour in a 60 zone, and I notice one of your brake lights is out, so that amounts to three offences. As well, and I'm sure you don't know this, it is an offence to swear at a police officer in a public place. Section 133 of the *Criminal Code of Canada* states that – 'a person commits an offence, punishable on Summary Conviction, when that person swears at or uses insulting language to a peace officer, and is liable to a fine of up to five hundred dollars and/or a term of imprisonment not to exceed six months.' (Of course, no such offence existed. 'A shame,' thought Kart.) If you're counting, this is the fourth charge I can lay against you. What do you have to say?"

While the driver was considering his reply, Constable Pete Moss in the Traffic car rolled up behind Bravo-14, put his lights on and lightly tapped his horn, letting Kart know he'd arrived and hopefully, the offending driver too. Walking up to his partner, he heard the driver say, "Sorry, officer."

Moss grinned at Kart and said, "Another Section 133 case? Gotta love 'em."

"Here's what I'm going to do for you," Al said to the driver, hiding his smile. "First, let me see your registration and driver's license. Then you can get out of the car and return that cigarette butt to its rightful place. Okay?"

When the driver got back in his car, he placed the butt in his ashtray.

Meanwhile, the Traffic member had responded to the dispatcher's call with the RO's name and address and gave it to Kart, who thanked him for being present.

On this occasion, he elected to write up one ticket for speeding, rather than give a warning. He wasn't *that* generous. He also gave a warning about the faulty brake light. The swearing, of course, didn't bother him. He'd come to expect it, like most officers, when dealing with a certain element of society. After all, police often said the same things to each other, only in jest, of course. As he drove away, he felt good, and humoured.

34

The following appeared on the Detachment Bulletin Board:

SECTION HEADS MEETING NOTICE
PARKTON CITY DETACHMENT
MARCH 21, 1989 – 1900 HRS
SUB DIVISION TRAINING ROOM
CHAIR – S/Sgt JIM HALL, OPS NCO

AGENDA

INTRO REMARKS	Inspector AL EDWARDSON
PATROL WORK COVERAGE	OPERATIONS NCO
GENERAL DUTY CARS & TRAFFIC, PROPERTY CHECKS	OPS NCO
PAPER WORK & DIARY DATES	ADMIN NCO
MEMBERS BEHAVIOUR	OPS NCO
COMMUNICATIONS	OPS NCO
SERIOUS CRIME	GIS NCO
PATROL VEHICLES	ADMIN NCO & TRAFFIC NCO
DRUG ENFORCEMENT	DRUG NCO
POLICE SERVICE DOGS	NCO I/C PSD
AUXILIARY POLICE PROGRAM	'A' WATCH NCO
COURT CASES	COURT LIAISON OFFICER
COMMUNITY RELATIONS	Cst. HEATHER JOHNSTON

◆   ◇   ◆

MARCH 21, 1900 HOURS

Staff Sergeant James Hall, Operations NCO, stood up and said, "Okay, lady and gents, let's get the meeting underway. Inspector Edwardson has a few remarks. Sir."

"Thanks, Jim. Thanks to everyone for coming, and being here on time too. As we all well know, the Treasury Board in Ottawa doesn't know how to spell the word 'overtime' when it comes to the RCMP. Oh well. We all love our jobs and wouldn't accept it anyway."

Someone said, "I don't know about that, Sir," which caused a chuckle.

"Hopefully you've reviewed the Agenda topics and are ready to add your two cents worth. Some general remarks before I hand the meeting over to Staff Sergeant Hall. Overall, I'm generally pleased with the performance of the detachment. I'm fully cognizant, as I know you are, of the fact that we can all improve our efforts and results. This kind of activity takes place in small increments, provided they don't result in taking one step forward and then two steps back, in our efforts to provide our citizens with a fair degree of protection and a reduction in our crime and motor vehicle accident rates. I regard our General Duty and Traffic members as our 'front line troops.' Together, they represent almost eighty percent of our total complement. They're the people the public generally comes into contact with initially on police matters.

"I mention at every meeting of the need to maintain our patrol work. That does at least two things for us – a greater ability to respond quickly to complaints, and puts more police presence on the streets. This is even more important now that we have an arsonist on the loose which is to be discussed. We need people to get away from that old phrase – 'Where the hell are the cops when you need them?' I know, I know, it's a bit of a pipe-dream, but we must make the effort and maintain a high level of presence and competence in all that we do.

"We operate at considerable expense to the taxpayer and I want us to give them their money's worth.

"There are thirteen items to be reviewed. Let's try to be succinct and not drag this out. I'll need you, Jim and Fred, to write up an account of the meeting to circulate to the others detachment members. I'd like everyone to initial that he or she has read and understood these notes. Of course, I'll leave it to all section heads to do any discussion you think is necessary with your people. As well, if any of you have private concerns, arrange an appointment with me. Any questions?

"Okay, I have to attend a City Council meeting on budgetary matters. Hope you have a good discussion."

The meeting was turned over to the Operations NCO and the members rose as the inspector left the room.

"Okay, folks, Item 1, Patrol Work coverage," said Jim Hall. "I know very well how difficult this can be for the watch commanders.

"This is a constant source of irritation for you. Lack of police presence on the road is obviously partly due to shortage of personnel on shift, and to some extent, waiting around in Courtrooms. There may be some instances, however, where you can reduce the number of absentees at one time. You have some latitude in approving Days Off, Annual Leave, and Training Courses, etcetera, so as not to leave yourselves critically short on any one shift. You may have to be a little 'hard-assed' in some cases in turning down a request – for a later time.

"We are particularly affected during the summer months when we're busy, when school is out and members with kids need to go away for a vacation. Try to find training courses in the 'off-season' winter months, preferably. If you don't already do this, consider asking your people to put in for Leave time at the beginning of the year so that you can do some degree of manpower planning. Just do your best, please.

"The next item is an important one for the detachment – General Duty and Traffic patrols. With all due respect to the other Sections present, without whom we could not be effective, I regard patrol work as the *raison d'être* – the bread and butter of our existence. The combined use and effectiveness of all these people shows how well, or not, we serve our community, and an important by-product of that is reflected in the leadership and abilities of those who run the show – you and me, folks. End of sermon.

"First, I'll have Don Michaels talk about Traffic concerns, then I'll finish with General Duty items with input from any of the Watch NCOs. Sergeant Michaels?"

"Alright, two things from me. First, our primary duty as you know is concerned with traffic enforcement within the City. Highway Patrol covers the highways and rural areas. Let me say that while my staff focus on that duty, they are also available to assist General Duty members when necessary, largely as back-up, time permitting.

"Likewise, we occasionally use GD members as traffic ticket writers when we operate radar units and there is no second Traffic car to do this.

"The watch commanders present understand that?" he asked, glancing around at his peers, to nods of agreement. "Good," he said. "By the way, regarding Jack's pending comments on the auxiliaries, we certainly like to take them out with us. They're very useful in helping direct traffic around accident scenes, attending to injured people and helping take measurements, etcetera.

"The second item I want to mention is about MVAs. We're averaging about fifteen reportable traffic accidents a day – that's over 5,000 annually. Incidentally one of my goals is to reduce that by ten percent in the coming year. It can be done.

"One way is through enhanced enforcement effort, and, at my suggestion, the City Traffic Engineer is undertaking a street safety survey, including, obviously, traffic light controlled intersections where many of the accidents occur.

"As we all know, General Duty members also handle accidents – many of them. There's just not enough Traffic people to cover them all and I for one really appreciate their efforts. A couple of things to mention in this respect. My section tries to investigate injury MVAs and, of course, fatals. At times, we may have three or four accidents occurring almost simultaneously, to say nothing of multi-car fender benders in rush hour.

"What I'd like to point out is that when GD members have to handle serious injury accidents without a traffic member present, a note to the watch commanders that would be helpful is to instruct your people to review these with one of us. We've taken more courses including traffic analyst training, and will be able to help in suggesting what *Criminal Code* or *Motor Vehicle Act* charges should be laid, etcetera. Likewise, Traffic members certainly appreciate the help of a General Duty member if he or she is available.

"Now, speaking of those people, I know that some of your crews," he said, looking at the four watch commanders present, "don't mind doing traffic enforcement. Some, however, do mind and seem to think it is the sole responsibility of Traffic Section – to the point where they'll ignore red light and stop sign runners, and excessive speeders. In saying this, I may get some disagreement but to my way of thinking, General Duty work includes a plethora of matters – plethora, don't you love that awkward sounding word? – I picked it up yesterday while talking to a Traffic statistician in 'E' Division – that also includes the absolute need to do some Traffic work. Comments, anyone?"

"No disagreement from me," replied Sergeant Dunn. "I'm cognizant of that and constantly remind some of my guys to do more traffic enforcement." The other watch NCOs nodded and made a note.

"While I'm on the subject," continued Don Michaels, "it is also important for all people driving police vehicles to obey the law. When I'm on the road it annoys me to see a few members failing to signal or rolling through stop signs and other minor infractions. It makes a traffic member's job more difficult when he or she has to stop and ticket someone for the same offences, only to be told by the driver that he saw a police car do the same thing some time earlier.

"Police officers have to be models of driving etiquette. A strong reminder to your folks would help, I hope. That's it for me. Thanks."

"Just a few words to finish off this subject," Jim Hall said. "The Mounted Police have been in the business of patrol work for a long, long time. I know just how it is, having 'been there – done that' for a number of years. In my view, it takes a certain mind-set to be an effective patrolman, not the least of which is the need and ability to be inquisitive. I'm not sure that all the members at this detachment have that ability. A few are lazy and a few are in the wrong profession, but that's subject of a later debate. By and large though, we've got pretty good, dedicated crews, thanks to your leadership. Stay on top of it, please.

"Down the list you'll see 'Serious Crime'. Sergeant Jones will be talking to you about some recent crime developments that are starting to cause some concern, which may have an impact on how we operate, and has some suggestions to counter this activity.

"I think if members follow them, it will increase the effectiveness of our patrol work, and certainly assist our 'detectives' if I can use that city police label.

"Property checks. To be done religiously. You know the OIC's feelings on this issue – and I concur. In this case, watch commanders might take the odd patrol on some night shifts to check whether this is actually being done by your people or is just reported as being done.

"We all know there are some people who dislike getting off their asses and out of the car, especially on cold, wet nights. This kind of activity earns us a lot of 'gold stars' from the business public and offsets to some degree some of the shitty brown ones from the general public when we screw up.

"Oh, one thing I haven't mentioned, and before I forget: Anything of a confidential nature said at this meeting should not be discussed with other members. Understood?" Some murmurs of affirmation were made. "Let's move on to paperwork and diary dates. Staff Sergeant Batick will cover this."

"Thanks, Jim. I'll be brief. I'm responsible for the paper flow in this office which includes making spot checks of classification and the filing system. At times it can be voluminous, as you can understand, with one hundred and ten of us contributing. I *do not* read all reports. Don't have time, so I really have to rely on all of you to ensure they are read and completed properly. By that I also mean ticking off appropriate blocks on the reports, especially the one that indicates the complainant has been notified, that the writing is done in readable English, as succinctly as possible. If any of you don't know what that last adjective means, look it up in the *Oxford Dictionary*, so thoughtfully provided for you at public expense."

"What's an adjective, Staff?" someone asked. A few smiles were observed.

"Continuing – I note that some constables tend to be a bit lazy and don't go far enough in an investigation, hoping perhaps that they can bullshit their way into closing a report off a bit early, when more could be done, and a crime, however minor it may be, is still worth the effort of trying to solve. In this respect, the odd phone call to a complainant to find out what was done would be useful, and to determine the level of 'customer satisfaction'.

"I imagine Sergeant Michaels concurs with my remarks concerning MVA reports which he vets, right, Don?"

"Yeah, generally they're okay but we still get a few returned from the Motor Vehicle Branch," he replied. "If watch commanders could take a closer look at them before sending them to me, I'd appreciate that. Thanks."

"One last reminder about Diary Dates. SUI files need to be pursued on a regular basis with ongoing investigations so that a conclusion can be reached. If a file requires a longer due date, that's okay, as long as an explanation is given for this request – questions?"

"Yes," said Sergeant Ed Miller of 'B' Watch, "is there a proposed start date for the new Mobility Data Terminals – MDTs – computer system?" Several people nodded at this question. "I imagine we'll all need to take the course. In principal, the system sounds good but complicated too. Apparently it will get rid of the need for a lot of paperwork?"

"Yes, we expect to hear from 'E' Div HQ soon on the matter. You'll be the second to know. Moving right along; I've decided to move the serious crime item to the end of our meeting. This way, we can give it more attention. There's no need for you, Rusty, Dave and Heather, to stay for this unless you wish to.

"So to the next item, briefly, dress and behaviour. To repeat, head-gear must be worn outside the police car. Members look 'undressed' without caps and it's unprofessional too. Some of your overweight people tend to look a bit sloppy, with baggy-looking pants. Can we ask them again, to try to lose some weight?

"Swearing. I know, it's part of our lexicon but we must be cognizant of foul language, especially when around the general public. I remember when I was a young constable at a small detachment. The Section NCO came around on one of his regular inspection trips and told us that he had a message about this issue from the Officer Commanding the Sub Division which he quoted verbatim. 'Staff Sergeant, I've had a complaint about foul language. When you visit detachments, please, tell the men to cut out the fuckin' swearing for me'."

After the laughter finished, he said, "So, for the next day or two, the words 'excrement' and 'fornication' were substituted with much humour, gradually returning to the unambiguous ones again. It was endemic in my day – getting a bit better now. Remember, there's more 'eyes and ears' out there now in the form of listening devices and the new digital cameras and video-cams. I think we're in the era of George Orwell's *1984*.

"Regarding communications. Keep chatter to a minimum and

use radio protocols when required, keeping in mind Orwell. Non-police people are probably listening in. Any remarks about these two items?" There were none.

"Fred, you have a word or two about patrol vehicles?"

"Yes, thanks, Jim. The usual reminders. Try to keep them as clean as possible. Near the end of shift, members are to gas up for the next watch. This sometimes is not being done. For minor repairs, replacements – i.e., light bulbs – go to our service stations and get it fixed right away. Anything more serious, fill in Form MC 201 and put it in the Admin NCO basket. I'll get at it the next day. It looks like hell for us to be driving around in defective vehicles, when we stop people for the same thing. As the old saying goes, 'Little things mean a lot.' That's it for me."

"Drugs is next. Corporal Brandt, you're up."

"Nothing much to say," said Rusty Brandt, "except to remind you we have a covert operation going on in the City. There are four members from the Vancouver Drug Squad here, who shall remain nameless. They're gathering intelligence but also looking for any drug activity worth looking into. There has been an increase in usage and distribution in our area and I'd like to keep the lid on as much as possible. The Vancouver people are all disreputable looking and good actors. If the members think they are checking one, better not to push the issue. Any doubts or help required, I can be reached on my mobile twenty-four/seven."

"Alright. Dog Section next. Corporal Marinaro."

"Thanks, Staff. As you're aware now, we have a third PSD and handler on staff, Constable Schneider and Police Service Dog Silver, enabling us to provide much better dog service. This will mean that much of the time we can have a dog available for the day and night shifts and possibly two on Friday evenings/nights. Members have expressed appreciation for this.

"A couple of other things. If the watch commanders wouldn't mind reminding your people that when it comes to searches with a PSD, the dog man is in charge of that event, otherwise confusion reigns. Secondly, I'd appreciate you telling your people not to interfere with the animals. Some members seem to delight in going face to face with them, through the rear window glass of the dog wagon, making stupid faces, sticking their tongues out and barking like mad, resulting in the dog going ape shit and drooling foaming saliva and snot all over the glass – that we have to clean up. Next time that happens, I might just turn the dog loose."

One or two of the sergeants looked down while Marinaro was saying that. Déjà vu?

"Well said," said Jim Hall. "Next on the list is the Auxiliary Constable Program. Sergeant Sterling?"

"We have forty-five men sworn in," Sterling said. "As you know, there are no women even though we've tried to recruit some. About thirty-five of them are regularly active. Three or four of them rarely show for duty and I'm in the act of releasing them. I'm also trying to get these people a bit more evenly distributed throughout the week, so that we don't end up on Friday and Saturday evenings with an overflow and not enough patrol cars and members to send them out with. Part of the problem as you know, is that most of them work daytime in their regular work and don't like to stay out late, like they can on weekends. I don't know about the other watch commanders but I send them out in pairs sometimes, with a portable radio, to foot patrol the three malls until closing and then on Main Street, for an hour or two. Their presence does make a difference.

"I've recently appointed a senior member, Auxiliary Constable Mike Bailey, as my liaison person. He is also chairman of their committee. His responsibility is to organize the shifts as fairly as he can, and to prepare a weekly shift list, to be posted on the bulletin board. I've told him to allow a few more people on shift on the weekends. If we don't do that, the keener auxiliary members won't get as much 'action' as they would like, thereby losing enthusiasm and interest, and end up leaving. After all the time, training, effort and money that we and 'E' Division HQ put into the Program, I don't want that to happen.

"A question I have for watch commanders and the Traffic NCO is – Do you think they are a useful asset to us?"

"Yeah, I have no complaints," said Sergeant Lockhart. "I sometimes wish a couple of my members were as enthusiastic. Yes, they are definitely a help especially as backup."

There was no disagreement.

"Before finishing," said Sterling, "just one thing to ask and that is to make sure you thank them before going off shift. They are doing it for free."

"Dave. Something to say about Court work, cases, etcetera?"

"Not much, Staff," replied Beauchamp. "Again, general reminders. Three or four items. Court Appearances. Punctuality is a must, so I'd like members to be waiting in the witness room or hallways at least twenty minutes before scheduled appearance. If he or she is inadvertently delayed, please make contact with me or the Court Clerk. No frivolous reasons, please. Conversely, if the member is not required, I will advise that person as soon as I know. If Crown Counsel wants you here earlier he'll either let the member know or ask me to.

"Court Dress – uniform or civvies – men and women – preferably in suits or sports jacket and slacks with tie – goes without saying. Have notebooks handy if needed. Ensure that only the pages in the notebook to be referred to is available to the Crown, Defence or the Judge if asked for. Separate those relevant pages with elastic bands.

"Regarding RCC's. Reports to Crown must be well written and any physical evidence to be introduced in Court must be included, along with a written description. Please remind everyone to pay close attention to the little things – in some cases, lack of care could mean dismissal of Charges and of course, make the witness and the Force look unprofessional.

"It's hard enough sometimes to get a conviction and no one likes to see the accused 'walk' as it were, and on the way out of Court, smile at the member and raise a middle finger. Not a good feeling.

"In a way, it's a pity every Constable couldn't do this job for a short while. It's an excellent learning experience, having to sit and listen how witnesses, and sometimes the accused, give their evidence, and to watch how Defence Counsel and the Prosecutor interact. I can personally vouch how much this would greatly improve their preparation and presentation and even investigation techniques, and I'm convinced, result in more convictions. That's it for me. Questions? No? Thanks for listening."

"Thanks, Dave. Alright. Constable Heather Johnston. Second to last but certainly not least. Some wise words from you about Community and Media Relations, a crucial part of the interaction between the police and citizens of Parkton. Let me say that it was not just because of her good looks and intelligence that she assumed this role. I mean I could have taken the job, too, you know…." Hall said facetiously.

"Yeah, right," someone said.

Ignoring the comment, he continued, "Heather holds an under-graduate degree in Journalism and I think you know I don't. Also, she spent five years in two small northern B.C. detachments before being transferred here and, as we like to say in the Force, 'has earned her spurs,' so she's not just another pretty face. Go for it, Heather."

She preferred to stand when addressing a group of people. At five feet seven inches and 130 pounds, her auburn hair in a page-boy cut, she was dressed in a mid-blue high collar silk blouse with pearl buttons, slim black slacks supported by a wide, black patent leather belt with a small sliver 'H' for a buckle (presumably for 'Heather') and complete with black, patent leather high-heeled shoes, she looked both professional and glamorous.

The room was very quiet. Eleven pairs of eyes were gazing intently, and with some degree of rapture, truth be told, at Constable

Johnston. It's unknown, of course, whether or not her words got through.

"Thanks, Staff. I'm glad you saved the best for almost the last," she replied. "Something about me you may like to know – or not. When I graduated from McGill in Montreal, I had no particular job in mind. In fact, I took six months and toured Europe which was the thing to do then, if you had time. A friend of mine said she had applied to join the Force and I wished her good luck. I moved to Vancouver and found a job as an assistant reporter for the *Vancouver Sun*, and later met up with Maureen who had been posted to a Fraser Valley Detachment. End result: she convinced me to apply and I did and here I am almost six years later. To anticipate a question, no, I wouldn't do anything else. I just love you guys so much," she said with a coy smile.

"Down to business. Inspector Edwardson's policy in dealing with the news media, is to route much of the information through the Community Relations Officer. On serious matters, like police policies and procedures, members in some purported trouble and so on, I liaise with him and he decides how the news will be handled and what to say. In lesser issues he relies upon me to use my own expertise, discretion and common sense when I am before the camera or being written up in a reporter's notebook. I can certainly see why a police officer needs at least five years of service before he or she is considered 'seasoned' so to speak. It takes that long to become accustomed to all the idiosyncrasies of police work and the policies and procedures of the Force before you put that first service star on your uniform, proudly I might add.

"Most of what I do, or rather say, concerns the more serious criminal matters and I don't need to list them for you. Most of the time I can be straightforward in supplying all that I know, usually gathered from members at the scene, and sometimes witnesses. In my position as a member of this detachment it sometimes isn't easy to be free with my information. The obvious reason is that I don't want to compromise the investigation, so you'll see or hear me sometimes 'hedge' around what I tell people. To a few of them, it may seem as if I am hiding something, or protecting perhaps a member, who for example, may have had a difficult time making an arrest and had to use force to do so. Some percentage of our population doesn't understand, or ignores the fact that police officers have to use force at times to gain control of an offender. To them, it always looks like an assault and some of the video that is shown can make it look that way. In spite of my repeating the 'Use of Force Continuum' that police are obliged to follow, it doesn't satisfy everyone.

"We have to do what we have to do, to be effective. I also think – I don't know if you agree – that this kind of public reaction about use of force, has had, to some extent, a cooling effect on a few members of the Force across the country. Rather than carry through and make a lawful arrest, they allow the person to 'get away', thereby avoiding the possibility of an injury to themselves, or a Charge being laid against them and/or facing a lawsuit."

Some murmuring from among the group seemed to indicate agreement with this sentiment.

Johnston continued, "Not that long ago, no member worth his salt would have considered that option. One had to carry out one's duty to the best of his ability and if you got hurt in the process, so be it. To do otherwise means that you could be labelled a coward and even more importantly, that the offender would try the same thing with the next peace officer they meet. Do you agree with that assessment?" she asked.

"You've hit the nail on the head, Heather," said Sergeant Miller.

"Okay then," Constable Johnston continued. "In the back of the mind of anyone engaged in law enforcement work should be an awareness of these possibilities that you need to do some degree of thinking about what you might say to the media. I know it's not easy in tense situations, but you can school yourself to think that way.

"In saying this I also want to stress that you should not unduly worry about that. Just be conscious of a few rules as guidelines and you'll do fine. You always have a fall-back – me or Inspector Edwardson. The people who work for you also face the same distinct probability. A reporter arrives quickly on site and shoves a microphone at the member expecting a response in detailed and eloquent English. Same advice from me applies. If members can save a little bit of room in a corner of their brain in anticipation of news media presence, then 'babble' can be avoided. That's why I encourage members becoming involved in public speaking, to all ages and cultural groups. The more you talk to the press the better you become at 'stick handling' their questions. If you show hesitancy or reluctance, they'll do a 'piranha' number on you – you know, the small ferocious fish that eats human flesh. This brings me to make a comment about the Rule of Law, of all the things for me to talk to you about – but it fits in with my final remarks.

"While in school, I had to do a paper on the topic of Freedom. In my research I came across the Royal Bank of Canada Monthly *Newsletter*, June 1969, entitled *Let Us Enjoy Our Freedoms*. If anyone is interested in reading the whole four pages, I'll be happy to provide a copy. Let me read you a couple of paragraphs from this well-written article.

"The first is under the heading *The Rule of Law* and says, in part:
It is a great ideal, with the Will of the people as the source of its great authority. Freedom is not liberty for everyone to do what he pleases without being subject to any law. [It] means that there is one law for all, that all are equal before it and that no one can be punished except for the breach of it.

"Under a heading *The Law of the Land* the article makes this point:
We have so much freedom that our liberties must be circumscribed. Laws are vital to the functioning of society, and that must be respected as a condition of freedom. The only alternative to the Rule of Law is the tyranny of the strongest.

"In other words, dictatorships," added Johnston. "Those are very succinct and meaningful words and one major reason why I'm glad I live in a democracy like Canada's. I know I don't need to remind you about the impact of those words, and am sure that every member of this detachment is aware of the sentiment contained in them when he or she steps out of their residence to go to work each day. When it comes to Rights and Freedoms, it is us whom the public comes into contact with on a daily basis, the so-called 'Thin Blue Line' or in our case, I suppose, the 'Thin Red Line' – and the need for us to practice them. Food for thought, gentlemen. Finally, let me say 'thanks' for all the effort the members put into community relations. It's essential work and I think, here at Parkton at least, we do it well.

"That's it for me. If you or your people need any help prepping material for talks to the likes of local clubs, Chamber of Commerce, business associations, schools, etc., I'd be glad to do so. Any questions?"

"Okay, folks, take a ten-minute stretch," said Hall.

◆ ◇ ◆

"Alright," Staff Sergeant Hall called out, bring the group back to order, "we're down to the last item: serious crime. I believe all of you are aware that we've had a few structural fires and some attempts at arson, in and around the City over the past few months, as well as the usual criminal mayhem that we have to constantly try to contain and control. With a combined total of 110 people at this detachment, we should be able to do that in an adequate fashion, I should think, with the possible exception of the drug trade, which seems to grow almost exponentially.

"That brings me to mention about the drug undercover operation in progress here, a combined effort of Corporal Brant's squad and the Vancouver Drug Section. Advise your people to be circumspect about this, please.

"Putting that aside for now, it seems we may have an arsonist on the loose and, if we do, we need to catch the son-of-a-bitch before he kills someone."

Looking at Sergeant Jones, in charge of GIS, Hall said, "Trevor, why don't you give your thoughts on this and other criminal matters?"

"Okay, Jim, thanks. In my view, major crime has not been too much of a problem in the last six months. We've had one murder as you know that was solved quickly thanks to some observation and follow-up by a watch member. I fully believe it's through our 'front line' people that we can do effective policing using the two basic police tenets – prevention and detection. I'll be covering that in a bit more detail shortly.

"Regarding the fires. Let me remind you of these incidents over the past six months or so. The first goes back to October last year when a private garage was set alight on the north shore of Parkton Lake just beyond the airport, and burned the owner's car. It was a collector's model under repair and not insured. The second and third fires were sheds, one on a farm property way out in Valleyfield and the other in the Highlands area. One contained farm equipment, and the other held furniture and personal items in storage. Not much value overall, all three fires suggesting that insurance coverage was not the intent. The last one concerned a waste disposal bin, on wheels, in a back lane, filled with crushed cardboard, was set alight around two a.m. and pushed into the alcove of an adjacent business building between Victoria and Spruce streets.

"It was quickly extinguished and caused relatively little damage, but did create some concern as a person was staying in the building in a small bachelor apartment. He luckily woke up in time and escaped through the thick smoke. However, all of these pale into insignificance when compared to the last fires we've had recently.

"Let me say here that we are not certain that these fires were set by one person, although who knows what goes on in the minds of people like that, but there are two insignificant common threads to them. Because they occurred in disparate parts of the City it strongly suggests that transportation was needed. I know that you're thinking, that it could be three separate people, living in each neighbourhood but the fire investigators don't think that is probable at this time. Something a little more significant, however, was the approximate time the last fires were lit – Thistle at about 2 a.m., then Surplus Harry's and Miss Congeniality at around 10 p.m. or so – suggesting a change of tactic.

"Our police experience teaches that, fortunately for us, most people's behaviour, criminal and non-criminal, follows a general pattern. Humans are creatures of habit which, for the police profession, often allows us to find perpetrators once we determine what their *modus operandi* is, but of course, we can be fooled too. Knowing this, a small percentage of the criminal element try to be clever in disguising or altering their methods and to be truthful, it sometimes works.

"We aren't exactly clairvoyants but if we apply ourselves to criminal matters, we can give the crooks a run for their money – that's an intended pun." Looking around at their blank faces, he added, "It's not really their money…."

A few groans were heard.

"Now," continued Jones, "regarding arsonists. The FBI, through its National Center for the Analysis of Violent Crime – NCAVC – has developed some very comprehensive information about arson – one on the methods of fire setting and the second, on the setters. Investigating fires is a two-agency activity – trained fire investigators responsible for determining cause and retrieving evidence, and the police for criminal investigation if arson is suspected. Arson is one of the most difficult of crimes to investigate and conclude successfully. These people often light many fires before they are caught and statistically, ninety-five percent of arson offences are committed by males. This act is one of the more serious *Criminal Code* violations and Section 433 provides for a life sentence where it results in the death of a human being, accidentally or on purpose.

"Basically there are six common motives: vandalism, profit, crime concealment, revenge, extreme action, and excitement," Jones said, showing them on the overhead screen, "and these are committed by three kinds of compulsive fire setters labelled as follows" – showing them in large black letters on the screen – "mass, spree and serial. Taken together, that's a potential of an eighteen element mix – quite an assortment of motives and people. I'm not going to discuss these labels now except to say that most fires are set by serial arsonists.

"You and your people can read up on them in the handout material. I'd appreciate it if you would ensure this is done and that everyone reads the words. Some of it is on a 'need to know' basis and some of it will be 'nice to know' stuff – background material if you like.

"Also, remind all your staff about their responsibility for confidentially. And while I'm talking about that, remind your crews to be mindful of what they say over the police radio. Confidential info should not be transmitted that way. To update that old war-time saying, 'Loose lips sink investigations.'

"So, regarding the arsons, the only common thread linking the last three occasions I mentioned, is the time frames and that is pretty slim.

"Graveyard shift members should try to be extra watchful around this time and use the Daily Patrol Report that I'm going to discuss next. It will mean having to get their arses out of their comfortable patrol car seats a bit more often.

"One last thing which I feel is important if we wish to be more effective in our investigation efforts that I've already discussed with Staff Sergeant Hall, is a simple data collection system that I'd like to put into effect on a daily basis, starting in two weeks. I'll review it briefly with you now on the overhead. You don't have to write this down as I have a copy of the form for you. Let's review it," he said, turning on the overhead projector. "As you see, it includes all the tombstone data suitable for police purposes. If the people on your watches have at least grade one English, they can read and understand it. To reiterate, these forms *must* be turned in at the end of every shift.

"So, while the members are on patrol, they can jot this information down on their foolscap pads even while they are driving. At or near end of the watch, they can transfer the information to the DPR sheet. A GIS member will peruse them on a daily basis and we will retain the paperwork for three months. Please remind your people not to confuse this with notebook use. These will, of course, have to be used when criminal activity is found or suspected. Let's be diligent about the use of these reports. It's our best kind of contact with your patrol people and a good source of ready intelligence. Let's bear down on the arson thing.

"That's it for me. Take this information with you and peruse it. Let me know about any changes you propose in a day or two. I'll get back to you in three or four days. Any questions?"

Seeing there were none, Hall said his thanks and the meeting broke up.

35

At Parkton Detachment, the Inspector in Charge insisted on having property checks made at night. The written policy was that all reachable business premises were to be hand checked at least once on the graveyard shift. After each area had been checked, it was to be called in by radio – 'such and such checked and secure' – which would be recorded on the Radio Log together with the time.

It wasn't Rick Taylor's most favourite police activity but he knew it was essential – as much as for security as for public relations – so he religiously shook every door handle or pushed every door. Most business people left lights on inside to enable better viewing of the premises but not all, so he had to use his long, heavy, 4-cell flashlight. It could also come in handy in light of an imminent assault.

Statistically, at least in Parkton, approximately 97 percent of businesses were found locked, or 'secure' in police parlance. Just under the remaining 3 percent were found unlocked or insecure and the remainder were break-ins. With the several hundred places to be checked however, that tiny percent of B&E's as they were referred to, could amount to quite a few in this spread-out municipality.

When a place was found unlocked or broken into, the name of the business and the owner's name – usually found by checking the Business Permit or a receipt book – was called in.

The member would then have to wait, however long, for the sometimes grumpy owner to arrive at an ungodly hour, check the place out and lock up. Most of them were grateful however for the check but it did tend to waste police time. As well, it was considered much better for the night shift to find these situations, than the day shift to have to respond to them. It meant that the night shift had been lazy or sloppy in their checks and Sergeant Sterling did not want that kind of reputation for his watch. To that end, once in a while, he would take out an unmarked traffic car and check on the 'checkers' to ensure that they weren't 'BS-ing' about their duties. He didn't like to have to do this but wasn't sure how else to confirm what they did.

In the world of business checks, two things were considered by police to be 'better', which would be finding an actual break-in and 'best', a break-in in progress. In the first kind of incident, most owners/managers appreciated the call especially if there was damage and goods stolen. Some of them took the time to either call the detachment during the day to express their appreciation or to write in. This information was usually conveyed to the member concerned through his or her watch commander, together with a few nice words – a 'gum drop' note, as it was called. Of course, catching the perpetrator in the act was the 'cream on the cake' so to speak, and because it happened infrequently, led to a glowing feeling of accomplishment by the officer(s) and to uttering words to the bandit like "Ha! – gotcha, you son-of-a-bitch!" usually administered before giving the police caution.

Malls were quicker to check than shopping centres. Most of it was done by walking around the perimeter checking the solid rear doors. However, often there was no visibility inside, except for the glassed main entrances. Most businesses had an alarm system, silent or loud, and some were connected to an 'on-call' private security company. Mall stores were therefore seldom broken into, nevertheless hand-checking still had to be done.

It was usually the smaller shopping centres and small, separate independent businesses, such as service stations and convenience stores that were more prone to break-ins and, of course, hold-ups. Most of these were 'smash and grab' – noisy, but quick.

It's surprising what can be heard 'in the still of the night.' Rick

Taylor had learned from his mentor, a senior constable, about three years ago when he was transferred from training to this his first posting, about what he called 'strategic approaches' to conducting night checks.

"Make a mental game of it," the mentor had advised. "Play 'cat and mouse' games and assume that the bad guys are always out and about trying to outwit the police. Here's some suggestions to follow. As you approach the commercial area you want to check, douse your lights and pick a spot where you can do a visual of the area and *not* be seen yourself. Make sure no other vehicles are on the road when you do this. Turn off your motor, turn down your radio and get out of the car, look around and especially listen. As I said, sounds carry better in the night air. With little or no traffic in the area and the same with human activity, even small amounts of noise can be heard.

"So look and listen carefully for a couple of minutes. Are there vehicles parked on the lot or next to a business? What you will see, or not see, is sometimes weather-dependent. What do I mean by that?" he asked Taylor.

Taylor thought for a minute and said, "Well, one obvious thing would be frost on a vehicle, or lack of it, if it is a frosty night. That should tell if it has been recently parked and what is it doing in that position at this time of night?"

"Good. Any others?"

He thought again and reflected on 'dates' that he'd taken out in his car and how the windows became fogged up when they were stationary for a time, doing some 'heavy breathing.'

"Yep, we've all done that," agreed the constable. "You can also do the reverse of this kind of check. That is, drive right into the parking area, lights on, so as to be conspicuous and start doing your walk around. When you've finished, leave, and drive the PC a few blocks away, turn around and drive back again to a secluded area, lights off, where you can survey the business premises again. Why bother with this second check, Rick?"

He replied, "The obvious answer is that the crook thinks you've left the area and won't be back for a while, if at all, so he's 'home free' so to speak."

"That's right and once in a while, you may get lucky and see or hear the break-in take place and collar the guy. It's a beautiful feeling. To paraphrase Clint Eastwood, it'll 'make your night.' By the way," he said with a straight face, "I learned most of my police work from watching his *Dirty Harry* movies."

♦   ◊   ♦

It was an early Monday morning, statistically the quietest time of the week for most police agencies and Parkton wasn't any different. Four minor complaints so far on the night watch.

Constable Taylor was driving 10-Bravo-2 and Andy Oliver was riding shotgun. Because of the lack of 'business', they were early and had almost finished property checks in their patrol area tonight, the South Zone. This part of the City encompassed a large part of their zone, south of the City Centre and the main east-west railway line, large tracts of residential areas, malls and shopping centres, and two light industrial parks. The two police officers were currently on the eastern edge of the city where businesses were spaced out along the Trans-Canada Highway.

Coming up on their right was a company that sold rugs and carpets – called 'Rug City' of all things – housed in a fairly large building with a full-width glass front where the showroom was and cinder block walls down the sides and back.

Taylor drove into the front parking lot and while he was pulling up, his partner eyeballed the glass. It took a second or two for Oliver's mind to register that something was wrong – the glass door did not reflect the image of the police car in the bright store lights – the glass was missing! He was about to say, "Holy Shit!" but Taylor beat him to it and as he uttered these two immortal police words he saw someone inside – an individual momentarily frozen in place like a deer in headlights, at the sudden arrival of a police car.

"Andy, go 'round the back and I'll take the front. Radio me if he comes out that way," he said quickly as both baled out of the car on the run. On his way in he reported the situation to Dispatch on his portable radio.

Seeing the two policemen leave their car galvanized the individual into action. He turned around and ran further into the store, disappearing behind large rugs suspended on rollers from the ceiling and smaller rolls piled on the floor. Taylor, running through the glassless front door, almost slipped on the shards of plate glass lying scattered over a wide area. His brain subconsciously tucked that fact away for later review. Corporal Bibermann, South Zone NCO, advised he was on the way but got no acknowledgement.

As Taylor reached the hanging rugs area, where it was dark, he swung his flashlight in an arc searching for the culprit. He didn't want the bad guy to get past and escape out the front door. As Taylor was doing this, his radio came to life as his partner yelled, "Rick, he's trying to get out the back door!"

"Okay, I'm coming through. Hang in there!"

He made his way as fast as he could through a minefield of stuff left on the floor – wood pallets, scattered roll-ends, dollies and boxes – slowing him down a bit. At the end of his flashlight beam, some forty feet away, he could see the man pushing frantically at the crash bar across the door. Just as Taylor was reaching out to grab him, the door swung open quickly and the suspect fell through, right into the waiting arms of Andy Oliver. There was a brief tussle, then the man quickly gave up and was handcuffed.

Both their police portable radios cackled alive with the voice of Walt Bibermann saying he was at the front of the store and, "what's the situation?"

The person, now officially called the 'prisoner', was placed in the back of the corporal's car – the 'cage' as it was called because of a screen partitioning off the rear from the front seats – after he had told them he would take the man to the detachment. As well, in the interest of efficient use of manpower, he told Oliver to go with him and take out another car to continue patrols of the area while Taylor completed the investigation and waited for a company representative to arrive and secure the place and for the Identification Section member.

Before they left, Taylor couldn't help himself. He opened the back door of the corporal's car, leaned over it and said to the man, "Don't tell me. Let me guess. You've just bought a new home and a bunch of furniture. You're maxed out on your mortgage and credit card and your wife badly wanted a new Persian rug. You were just driving by this store and out of the goodness of your heart, impulsively stopped to do a bit of late night shopping for her, right? Why the Hell would you break into a RUG STORE!?" he finished in an incredulous voice. Anyway, he felt good about catching someone during a break-in – it 'made his night.'

36

Dick Ketchum was holding court – his own that is. For Ketchum, being centre stage and to have the rapt attention of all those around him, however large or small the group, was the elixir by which he lived. In the grand scheme of things, he was an actor in policeman's clothing, a person whose vocation was misplaced. He could have been a successful jester in the Court of King Arthur, or a stand-up comic on the *Tonight Show*. Ribald storytelling was his forte, often as not told in a loud and raucous voice, often interrupted with good humoured cries of 'No shit!' from his listeners. He would never actually lie about anything he told. It was more or less the truth, but with a certain degree of embellishment, that while sometimes obvious, never seemed to bother his audience; if anything, it was expected.

Life around the 'Incredible Hulk' as he was nicknamed, was always entertaining, and, on patrol, sometimes surprising. He was often the catalyst that held "A" Watch together in a collegial way, never imposing his seniority. When he was not on shift with them, life for the remainder was rather staid and quiet. All this is not to say that he was a fool. He was not. He was an astute and effective policeman.

The first morning he reported for duty on the watch, after being transferred from plainclothes duty on the General Investigation Section back to uniform, one of the wags on the squad said to him, "Dick, how many cows did they have to kill to make your Sam Browne?" He was just short of being rotund. At six feet, one inch, weighing 250 pounds, he had a commanding presence.

He filled his shirt to capacity to the point where the buttons threatened to pop. His short sleeves were skin tight and if he flexed his biceps, could rip them apart. Of course, there was an overhang on his belt. It was only natural that he was attached with that label. Some even said he looked like the legendary Hulk figure, especially when he got mad, which wasn't often.

With going on twelve years service, he was a senior member on the watch, and one of the more senior constables on the detachment. As such, he was assigned a recruit for the twelve months field training program, whereby the new man, just out of Regina, would 'learn the ropes.' This was a far cry from the old days when they were given a flashlight and a set of keys to a car and told to go and do police work. There was still a debate about the wisdom of which method was best. Older members were inclined toward the 'sink or swim' theory, be-lieving that if the member had any degree of spunk and intelligence, it would manifest itself in the end result of whatever he did and he would thereby survive, or go under. 'Babying' the man along would do nothing for his self-reliance and effectiveness when he was even-tually cut loose by his 'big brother' to face the world on his own. If the trainer had some bad habits, was lazy or too officious, inevitably the new man would pick up those habits and attitudes.

The not-so-senior set were inclined to the opposite view that the new people could be guided along by experienced members in a controlled training environment, and avoid some of the horrendous mistakes they had fallen into.

In any event, all trainers now had to take a one-week course in the philosophy and psychology of training their new charges which, in theory at least, was intended among other things, to reduce those negative possibilities. In any group discussion on the subject, reference would often be made, in an oblique but pointed way, about some of the 'monumental screw-ups' committed by the more senior members who had not had trainers. Actually, both arguments contained ele-ments of truth and, indeed, there was something positive to say for both methods, but any objective analysis would have to conclude that the 'buddy system' of training was superior.

In this instance, his buddy was a 22-year-old prairie boy of Dutch extraction, Henry 'Hank' Deleeuw. Initially, Ketchum was referred to as 'Dad', or together they were called the father-and-son team. This was partly because this was a euphemism applied to many training teams, simply because the senior man was quite often much older than his sidekick, but in this particular case, because Ketchum often use the words 'me son' as in, "C'mon, me son, let's hit the road."

In a way, Richard Haliburton Ketchum enjoyed having a recruit along because it gave him an opportunity to reach into his bottom-less bag of awe-inspiring 'war stories', inspiring at least to this young listener, and for Ketchum to relive, with relish, some of the more mo-mentous and some not so momentous, occasions in his police career.

Some incident, some face, some remark, some passing scenery seem to trigger one of his inexhaustible supply of stories and the recruit, if he had heard it before, would nod and grunt, 'Uh huh' or 'Yeah' or 'You're kidding' out of deference to his partner's seniority, as well as for his feelings. An occasional sideways glance by Deleeuw would reveal a look which said, "Christ, you must be getting senile, you've told me that bloody story three times already!' Even if the re-cruit was so bold as to say that, it wouldn't faze Ketchum, who would plunge headlong into another epic experience.

Ketchum had always tried to keep his middle name to himself, and just used the 'H' when necessary, but when the watch command-er inadvertently left one of Ketchum's personal documents showing his full name on his desk for a few minutes, the secret was out.

"Haliburton! What the hell kind of name is that?" someone asked him, and he mumbled something about his old man gave him the name because he was born there, in Ontario.

And so it came to pass that Dick H. Ketchum started training his third recruit.

"Okay, me son, let's go. I'll show you some of the sites of our fair city and introduce you to some of its citizens," emphasizing the last word. Grabbing a portable radio from the rack, the father and son team went into the parking lot and climbed into Ketchum's pride and joy, his brand new Ford LTD patrol car, labelled 10-Bravo-6. Putting their hats on the top of the back rest between them and the rear of the car, they prepared to depart. Ketchum checked the 12-gauge shotgun mounted in the vertical position on the right side of the transmission hump, making sure four rounds were in the magazine and none in the breech.

This was contrary to policy, it requiring that a round would be left in the spout, safety on, but Ketchum thought that too damned unsafe, with some of the idiots he had known in the past, and besides, if necessary, he could pump one in and aim the gun before you could blink an eye. He was brought up with guns and was an avid hunter.

"Well, the heavy artillery's okay, and the last guy left some gas in the tank, so I guess we can roll. Tell Radio we're 10-8."

Duly instructed, Deleeuw took the hand mic off the hook near the ashtray, turned the squelch button to check the volume and said, "Dispatch, Bravo-6, 10-8, Ketchum and Deleeuw, Centre."

Centre, in this case, was largely the downtown core of the City, referred to as the 'Zoo' because it was the gathering place, especially at night, for all the human 'animals' and where much of the heavy action was.

Hank was almost as big as Dick and when they got out of the patrol car, they looked like they meant business. They were detailed to the Centre Zone for a week in the absence Gordon Finch and Al Burns, one on Leave and the other on a Constable's Advanced Course in Vancouver.

It was a beautiful summer morning, with a clear blue sky and the promise of being a warm day. Ketchum eased into the morning traffic, saying to Deleeuw, "Hank, have you written a traffic ticket yet?"

"Yeah, last week, Dick, when you were away and I was out with Corporal Hawkes, I wrote a guy up for a stop sign."

"Wow! You really were busy, eh. Well, I'll show you a few spots where you can pick 'em off anytime."

So Ketchum took him down the main street and showed him all the 'No Left Turn 7 A.M. – 9 A.M. Monday-Friday' signs, and by eight, they had knocked off a half dozen drivers who took the chance. At 9:15, after school patrols, it was time for coffee with the members in a couple of other cars, and another session of either bitching or story telling. If it was payday, the mood was generally more magnanimous among them and they might play the game of 'guess the correct number' which really meant that you had to avoid calling the right number because that meant you lost, and paid!

After coffee, it was back to the office to write up a couple of minor complaints they had attended, and then to the Court House for a 10:30 trial.

In this case, Ketchum had arrested a man for driving a motor vehicle while impaired by alcohol and for refusing to give a breath sample when taken in to the breathalyzer room. The matter was now six months old and the constable had not seen the accused since the night of the offence, and then only the one time. While a camera was set up to take pictures of people charged with criminal offences, often it was not working or there was no film left. Sometimes too, over a long period of time, a person's appearance might change. A man might have grown a beard or shaved one off. A woman could be wearing a wig when picked up, or conversely, wear one on the day she appeared in Court, so the photographs were not always infallible in identifying an accused person later on.

Having lost a similar case sometime before because he was unable to positively identify the driver in Court, he now made it his business to approach an accused outside the Courtroom. He did this by simply calling out the name and when the person responded, Ketchum would introduce himself, whether necessary or not, and say something like, "Hi, I'm Constable Dick Ketchum. You no doubt remember me, I suppose. How are you today?"

If at all possible, he would indicate somehow to the person that he wanted him or her to stand up and walk along with him and talk. As he explained to Deleeuw, he would observe the person's general demeanour and physical condition, even getting close enough to smell breath.

"Why do all that again?" asked Hank. "You already know what his condition was like the night you arrested him. Isn't that enough?"

"To make sure I've got the right person," he answered, "and for comparison purposes. You see, I give his physical condition and attitude on the date of the offence in my evidence-in-chief – you know what that is, eh?" – a question to which his partner nodded.

"Okay. So when the Crown Counsel is finished with my evidence, I'm turned over to the Defence Lawyer, right?" Without waiting for a response, he continued, "Well, you sit in on today's trial and maybe you'll see what I mean."

And Deleeuw did see what he meant. It was almost as though it was a prophecy coming true, as he listened to the following exchange between Ketchum and the Defence Counsel.

"Now, Constable, you've explained at length concerning the physical condition and attitude of my client. You said his eyes were bloodshot, speech slurred, clothing disarranged, a strong smell of alcohol on his breath, and that he was insulting and uncooperative with you. Those last two things bother you, don't they?"

"No, Sir, they don't. I'm quite used to them."

"Why bring that out in your evidence then?"

"Because it's been my past experience, particularly with people under the influence of alcohol, that their inhibitions are relaxed and they often become belligerent. When they are sober, they don't, at least not often or to the same extent," replied Ketchum.

"I see. Had you ever met the accused before?"

"No, Sir."

"So you don't know what kind of a person he was before the night in question?"

"That's correct," he replied.

"Have you met the accused since you arrested him on January 16th?" the Defence Counsel continued.

"Yes."

"When?"

"Today."

"Where was this?"

"Outside the Courtroom in the hallway."

"Did you speak with him?"

"Yes, I did," replied Ketchum.

"I have no further questions of this witness, Your Honour," Defence Counsel quickly said, realizing he was putting himself into a checkmate position with his questions.

This was the moment for Anne Blair, the Crown Counsel, to rise up and say, "I have some re-examination, Your Honour."

With a slight nod from the Judge, she then asked Ketchum the kinds of questions he hoped she would.

"When you spoke to the accused today, Constable, did you notice anything about him as opposed to the last occasion you saw him?"

"Yes, I did."

"Objection, Your Honour, she's leading the witness," Defence Counsel quickly interjected, "and besides, this line of testimony is not relevant here."

"You raised the issue, Counsellor. Miss Blair, what's the purpose of your re-exam, and you were leading a bit," the Judge asked, knowing full well what the answer would be.

Blair, in turn, knowing full well that the Judge knew the purpose of her further examination, nevertheless had to respond, and said, "The constable's evidence might show very distinct differences between the accused's behaviour and appearance on those two separate occasions, Your Honour, from which certain inferences may be drawn."

"Very well. Your objection is overruled, Mister Johnston. Miss Blair, continue, but be careful, please," the Judge replied.

"Thank you, Your Honour. Let me re-phrase the question, Constable. At the time of his arrest, you testified that the accused appeared to be heavily under the influence of alcohol, was staggering and extremely obnoxious. You described certain words spoken to you by the accused including two words telling you to leave. Did you see and hear similar things today when you spoke to him?"

"No, I did not," replied Ketchum, trying his hardest to keep the smile off his face.

Later, after lunch, when the two were back in the patrol car again, Ketchum asked Deleeuw what he thought of the case.

"I had to admire the Prosecutor there. She had a neat way of introducing the driver's language telling you to fuck off without saying it. Anyway, you were right, but surely this kind of verbal sparring doesn't go on like that in every case, does it?"

"Oh yeah. It's a Defence Lawyer's duty to 'get at the truth of the matter,' as they would say, but if they can sink your testimony, and your credibility too, they'll do it every time. But you can see what I mean about this business of comparisons, eh? Some of the younger lawyers fall into that trap before they realize it. The more experienced ones are more subtle. They'll continue with a line of seemingly innocuous and easy to answer questions, then zing one at you that you can only answer one way, which might tend to discredit or even destroy the evidence you've already given. Your credibility can suffer a bit. It's worse if it's a jury trial. So you've got to pause and really think about each question before you answer. You can get some of them pissed off at you by saying, 'I'm not sure I understand your question' or 'Could you repeat the question, please?'

"It's an adversarial position you're in, strictly cat-and-mouse tactics. Anyway, if you feel you can't mentally compete with that kind of rhetoric, then just play it straight and don't volunteer anything more than you are asked. If the Lawyer continues to badger you, either the Prosecutor or the Judge, if they're worth their salt, will jump in and get him off your back. The more often you go to Court, the more effective and reliable witness you'll become and eventually develop a reputation as an honest and competent witness, one that most Counsel won't 'tamper with' on the stand."

"Yeah, I suppose you're right. By the way, what did the accused get? Remember I had to leave before the case was concluded."

"Three hundred for the impaired, three hundred for fail-to-blow, six months suspension of his right to drive, and to take the drunk driving course. Judge even told him he was unimpressed with his behaviour. Unimpressed! – hardly the word in this case. Christ, I'm unimpressed with my salary! Good thing I wasn't sitting on the bench or the son of a bitch would've got three months in the slammer and a year's license suspension."

"So he did get to you, eh?" asked Deleeuw, with a slight smile on his face.

"Yeah. You know, in spite of all the training we get and the amount of patience we try to develop, and with the realization that it's often the liquor that talks, there's always some asshole that gets under your skin. I defy anyone to go through even one year of active police service without once having the strongest desire to flatten somebody out. It's at times like that when it's good to have another member along to act as a restraint on your behaviour, and your mouth. In any case, you can't say that in Court."

They fell silent for a while, a rather unusual event for Ketchum, but he was preoccupied in this instance with reliving his vexing experience with the drunk driver and the events as they unfolded in Court. What took his mind off the subject, as was often the case, was something he spotted across the street from them in the downtown.

"Jesus, would you look at that!" he exclaimed, nodding his head out the right window. It was a warm afternoon and the beautiful woman he was looking at was dressed only in a brief halter top and short pink shorts. Gorgeous!

Deleeuw shouted, "Watch out, Dick!" and Ketchum braked quickly, avoiding another intersection police car accident. After he regained his breath, Deleeuw said, "You know, for a fairly small city, this place has a lot of good lookin' women roaming the streets."

"Second the motion," replied Ketchum, carefully going for another quick glance.

37

"Radio, any car on or near the Reserve area?" the dispatcher asked.

Silence for a few moments.

"Bravo-3, I'm on River Road close to the bridge. I can be there in three – four minutes," responded Joe McKillen.

"Ten-four – attend please. Report of fire in progress at a warehouse complex on Tundra Road. Fire Department on its way, please meet."

"Bravo-3, I think I can see the smoke from across the river. Be there shortly."

It was 10:30 Sunday evening. Sergeant Sterling said he'd meet McKillen there in 10 minutes or so.

The first of an eventual six fire trucks had arrived ahead of Bravo-3 at the Modern Furniture store, and their preliminary finding, after entering through the front workshop door, which they found had been forced, was that the whole of the interior was filled with thick, toxic-smelling smoke requiring the firemen to wear their breathing apparatus, and proceed in pairs with extreme caution. Smoke rises, of course, and at the six-foot level from the floor, they could just make out a large glow ahead of them indicating the source of the fire. The senior of the two men radioed this information to his unit, who by now had hoses at the door, ready to enter.

Constable McKillen arrived and spoke to the Deputy Fire Chief who had just got there ahead of him. His first words were, "Is there anyone in the building?"

"We're presuming not, as there's no vehicle in the parking lot but we've had no time for a real search yet."

"Have you ever been in here?" asked McKillen.

"No, we don't know the layout but it looks like an inferno inside. Don't know yet if we can save it," replied the Chief.

"Okay, I've asked our office to advise the owner and get him here."

When the police dispatcher got back to Bravo-3, she said, "Be advised owner on way. He confirms the presence of a night watchman, Jimmy Eagle, who is supposed to be on the premises upstairs at the end."

"Shit!" McKillen said to himself. He found the Chief in the bustle of all the activity and told him, and asked if they could begin looking for the man.

"Jesus, that's not good news. Okay, as soon as the owner arrives we'll find out how to get there from here. In the meantime, I'll tell the crew inside. It's hotter than a bitch in there and toxic. Visibility is almost zero. We'll do our best. As you can see, we've got a number of fans going at each of the building exits to draw the smoke out but they are only marginally effective for a time," he explained. "Most of the remaining smoke will rise and gradually dissipate but that could take some time."

It took an hour to get the flames out and the source of the fire determined. A preliminary investigation of this indicated no apparent reason for accidental combustion – no electrical outlets nearby and no other heat source.

Sergeant Sterling was on scene and had a strong feeling that this was the work of their serial fire man. In thinking about this, he called Shelley Prentice patrolling the North Shore and asked her to check on Rifell's residence.

Identification Section members attended at the fire scene but could do little until the all clear was given and it was safe to enter.

The building shell was intact. It was constructed of corrugated aluminum and was largely untouched by the flames. The fire, in itself, was not large and the flames just barely reached the high ceiling. A huge, heavy plastic divider, in three sections, that ran from floor to ceiling, had burned, creating thick, black and toxic smoke filling the interior.

The owner, Ralph Simmons, arrived in the parking lot amid a swirl of dust and squeal of brakes, visibly agitated, not just because of the damage – much of the finished and unfinished furniture was damaged by fire, smoke and water and was largely covered by insurance anyway – but particularly because of the possible loss of life and the fact that he would have 25 unemployed people on his hands.

Also waiting in the parking lot was Jimmy's mother who had hobbled to the building from her house on hearing the sirens and seeing the fire trucks stop at Modern – where Jimmy worked!

It was not until about midnight that firemen were able to climb the stairs to the loft area – untouched by the fire – and found Jimmy. He was lying on the platform with his head and outstretched arms hanging down over the top step – dead.

The news was conveyed to Mrs. Eagle who collapsed and to Mr. Simmons, who buried his head in his hands and shook his head. He did not know Mrs. Eagle but presumed it to be her and approached her to confirm this fact and knelt down to try to comfort the elderly woman for a minute or two after she had been revived by one of the firemen. He asked her if she would like a ride home but she shook her head and said that she'd wait until they brought Jimmy out.

By now, the front of the building had been cordoned off with yellow 'Police – Do Not Enter' tape. Removal of the body and mop-up operations were over by 3 a.m.

Constable McKillen was asked to remain on duty at the site pending the arrival of the Fire Investigator and members of GIS at seven o'clock. Jimmy Eagle's body was taken to the morgue at the hospital for later autopsy.

♦   ◊   ♦

Mark Rifell saw the first fire truck as it came across the North
Thompson Bridge.

'Time to go,' he thought and pulled out of the parking lot, going east toward the north highway, which, if you turned right off the
Reserve land, could bring you back into the City. He wanted to stay
away from the police and fire presence arriving from the west. He felt
'satisfied' with his work. Still a fair amount of traffic on the roads, he
noted, all the better for me. He was famished and fancied a thick crust
pizza, liberally smothered in mozzarella cheese, covered with pep-
peroni sausage, tomato, mushrooms, olives and red and green peppers.
Couldn't wait to sink his teeth into its hot deliciousness. He'd try to
save a piece for his friend and fellow work-mate, Ronnie Sheppard.

Stopping downtown, he fulfilled his gastronomic wish at the
Boston Pizza on Victoria Street, washing the food down with a large
Dr Pepper. Unable to eat more than three quarters of the pie – it was
a large – he had it doggie-bagged, paid and left, making his way to his
buddy's rented condo downtown.

♦   ◊   ♦

Constable Prentice had driven by Rifell's residence early in the shift,
around nine, saw the truck and made note of it and the date – April
9 – on her DPR sheet. When she was later asked by her sergeant to
make another check at 10:30 p.m. after the fire had been reported on
the Reserve, she was dealing with a noise complaint and was not able
to drive by until close to 11:00. Everyone, it seemed, was busy. When
she did, his vehicle was not there and it did not reappear for the remainder of the night. All cars were asked to BOLF but by the end of
watch on Monday morning, it was not seen.

The Identification Section constable was not able to glean much
physical evidence at the building. Examination of the tool mark

impression on the door and the door frame revealed it to be quite distinct and he was able to get a good, clear photo and measurement but its probative value as evidence was limited. Most tire irons and crow bars were of standard make and size and difficult to compare unless there was a distinction, such as a nick at the sharp end. No fingerprints were found on the master switch in the tool room, however, faint imprints of several pairs of footwear in the floor dust were visible and similarly photographed.

The point of ignition of the fire was minutely examined and yielded nothing but a slight residue of a wax-like substance, which was scraped from the blackened concrete floor and bagged.

◆ ◇ ◆

On Monday morning at 06:45, Sgt. Myles Lockhart, i/c 'C' Watch, which was arriving on duty, was filled in about the fatal fire and asked if his North Shore crew could take a run by Rifell's place during the day. He had not been home last evening or night.

At 7 a.m., Sergeant Jones and Constable Todd had already been at work an hour, reviewing the fire reports – there were two: the Fire Department's and their own.

"Let's apply for a search warrant for Rifell's place first thing this morning. Is he at work or home today, Ralph?"

"I think he's on the afternoon shift. Let me confirm that." Checking the file he said, "Yes."

"Great," said Jones. "Lockhart must have a car in the area."

◆ ◇ ◆

An 08:30 meeting was scheduled with Inspector Edwardson, the Operations NCO, Sergeant Jones and Constable Todd. The purpose was to consider the next investigative steps to be taken in what had finally turned into something they had feared – the death of an innocent person. Of the four people present, Trevor Jones probably felt the worst. Serious crime was mostly his squad's responsibility at this detachment and he couldn't shake the feeling that he could have done more, earlier, to prevent this tragedy. He found that he was continually second-guessing himself: 'Should I have brought Rifell in for questioning?' 'Should I have searched his residence earlier?' 'Should I have maintained a much tighter surveillance?'

"Get the Warrants Forms ready and signed," directed the Inspector.

◆ ◇ ◆

"I'm going to hold my nose while I sign your Application for a Search Warrant, Constable Todd. Your reasons seem a bit slim and I'm not entirely certain they would withstand approval if challenged, but in view of the circumstances of this fire I'm going to allow it," said Justice of the Peace Charles Stewart at his residence, as he scribbled his signature at the bottom of the two forms and stamping his authority underneath. He was the judge on call for this purpose.

"Thank you, Sir," said Todd.

◆ ◇ ◆

Rifell was observed arriving home at 10:30 a.m. by the surveillance car and the information passed to Sergeant Jones. He told Todd to take a 'uniform' along with him.

At 11:10, the two police officers arrived at the residence and banged on the basement door. The surveillance car left.

It was opened by a young, slim, dark-haired male, about five-nine tall, with a bad case of acne on his face. The strong smell of sausages and garlic wafted out, suggesting that breakfast was being prepared. Upon seeing the uniformed constable and the man in plainclothes, Rifell's eyes noticeably widened and he looked apprehensive. A passing thought told him to slam the door, overtaken a second later by another thought that said, 'Calm down, you can bullshit your way through this,' knowing full-well the purpose of the visit.

"Mr. Rifell? Mark Rifell?" asked the guy in civvies.

"Yeah, what's the matter?"

"I have a Search Warrant for your residence. Here's a copy for you. We'd like to talk to you for a few minutes and explain. May we come in, please?"

"I guess so," Rifell said hesitatingly and stood aside to let them in, profoundly unhappy about the intrusion.

As they entered, the GIS member introduced himself and his uniformed partner. "Are you in the middle of making breakfast?"

Inside the residence, the smell was noticeably stronger – 'pungent' didn't do it justice – to the point where both members were thinking maybe they should return later to give the odour time to dissipate, but of course, it was too late.

Rifell took them into his tiny living room, not offering them a seat. Given the untidy look of the place, the police officers didn't mind.

"We'll try not to keep you long so you can get your meal. Mark, would you mind telling me where you were last night?"

"Why do you want to know?"

"We're investigating a fire on the Indian Reserve."

"I was with a friend."

"All night? Was it a girlfriend?"

"No, it was a guy I work with at the mill."

"What's his name? We'd like to verify that."

"Ronnie Sheppard."

"Where does Ronnie live?"

"On Dominion Street, 1221."

"Phone number?"

"He don't have no phone."

"Alright, why don't you finish your breakfast?"

Rifell picked at it for a minute or two, then laid his knife and fork on the plate. His appetite had disappeared.

While this conversation was going on, the uniformed member took a cursory look around the room which showed no overt evidence until he noted a large red textbook on the cluttered side table beside a ratty brown corduroy couch. He read the title – *Criminal Investigations*. 'Hmm, interesting,' he thought as he picked it up and started to leaf through it. He found a bookmark at Chapter 20, entitled *Arson* and noticed several paragraphs outlined in yellow marker. 'Bingo!' he thought. This was the first item seized along with a yellow marker found lying on the small wooden coffee table. In a drawer under the kitchen counter they found a street map of Greater Parkton with a half dozen locations outlined in red pen including the sites of the four arsons.

In the tiny bedroom, on the clothes closet wall hung *Parkton News* photographs and accounts of the three previous fires – Thistle Heights, Surplus Harry's and the Commercial Block. Last night's fire would undoubtedly be in today's later edition, the article and photo too late to assume its position on this gallery.

In the kitchen pantry on a shelf the following items were found: a ball of thin hemp string, a package of small birthday candles, a box of 'Eddie' brand matches and a twelve-set box of latex gloves, opened. These were photographed in place, removed from the shelf and bagged. The gloves were counted and eight pairs remained.

Near the back door, on the floor, a small pile of newspapers was noted and photographed. Rifell owned three pairs of footwear – black oxfords, sand-coloured steel-toed work boots and the runners he was currently wearing. The shoes and boots were seized for later footprint comparison purposes. All of these findings were written into the officer's notebook. At this time, Mark Rifell, with the evidence gathered, was now a suspect, and officially cautioned.

When the two policemen were finished in the house, Rifell was asked to accompany them to the police office.

"What if I don't want to?" he said.

"Well," he was told, "you don't have a choice, I'm afraid."

He acquiesced, was handcuffed, placed in the back of the marked police car to wait while the officers checked his vehicle. No evidence was found but the plainclothes member did notice the absence of a red plastic gasoline can, this having been mentioned as being strapped down in the box, on one of the night checks mentioned in the DPR Reports. Duly noted.

Rifell was returned to the detachment and placed in the holding cell. Todd telephoned Hannah Priestly at the mill to tell her he was sorry but that Mr. Rifell, the dust control engineer, would not be reporting for work later today. He would explain the situation to her later, he said, and she replied that she'd looked forward to that.

♦   ◇   ♦

"How are you going to do this interview, Ralph?" asked Sergeant Jones.

"Well, I thought I'd use the 'Come-to-Jesus' approach. He's Catholic and it might work. I'll go in with the file" – the name RIFELL was written in large black marker pen letters across the front of the thick red folder – "and just place it on the table. Shouldn't have to refer to it. I know the details pretty well. Our evidence is 'okay' but it would be nice to seal the case with an admission."

He and the sergeant had just reviewed the file and Todd was primed to go into the interview room to talk to the suspect.

"Alright, good luck."

38

Entering the interview room, Constable Ralph Todd said, "Hi, Mark," and re-introduced himself. "How are you? Okay?" he added, sitting down on a wheeled chair at a corner of the desk nearest Rifell. Part of his interview techniques training had suggested this method, to appear to be less formal, but at the same time a bit intimidating due to close proximity to the suspect – 'In his face without appearing to be in his face,' as the instructor put it.

"Okay," Rifell said, definitely not looking okay.

"Would you like some water, coffee? – Water? Okay."

Returning with a glass of water, Todd continued, "I'd like to have a chat with you about these fires. That alright?" he asked, nodding his head.

Rifell said, "I don't have nothing to say."

"That's okay, you don't have to say anything. You'll notice a tape machine on the table and I'm going to turn it on just so we get everything recorded accurately. I'll introduce myself and you before we begin. I do have a formality to follow. I know you've already been cautioned but I'd like to do it again to make sure you understand your rights and to get you to sign the caution at the top of the Statement Form. All that does is confirm that you have read the caution and understand what it says – nothing more. Okay with that?"

A nod.

Todd pressed the tab down and introduced himself and Rifell.

"I'm going to read it to you first," and he did so. "Do you understand what I've just read?'

"Yes," replied Rifell.

"Alright, would you please now read the Caution on the Statement Form and again, if you understand it, sign to that effect and put today's date below. It's April 10, 1989."

Rifell complied. No request for a lawyer was made.

"I see your original surname was Rifelli, with an 'i' – must be of Italian origin?"

Another nod.

"You must be Catholic then?"

"Yes."

"Me too. Which church do you attend?"

"None right now."

"Oh, that's too bad. I go to Saint Joseph's Parish. Try to go to Confession every week if I can – you know, get the bad stuff off my chest. Funny how that makes you feel better, isn't it?" said Todd, nodding his head again.

A slight nod of agreement by Rifell.

"Jeez, by the time you go back to church you'll need a couple of hours of the Father's time!" Todd said with a chuckle.

Rifell gave him a funny look and Todd quickly said, "Just kidding, just kidding," and with a smile, momentarily patted one of Rifell's clenched fists resting on the table.

"Okay, Mark. I'd like to chat with you about the fires over the past few months, the three small ones last fall and the four recent large fires.

"It's the last one that has me concerned. As you know now, someone was in the building. Mark, would it be fair to say that you took care not to set a fire with a person in the building?"

No answer.

"Would it be fair to say then that you *didn't* care if someone died?"

"No!" Rifell replied quickly, his voice quavering and his eyes wide open. He stopped speaking, quickly putting his hands up to his mouth as if to staunch a flow of words. He realized what he'd said and remained quiet for a few seconds, his mind working overtime. Todd wisely allowed him this time to think.

Rifell continued, "I didn't want to hurt no one," he said, looking into the constable's eyes as if seeking understanding and the policeman, catching the import of what he said and the look, said nothing and let him continue. "There was supposed to be no one in that building. I cased it several times and never saw a light upstairs at night."

"That's alright, Mark, take it easy. That's a good thing in your defence that you took care not to hurt anyone. I mean, no one died in your first three big fires, did they? So that goes to show how careful you were. Get you more water? No?"

Todd said, "Can we continue now, Mark? Shouldn't be much longer with you I would think. You know, I read you as a sharp guy, thoughtful and careful about what he does. Am I right?"

"Yeah, I guess so."

"I'm kind of intrigued, mystified if you like, about how you got started and how you went about planning and doing these activities. Care to tell me about that?"

Taking another drink from his glass, Rifell thought for a minute and said, "Well, I guess I've always been attracted by fire. My mom let me strike a match and light her cigarette sometimes. I was only about 5 or 6. I used these long wooden matches. I used to play with them in my room when she was not in the house."

"Let me ask you something. Where was your dad?"

"Oh, he buggered off and left us when I was about four, I think."

"So your mother brought you up. Is her name Rifelli?'

"Not now. She changed it back to her maiden name, Rossilini, long time ago."

"Where's your mother live?"

"Oh, she found another guy after I left school and moved to Vancouver."

"Okay, go on, please."

"Well, one day when I was a bit older, I accidentally lit some newspapers and they scorched the rug in my bedroom and the whole house stunk of smoke. When my mom come home she beat me with a belt and wouldn't feed me for a day."

"Did that make you stop?"

"No, I took the matches outside and played with them when she was away."

"So, is it true to say that you've always liked fire, flames?"

"I guess so."

"Alright, I'm going to ask you an important question now. What made you light all these fires?"

Mark thought about the question for a few seconds and replied, "I think it may have been because of a book I was reading that I found in a second-hand store. It was a college textbook, you know, the one the officers took, and it was called *Investigation Methods* – or *Techniques* – something like that. I bought it because at one time I was interested in becoming a police officer and I like police and detective shows on TV.

"I found a whole chapter dealing with arson and it told how people set fires and what they did to stop from being caught. I read the chapter several times and decided to test out what the book said about starting fires – the various ways. I experimented with a fuse delay method and it worked real good."

"Yes, we found the remains of the one in the clothing store fire. Quite well done. By the way, did you get that from the textbook? We noted you underlined several sentences in the arson chapter that we took from your place today, along with all the newspaper photos on your wall."

"No. I figured it out on my own," Rifell replied.

"Just a few more questions to complete my investigation, okay?"

"Uh huh."

"Why did you pick these particular buildings?"

He shrugged his shoulders. "No real reason. I just wanted big fires."

"How did you go about making sure no one was in any of these buildings?"

"Well, I checked each place out at least three times, except the ladies store, once in daylight and twice at night. At night, I sat in my truck near the buildings and watched for anyone going in or out of them. They were all empty by eight o'clock."

"Alright. Tell me about the warehouse fire on the Reserve. Did you case that place? And tell me exactly what you did."

"I checked a lot of places and finally chose the Modern Furniture store because it made and stored house furniture – you know, tables, chairs, bedroom suites, kitchen cabinets, etcetera – easy to burn. Many of the other buildings on the Reserve were not like this one. Either they had nothing to burn or were hard to get into and often they were surrounded by high steel fences. This place had a mesh fence around the back yard, but there was a large parking lot in front of the building entrance, which was unfenced, of course.

"I walked inside one day and told the salesman I was interested in buying some furniture as I was getting married soon, so he let me look around. This building had a sprinkler system, so I carefully checked the place and found the power switch to turn it off in the tool room to my right when you enter the front door. There was also an alarm breaker. The room was empty when I checked it. The offices for the store were located on the upper floor at one end of the building."

"How could you tell that for sure?" asked Todd.

"Well, I could see people working up there, answering phones and walking out with paper in their hands. I hung around for a few minutes to make sure that's what they were – offices. Half of the ground floor was used for making the stuff and the other for a show room. There were long, floor-to-ceiling thick plastic sheets hanging down to the ground and I figured they were there to keep dust in the part where they were making the furniture."

"Were there any windows in the upper office area?"

"No, I didn't see none on that end of the building, just on the inside that overlooked the main floor area."

"Okay. You say that you checked the building out in the evening when it was dark. Were there any lights on inside the building?"

"No, at least, I couldn't see none."

"Did you look through the front glass door?"

"Yes, but I couldn't see nothing. It was dark. I shone my flashlight in but the light didn't reach very far in."

"What time of night were you there when you entered the place?"

"Oh, around ten o'clock. It was quiet and there was no traffic."

"Were there any vehicles parked outside in the driveway area?"

"No. That's why I really thought no one was inside."

"Where did you park your vehicle?"

"Down the road a bit. Pulled it into another business parking lot. It was pitch black – no street lights."

"Tell me how you got into the place."

"To the right of the main entrance, there was a wooded side door. I jimmied it open with a tire iron. It was the tool room. As soon as I got in I turned off the sprinklers and alarm and then went into the area where they make the furniture to set the fire. It was dark inside with only one small light on over a work bench at the back.

"Setting and lighting the fire was a cinch. There was lots of wood all over the place – lots of small pieces in a big bin. I dipped the three-foot piece of string into the gas container and set out the fuse. As I did before, I scrunched up the newspaper I carried in with me, and then took the pieces of wood and made a pyramid over the whole fuse area, you know, out along the top of the string, poured gas all over the wood blocks and then over to other furniture in the area. I guess I really didn't need a fuse for this one – there was no one around. Anyway, I made one and lit it. I threw the empty plastic gas can and my rubber gloves on top of the wood. I threw my overshoes into a bush area as I drove away."

"Can you remember just where you did that?"

"Not sure. Might be able to."

"Did you stay and watch the fire?"

"Yeah. I ran back to my truck and watched from there for a few minutes to make sure the fire was going and left before the fire trucks arrived."

"Just one last question, Mark. We noted that these fires were set exactly six weeks apart. Can you tell me why that was?"

"No. I just felt like doing them when I did, that's all."

After a moment or two of silence and a change of expression on his face, Rifell said to the policeman, "Constable, how much time do you think I'll get for this?"

Todd replied, "Mark, there's no way I can give you a definitive answer. The Prosecutor will make submissions – statements – to the Judge as will your Defence Lawyer. What I can tell you is that the *Criminal Code* allows Prosecutors to proceed with more than one criminal offence of a similar nature on one Information or Charge sheet. These are known as 'Counts' meaning one Count for each offence committed. If the person is found guilty, the sentences imposed on each of the 'Counts' *can* be set 'concurrently – that is to say, to run together – or they can be imposed 'consecutively' – one after the other which can mean more time to serve. I can tell you that in my experience, the Courts generally impose concurrent sentences – joined together as one period of time but, like I say, not always. I'm sorry I can't give you an idea of the time you might have to serve, and I'm not allowed to speculate on that kind of thing anyway. You will most likely have a lawyer representing you and it's his job to advocate for you, in this case, 'speak to your sentence,' as it's called. Alright, Mark, just to briefly recap then…."

When the statement had been typed up, Rifell read it through, initialled each page and signed the last page in full which was then witnessed with Constable Todd's signature.

PART FOUR

39

It was a Sunday evening in early May. The days were getting long and the summer solstice would arrive in six weeks along with the long, hot dry summers. "A" Watch started its tour of duty at 1900 hours. After he had dispatched his fifteen members to their respective patrols, and cleared up some paper work, Sergeant Sterling decided to take a drive for an hour or so, leaving the office at eight-thirty while it was still light. The radio was quiet and there was no 'business' to speak of. His favourite place to go was west along the Trans-Canada Highway, about ten kilometres from downtown, and still within the City limits. Along here, the highway steadily rose to a plateau among the bare, high rolling hills. It was sage-brush country. He loved the aroma of this particular plant, especially after a rainfall which seemed to release the pungent smell even more and turned the brush from a dusty grey to a burnished jade green.

Unusually, there had been a light summer shower in the early evening, and as he rolled along the highway, windows down, he took in the beautiful scenery which included the Thompson River Valley and the lake off to his right. 'I could settle down here,' he thought.

Pulling into a gravelled area, he got out of the car and stretched his arms and legs, breathing deeply. Except for a light rippling breeze and the occasional cry of a circling Chukar bird looking for a place to settle down for the night, it was quiet, outside the car and inside, with no radio chatter – just the way he liked it.

The quiet was now and then interrupted with the sound of an approaching twenty-eight wheeler transport truck, slowing down as the driver saw the patrol car, even if it seemed that he wasn't speeding.

Sterling justified these drives with the knowledge that he was doing 'preventative' police work, which was true, of course. He wasn't 'stealing time,' as it were.

The evening sky to the west was streaked with thin, bright yellow, pink and orange cirrus clouds, interspersed with grey-blue stratus that gradually infused itself into the kaleidoscope of colours as the sun slowly set. It was fascinating to watch these beautiful changes. He thought it was almost surreal and worthy of a canvas.

Strangely, it left him feeling a bit melancholy, or did he feel that way before he arrived? He didn't know. In a few months he'd have completed twenty-five years of service when he would be forty-nine. He'd recently begun to contemplate what he should do with the rest of his life – stay on the Force until age sixty, or quit and find something else to do – an age-old dilemma for most people in the Public Service. Maybe this was a good moment to reflect on this.

He could serve another ten years for a fairly good pension and maybe get his staff sergeant's position. Lately, he'd noticed that doing General Duty police work, that nice euphemism used to describe doing almost any kind of police activity, and the vicissitudes of the job, were slowly eating around the edges of his life. 'Have I become a 'Jack of all trades and master of none?' he wondered.

For the most part, he still enjoyed the challenge of the work, and supervising people, but the 'same-old, same-old' recurrences were beginning to make him feel jaded. 'Maybe I need another challenge? What kind of work could I do, or get if I stayed in the Force to say age sixty and then quit? I'd be too late to embark on a long term career on civvy street. However, if I left now, I'd have at least fifteen years, to age sixty-five, in some other profession.' As he sat down in the patrol car, he reviewed his qualifications and experience.

He held an undergraduate degree in sociology which qualified him for teaching management subjects to mid-level ranks of Canadian police forces at the Canadian Police College in Ottawa. He'd enjoyed that job and was reluctant to leave after serving four years there, due to a time limit policy set by the Director. It was too bad because he'd felt competent and confident as an instructor. When he was transferred to Parkton, the Officer in Charge had asked him, because of his training expertise, to take over the role of the NCO in charge of Auxiliary Police recruitment and training for the detachment in addition of course to his main function as a watch commander.

As well, he was called by Division HQ to lecture occasionally at supervisory training courses in Vancouver. He'd enjoyed doing both these extra jobs, even though they did eat into his time off.

He'd also been involved in 'show business,' as he called it. Over one Christmas period, he'd been approached by the general manager of the local radio station to do a number of public service 'spots' on the air concerning safe driving issues. He had a good, clear, well-modulated voice, he was told. He also assisted in creating two video presentations, produced by the same station.

The first concerned impaired driving and the second was about drinking and driving at high school graduation time. It was a rather graphic account of a seventeen-year-old girl who was killed at age 17 while riding in her impaired boyfriend's car on grad night, and aptly called, *Please God, I'm only 17!* Sterling acted as the 'first officer on the scene' and, as he vividly recalled now, had to bend over the 'body' to close the 'dead' girl's open eyes. Surely this experience is worth some consideration for future employment, he asked himself sardonically.

He thought about his private life. He was making decent money. He and his wife had a nice house on a hill overlooking the City and the north valley. At night, the lights were pretty to look at, especially in the winter when they seemed to twinkle in the frosty darkness. Jocelyn was a secretary at the local college, again with good pay. They had two vehicles, one of which was a truck and camper which they used for longer trips into the United States.

They had it 'pretty good' in reality. Greg, his oldest, had started college this spring, studying surveying. He was out of town over the summer months, fighting forest fires in eastern British Columbia, for the Ministry of Forests. Jeff and Brad were still in school. 'Why change anything?' he thought. 'Am I looking for change for the sake of change – fields always look greener on the other side of the fence – or is my unrest deeper than that? What discontented animals we human beings are!'

As the bright pink sky deepened to blue-grey and night was slowly creeping in, he caught the gleam of the sun's corona in the last few seconds as it sank behind the mountains in the far distance.

Taking one last look and one last deep breath of the sagebrush, he put the car in gear and headed back into the City, feeling a bit better, but still slightly discontented.

40

'A' Watch was back on day shift, after three days off.

Arriving early, Sergeant Jack Sterling had briefly gone through the wad of complaints accumulated over this time period to bring himself up to date on what had happened and how it may affect his part of the operation, and noted something that disturbed him.

On the morning following their last night on night shift, three businesses in the downtown area had been broken into, one reported by a passing pedestrian on her way to work at eight — a front door smashed in. He knew that it's not possible to find all break-ins but obvious ones like this and the other two — both rear doors — absolutely should have been noticed. He checked the duty roster for Centre Zone and noted that Gordon Finch was responsible for this area unless Corporal Bibermann had changed him. He'd made arrangements this morning for Corporal Hawkes to see him regarding Constable Frank Smith on another matter and in view of his discovery about the break-ins, asked Bibermann to see him as well, after school patrols were over.

Sterling didn't like to interfere with his NCOs in how they operated their shifts. He let them run their own 'shows' but naturally kept an eye on how they did that and was reasonably satisfied with their performances. He had to do an annual appraisal of their work and knew that he had a couple of conscientious people.

He suspected that they too, didn't like to interfere unnecessarily with their constables — 'let them take a long leash,' as Dog Masters are wont to say. They were mature enough people and would resent over-supervision.

Personnel matters were always delicate and required sensitivity in handling – not an easy task as he'd learned at the CPC in Ottawa.

"Have a seat, Al," he said as Hawkes entered the sergeant's office. "Shouldn't take long. Haven't had much of a chance to talk to you lately. Is everything going okay?" – by which he meant everything; police work and if necessary, his private life. He'd found that it was generally more the case of difficulties with the latter that led to problems at work. Asking the question like that gives the individual the opportunity, if inclined, to venture into discussing family issues, provided there is a degree of comfort and an understanding about confidentiality.

Sterling had tried to mediate a few husband/wife, girlfriend/boyfriend problems, with mixed results. Police personnel were not at all eager to go through counselling, fearing they would be viewed by their compatriots as being unable to handle their home situations, or, that it was no one's business and because of that, moderating such incidents was generally more difficult than with civilian cases. Until recently in the Force, no family counselling at the elementary level had been available other than through the provincial Ministry of Health.

Responding to his question, Hawkes said, "Sure, everything is fine with me, thanks. You wanted to discuss Frank Smith, I imagine?"

"Yeah. I know you've only been back a week from your two-week supervisory course in Vancouver. You may not have noticed Smith's behaviour, or rather, his demeanour."

"No, can't say I have or it's not apparent when I'm around him, and we have been run off our feet, as you know. Frank's an even-headed kind of guy and seems to get on okay with the other members on the North Shore. Can you be more specific?"

"That's the problem. It's hard to find something specific. As you've learned, trying to discern human behaviour is not easy and I find myself using words like morose, argumentative, quiet, maybe even sullen, to describe his behaviour lately. I'm wondering if he's got marital problems, Al."

"If he does, it's not evident to me."

"How about financial?"

"Same thing. I've no way of knowing, but I shouldn't think so, with Janice working at a responsible position with Bartwell & Company – unless they are overspending, or she is. The business clothes she wears are not cheap."

"Alright. As much as you can, I'd like you to keep a closer eye on the man. If his behaviour continues, say for the next two, three weeks, get back to me and either you, if you feel up to it, or me, will take him out for a coffee and start digging. Maybe try to double him up with Al Kart or Joe McKillen, and take a reading. I know Shelley Prentice prefers to patrol alone. What do you say?"

"Okay, Jack, I'll let you know."

♦ ◇ ♦

"Hi, Walt. Have a seat. Won't keep you long. This is about business premises checks on night watch. When I got to work this morning I quickly reviewed the complaints received for the past three days that we've been off. I noticed three reports of break-ins in the downtown area the morning after we finished our last night shift, one being called in by a passing pedestrian on her way to work at 8 a.m. – the front door glass smashed in. That may have been a case of vandalism. The other two were reported by the owners, entry gained from the alley, by kicking in back doors. Point is, of course, they were not discovered by us as they should have been. It's not like they weren't obvious either. In checking the shift rotation I believe that Constable Finch was covering that area – right?"

"Yes, I believe so," replied Bibermann.

"Finch knows full-well the detachment policy about night checks so I'm wondering what happened? On the surface, it seems that he got lazy and/or tired that morning – by the way, was it raining? As you know, some people don't like to get out of their cars when it is."

"No, I don't think so."

"Alright. He's on duty today, so have a word with him, please. Remind him that this kind of slackness doesn't reflect well on the detachment, especially on you and me. Has Gordon been having any problems?"

"Not that I'm aware of, Jack. I hear he has a new girlfriend and that could be acting as a bit of a distraction but I'll speak to him. I think this may have been an untypical lapse of behaviour on his part. I'll let you know. I feel I should apologize. It is my ultimate responsibility."

"Okay, Walt, let's try to keep ahead of the game if we can."

Sterling had not been left a note on this matter by the Operations NCO and felt relieved about that. He preferred to keep his own counsel.

41

Wally Rheingold was not Jewish. His surname looked that way and you couldn't blame people for making that assumption, they being quick to label people based on little or no factual information. He didn't mind so much. 'You get used to it.' He had nothing against Jews, Japanese or Maoris. His dad had experienced the same treatment and had learned to live with it and deal with it. He thought that the name may have originated with Saxons of Germanic origin who intermittently invaded Britain during the Roman occupation to about 500 AD. Over the years, many migrated to other parts of Britain carrying their names with them.

What irked Rheingold was to be labelled anything. If he did answer other than by saying 'No' to the question, he'd reply something like, 'No, I'm just a Canadian with no affiliation to any religious or ethnic group,' and a little sarcastically added on, 'I hope that's okay?' Most people would be a bit embarrassed.

An only child, he was born in Calgary twenty-five years ago, an event registered with the Alberta Ministry of Births, Deaths and Marriages with his Christian names recorded as 'Wally' (not Walter) Arnold (after his grandfather). He was fourth generation Canadian of British stock, from the Midlands.

Measuring six feet, two inches, at 210 pounds and formerly his high school's heavyweight boxing champion, he was a formidable presence. His boxing instructor at Depot Division in Regina had picked him out of the troop to demonstrate his pugilistic skills with the new recruit. After a one-minute bout, the instructor found himself on the gym mat in a bit of a daze.

Poor Rheingold. He wished he hadn't done that but instinct and training had kicked in. He knew he was in shit, but to the corporal's good nature, Wally was asked to assist with some of the rudimentary boxing training. He respected his instructor for that – but he didn't fight him again.

He had four years service, the first three being spent at a Vancouver Island detachment. It was one of those so-called 'retirement posts' with little action, and boring. Assistance to the General Public – AGP – calls were more prevalent than crime-related ones. As well, the weather was gloomy and the rain one winter ran to 43 days straight. As a Calgarian, he was used to cold but sunny days. When he got the call to transfer to Parkton, he was pleased. It was a comparatively large community with some similarities to the Stampede City – climate, geography and situated in open rangeland and, importantly for him, a much larger variety of police work, and busy. He got on well with his peers and thought his sergeant 'an okay guy.' He was reasonably contented, made even more so when he was with his new girlfriend, Nancy. 'Yep, couldn't be much better,' he thought, 'accept maybe for more money.'

In his year at Parkton, he'd learned to deal with the 'local yokels' as he referred to those who inhabited the lower social strata. He tried to use the three F's of people interaction – firm, fair and friendly – and if they didn't work, he'd call upon his second or fall-back position, his height and strength, to achieve his objective, which usually meant a trip to the cells, sometimes unceremoniously carried out. Unlike some police officers, he didn't mind 'mixing it up.' Good guy to have at your back, thought his shift mates.

It was the start of a new series of shifts, beginning with the grave-yard. Rheingold liked this shift because it gave him more time for patrol work. Days were more spent on conducting sometimes boring investigations – like False Pretence complaints (bouncing cheques and similar white collar stuff), administrative matters, school patrols, traffic work and so on.

Today was Monday, with far fewer 'ants' out tonight as Rheingold sometimes referred to humans. The sun had gone down at 8:15 – the country was now on Daylight Saving Time – and by the time he had got his car, Bravo-1, on the road, it was getting dark. His partner, Al Burns, was off this week and because South Zone was one man short, he was asked to overlap the two zones. The reporter, Charlie Preston, was riding with him tonight.

Centre Zone was not large in area but in daytime and evening hours, contained a disproportionate number of people, for obvious reasons. The mix of buildings was about forty percent commercial and sixty residential. Unlike the business area, the residential part of Centre Zone was fairly quiet. Many of the houses were quite dated, some built before 1900 and largely occupied by older and retired people, a cohort that was statistically quite law-abiding. Most of the younger families lived in the 'burbs' where delinquency was a problem.

The business section was quite the opposite. Several hotels, pubs, night clubs, pool halls, a large mall, and dozens of eating places all contributed to a steady demand for police services. Fully 80 percent of an officer's time in this area was spent answering calls. Constable Rheingold was astute enough to realize that, and when he was patrolling Centre, he tried to 'show the flag' as often as could be managed in the residential area. He reminded himself that people living there were taxpayers too, who deserved attention. And so it came to pass, that he found himself guiding his patrol car through the back streets, on the lookout for anything 'out of place.'

His sergeant had told him when he arrived in Parkton that he was to 'make it his business to learn all he could about his patrol area and inhabitants and that he would soon begin to understand the 'rhythm of the place' and become an effective police officer.' Reading situations and people was a vital part of police work and it took time to assimilate in an officer's mind, all the myriad incoming information – visual and sound. It was a challenge and at times, a game of wits.

Take chasing stolen vehicles, for example. It was possible at times to predict which direction they would travel. If the officer could get close enough to read the license plate, it may indicate whether it was a local issue or out-of-town or -province. Its direction of travel could also help predict where it may go.

If it was a local plate, it was unlikely that the driver would head out of town, more likely to abandon it near his place of residence. It meant staying on his tail, thinking ahead where he may go and lining up assistance.

In one such case, Rheingold had an indication that the culprit he was chasing had stolen vehicles previously, and, knowing where he lived, drove to his residence, backed into his driveway and waited. Sure enough, the idiot drove down the street, parked a block away and nonchalantly sauntered down the street, hands in his pockets, certain that he had outwitted and out-driven the police. Surprise!

With out-of-town or out-of-province plates, it was likely that the driver had stopped in Parkton to re-fuel, eat, use a toilet and carry on, which meant going east or west (more likely) or the main highway north and it was a simple matter of setting up police check points. He had been successful that way too. He enjoyed the mental challenge. Tonight was to be another one.

He was on the road again, riding with the *Parkton News* reporter, and had just taken a quick break at the Dairy Queen in the Evergreen Mall just west of the city. The Trans-Canada Highway here was four lanes wide for several miles as it by-passed Parkton through the hilly, timbered section on the south side. Speed limit was 100 km. It was 10 o'clock and not a lot of traffic out. Three miles east was a smaller shopping centre – called Hilltop, because it was at the top of a long hill above the city. To the left and paralleling the TCH was Columbia Street which went steeply downhill into the City Centre. Three sets of traffic lights controlled the intersections here.

Rheingold drew up to the first red light. His right side window was half down and through it came the ear-splitting noise of rubber on pavement. Looking quickly right, he noted a new, bright silver BMW convertible, top up, speeding out of the Chevron service station leaving a pall of blue smoke hanging in the cool night air.

It drove to the intersection, turning right at speed, the back end swaying hard left until the driver corrected his steering and continued east, picking up speed and running the next red lights.

Rheingold turned on his emergency lights but was second in line at the light, still red. He honked his horn and motioned to the driver looking through his rear view mirror at him, to turn right and he obligingly did so. Punching his accelerator to the floor, the back end of Rheingold's car dipped down as the rear wheels spun for a moment before getting a grip on the shiny pavement and, like the BMW, creating a loud squeal and a small cloud of smoke as it shot forward. He'd had a glimpse of the rear license plate – possibly Washington State.

"Better cinch your seat belt up a bit, Charlie. This might get a bit hairy."

The car had gained some distance and was going well over the speed limit.

'Okay,' Rheingold thought, 'the driver will no doubt stay on the TCH and try to outrun me.'

He radioed Dispatch with the details and asked if there was another car east of his position. Charlie-2, a Traffic car, responded and said his 10-20 was in Valleyview and asked what Rheingold's ETA would be. Before he could reply, the dispatcher advised that the driver of the car was a suspect in a 'gas and dash' from the Chevron station.

Rheingold called Charlie-2, told him he was travelling at 160 km, his top speed. "I have the car in view but not gaining and unable to read the plate number. Can you get to the Highway 5 overpass in case he makes a left to go north? It could be a Washington car, so be careful."

"Bravo-1, roger that. You'll be at my location shortly. I don't have time to deploy my spike block, and no one appears to be east of me."

"This is Bravo-7," said Sergeant Sterling. "I'm heading your direction, Charlie-2. Closest North car to the river, head over the bridge to 5 and set up there. Copy?"

"Bravo-14, I'm close to the bridge. I'll take it," replied Constable Al Kart.

Sterling came on the air immediately again and said, "We may have to ask for assistance from Salmon River Detachment. Dispatch, will you please call and alert them and see if they have a car available, with spikes, to head this way."

"Bravo-1 and -7, suspect vehicle coming down hill toward my position," called Charlie-2. The blue and white colours of the Traffic car were clearly visible under the bright highway halogen lights.

Before either of those two cars could acknowledge, he said quickly, "He's spotted me and turning to take the overpass exit at full speed— shit! He's hit the guard rail – going over onto Valleyview Drive!" he yelled.

◆ ◇ ◆

The scene on the road beneath the overpass was a mess. The suspect's car was flattened and lying on its roof. Just behind it, blocking the road, were a jack-knifed semi-trailer, which had attempted to avoid the 'car from the sky' as the injured driver had called the BMW, and a mini-van which had struck the rear of the semi. In the one minute it took for the City and Traffic cars to drive around to the scene, traffic was beginning to back up in both directions and people were starting to mill around the smashed vehicles.

"This is Charlie-2 and Bravo-1 – at the scene. We need assistance. Out of cars."

Later, after the body of the car driver had been removed from the sports car, using the 'Jaws of Life,' or as Wally Rheingold called the machine tonight, the 'Jaws of Death,' and the mandatory photographs, diagram, measurements and statements had been completed, the compact car, now more so than ever, was hooked onto a flatbed trailer and taken to the local impound lot. Once there, Rheingold said to his ride-along, "Let's see if he's carrying anything."

He managed to pry the small trunk lid open and found, in the spare tire well, what turned out to be a six-kilogram package of 'H'. An Indices name check revealed the registered owner – and driver – to be Jesus Jorge Estrada – formerly of Nogales, Mexico, now living in Vancouver, who had two previous charges but no convictions in British Columbia for 'possession of heroin for the purposes of trafficking.'

"Well, Estrada *still* has a perfect no-conviction record," Rheingold noted. "But sometimes there is Justice, Charlie."

42

Peter Standing, 26, and Caroline Sparrow, 24, had been 'going together' as they told people, for the past two years. Sometimes they slept at his place, sometimes he at hers. Both lived on the Parkton Indian Reservation on the northeast side of the confluence of the North and South Thompson rivers, adjacent to the City.

They were part of the much larger Shuswap Nation which included 27 Bands covering much of the lower central part of the province. Half of the Reserve was residential and the other light industrial and storage facilities which provided a fair degree of rental income to the Band. Most of the land consisted of river silt, settling here over the ages, the result of snow runoff bringing sand down from the Cariboo Mountain Range to the north.

Both Standing and Sparrow had part-time jobs and that suited their life style. 'Pete' got about in his 1974 Mazda pickup, held together by mechanical ingenuity and bailing wire, as he said. It was destined to live its last day on the Reserve soon, left to die where it quit running, but for now, it was wheels.

They were what could be called 'light gamblers', that is to say both played the twice-a-week 6/49 draw – choosing 'Double Dip' at ten bucks a ticket on the 'Quick Pick' method – every Wednesday and Saturday. They'd been playing for about three years and seldom won, even the ten dollar prize. But it was fun and both lived in perpetual hope of winning the 'big one'.

Today was Thursday and they'd driven over the two river bridges into downtown in the late afternoon, finding a spot to park on Victoria Street, near the Grand Hotel which they frequented.

Before going in for a drink or two, they'd checked their Wednesday 6/49 ticket at a small Chinese-owned general grocery store close by. The clerk ran the two tickets through his machine and declared one of them a winner.

"How much?" Caroline Sparrow squealed before the man could tell them.

"Don't get too excited," he said. "Ninety-six dollars."

"Wow!" she exclaimed and Pete Standing smiled.

"More than we've ever won," he said as the man opened the till and counted out four twenties, one ten, one five and a Loonie and got Pete to sign the back of his ticket, which had produced the prize.

Exiting the store, Sparrow said, "What are we going to do with the money?"

"What do you mean 'we'? I won it," said Standing with a straight face.

She smacked him on the shoulder and said, "Share and share alike," as he broke into a smile.

"I don't know… Let's have a party – okay?"

And so they did.

Standing called his long-time friend, Mickey Wood, and told him he was going to bring four boxes of Okanagan Spring beer, a couple of bottles of Black Label and that he'd see him at Wood's house in about half an hour. His friend's house was a bit bigger than Standing's and had a fireplace.

"Where'd'ja get the money for the booze?"

"Won it on the 6/49 draw. Call up Tommy and his girlfriend – what's her name? Wanda? Okay? See ya soon." Wood had no current girlfriend.

◆   ◇   ◆

The happy group, with a big log fire blazing away and the wood crackling, had consumed two cases by 9 o'clock and intended to finish the remaining two before calling it a night. Their degree of inebriation got higher and so did the fire as they kept putting on fir logs before the bottom ones had fully burned, pretty much filling up the small fireplace. At one point, someone forgot to replace the mesh screen in front and several large pieces of red-hot embers flew into the living room and onto an oval wool rug, one of them causing it to smoulder. Standing's logging boot came down and smothered it.

Tommy and Wanda staggered out of the house about one-thirty.

By two-thirty in the morning, only Wood was awake but close to nodding off. Standing and Sparrow had fallen asleep on the couch. As host, he just remembered to stoke the fire one more time before staggering into his bedroom, failing to replace the screen.

The nearest neighbour, up to go to the bathroom at 4 a.m., looked out his front window and saw what looked like flames inside Mickey Wood's house. He knew a party had been going on through the evening. Quickly calling the Parkton Fire Department on 911, he then ran over to the house and pounded on the front door. By now, flames had taken hold and the fire seemed larger.

He shoulder barged the door open and the oxygen rushing in instantly fed the flames and thick grey smoke roiled out through the opening. These two elements prevented him from entering this way. Running around to the back door, he turned the handle and the door opened.

Getting onto his hands and knees he crawled into the smoke-filled hallway a few feet yelling, "Mickey! Mickey! Where are you?"

No reply.

He moved forward slowly, still on his knees when his right hand felt something. Clothing. A person's shoulder.

Putting his left hand out too, he grabbed the clothing and started pulling the individual back toward the door and got the head onto the top level step. It was Wood, who began coughing, spluttering and gasping for air.

Leaving him in this position, below the level of the billowing smoke, the neighbour tried to enter the hallway again only to be driven back. At the bottom of the outside steps, he pulled Wood down to the ground, checked him for a few seconds to make sure he was breathing and ran around to the front door. No way in. The flames were by now licking out around the door frame. Backing away, he threw up violently, in one level of his mind because his lungs were full of smoke and at a higher level, because he knew his compatriots were dying in the inferno that had now overtaken the house and that he was powerless to do anything about.

♦   ◊   ♦

On the morning after the fire, 'A' Watch had been on duty and when his routine office morning chores were finished, Sergeant Sterling telephoned Band Chief Henry Sparrow and asked if he could see him.

On arrival, he parked on the gravel turn-around driveway, mounted the thick cedar steps to the house and was about to knock when the door opened and Sparrow stepped out onto the covered deck to meet him.

In his service at Parkton, Sterling had seen the Chief on a few occasions dealing with Reserve problems, unfortunately mostly criminal ones. The two men got along well and respected each other. Today they hugged briefly and the sergeant detected moist eyes in the man's weather-beaten face.

Sterling patted him on the shoulder as they entered the house and said, "Henry, please accept my deepest sympathies for your loss. My heart goes out to you and your family. Has a date been set for the services yet?"

"Yes," he replied, "a week this Saturday, at 2 p.m. at the Long House."

"I'd like to attend and bring two of my watch members with your permission?"

"That would be kind of you, Jack. I'm sure the folks would appreciate your gesture. Thank you."

Caroline had been the Chief's only daughter.

Sterling received permission from Inspector Edwardson and detailed Constables Bernie Wardlow and Shelley Prentice to accompany him, dressed in Review Order.

♦   ◊   ♦

Saturday was cold and sunny. Six doe-skin-covered drums were pounding slowly and rhythmically inside the Long House which was filled to overflow. Many people sat on hastily-assembled chairs and wood benches outside. A large number of the approximately 300 people were out-of-town visitors, mostly relatives, obscure or close, to the deceased who were 'lying in state' in closed coffins, lined up side-by-side just below the dais. The coffins were covered by Canadian flags over which a small ceremonial head dress of eagle feathers had been placed.

Among the crowd in the building, those three members of the Force, dressed alike in Stetsons, red serge jackets, dark blue breeches, and highly polished brown leather riding boots and silver spurs, contrasted smartly with the ceremonial apparel of the dancers. Henry Sparrow delivered a very thoughtful eulogy.

As *Oh Canada* was played by tape over the loudspeakers, Sergeant Sterling gave a salute on behalf of the RCMP. When it was finished, he turned his head slightly to his left and whispered to Wardlow and Prentice, "Remove – head dress." Three hands went up in unison, simultaneously removing Stetsons and tucking them smartly under their left arms, bowing their heads for one minute of silence as Bishop Steen intoned the final prayer.

◆ ◇ ◆

"It's been an experience for me. Highly emotional in there, wasn't it, Sarge?" said Shelley Prentice as they left the Reserve.

"Yeah. I like Henry Sparrow, and his daughter was a good person at heart. It's a shame this kind of thing happened. I'm glad we showed up to lend our support; it's important that we do. I appreciate both of you being with me."

43

Two weeks later, Sterling found himself patrolling again with the newspaper reporter, on the evening/night watch. He'd gotten used to his company and felt that Preston would report his findings, in whatever form they may take, in a fair and objective way. By now, the man had been on ride-alongs with almost everyone of his watch members, including the two corporals. He was amassing a great deal of information and it was going to take some time to sort it all out into a useable, readable, interesting account of his experiences, from a reporter's and a citizen's viewpoint.

How to present this to the public was the question Preston was trying to come to grips with – one of two formats, he thought: an anecdotal historical account or in a novel format. He was leaning toward the latter, he told Sterling.

"If you choose the novel format, what would be the focus of the story, Charlie?" the sergeant asked, as they drove along River Road north-bound.

"I think the primary purposes would be to show how the RCMP handles its General Policing services through a group of people at a large detachment, focusing on the human aspects of the job more than the legal and technical applications. I've learned that they do their work guided by an extensive set of *Policies and Procedures*, called *Rules, Regulations and Orders* – 'RR&O's' as you call them, which is their 'operational bible' in short. Those, as you well know, apply to all their operations and, in my view, allow for a standard approach to police work across Canada but, it seems to me, also allows for individual approaches and idiosyncrasies.

"To illustrate that, I will select a variety of operational occurrences – stories if you like, and a few administrative activities, mixed in with my own experiences I've gained with the ride-alongs, my observations and recordings of events we've been involved in, and, importantly, add the necessary human dimension to give them and their stories substance."

"I don't suppose it'll be a Joseph Wambaugh LAPD kind of story?" chuckled Sterling.

"No. He's a very funny police story writer but a bit 'over the top' for my purposes. I shall make mine a bit more muted, but no less interesting, I hope, to suit the reality of police work in this country.

"By the way, one thing I'd like to confirm with you while I think of it. I read an article recently in the *Globe and Mail* about something called 'DNA', used by the British police in securing a conviction in a murder case last year. You know anything about it?"

"Yes, I do. The case was circulated by HQ, Ottawa. DNA is a very short term for Deoxyribonucleic Acid. It contains all the genetic makeup, called 'genes', in the human body. These are slightly different in each of us. The discovery of this evolved into something labelled 'genetic matching' as I recall and led to forensics people being able to match body fluids, hair, etc., found at a crime scene and link them to a suspect, sufficient to an absolute degree of certainty."

"How do you remember this, Jack?"

"Well, strangely enough, the murder took place in Enderby in the County of Leicestershire, and living in its namesake in B.C., I guess it stuck in my mind."

"What a coincidence," replied Preston. "This matching ability bodes well for future murder investigation."

"Yes. We can use all the help we can get."

"Anyway, where did you go from Richmond Detachment?"

"Right here to Parkton in 1972. By now, I had two sons, who were ages 6 and 2. Number three son arrived a year later. My wife and I were lucky to be able to rent an old wartime military house up on the hill for cheap rent, and Jocelyn worked part-time at the downtown Hudson's Bay store. While we were still not paid to City police levels, we did okay financially and were able to buy a second-hand truck and camper. We used it a great deal, going away on trips in the spring and summer, exploring parts of the province and taking a summer vacation along the beautiful Oregon Coast and down to Disneyland at Christmas one year.

"I liked the area, the countryside and the climate and enjoyed my time here, gaining a great deal of experience in having to deal with just about every kind of criminal offence. I also spent one year prosecuting Summary Conviction charges, under the tutelage of the Prosecutor, Patrick Dean, small stuff like motor vehicle and government liquor act offences.

"For me, it was challenging work and I learned a great deal about the intricacies of Court procedures, especially how important it is for a police officer to be careful about his Court brief and giving evidence, particularly relating to statements given by an accused person. There can never be sufficient training for that."

Preston agreed. "Yes, since I've been reporting Court cases in the paper, which has meant a lot of time listening in at trials, I've also come to appreciate the complexity of Court procedures. I believe that the British system of Justice, which most Commonwealth countries seem to follow, is about the best there is."

"Dispatch, car closest to River Road and Spencer?"

"10-Bravo-7," Sterling quickly replied, "I'm about half a mile south."

"Bravo-7, 10-4. Collision at that intersection, one car down the river bank and partly submerged – injuries. Charlie-4, are you able to attend?"

"Charlie-4, I'm on the North Shore – be about five minutes," replied the driver of the Traffic car.

"Charlie-4, Roger. Ambulance dispatched."

"Bravo-7, any North car?"

"Bravo-6, I can be there shortly," replied Dick Ketchum, who was accompanied by Hank Deleeuw.

"Okay, I'm almost there," replied Sterling. "Will advise the situation."

To his passenger he said, "This doesn't sound good. May have to get my feet wet."

Rounding a sharp bend in the road, they came upon a badly smashed car sitting sideways on River Road, just past Spencer. Flames were licking up around the engine and steam rising. A couple of people were trying to force open the driver's door.

Sterling cut the siren and slid to a stop just back from the car, leaving his emergency lights flashing. He quickly instructed Preston to grab the fire extinguisher down by his feet. "Go to the car, pull the pin out, press the cover guard down and spray the engine. Need to get that out ASAP. I'm going down the bank to take a look. Be okay? When you're done, assist the civilians."

The river bank at this point went down at about a 45-degree angle and from the road above to the water's edge was about forty feet. The car was nearly submerged in the forward position with only about the last two feet of the cabin and part of the trunk above water. In the twilight, scrambling down the steep slope, Sterling could see a person kneeling on the trunk by the back window, pounding on it, to no avail.

Wading into the cold, fast-flowing water, he yelled, "Police," at the individual and seeing that he had a rock in his hand, said loudly, "Gimme the rock! Wait on the bank. I'll need a hand when I call you, okay?"

The man nodded his head.

As Sterling was doing this, Constable Slater arrived on scene. Seeing him, Preston, who had doused the engine fire, ran over to Slater's car and told him that Sergeant Sterling was down the bank at the second car. Slater called Dispatch and asked if a wrecker was on the way.

"Affirmative," came the reply.

"Okay, call the company again and ask if this truck has a long tow cable and for the driver to get his ass here ASAP. Also, we'll need another GD car on site to help out with traffic control. I'm going down the bank to give Sterling a hand."

♦   ◇   ♦

The back door would not open. Sterling struck the side window hard, with two blows, and the glass shattered into tiny cubes. Reaching in, he felt for the door handle, found it, and pulled – still to no avail.

'Okay, nothing for it but to get a bit wetter, I suppose,' he muttered to himself as he hauled his body through the glassless window. The water was now occupying about four-fifths of the interior, up to the roof where the driver sat.

'No alternative but to submerge. Get a move on!' he told himself.

Taking a deep breath, he put his head into the murky water, his arms forward, first feeling over the front passenger seat for an occupant. Feeling nothing, he moved to the driver's side. His hands felt the shoulders and grabbing clothing, he pulled up but the person did not budge. 'Shit, the seat belt.'

He pulled back momentarily above the water, took a deep breath, submerged and felt along the driver's right thigh for the seat buckle. Finding it, he pushed the snap in, pulled the strap free and let it go.

Another big breath and he found the shoulders again. With his feet on the back floor, he stood in a half-crouched position directly behind the driver's seat and pulled up and back for all he was worth, feeling the body rise. With his head just above the water line now, Sterling was able to start breathing and kept pulling, feeling the person ease backwards a few inches with each pull.

Turning his head to the right, facing the broken side window, he yelled, "I've got him! Gimme a hand!"

Keeping one hand gripping the man's clothing, Sterling wriggled through the window. Then, assisted by the unknown civilian, they managed to pull the limp body through the window with great difficulty and onto the bank at the river's edge, where Slater had just arrived. Sterling laid down beside the victim gasping for air from the exertion.

He would relive that scene for the rest of his life with the realization that he had almost died, for, as soon as they were both out of the car, it slid silently down into the river and disappeared. The funny thing was, he didn't think about that at the time. What passed through his mind was an absolutely incongruous and irrelevant thought: 'Jeez, the tow truck driver's gonna be pissed – he lost a tow job!'

The driver was dead. Time was the enemy in this case, for it had been a full ten minutes since the accident had happened to the point where Sterling pulled the man's head above water. Having made the effort and not being successful made him feel sad and he couldn't help wondering if he had driven a bit faster, slid down the slope a bit faster and pulled him out of the car a bit faster, that those actions might have made the difference and saved a life.

He eventually got over those feelings, realizing that he was damn lucky on two counts – that he got there in time to pull the man out, and that *he* got out of the vehicle in time, saving his own life. 'Can't win 'em all,' he reluctantly told himself.

Two hours later, having gone home, once again with the reporter, to change his clothes – 'This is getting to be a bit of a habit,' he jested – they were back at the detachment where Sterling was completing his report on the fatal MVA. The lone driver of the other vehicle was in hospital with minor injuries and had later blown an alcohol reading of .18 mg/L, more than double the legal limit. Sterling didn't know if he had been informed yet of the death of the other driver. 'So many lives stupidly lost,' he thought. 'I wonder what the tox report will reveal on the deceased man. Would be ironic if he showed over the limit too. An accident absolutely waiting to happen, with deadly results. Who dies and who lives?'

◆ ◇ ◆

"You feel okay, Jack? You're understandably quiet," asked Charlie Preston as they were once again on patrol.

"Sorry, I was doing some wondering."

"Listen, if you need some space, I can go…."

"No. no. I'd like your company. Take my mind off what happened a bit. Let me continue with the saga of my service," Sterling said with a half smile.

"Well, that was certainly an example this evening, Jack. I had no idea what was going on down there until you came up soaking wet. Hell of an effort if I can say so."

"Thanks. Any one of us would have done the same thing."

Preston did not reply to that but wondered if it was true in this case.

Later, continuing, Sterling said, "In my first time here, 1972 to 1976, the City area and population was considerably less than it is today. The detachment had a complement of 35 members, as opposed to 110 now, some fourteen years later.

"As you're probably aware, the City annexed much of the 'unorganized' rural area, for several miles in any direction, in effect quadrupling the square miles and greatly adding to the population. I was astonished when I returned in 1985.

"I enjoyed my time here. Interesting variety of work and my kids grew like weeds. All three were members of youth organizations, Scouts and Sea Cadets. Brad, the youngest, started out in Beavers, whose motto is *sharing, sharing, sharing*, words that I often had to repeat as a father/referee during disagreements over ownership of a particular toy. I also enrolled them in swimming lessons and eventually, they all became lifeguards and got paid jobs at swimming pools.

"Three events stood out for me. The first was a float plane crash in the river just east of the bridge. I was on day shift and it became my file. I managed to get a guy with an 18-foot aluminum boat to run out to the plane with his buddy and effect a rescue of the pilot and passenger. Your paper got hold of the story right away and sent out a reporter to interview me. We stood on a street uphill from the scene with a view of the upside-down pontoons sticking out of the water.

"His cameraman took a photo of me, a close-up, above-the-waist shot, showing me wearing my cap, a pair of California Highway Patrol style sunglasses and a nice, pressed khaki shirt – a posed shot if ever there was one. It appeared in large format on the front page the next day. My wife said I looked 'dashing' and that she felt proud of me, my chest expanding a little when she uttered those kind words, but I got some quite dissimilar comments from my mates. For a day or two I was called 'Chips' from the old TV series of the same name, about the California Highway Patrol, currently airing at that time.

"Two other events of significance for the Force occurred during this time. The first was introduction of a new computer system, called the Canadian Police Information Centre – CPIC, or C-PIC as it quickly became known. It was to provide all police departments in this country with information on crimes and criminals and outstanding Warrants. All detachment members had to attend a two-hour seminar on its operation. Most of us, young and old, were skeptical about its abilities – seemed too good to be true. It was similar to the U.S. system, called NCIC – National Crime Information Centre – based in Washington, D.C. We had heard of this but knew little about what it did.

"The federal government spent 20 million dollars on ours and apparently it was vastly superior to the U.S. one, to the point where their technicians came up for a look and essentially copied it.

"It came on-line July 1, 1972 across Canada. Terminals were situated at the larger police posts only. Previous to this time, police forces had to rely largely on paperwork for information. For example, we had 'hot sheets' printed up daily for stolen cars and property, missing and wanted persons, which was largely out-of-date when it was printed – next to useless really. With this new system, we were assured that we would get responses to our radio enquiries almost instantly. 'Yeah, right,' we said to ourselves.

"Turned out to be true; better than I expected. I was on patrol that day and decided to check out an Alberta license plate in front of me.

"About 8 seconds after I called it in, the response came back – 'Reported stolen, Banff.' I was suitably impressed and became an avid user of the system – a computer 'junkie' – a pain in the ass to the terminal operators, but a successful one. In another example, I was passing a campsite just east of the City when we had a BOLF call – Be On the Lookout For. In this case, cars were asked to look for a certain make of truck and trailer, the occupants believed camping in the Parkton area and advise the occupants to call home regarding a family emergency. I swung into the site for a check, found the vehicle immediately, delivered the message and replied to our Terminal to that effect. It took 30 seconds to do. Good stuff. Another score for Sterling. Overnight, the Force had entered the age of modern electronics."

"I can understand why," replied Charlie. "The more you check the greater your success rate, eh? What was the second big event?"

"Well, that would be the RCMP Centennial in 1973 – a banner year for us, or as some wag put it, 'starting our second one hundred years of grooming horses and sweeping up horse shit,' referring of course, to the Musical Ride stationed in Ottawa.

"Most detachments across the country took part in some type of celebration. In Parkton, a small squad of us rode in our scarlet Review Order uniform on borrowed, standard size black Quarter Horses and saddles. The RCMP in Regina provided us with blue and gold shabracks – saddle blankets – bridles and reins and lances with pennants. We led the parade through the City on the first of July. Took my thoughts back to training days in Regina, and, I have to say, made me feel proud as we rode down the main street through the cheers of the local population."

"Wow! I'd liked to have been there to see that."

"I guess I should mention the RCMP Ball, held in May. There were over 100 members present in their formal 'Walking-Out Order' uniform – Stetson, red coat, long blue pants and a pair of shiny black Congress boots complete with gleaming silver miniature spurs attached to the heels – accompanied by their female partners dressed in a huge variety of colourful formal gowns. A highlight of the social season here.

"The final icing on the cake for that year, was that every member of every detachment, Sub Division and at 'E' Division HQ in Victoria, posed for a photograph at his respective post – no women in the Force until the next year – and these were published in the Division Centennial book. A great keepsake."

"Wonderful. If you have your copy, I'd like to have a look at it, Jack."

"Sure, I'll bring it the next time we meet. There is one final thing I perhaps should mention. While stationed here then, I decided to begin advancing my education and enrolled in an undergraduate degree program, by correspondence, with the University of Waterloo in Ontario.

"I started out by doing two courses at a time and found that that was too ambitious. I could not find enough time to study properly, due to the pressures of work and raising three sons, so I reduced it to one per semester, which included taking three of them at the local college and transferring them to the U of W.

"I hadn't studied for a long time and had to develop disciplined learning habits to continue. In retrospect, it turned out to be a good decision as I'll explain later.

"Listen, I think I've covered enough for now. I don't have a whole lot more to tell you to bring you up to date. I need to go back and finished up my paperwork and get home on time tonight. I'm beat. Mind if I call you?"

44

There were twelve pubs in Greater Parkton. That equalled almost one per ten thousand residents – not a large number on a per capita basis, but more than enough for the police, especially during the long, hot summer days and evenings, with temperatures often hovering around 30 degrees Celsius plus, even after midnight.

The City was, after all, just within the boundary of the northern end of the Great Sonoran Desert, which stretched south to Mexico. Rattlers slithered along in the grassland, mixing with sagebrush and short-stem cactus, co-existing with the beautiful Red Fox, Black Widow spiders, and ferocious large red ants prowling the nap of the earth.

Pubs emptied their patrons out at 1 a.m., sometimes unceremoniously, assisted enthusiastically by bouncers. Friday night was by far the busiest for these establishments when drunkenness prevailed, leading to fights and assaults – hence the label 'Friday Night Fights' used by the police.

Five of the pubs were located downtown, all of them on the main street. One, the Grand – if ever there was a misnomer – was rightly described as a 'shit-hole', attracting many of the local undesirables, who, mixed in with mill workers, ranch hands, loggers, general labourers and a few of the local First Nations folk, made for a potent mix of alcohol-filled human beings.

The natural outcome, of course, was the use of force against each other by fist or boot or both, and occasionally, bottles and knives. The

Parkton General Hospital always had extra emergency ward staff on duty at this time.

The detachment had a very useful van in service, called the Bunwagon. The word 'bun' was a slang word for 'drunken condition' and this was its primary use. Painted a dull black, it was officially designated Alpha-One. It was a very utilitarian van with a bare metal floor and metal benches along each side. Easy to sluice the puke and excrement out, which was part of the junior constable's job description – unwritten, of course. It patrolled mostly along Victoria Street, manned by two large, generally young constables. Tonight, Wally Rheingold and Gordon Finch filled that role. In case of brawls, they were backed up by two equally beefy constables, Taylor and Burns. For the purposes of drunk patrols, they were called the 'Four Musketeers' and very effective they were too.

This evening was no different, having to deal with stupid mayhem; almost always involving males – who were, incidentally, generally easier to deal with than fighting females. Motor vehicle accidents, drunk drivers, family fights, shoplifting (sadly, mostly juvenile females) and occasionally, to make police work a little more challenging and interesting, a murder or suicide, added to the work load.

♦ ◊ ♦

At the detachment, 'bedlam' might be the appropriate noun to describe conditions. The male cells and the drunk-tank at the detachment were especially vociferous, with people shouting and swearing and from the female cells, full volume screaming. It often wasn't until 4 a.m. that things began to settle down. At six, the noise level rose again with the clanging of cell doors and the release of overnight drunks from the tank.

To cope with all this, watch commanders tried to ensure they had maximum crews working. So too did the other sections: Traffic,

General Investigation, Drug Squad, Identification (Forensics) and, if possible, a Dog Master. All were obligated to assist General Duty members in serious situations and came under the control of the watch commander when these situations arose. GIS – the detectives of the RCMP – usually handled the more serious types of crime, and Traffic people, major accidents. As well, Auxiliary Police members were on duty; upwards of eighteen or so on these nights providing good, useable service to assist the detachment members.

It could be problematic at times in placing auxiliaries with the regular police officers. Not all of the members felt comfortable in their presence, claiming lack of professional training and commitment to the job, in terms of regular turnout. They were after all, 'part-timers', some members said. Nevertheless, on busy nights and because they could not drive patrol cars, they had to be paired with watch members. On 'A' Watch at least, it seemed to work out well. In part, that may have been because Sergeant Sterling was in charge of the Auxiliary Police Program. This evening, more auxiliaries showed up than usual. After distributing them, including one to each of his zone commanders, he still had two people standing around. Each watch commander, in addition to his patrol car, Bravo-7, had an unmarked car available, but it was not used often.

'Dammit, what am I going to go?' thought Sterling. 'Okay, they're both mature people with over five years experience, so I'm going to try something, permission or not. I think I'll give them an unmarked car and cut them loose.'

He sat them down and gave them some strict guidelines in what they could, and could not do, in the operation of a police car. They were primarily responsible as back-up help when called upon or if they saw a 'situation' that called for their assistance. They were not to exceed the speed limit which meant no chasing speeders, just to report them. They could check a suspected impaired driver by stopping the person and waiting for a regular member to arrive and take over. In a situation like this, they were to make full and accurate notes of what they did, saw and heard, for possible use in Court if the case went to trial. Their car, 10-Delta-3, was equipped with a portable red flashing light with a magnet that could be placed on the roof in order to stop vehicles.

For these two auxiliaries, it made their night to be given this kind of responsibility and they stayed on duty for seven hours before being thanked and told to go home.

"You did well," Sterling told them, "especially getting that bunch of drunks off the road before they killed someone."

He was referring to an incident where they were patrolling in the downtown area, which included a few one-way streets. Around ten p.m., they noted a battered, rusted-out 1975 Dodge Charger, driving the wrong way down Pine Street. When they finally got it stopped, the auxiliaries found four people in the car. All appeared to be drunk.

As per instructions, they called a General Duty constable. The occupants had been 'pub crawling' since five p.m. and were on their way to finish up the night at the Grand. To their limited credit, they decided three of them were 'too pissed' to drive and elected the fourth, who was deemed to be 'less pissed,' as their designated driver. Because of their condition, three were placed in the drunk tank while the driver was introduced to the breathalyzer machine, where he blew .18 mg. After being processed, he joined his friends in the cells for the rest of the night.

Later in the week Sterling discussed with the Operations NCO the matter of allowing the two auxiliaries to drive, explaining what he had done, why, and how it had gone. He also talked to the three other watch commanders and they agreed they'd like to try it too.

A review by the OIC Detachment was positive and included a set of guidelines similar to Sterling's. It was to be a limited operation of one police car, marked or unmarked, per shift. He wanted to review and assess the Auxiliary Police Driving Program, as he dubbed it, in five weeks.

Things went well and the program proved its worth, so that it was expanded to two cars per shift if needed. Of course, this was particularly helpful on the weekends and when a watch was short of regular members. 'E' Division HQ was reviewing the matter.

For the auxiliary constables, it gave a renewed sense of worth – that their services were needed and valued – a win-win situation for everyone.

45

Resting his knife and fork in a parallel position on his empty dinner plate, he looked at his hostess and said, "Thank you, Shirley, that was delicious. I especially liked your Yorkshire pudding – it goes so well with roast beef and gravy and, of course, that eye-watering horseradish."

"You're welcome, Jack. Have some pumpkin pie and soft ice cream?"

"Thought you'd never ask," smiled Sterling in reply. He was a guest of the *News* reporter, and, on a day off, had been invited over to continue his narrative about his police service. Sterling's wife had also been asked but had to beg off due to night school classes.

His host thought it would be much more productive to continue this way, rather that in the patrol car, with the inevitable interruptions. "Not that I mind," he'd told Sterling. "In fact, I enjoy the calls we go on – well, for the most part. Don't care for the dead bodies parts of my ride-alongs though."

After desert was finished, Shirley Preston said, "Why don't you two go into the den, while I clear up? It'll be quiet in there for you."

"Very kind of you, thanks," said Sterling as he finished off his glass of Merlot. "Can I help with the dishes though?"

In the den, with the door closed, Charlie Preston said, "Shirley fully understands that washing dishes is women's work."

"Not in my house," Sterling replied. "I do them most of the time – well, the boys and I."

"Just kidding, Jack. I'm like you. I got off lucky tonight. I think we're fifty years too late for that. I'll turn on my recorder?"

"I think I've pretty much covered my first posting here. There's so many things to say. How does one become selective? I was a couple of months away from completing four years here when Staff-Sergeant Baker, the NCO-in-charge, called me into his office. When that kind of thing happens, you automatically think you're in shit and I'm searching my mind for something that I did, or didn't do. It was quite the reverse.

"'How'd you like to have your own detachment?' he asked right out. For a few seconds, I didn't say anything and then quietly said, "Er, yes, Staff" my heart thumping away.

"'Okay. You've got it. Superintendent Harrison called me today and wants you to take over Enderby – in the North Okanagan. It's a very busy 4-man post and he feels confident you can handle it. So do I for that matter. Congratulations,' he said, reaching across his desk to shake my hand.

"You'll get your corporal's hooks on the October Promotion List. Your transfer is effective August 1st. See Corporal Henderson at Sub Div for transfer details. No need to house hunt either. You'll have the pleasure of living with your work, in attached quarters. I'll give you a day as the time gets nearer to run down there and talk to Corporal Evans about the place. It's in this Sub Division so we'll no doubt see you occasionally. I wish you all the best, Jack."

"I checked the name Enderby in the *B.C. Gazetteer* and found, to my surprise that it was in fact a city – incorporated in 1905 with a population – within its boundaries – of 500.

"In B.C., all communities with that designation are required to have a City Hall, a mayor, council, a city clerk and a fire and police departments. Before 1950, Enderby, and much of the rest of British Columbia, was policed by the B.C. Provincial Police. Policing transferred to the Mounties that year when the B.C.P.P. was amalgamated with the RCMP. I found out later that the City's contract for policing with the Provincial government required them to pay fifty percent of costs. To help alleviate that financial commitment, all Court fines imposed for offences committed within the boundaries of the municipality, went to it. It's important for me to mention this now, as I'll explain later on."

"You must have been pretty pleased with the transfer?"

"Yes, but naturally apprehensive too. I was stepping into unknown territory, literally and figuratively, suddenly responsible for the operation of a police station. I knew it would be a challenge. When I met the Mayor for the first time, he called me 'Chief' and I thought that it was just an appellation that he liked to use. It wasn't. I was his 'Chief of Police' and that's the way he referred to me. My wife thought it amusing and periodically alluded to me as Chief – as in, 'What would you like for dinner tonight, Chief?' Up until this time 'I didn't get no respect' from the family, as the comedian Rodney Dangerfield likes to say. I kind of liked the title though. They say your first promotion is always the most memorable and I can say for certainty that it is."

"That's a great little anecdote. I'll make a note of it," said his host.

"Just to finished off some stats. The detachment area was about 1500 square miles and included Mabel Lake, the Shuswap River, part of the Heals Range of mountains, Highway 97A running from the U.S. border in the south to the Trans-Canada Highway to the north. The area population was about 3,500 and included part of the Shuswap Nation Reserve. People were largely engaged in farming – hay, dairy and beef herds – forest industry and tourism in the summer months. A very active social community and different in every aspect to Parkton.

"Getting to know my constituents became important, I realized, and to do that, whenever I went on patrol, I would stop and talk to people, find out who they were, and marked that information on my large relief map of the area. I find it's better to know people on a first-name basis, whether they're good citizens or bad. Easier to talk to when you've shaken their hand. 'Nice' produces better results than 'nasty', don't you think?"

"In my business," replied Preston, "that's generally true. Should apply to yours too, I suppose. Listen, can I get you another drink, Jack?"

"Thanks, but no. I have to drive home. Anyway, I started work on August 1st having moved my family and furniture into the detachment quarters, which adjoined the office and jail cells, two days earlier. I had asked the landlord, a building contractor, to have the interior repainted and he agreed and it had been completed already which made my wife happy, moving into clean premises. But, let me tell you what we had to put up with for four years. Noise!

"From the highway passing through right outside the office, a small saw mill just down the road cutting lumber, and from noisy drunks and other assorted assholes in the cells, no more than 40 feet away from the door into our quarters. As well, there was no air conditioning, so that meant open windows at night in the hot summer months to try to cool the place down a bit. A noisy hell.

"I went out for a patrol of the area on my first day, to begin to get familiar with it – I sometimes worked weekends to give my guys a break – when Vernon Detachment radio called to advise of a possible drowning on the Shuswap River, 6 or 7 miles east of town. I called for an ambulance – my wife answered the office radio as I'd asked her to stand by in case I needed assistance – and raced out to the spot but it was too late. The person, a woman, was dead. Four adults, ages around 25 years, had been picnicking and drinking at a small sandy beach area. One of them decided to wade into the river, but the bank dropped off steeply into deep water and she lost her footing. No one could swim and no attempt at rescue was made. She drifted downstream about 200 yards into shallow water and her clothing snagged on low-hanging branches, so her friends were able to pull her out by the time I arrived. I guessed that the remaining people were all over the legal alcohol limit and this was borne out later when the woman's autopsy report indicated a reading of .10. I don't know if you're aware of this fact but booze claims more victims by drowning than anything else.

"Anyway, the ambulance arrived, complete with a doctor on board, to my surprise. He injected adrenalin with a very long needle, through her breast and into her heart to try to revive it again. A sad and unnecessary death. 'Welcome to my new post!' I said to myself.

"I found out quickly that it was indeed a busy place, with more than our share of 'complaints'. That's a euphemism for 'occurrences' that require police attendance. We seemed to have an inordinate number of motor vehicle accidents, and speeding through the City was a constant problem as the main street was really an extension of the Okanagan Highway, north and south. Even with the occasional help of Highway Patrol units from other detachments, running radar checks, it still seemed like a tidal wave of fast traffic. We had no radar set and had to clock speeders with police cars in order to write a ticket – not the most reliable method, and time consuming for us. I think it's at this point that what I'm about to tell you ties in with what I said earlier about the police budget.

"About six months after my arrival, I was talking on the phone with the corporal in charge of Summerland Detachment and mentioned my speeding problem. His office was also on the main highway. He said that his municipality had recently purchased a new radar speed meter unit and the old one was for sale, for the price of $200.00 which would include the cost of recalibrating it.

"I told our city clerk about it and he said he would advise the Mayor who would have to have the approval of the council people to buy it. He thought that it was a bit too expensive! I called the Mayor and reminded him of our traffic problem and that the radar device was a steal at that price. It would only take the issuance of 8 traffic tickets to pay for it. "Sold," he said.

We began to use it after the four of us had taken the approved half-day radar course. In its first full month of use, we turned in $600.00 in fines – at $25 per – but were hardly making a dent in our speeding problem. Funny thing was, we had to raise the minimum speed at which we were writing tickets, from 40 (in a 30 zone) to 50 mph! We'd have been writing tickets all day long at that lower speed.

"In spite of what people think about police officers 'making their quota' – it was simply not true. The intent was to slow traffic down as it went through a congested city area, including a kid's playground, a hospital zone and past two schools. It was coincidental only that it added cash to the City's coffers.

"Interestingly, as time went on, our cheap but perfectly workable radar unit began to have an impact. We had feedback from a few motorists whom we stopped that Enderby was the place to watch for speed enforcement and we noticed a measurable decline in the rate of speed. Enforcing the speed limit became an 'ebb and flow' situation. When speeding increased we increased our use of the machine and vice versa when it declined.

"Over time, I noticed an increase in the 'income' of fines within the City, not only through traffic offences, but with *Criminal Code* ones too, especially impaired driving. Back then, the usual fine was $250.00 for that offence and some months, we'd have ten or more cases. The police budget for our operation wasn't really my concern. That was between the City, 'E' Division HQ and the Provincial Government, but after a year there, I became curious. I asked to see the costs of our operation, and, knowing the amount of money that was going to the City from penalties each month, I found that our efforts, completely unintentional, were returning fully fifty percent of the expenditures. A large part of that revenue came from traffic tickets. I asked the Mayor if he thought the $200 the City had paid for the radar unit was worth it. He only gave a diplomatic smile in response. In any event, that aspect of the revenue certainly did what it was intended to do – slow down traffic."

"How did you compare with other similar sized offices, Jack?"

"I never enquired about the financial aspects but I did in relation to the work load."

"More coffee?"

Looking at his watch, Sterling noted it was almost 9 o'clock. "Okay, just a half cup, thanks. Time's getting on and I should go soon. Let me finish up with my time at Enderby.

"With our heavy workload, I decided to write to six other four-man detachments and ask for their Stats – number of complaints received (over the past 12 months), reportable motor vehicle accidents, prisoners taken in to the cells, *Criminal Code* and provincial statutes violations, sudden deaths – natural causes, accidental, suicidal, homicide and traffic – and the number of hours per week worked by members. Remember, there was no such thing as 'overtime'.

"What I got back almost shocked me. In all those categories, our Stats were a minimum of 33 percent higher and as much as 50 percent. I guess that's why all four of us averaged 59 hours per week to deal with the work.

"I decided to put together a comprehensive report and submit it to Sub Division HQ requesting consideration for increasing the 'establishment' from 4 to 5 – in other words, another constable. I only expected an acknowledgement. Well, two weeks later, the Section NCO showed up to discuss the issue and we reviewed the Stats from the other detachments and mine. He was impressed and said he would recommend my request. It worked. About 3 months later, I had my fifth body in place.

"Flushed with success, I decided to push my luck and wrote away for permission to hire a half-time secretary – I was doing most of that kind of work and it reduced my time on the road keeping an eye on things – called 'walking the ship' in naval terms, and – don't go away, Charlie – also threw in a request for two half-days a week janitor. Got that too. What a difference these people made. We began to be quite effective in policing our area, with evening patrols on until 1 a.m. that included doing property checks, which went down well with the business community, even catching the odd culprit during a break-in. The Band Chief asked us to patrol the Reserve area more frequently and that had its benefits."

"Apart from what you've told me, Jack, what events stand out in your mind in your time at this detachment?"

"Nothing terribly unusual. I suppose we had our share of human mayhem – accidents of all kinds. Let me list a few. In the spring each year, we lost one or more snowmobilers to avalanches in the Heal's Range area, in spite of radio and newspaper warnings about snow conditions. Many young people, it seems, think – know – they are invincible. There were the usual drownings, a sexual assault and murder of a three-year-old girl, a love-triangle murder, suicides and an airplane crash one spring. A Cessna 4-seater en route from Calgary to Vancouver went down in our area. Air Force Search and Rescue, called SAR, sent up a large Chinook rescue helicopter and I went up as an observer, looking out the side through large bubble windows with binocs. We found it in dense forest after a three-hour search. Unfortunately, all four occupants had died on impact. There's two other stories to tell you – one humorous and one not.

"The first occurred on Christmas Day one year. Our family had just finished a big Christmas breakfast and were sitting around on the living room floor, beside the Christmas tree, opening presents when the police phone rang. I was on call. One of the native women, Mary Trueman, called to report the theft of a turkey from her oven, while she and her family were at church Christmas service.

"On my arrival, the poor woman was upset as she had planned a big dinner for her husband and five children. Not a lot I could do – of course I did not tell her that – but I took down a description of the big bird in my notebook, which I still have, by the way – for the record I told her – and of the pan in which it was cooking. She had no idea who would want to do this.

"Since I'd been called out, I decided to take a drive along Mabel Lake Road, where she lived, more or less to show the flag and look like I was at least trying. The next closest house to Mary's was half a mile away. I recall it was a nice sunny, cold day with a light snow on the ground and I had my right side window down a bit for some fresh air. As I passed this house, the smell of turkey wafted in. I drove past, thinking naturally that there'd be many a turkey facing the same fate today, but something made me stop – call it instinct maybe. I turned around and drove into the gravel driveway, got out and knocked on the door of a rundown shack of a house. It was opened by Billy Crowman, whom I knew.

"He looked surprised. I asked if I could come in, wished him and I presumed his wife a Merry Christmas, smelled the air and said something like, 'That sure smells good, Billy.'

"His lady opened the oven door to reveal a large turkey sizzling away in the roasting pan, identical to the one reported stolen. Bingo!

"Two small children came into the living room but she shooed them back into another room.

" 'I have to tell you, Billy,' I said, 'that I just came from Mary Trueman's place. She reported that her turkey had been stolen and described the pan it was in. The one you have in your oven matches it exactly. Anything to say?'

"He hung his head down for a few seconds and his wife looked away. 'Yes, I took it,' he said.

" 'Can you tell me why?' I asked.

"He remained silent so I said, 'Billy?' again and he slowly replied that he 'didn't have no turkey for my kids and couldn't help going into my neighbour's house when I smelled the turkey while I was walking back from the town.'

"I considered my options. Arrest the man and lock him up, or handle it another way. I found out in my tour of duty here that Native people tend to be very honest, as was the case here. 'Okay, what'll I do?' I asked myself. To me, there was really only one alternative – have Billy return the bird to Mary and offer her his apologies and with her concurrence, drop the matter. The Spirit of Christmas was upon me.

"So that's what I did. Bundled Billy, the turkey and pan into the back of the patrol car and gave it its last ride back to Mary's.

"There, Billy, his head lowered, admitted his culpability to her but said no more. I took Mary aside and told her why he had taken the turkey and asked if she could find it in her Christian heart to invite his family over to share the turkey. She did. Made my Christmas day."

"Great little story, Jack. What else?"

"Just two things, I think. One concerns an all-day manhunt and the second, how I came to go to Ottawa.

"First. One morning, I was awakened at three a.m. by Constable Chesterfield, standing in the doorway to our bedroom, back-lighted by the hallway light. He said something like, 'Corp, we've got an emergency. My police car's been stolen!'

"That woke me up quickly. I said I'd meet him downstairs in the office and got dressed, wondering to myself how anyone could steal a police car, occupied by a policeman.

"It was Saturday night/Sunday morning time frame. Chesterfield had been busy and was finishing off his shift by checking business properties just north of the City. He found an Esso service station broken into and got the owner who lived nearby to check and secure the place, while he checked the area. No vehicles were moving and no one was on foot. Driving down the back road toward town, however, he saw a figure dressed in a large army overcoat, walking in the misty rain. He stopped the individual and was confronted by a male from the Reserve, who pointed a rifle at him. Chesterfield immediately dove into a nearby ditch and scrambled up the far bank, hearing a shot fired at him. The individual, whom he recognized, got into his patrol car and peeled rubber as he drove into town. The policeman had to walk to a nearby farmer's house to use a phone (police portables would not transmit in the area) and called another member to advise what had happened and for a ride to the office.

"In the office, he looked a bit shaken and quite worried, so I tried to reassure him that what happened could even happen to a corporal. At least I got a bit of a smile back. I called the emergency line at Sub Division in Parkton and gave the operator brief details, and then got the other two members out of bed, and, with the remaining patrol cars, began a systematic grid search. The Section NCO meanwhile had contacted surrounding detachments and organized a number of road blocks in a bid to seal off the area around Enderby. It was a good thing it was a Sunday morning, there being very little traffic out.

"When all this was in place, I counted 24 police officers in 12 police cars in operation, including a Dog Master and an RCMP helicopter from Parkton. Because it was my area, I was in charge, so I remained in the office doing coordination work. When the Section NCO arrived, he asked my wife if she could make sandwiches and coffee for everyone, which she willingly did, of course, and we shuttled the food around throughout the day.

"As the day wore on, I began to think that the thief had gotten ahead of our road blocks. Then our luck changed. At three o'clock, I took a call from a couple of people who had left early in the morning by car, for a hike at Mabel Lake. They heard a news report of the stolen PC on their way back and recollected seeing a large black car on the side of the road pointed east in the direction they were headed. It had no 'red lights' on top but in thinking about it now, they thought it a bit odd.

"I re-directed a couple of cars out that way, including the Dog Master. Our stolen car was found an hour later, partly hidden off-road in the trees and camouflaged with fir branches. Upon examination, the emergency equipment on the roof was missing, the police crests on both doors had been covered with black grease and the radio smashed. About half an hour later, as it was getting dark, the police dog found the suspect hiding inside the hollow trunk of a Douglas fir tree lying on the ground. With the dog barking like mad, standing on the trunk, the guy gave up and as he was crawling out of his hiding place, big gobs of foamy drool from a furious German Shepherd dropped all over his face.

"The end of an exciting and exhausting day. He got 8 years in prison for the service station break-in, discharging a firearm with intent (not enough for attempted murder, thought the Crown Prosecutor)

– in his statement, the culprit said he only wanted to scare the policeman off – and theft of the police car."

"That's quite a story. I imagine Constable Chesterfield was glad when it was over. Did it affect him?"

"No, I asked him if he wanted counselling and he said, 'No, I'm good. It's all in a day's work.'

"So let me finish off with Enderby. Early in May of my fourth year at this post, I had a surprise visit from the Staffing Officer from Victoria. He said I was being considered for an instructor's position at the Canadian Police College in Ottawa – 'What did I think of that?' For a few seconds I didn't know what to say and from the dumbfounded look on my face, he must have been reconsidering the offer.

"He explained that it was a sergeant's position with a three- or four-year term and involved teaching, of all things, 'management theory' to senior NCOs and officers up to the rank of superintendent.

"Recovering, I said, 'Sir, the only thing I know about the subject is how to spell 'management theory.'

"He chuckled and said he thought I was bright enough to pick up the academics of the job and that I'd be understudying someone for six months. He said the position required an undergraduate degree and, to my surprise, asked me how much longer I had to go to achieve mine. When I told him one year, he said, 'Good, we can get you in on that basis. You've got two days to consider.'

"And it came to pass. Jocelyn was okay with it, ready to move on and lucky for me, did not mind these transfers. The boys were excited about going to live in Canada's Capital."

"How about you, Jack? Must have come as a surprise and quite a change of police duties. Did you have some doubts?"

"Oh yeah, I was really apprehensive about doing stand-up teaching, especially on such subject matters. I thought I'd spend the rest of my career on General Duties work, which I like. My wife said, 'Go for it, you can always return to B.C.,' so I did — both. Just before we left, people in the community put on a farewell party for us at the Canadian Legion Hall, which was also attended by the Band Chief and a delegation of men and women from the Reserve.

"I was surprised and delighted and quite nostalgic too. Anyway, more to follow. I should get home. Thank you for a pleasant evening."

46

A week later.

"Let me tell you, Charlie, that when I left Enderby it was with very mixed emotions and some degree of sadness. I'd made many friends in the community, had been involved with the Junior Baseball League, was a volunteer swimming instructor at the local outdoor pool, coming to know many parents. Even my wife gained some police experience – from her unpaid labour in the office – in helping to run the place. At times, she was indispensable, acting as Matron for female prisoners, feeding inmates meals, answering the telephone and police radio. When we pulled out of town in our truck/camper for the long drive half-way across Canada, I had a lump in my throat. I think out of respect for my feelings, my wife remained quiet for a while, letting me remember. I could tell too that the boys were feeling down as they were unusually quiet too."

The reporter was out for another ride-along and knew that Sterling was getting to the end of accounts of his police service. Charlie Preston had his tape running and listened.

"We had a surprise waiting for us in Ottawa. My family had to stay in a hotel for ten days, pending our move into our rented house. The first morning I got up to drive to our headquarters office I found my truck and camper unit had been stolen from the hotel parking lot. It was filled to the brim with personal effects, including several hundred dollars worth of new clothing for the boys for the new school year, some of my uniform and many other items of value. It was our only means of transportation. The vehicle was never recovered and I had to wait weeks for my insurance claim to be finalized and get my cash – devalued to seventy-five percent of the claim. Welcome to Ottawa!

"After taking an intense instructors course I started by sitting in a classroom, listening to an instructor and making notes, and gradually assumed his portfolio of lectures. I found myself not only studying and producing assignments for my degree but also having to read about, and get into my head, 'management theories' – no easy task. In a short period of time my work had gone from functional to cerebral. I was on brain overload. I had difficulty expressing my new-found knowledge and at first, regretted accepting the position, in spite of the sergeant's stripes. It took about a year for me to get comfortable and knowledgeable and from that point on until I left, I was 'on a roll' and enjoyed teaching. One other thing I should tell you is that the college also accepted police personnel students from many Commonwealth countries and the United States. There was often an FBI agent on management courses. Happy to say I've made friends with some of them."

"I can imagine it being a difficult transition," said his reporter friend. "You know, I've noticed a curious thing about Mounties. There seems to be a mindset that believes you're all capable of performing well, whatever job you are assigned. It almost seems to be axiomatic. It certainly speaks well of the Force's trust in its members – and a challenge for them to meet these expectations. You feel that way, Jack?"

"Well, I've never considered that. An interesting observation. Maybe it takes an outsider like you – no offence – to pick up on that kind of behaviour and attitude. I'll have to consider what you've said. Anyway, to continue.... We enjoyed Ottawa for its appearance and amenities. It's a good place for kids to grow up in, with generally good schools and two first-class universities, Ottawa U and Carleton.

"School students are lucky in that all schools' curriculum taught something of our parliamentary system and, of course, kids enjoyed school bus trips to Parliament Hill and a short session in the House.

There's also a concentration of major museums and a beautiful concert hall, the National Arts Centre.

"For nine months of the year however, the weather is an abomination – four months of snow on the ground and five months of oppressive heat. It's got to be the fly and mosquito capital of the world! There are some benefits. Snow in the Gatineau Hills across the river in Quebec provides excellent cross country skiing and the Rideau Canal freezes solid, allowing good ice skating for two or three months. While we were there, we took advantage of the geography and, one summer, spent a month visiting beautiful Atlantic Canada and the next summer, drove down the eastern U.S. to Florida, stopping for three days in Washington, D.C., to see the history of the place, including a visit inside the White House, went to the top of the Washington Monument for a spectacular view of the city, and visited all eleven of its famous museums. In the Sunshine State, the kids being of an age, we spent five days visiting the fairly new Disney World. A memorable trip."

"I take it you finished your undergraduate degree?" Preston asked.

"Yes. In May of the next year. I took three days off and drove to Waterloo, stayed on campus and joined 500 other graduates at the Convocation. I finally visited 'my' university and it was a rewarding experience."

"So you finished your mandatory four years at the police college and returned to B.C. and Parkton. How did that come about? I mean returning to this City?"

"It was the luck of the draw, caused by vacancies. I was on a transfer list and probably my name popped up and filled the next position. I was told in Ottawa that the watch commander's positions as sergeants were to be raised to staff sergeants in view of the increased size of the detachment, so it was potentially a promotion transfer."

"Did you mind going back to the same place?"

"I had mixed feelings about it. Would have preferred another posting but was okay with this one. Jocelyn and I went on a house-hunting trip and managed to buy our first house, on a nice street, high up on a hill with a magnificent view of the City, the valley and the snow-capped Cariboo Mountain Range to the north. Frankly though, I could have stayed on at the college for another year or two. As I said before, I liked what I was doing and, I believe, was good at it. The test of an instructor's ability, I believe, is manifested at the end of a session when people stay after class to discuss the topic further and ask for advice. I enjoyed those talks."

"So, my friend, it looks like we've come full circle in your career. You're coming up on twenty-five years service shortly, I believe?"

"Yes, on August 5."

"Going to stay on for a while yet?"

"I'm unsure, Charlie, but I've been giving it a lot of thought. I'm in a mental turmoil but I'm considering jumping ship here and going to greener pastures, to mix my metaphors. When I decide, after my wife and kids, you'll be the next to know."

"Well, well, well, if you're gonna pull the pin, Jack, we'll miss you."

"What's it been?" asked Sterling. "About ten, eleven months since our first connection about 'A' Watch and its members? I take it you've done some preliminary writing on the matter?"

"Yes to both questions, Jack. As you may well understand, I have a great deal of information to plough through and sort out. It'll be a bit of a challenge but a pleasant one I think for me. You'll eventually see a first draft."

"Alright. Good. Listen, just because you've completed your 're-search' so to speak, don't feel that you can't go for a ride with me. You certainly can, Mister *News* reporter."

"Thanks, I appreciate that. I'll give you a call. 'Night, Jack," Preston finished, and shook his hand.

47

At 7:15 p.m. on a Friday in early June, Cathy Johnson, 23, and Sherry White 24, lay on the golden sandy beach at the downtown Riverside Park, which was adjacent to the Thompson River. They were not dressed adequately. As well, on the female anatomy scale of rating, both came close to the top of the chart – '10s'.

After finishing their work at 5 o'clock, they had walked from their downtown office complex to the park. It was hot with the temperature hovering at 32 degrees Centigrade. Choosing the western end of the beach area, they laid out their blankets in order to get some sun tanning in for an hour or so, away from the crowd and the kids play area. They'd brought along a small cooler, packed with ice from the ice-making machine in their office and six beers, plus, of course, a variety of personal music complete with the requisite ear plugs. They were cognizant of the need to keep the noise down. Slathering themselves with a high number sun tan lotion, they lay down, with big, white-rimmed beach sunglasses on, each with a pocket book, listening to their choices of music and sipping beer. Contentment.

♦ ◊ ♦

"10-Bravo-2."

Rick Taylor answered, "Bravo-2."

"Report of indecent exposure, two women, Riverside Park Beach – see the complainant. She's at the entrance wearing a pale blue sun dress and large white floppy hat. Name is Dorothy something," said the dispatcher.

"Radio, Bravo-2, we're on it," Taylor replied. He was partnered this evening with Constable Gordon Finch, who had been assigned to patrolling Centre Zone, much of which ran parallel to the river. They'd been on duty fifteen minutes.

"Bravo-2, Bravo-1, can we cover you?" requested Constable McKillen who was partnered with Constable Portal.

"Bravo-1, negative. If we need assistance, you're the first in line though."

The two Mounties found the woman, Dorothy, in her sixties, who told them she thought it was 'not right' that women should expose themselves in public. When Finch asked her how they were 'exposed', she said that they were not wearing their bra tops and had very little else on 'down there, you know,' pointing downward with her index finger, and then showed the members where the women were at the end of the beach. They thanked her and conferred for a minute.

"Look, Gordon," Taylor said straight-faced, "I can handle this. Why don't you take a brief statement from this lady?" which was not meant as a question.

"Are you kidding! You're gonna need my help in handling this situation. If anything 'untoward' should happen, you may need a witness if you get my drift. Let's go."

And so they went about their sworn duty.

"Uh hum," grunted Taylor, who with Finch, was standing next to and almost over, the two semi-nude women. A little bit of math here might serve to clarify for the reader just how scantily clad they were. If it is a given that being clothed from shoulders to the knees represents one hundred percent coverage, these two females, each wearing a triangle of cloth on their lower fronts, had, at most, two percent and that may have been a generous estimate on the part of the examining constables.

By now, both girls were trying to nap and didn't hear the police arrive, until Cathy heard Constable Taylor's 'Uh hum.' Opening her eyes and looking through the dark glasses, she was startled to see two large men in uniform staring down at her and immediately said, "Oh shit!" which alerted Sherry who repeated her friend's exclamation.

"Hi, ladies, taking advantage of the nice weather?" said one of the men in a very friendly tone.

"Er, yes," replied Cathy. "Sorry," she continued, "we thought we would be okay at this end of the beach," as she sat up, thereby completely changing the constables' view of her. She was followed by Sherry. The men's perspective of the two women changed again when both girls stood up and faced them to continue the discussion.

The policemen astutely observed that the two triangle patches were held in place, supported by spaghetti-strap cords around their waists and through the buttocks. Using a sideways glance to his partner, Taylor rolled his eyes up to convey thoughts – 'Oh my God!' – he didn't say.

The interview took all of fifteen minutes and while Cathy replaced her top herself, Sherry, standing very close to one of the men, turned her back to him and asked for assistance in tying the string into a bow at her back. For a nanosecond, he thought about his position as a member of the Force and then his responsibility to assist the general public. No contest. He complied but awkwardly, having to make two attempts with his fumbling fingers.

While explaining the law on public nudity to them, Constable Taylor took their names and addresses. Sherry asked him if he needed their telephone numbers too, and, after pausing for a second or two, he said that might be a good idea, so the numbers were promptly recorded in the constable's notebook. In view of their consideration in selecting this spot to sunbathe, they were advised that no charges would be laid, just a 'Caution' issued. The two officers wished the girls a pleasant evening and reluctantly left.

As they were walking back along the beach, Taylor said to his buddy, "Jesus, Gord, my metabolism's gone to hell."

"Me too – I'm in love again!"

"What do you think? – a pair of D plusses?" asked Taylor.

"Yeah. Sherry may even be E's," his partner said.

"You think?"

"You know, I've often wondered why, how a D cup size could have a 'minus' rating. I mean, isn't it a given that they would always be a plus?"

Before Taylor could impart his wisdom, the dispatcher's voice interrupted them.

"10-Bravo-2, are you clear yet?"

"Bravo-2, 10-4," replied Taylor on his portable radio.

"Was it a difficult investigation?" she asked, with a hint of sarcasm. No reply.

"Okay. Report of two drunk males near the kids' swings. Check it out, please. Delta-1 [the prison van] – see if you are needed."

"Back to the real world," sighed Taylor.

♦ ◊ ♦

Meanwhile, Constables Kart and Austmann were called to deal with another young woman. The mall stores were open until 9 p.m. Just before closing time, they went to a shoplifting offence at one of the department stores. Reporting to the store security office, they found a young teenage female suspect tied to a chair, and gagged. A little taken aback by what they saw, they told the security female to untie her and remove the gag.

She said, "Okay, but you're going to get an earful from this bitch," and she was right.

The girl, about 14 years old, let go with a string of obscenities that would have embarrassed a sailor. She also got up from the chair and slapped the woman hard on her face and then went for her hair all the while screaming at the top of her lungs. Kart grabbed her from behind and lifted her off her feet, at which point she started kicking at anyone who was near her and that included Constable Austmann who took one on his left knee. He winced at the pain, but bent down and managed to corral both her legs. Together, he and his partner carried her to the patrol car, still screaming and struggling. Finch shouted over his shoulder to the security people that he would be back for the details as soon as they lodged her in the cells. One of the staff carried both policemen's hats back to the police car for them.

At the detachment, she was placed in the holding cell, a place where people waited to be processed into the cells. A matron was already on duty and one look by her at her 'charge' told her she would need help to get the girl into the juvenile cells. It took two constables and her to accomplish that.

The girl had no ID and screamed, "Fuck you," when asked for her name. It was Friday evening and most of the four separated cell block areas – adult male, juvenile male, adult female and juvenile female were filling up, mostly with drunks and druggies.

As her screaming continued, some of the inebriated and stoned people, when the noise penetrated their fogged skulls, began shouting, "Shut the fuck up!" and similar vernacular, turning the back of the detachment where the cells were located, into the dictionary definition of a living hell. The noise was beginning to penetrate the plate glass enclosed area of the dispatch centre.

"Okay," said Sergeant Sterling, "enough of this shit!" Looking around the bullpen area of the office, he spotted Constable Prentice trying to do some paperwork. "Shelley," he called out to her, "I need you to do something."

"Yeah, Sarge?"

"This is getting chaotic in here," he replied. "We'll have to remove the female juvenile from the cells. Tell her if she stops screaming and fighting, we'll take her out of the cells. Take her into my office and try to quiet her down. She's seriously disturbing the population back there. Take Constable Austmann with you and get her out now. You'll have to stay with her. If you can do that, we might just be able to let her go home in the company of one or more of her parents. Dispatch is trying to contact them now. Be careful," he finished.

The back door in from the garage swung open and Corporal Bibermann entered with an impaired driver in tow and took him into the breathalyzer room for a 'blow job' as it was euphemistically called, using the Breath Alcohol Testing machine – the BAT. The mobile version was called, naturally enough, the BAT mobile. Hearing all the turmoil, he said to himself, 'I've got the feeling this is going to be a bitch of an evening. Must be payday weekend.'

48

It was sentencing day for Mark Rifell. He'd been held in custody since his arrest some weeks earlier and subsequent pleas of 'Guilty' to four Counts of Arson, one Count including the death of a person.

Crown and Defence Counsel had earlier rendered their submissions on sentencing – the Prosecutor for a minimum of fifteen years and Defence for a maximum of ten. The Pre-Sentence Report had also been prepared for the Judge's guidance. The Courtroom was full and included a number of press people, including Charlie Preston.

When Provincial Court Judge Elizabeth Cunliffe sat down, the Bailiff asked the defendant to rise as did his Counsel. Looking across the Courtroom at him, the Judge said, "Mr. Rifell, these are serious Charges that you have admitted to, including the one Count of causing the death of a person. In my view, the offence of arson always has that potential attached to it. Such activity also puts firefighters' lives at risk and causes collateral damage, often unintended, to other property, creates the loss of employment and causes financial hardship. There is generally nothing about this kind of offence which warrants a positive consideration in sentencing.

"However, from the evidence introduced, particularly that of your statement of admission wherein your actions seem to support your claim of some degree of care in ensuring the buildings were unoccupied, is the only mitigating factor I am taking into consideration in passing sentence. Your probation report discusses this aspect of your activity and asserts the notion that you show remorse for your behaviour.

"I am hopeful that, in your case, you will truly benefit from the therapeutic care offered during your incarceration. Do you have anything to say before I pass sentence?"

"Yes, I have, Your Honour," he said, trying his best to keep his head up. "I'm sorry for what I done and I'd like to apologize to Mrs. Eagle for the loss of her son. I just wished that it hadn't happened," and tears rolled down his cheeks.

The Judge then said, "I sentence you to ten years on each Count, to run concurrently."

Rifell's mother burst into tears when the Bailiff said, "All rise," and the Judge left the Courtroom. The Sheriff's officer took charge of the prisoner after a brief discussion with his lawyer, and led him away through a side door.

"What do you think, Jack?" asked the *Parkton News* reporter outside the Courtroom. He and Sergeant Sterling had sat together during the sentencing.

"Fair enough in the circumstances. I can't see the kid repeating this kind of offence, but that depends upon the social conditions he finds 'inside'. Hopefully the staff will steer him clear of the repeat offenders. If he keeps his nose clean, he may make parole in five or six years. In any event, he'll soon learn what to do to apply for early release."

"What's that?"

"Parole Boards love to hear that you've done the following three things – reiterated your guilt and remorse to one or more of the prison staff, taken some trades or academic courses for a job prospect, and that you've 'found Jesus' – go to the Chapel regularly."

"Well, I have another dramatic Courtroom scene to report."

"I know you'll do an excellent job, Charlie. See you later."

49

Sterling entered the Provincial Government Building on Connaught Drive, just down the hill from the police Sub Division building. At the receptionist desk he asked to see Mr. Andrew Atkinson, the senior game warden in the district, in the Ministry of Environment.

The woman took him to his office and at the open door, Sterling said, "Hello, Andy, how are you?"

"Well, thanks, Jack. Come in and sit. Good of you to drop by. Pleasant weather, eh?"

"Indeed. June is a nice time of year here. Just wanted to touch base with you regarding those two game bandits my people nabbed on the weekend. Your memo to our office regarding these poaching suspects, and to BOLF, worked.

"Two of my men, Constables Portal and Oliver, took an unmarked car out yesterday and patrolled the hills south of the City on the off-chance of seeing some poaching activity. They got lucky. Spotted the suspect pickup hidden among the Ponderosa pines and decided to back off a bit and wait to see what might happen. Sure enough, the two returned to their vehicle, driving it further uphill, over the top and down the south side, eventually stopping. They were 'glassed' and observed cutting up an animal and loading up the parts. It was 'game over' – no pun intended – and they were taken into custody. Our guys took photos at the scene and statements of admission from them. Seeing that they are local they were released on a Recognizance. Here's a copy for your file. We'll cc you with copies of the other paperwork. The meat is in your compound locker, as you know."

"Wow, what can I say? Seems like an open-and-shut case. I'd like you to thank the two members for me and I'll be writing a note of appreciation to Inspector Edwardson. Thanks, Jack – damn good work by your guys."

"Okay, but you owe them a beer, Atkinson."

"Done. Listen," he said, "I have something you may be interested in. Our headquarters in Victoria recently hired a new chief, an ex-Mountie named Ralph Alderson, who did his service in Ontario. Don't suppose you know the name?"

Sterling shook his head.

"Well, up until now, game wardens have been taking whatever law enforcement training and specialized courses wherever they can get it, mostly via the city police training facility in Vancouver. While it's okay, it doesn't really meet the needs of the Fish and Game Branch. The chief has received authority to employ a full-time training officer to create our own programs. The job is going to be advertised shortly and in view of your Police College experience, I wonder if you would be interested?"

"Thanks, Andy. You never know. Do you have a copy of the job description here?"

A week later, Sterling was reading about the job with Jocelyn. They'd had some preliminary discussions about his career and staying in the Force beyond his 25th anniversary. One of the reasons he loved his wife was for her easy going nature. 'Whatever you think is right sweetheart,' she'd say. He knew this decision was to be a major consideration in their lives and to a lesser extent, their sons, who by now were young adults, with Brad, the youngest, going into his last year at high school.

It sounded like a good challenging job, less money than he was currently earning, but his gross income would rise when he started receiving his police pension income.

"Why don't you apply and if you're selected, go for an interview at least. Nothing ventured, nothing gained, as you are fond of saying, Jack," she said.

So he did and was quickly invited to go to Victoria. The interview went well and Sterling felt confident that he might be offered the position. The problem was, he felt 'at home' as a member of the Force and still liked his work. He reflected on the thoughts he'd had a few weeks ago in May when he was sitting in his patrol car on a quiet Sunday evening out on the highway, watching the sun go down and wondered if that sunset was synonymous with his time in the Royal Canadian Mounted Police.

Ten days later, he received an 'offer of employment' from Alderson, with a suggested start date of no later than September 15th. On reading the letter to Jocelyn, he experienced two very distinct feelings – elation at being offered the job and sadness if he accepted it. "I just don't know what to do, Jocelyn."

She held him in her arms for a few seconds, looked up into his eyes and said, "This may be a golden opportunity for you. Why don't you accept it, darling?"

He reiterated his feelings to the reporter over coffee a few days later, who said, "Well, one benefit that I can see, at least for me, is that it makes a nice ending to my story!"

Sterling spoke to Staff Sergeant Batich, Administrative NCO, who advised him to submit a formal letter of retirement to the Officer in Charge, to include his last date of service. He did that but kept the letter back a few days, still not willing to let go and knowing that when he sent the memo in, the umbilical cord would be cut; there would be no going back.

One morning he woke up, after a sleepless, restless night and irreverently said to himself, 'Goddamnit, let's go for it.'

When he was picked up at seven a.m. for his ride to the office, he was quiet. Constable Marv Petersen picked up on his mood and, glancing over at him, said, "You okay, Sarge?"

"Yeah, couldn't be better, Marv, couldn't be better."

◆ ◇ ◆

His remaining time at Parkton went by fast. Summers were a busy time – lots of visitors and traffic – to be dealt with by reduced members on watch, some of the senior people away with their families during the long summer school break. Jocelyn had to give notice at the college, there was the house to sell, finding a place in Victoria and eventually, packing for the move. His report date for his new job in Victoria was the week after Labour Day, September 11th. He managed to get in a couple of visits with the reporter, who knew of his pending retirement.

On his last ride-along with the sergeant, Charlie Preston reflected on his many experiences with 'A' Watch and how privileged he felt about being allowed to take part in such varied, interesting and often dramatic experiences he'd had with Sterling and his 'band of brothers'.

"You'll be giving up your career as a policeman soon, Jack. I can imagine the feelings you must have. I also think, by and large, you've enjoyed your service in the Force. How do you feel about that?"

"Hmm, good question. How can I reply? I guess the answer is – I feel good, especially where I know I've made a difference helping people. You know, in a way, I think the police are like those tall, stove-pipe rocks in Arizona's Monument Valley, standing like sentinels keeping watch over the desert. In the hundreds of night shift patrols I've done, I've felt like the human equivalent of one of them."

'What a fitting analogy,' Preston thought, making a mental note to include that in his book, as he wished him well in his retirement from the Force and his new venture in life. The reporter had a feeling there were a lot more like Sterling in the Mounted Police.

50

"Alright, Sweetheart," Sterling said as he rose from the dining table, "I'm off to work. Thanks for a good dinner."

She also got up – none of their sons were at home – and gave him a hug, an extra long one it seemed to Jack, and said, "Be careful out there tonight, honey," in a meaningful way, implying, *please come home to me tomorrow morning.*

"I will," he replied. "Should be a quiet night." He kissed her on her cheek before he walked out the door to the waiting patrol car. It was his last shift, from seven p.m. to seven a.m., Sunday evening through Monday morning.

♦ ◇ ♦

It was a quiet night – until one.

Constable Oliver, South Zone, called it in. "Dispatch, Bravo-13, there's a fire in one of the new townhouses up above Pacific Ridge. I'm downhill from it and going up. Advise fire department, please."

"Bravo-13, Bravo-7. Andrew, I'm on my way up there," said Sterling as he turned his car round quickly and made his way up the long, steep hill. He was thinking, 'Jesus, shades of Rifell! Hope the little bastard hasn't escaped! Can't be him? A copycat maybe?'

At a certain point on his way, he had a good view of the new complex and could see several units on fire, flames being fanned by a rising wind.

"Andy, any vehicles or people on the road up there?"

"Not yet, Sarge. None of the homes appear to be occupied. Fire's really catching on now. It's the first row burning. There's another two rows behind, close to them. Any sign of the fire trucks?"

Sterling glanced in his rearview and just caught a glimpse of flashing red as he rounded another corner. "10-4, they're on their way. Be there shortly."

As Sterling turned onto the dead-end road between the first and second rows of buildings, he saw Oliver coming at him and pulled up as he approached.

"Sarge, don't go any further. The wind is pushing the flames this way and it's too damn hot."

Sterling turned around. There was no other way in.

As it turned out, the fire trucks, eventually six of them, were virtually useless for the same reason.

At the front of the first row, the ground fell away sharply, downhill, denying access that way in too. The Fire Chief conversed with the sergeant about tactics, but both agreed little could be done. They couldn't get close enough.

"About the only thing for us at the moment is to pour water on the second row and hope that stays safe," the Assistant Chief said.

By now, the wind had reached almost gale force velocity which often happens with large fires and all of the units in row one were burning wildly, with huge showers of sparks and embers flying around. Downhill from them was open space covered with bunch grass and young pine trees, bordering on the Trans-Canada Highway. The flames, being blown almost sideways, were now starting grass fires in several places.

"Shit, this is getting out of hand, Andy. I'll ask the dispatcher to call out the forestry people. This is Crown land, I believe. Although there's little traffic I don't want to have to close the highway," said Sterling, activating the mic on his portable radio. "Dispatch, Bravo-7. Call the Forestry people and ask them to get their fire suppression crew up here ASAP. Call me on frequency two when they come on air. Bravo-12, drive along the TCH and keep an eye out for debris flying over the highway."

He noticed the fire trucks pulling out from the second street where they'd been watering down the units on row two. One of the drivers pulled alongside the police car and said the paint was blistering and conditions were too hot to remain especially with the unpredictability of the wind. "We're gonna try to keep row three from going up, but I'm doubtful we can save it."

"Bravo-12, Bravo-7."

"Seven – go."

"I see the forestry crew and tanker truck. They're on the way up via the logging road in order to get above the grass fires. Christ, Sarge, it looks like a scene from the blitz of London in World War Two up there. Is everything going up?"

"Kinda looks like it, Jim."

"Just to let you know, the TV and radio station people are on their way."

At five a.m., the fires had burned themselves out rather than being put out. Three of the detached houses nearby were badly damaged. Much of the grassy slope and a few of the trees were blackened. Both groups of firefighters remained at the scene in the event of any flare-ups. Sterling and the Fire Chief had been interviewed by Charlie Preston in front of the radio and TV people and would be heard and appear on both those media at seven-thirty.

◆   ◇   ◆

At seven-thirty, Monday August 25th, Sergeant Sterling was being driven home by Sergeant Miller, 'B' Watch Commander, in Bravo-7 when the newscast came on radio station CFPK. They had just arrived at his house and sat and listened.

Last night, at around one a.m., one of the largest fires ever to hit this city burned down three rows of unoccupied townhouses and damaged several detached homes in the Pacific Ridge Estates up on Pine Ridge Road. Fire trucks from all City fire halls attended, as did the Ministry of Forests fire crews, needed to put out grass and tree fires on the slope reaching down to the Trans-Canada Highway.

This reporter interviewed Sergeant Jack Sterling, who, with the Assistant Fire Chief, Mel Baker, agreed there was a strong probability of arson. The loss is estimated to run to twenty-eight million dollars. More later.

On a more personal note, today is the last day in the RCMP for Sergeant Sterling. Here's a bit of that conversation: 'So, Jack, you're retiring from the Force today. How do you feel? Will you miss it?'

'I feel good. I've had twenty-five years of service and it's time to move on. Of course I'll miss it, especially all the members that I've worked with. I'll never forget them.'

*'Well, Jack, that was quite a night to finish off your career. I guess you could say that you're going out in a **blaze of glory**!'*

Both officers chuckled at that.

Miller looked at Sterling and said, shaking his hand, "So long, Jack, it's been good to work with you. Best of luck. Do you want to do the honours?"

Sterling took the microphone off the dashboard hook, one last time, pressed the button and simply said, "Dispatch, 10-Bravo-7."

"Bravo-7."

"Sergeant Sterling, 10-7 residence. End of watch."

CPSIA information can be obtained at www.ICGtesting.com
Printed in the USA
LVOW060015170712

290317LV00001B/3/P